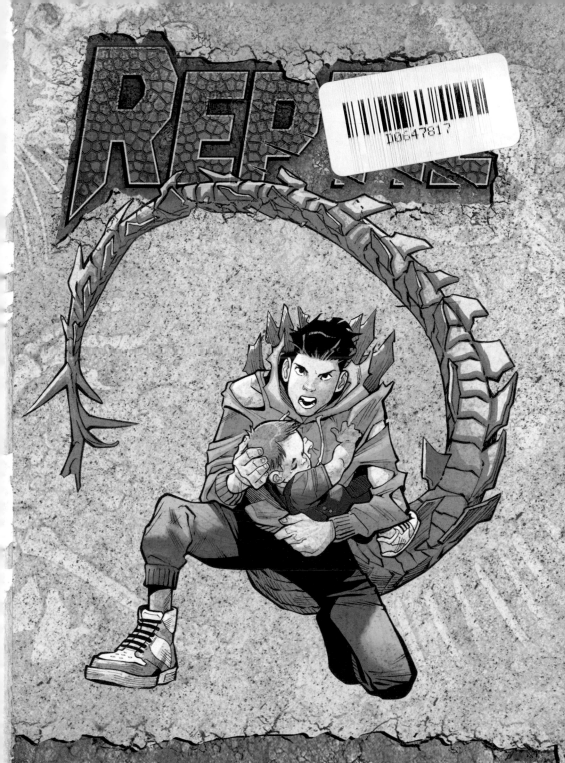

BRINK OF EXTINCTION

Humberto Lopez's life changed after discovering a mystical fossilized amulet that granted him the ability to transform into any prehistoric creature, as well as proportional strength and advanced healing when in those forms. Once hunted and tortured for his powers, treated as hero and villain alike and now flying solo – Humberto Lopez is...

REPTIL: BRINK OF EXTINCTION GN-TPB. Contains material originally published in magazine form as REPTIL (2021) #1-4 and AVENGERS: THE INITIATIVE FEATURING REPTIL (2009) #1. First printing 2021. ISBN 978-1-302-93017-2. Published by MARVEL WORLDWIDE, INC., a subsidiary of MARVEL ENTERTAINMENT, LLC. OFFICE OF PUBLICATION: 1290 Avenue of the Americas, New York, NY 10104. © 2021 MARVEL No similarity between any of the names, characters, persons, and/or institutions in this magazine with those of any living or dead person or institution is intended, and any such similarity which may exist is purely coincidental. **Printed in Canada.** KEVIN FEIGE, Chief Creative Officer; DAN BUCKLEY, President, Marvel Entertainment; JOE QUESADA, EVP & Creative Director; DAVID BOGART, Associate Publisher & SVP of Talent Affairs; TOM BREVOORT, VP, Executive Editor; NICK LOWE, Executive Editor, VP of Content, Digital Publishing; DAVID GABRIEL, VP of Print & Digital Publishing; JEFF YOUNGQUIST, VP of Production & Special Projects; ALEX MORALES, Director of Publishing Operations; DAN EDINGTON, Managing Editor; RICKEY PURDIN, Director of Talent Relations; JENNIFER GRÜNWALD, Senior Editor, Special Projects; SUSAN CRESPI, Production Manager; STAN LEE, Chairman Emeritus. For information regarding advertising in Marvel Comics or on Marvel.com, please contact Vit DeBellis, Custom Solutions & Integrated Advertising Manager, at vdebellis@marvel.com. For Marvel subscription inquiries, please call 888-511-5480. **Manufactured between 9/24/2021 and 10/26/2021 by SOLISCO PRINTERS, SCOTT, QC, CANADA.**

10 9 8 7 6 5 4 3 2 1

REPTIL

BRINK OF EXTINCTION

TERRY BLAS
WRITER

ENID BALÁM
PENCILER

VICTOR OLAZABA
INKER

CARLOS LOPEZ
COLORIST

VC's JOE SABINO
LETTERER

PACO MEDINA & FEDERICO BLEE
COVER ART

LAUREN AMARO
EDITOR

LAUREN BISOM
SUPERVISING EDITOR

COLLECTION EDITOR DANIEL KIRCHHOFFER
ASSISTANT MANAGING EDITOR MAIA LOY
ASSISTANT MANAGING EDITOR LISA MONTALBANO
SENIOR EDITOR, SPECIAL PROJECTS JENNIFER GRÜNWALD

VP, PRODUCTION & SPECIAL PROJECTS JEFF YOUNGQUIST
BOOK DESIGNER STACIE ZUCKER
SVP PRINT, SALES & MARKETING DAVID GABRIEL
EDITOR IN CHIEF C.B. CEBULSKI

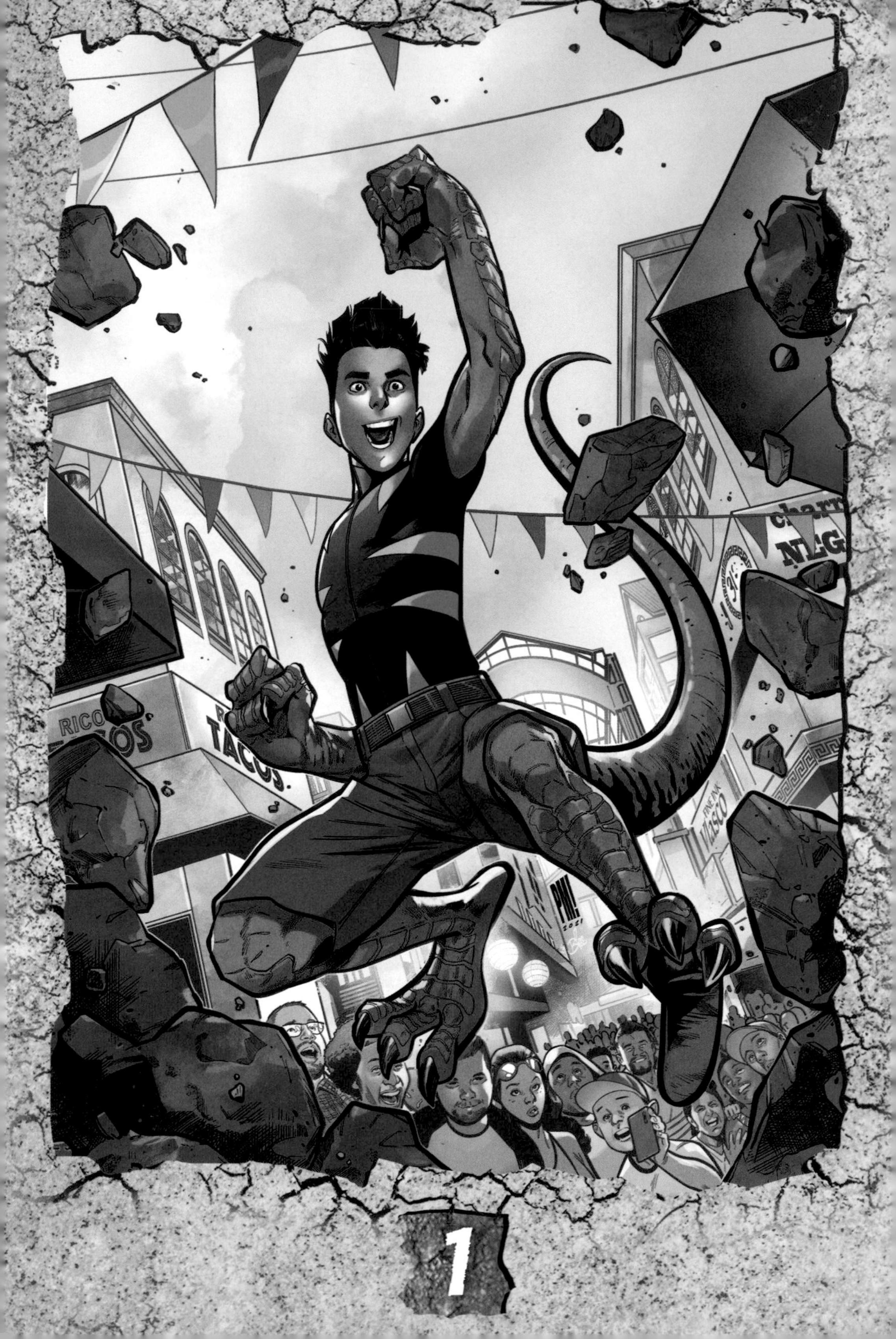
RICO
TACOS

1

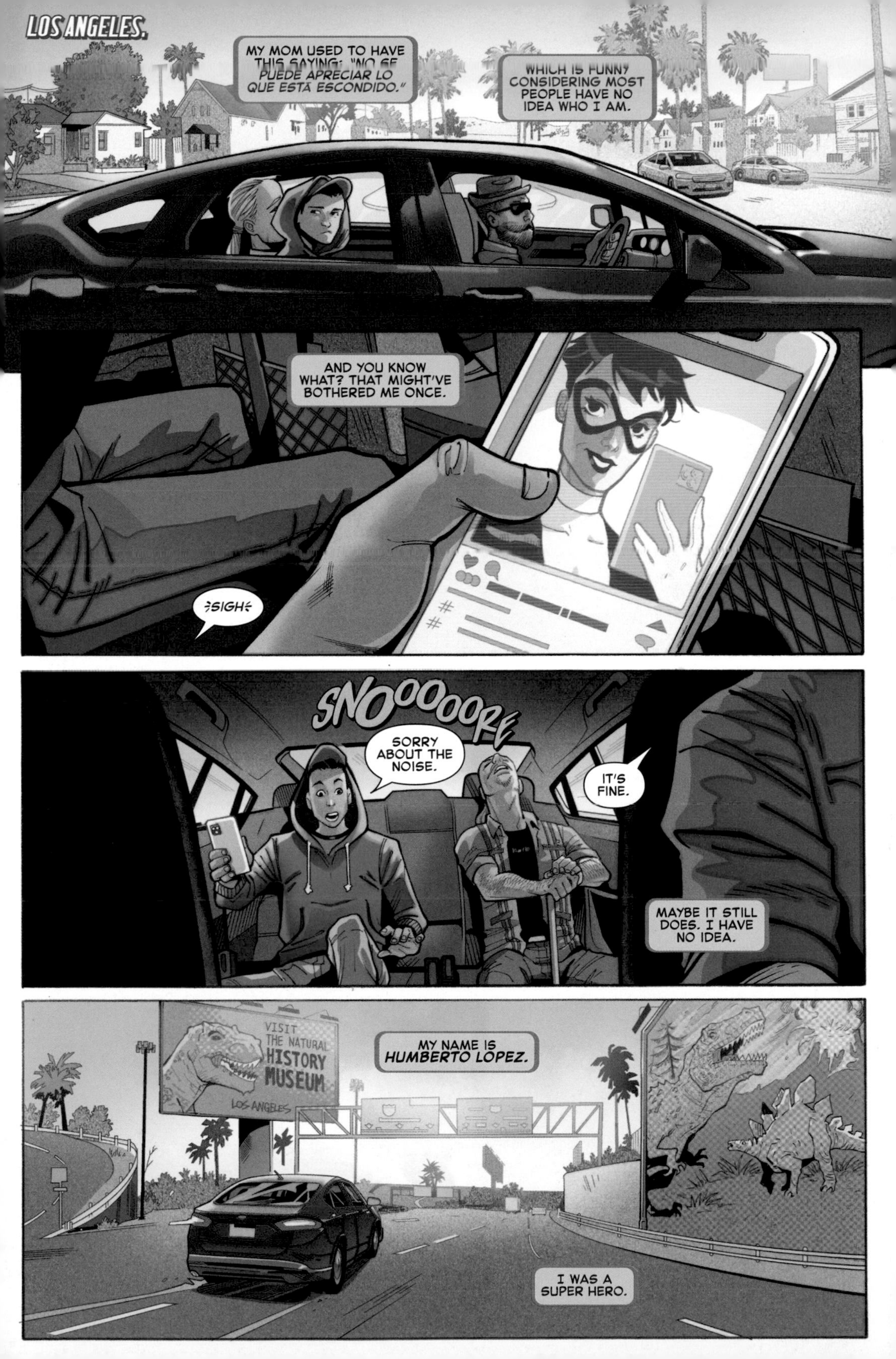
LOS ANGELES.
MY MOM USED TO HAVE THIS SAYING: "NO SE PUEDE APRECIAR LO QUE ESTÁ ESCONDIDO."
WHICH IS FUNNY CONSIDERING MOST PEOPLE HAVE NO IDEA WHO I AM.
AND YOU KNOW WHAT? THAT MIGHT'VE BOTHERED ME ONCE.
SIGH
SNOOOOORE
SORRY ABOUT THE NOISE.
IT'S FINE.
MAYBE IT STILL DOES. I HAVE NO IDEA.
VISIT THE NATURAL HISTORY MUSEUM
LOS ANGELES
MY NAME IS HUMBERTO LOPEZ.
I WAS A SUPER HERO.

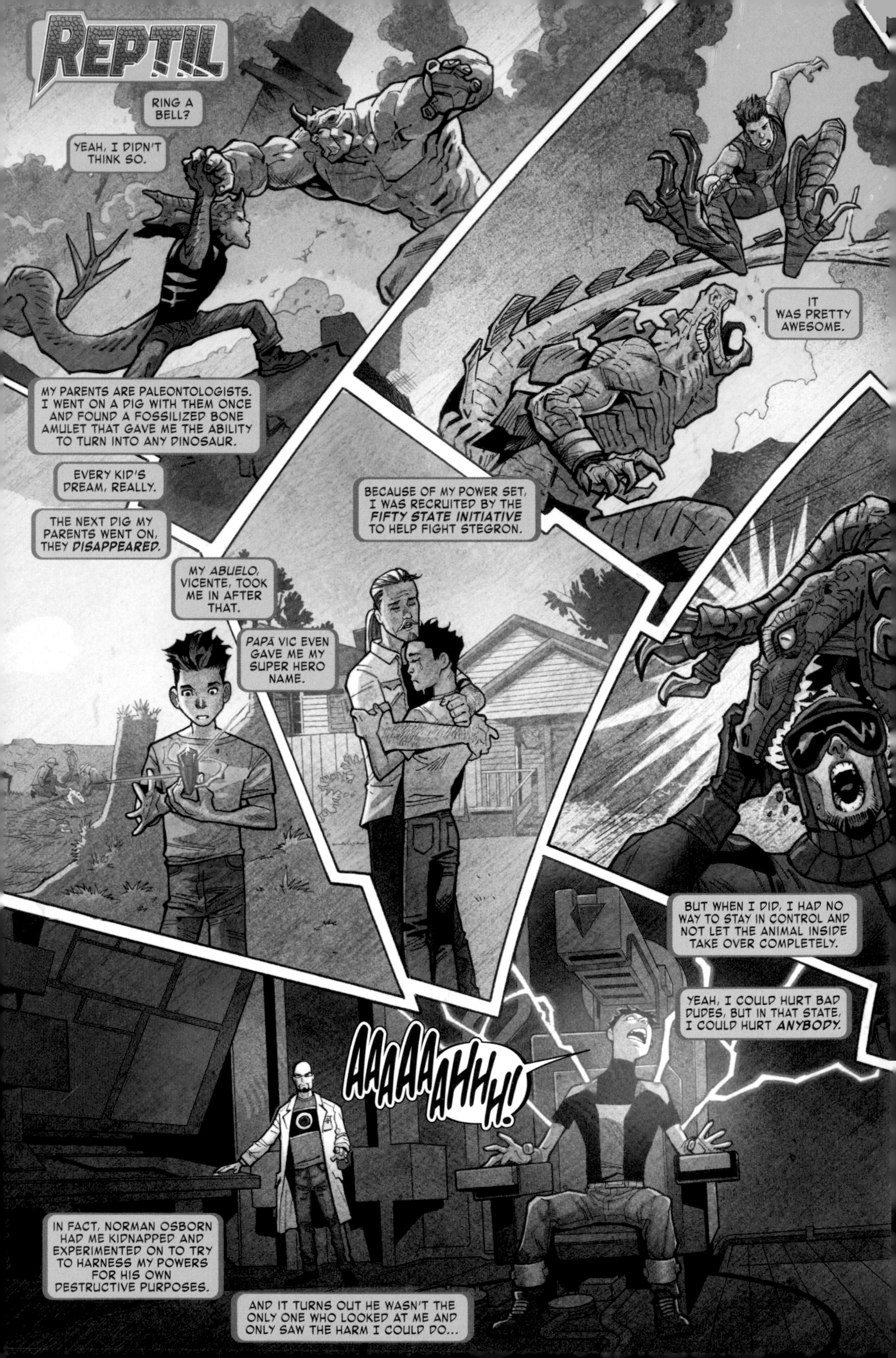
REPTIL
RING A BELL?
YEAH, I DIDN'T THINK SO.
IT WAS PRETTY AWESOME.
MY PARENTS ARE PALEONTOLOGISTS. I WENT ON A DIG WITH THEM ONCE AND FOUND A FOSSILIZED BONE AMULET THAT GAVE ME THE ABILITY TO TURN INTO ANY DINOSAUR.
EVERY KID'S DREAM, REALLY.
THE NEXT DIG MY PARENTS WENT ON, THEY *DISAPPEARED*.
MY *ABUELO*, VICENTE, TOOK ME IN AFTER THAT.
PAPÁ VIC EVEN GAVE ME MY SUPER HERO NAME.
BECAUSE OF MY POWER SET, I WAS RECRUITED BY THE ***FIFTY STATE INITIATIVE*** TO HELP FIGHT STEGRON.
BUT WHEN I DID, I HAD NO WAY TO STAY IN CONTROL AND NOT LET THE ANIMAL INSIDE TAKE OVER COMPLETELY.
YEAH, I COULD HURT BAD DUDES, BUT IN THAT STATE, I COULD HURT ***ANYBODY***.
AAAAAAHHH!
IN FACT, NORMAN OSBORN HAD ME KIDNAPPED AND EXPERIMENTED ON TO TRY TO HARNESS MY POWERS FOR HIS OWN DESTRUCTIVE PURPOSES.
AND IT TURNS OUT HE WASN'T THE ONLY ONE WHO LOOKED AT ME AND ONLY SAW THE HARM I COULD DO...

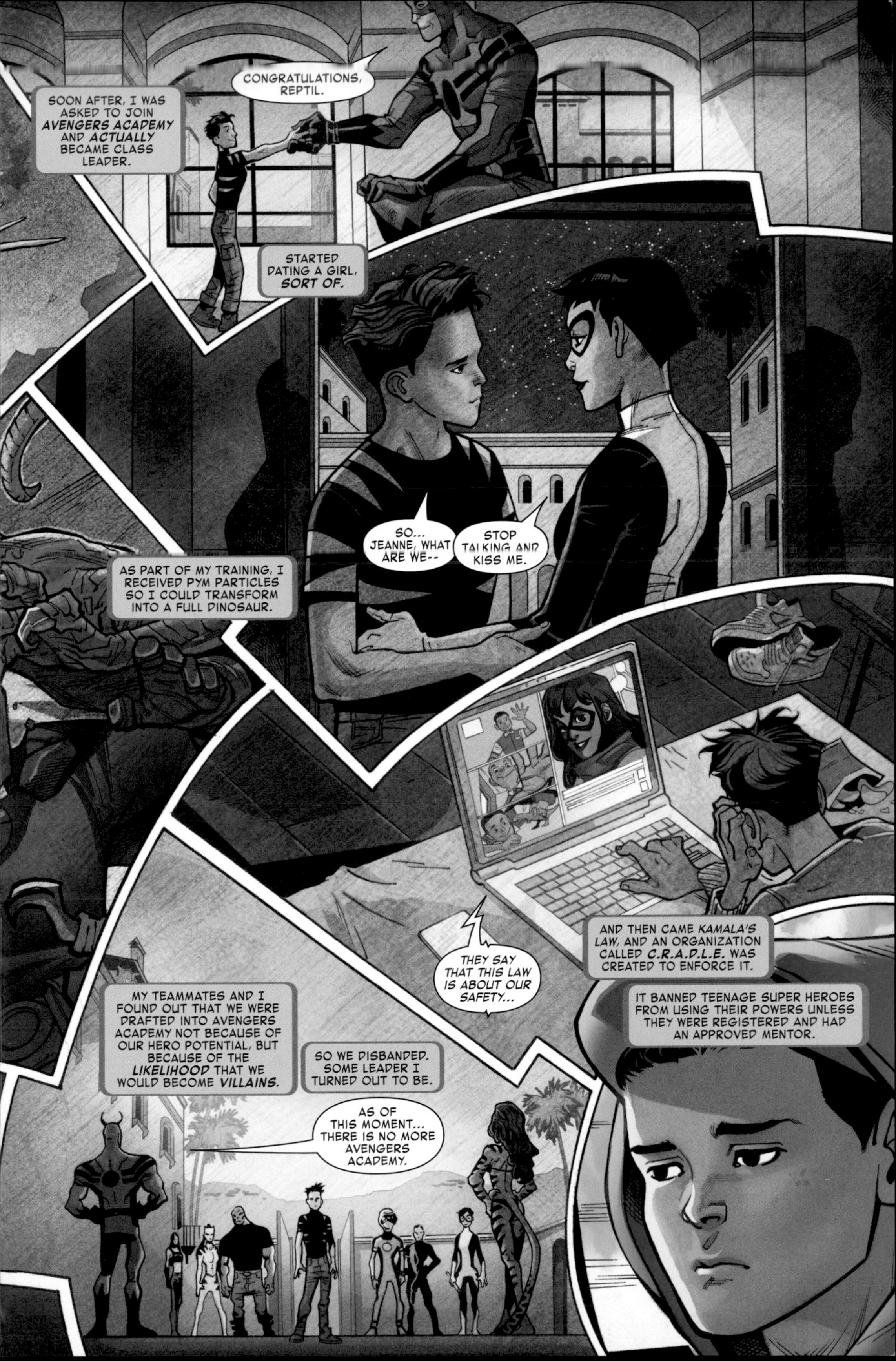
SOON AFTER, I WAS ASKED TO JOIN AVENGERS ACADEMY AND ACTUALLY BECAME CLASS LEADER.
CONGRATULATIONS, REPTIL.
STARTED DATING A GIRL, SORT OF.
SO... JEANNE, WHAT ARE WE--
STOP TALKING AND KISS ME.
AS PART OF MY TRAINING, I RECEIVED PYM PARTICLES SO I COULD TRANSFORM INTO A FULL DINOSAUR.
AND THEN CAME KAMALA'S LAW, AND AN ORGANIZATION CALLED C.R.A.D.L.E. WAS CREATED TO ENFORCE IT.
THEY SAY THAT THIS LAW IS ABOUT OUR SAFETY...
IT BANNED TEENAGE SUPER HEROES FROM USING THEIR POWERS UNLESS THEY WERE REGISTERED AND HAD AN APPROVED MENTOR.
MY TEAMMATES AND I FOUND OUT THAT WE WERE DRAFTED INTO AVENGERS ACADEMY NOT BECAUSE OF OUR HERO POTENTIAL, BUT BECAUSE OF THE LIKELIHOOD THAT WE WOULD BECOME VILLAINS.
SO WE DISBANDED. SOME LEADER I TURNED OUT TO BE.
AS OF THIS MOMENT... THERE IS NO MORE AVENGERS ACADEMY.

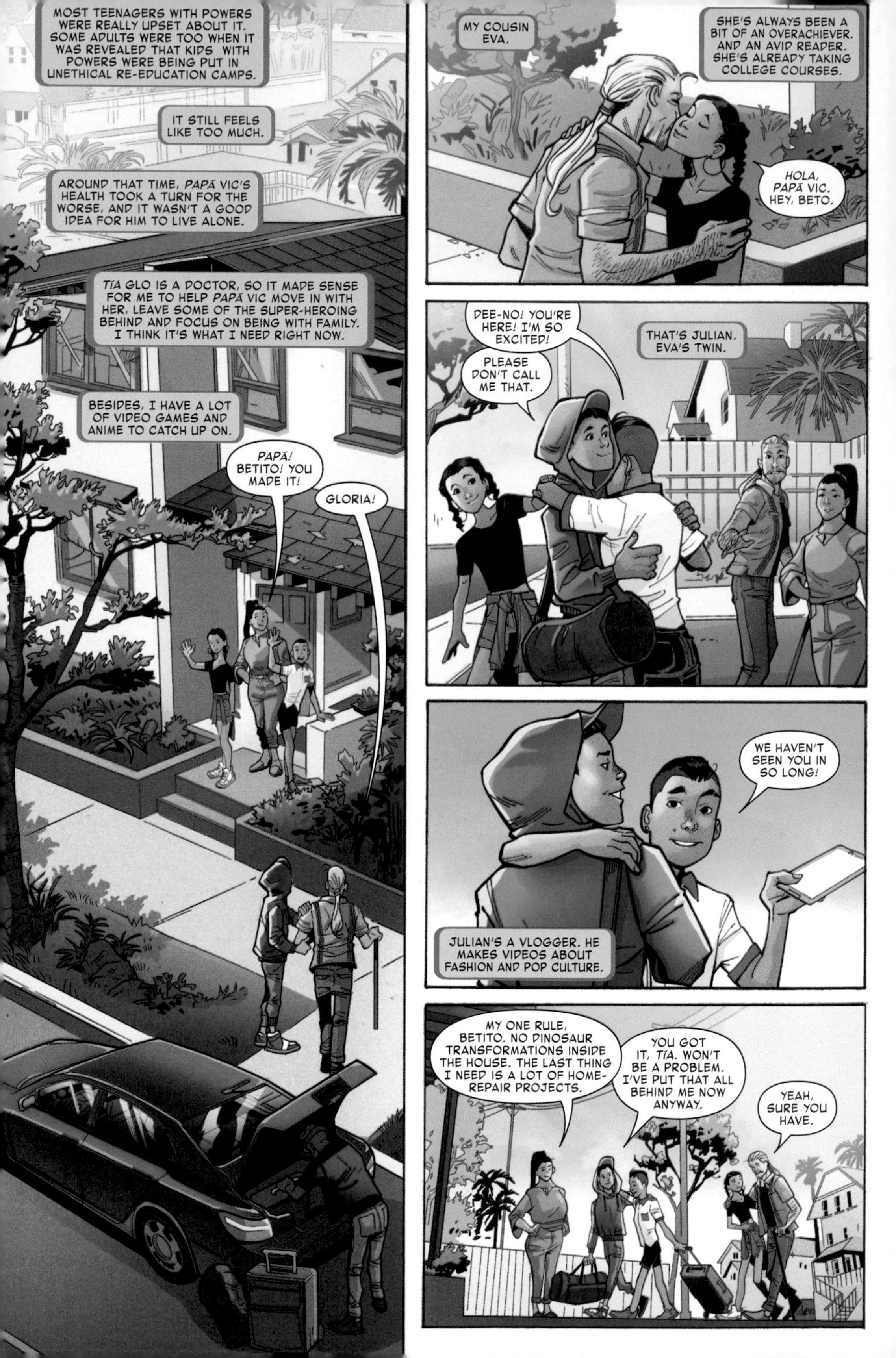
MOST TEENAGERS WITH POWERS WERE REALLY UPSET ABOUT IT. SOME ADULTS WERE TOO WHEN IT WAS REVEALED THAT KIDS WITH POWERS WERE BEING PUT IN UNETHICAL RE-EDUCATION CAMPS.
IT STILL FEELS LIKE TOO MUCH.
AROUND THAT TIME, *PAPÁ* VIC'S HEALTH TOOK A TURN FOR THE WORSE, AND IT WASN'T A GOOD IDEA FOR HIM TO LIVE ALONE.
TÍA GLO IS A DOCTOR, SO IT MADE SENSE FOR ME TO HELP *PAPÁ* VIC MOVE IN WITH HER, LEAVE SOME OF THE SUPER-HEROING BEHIND AND FOCUS ON BEING WITH FAMILY. I THINK IT'S WHAT I NEED RIGHT NOW.
BESIDES, I HAVE A LOT OF VIDEO GAMES AND ANIME TO CATCH UP ON.
PAPÁ! BETITO! YOU MADE IT!
GLORIA!
MY COUSIN EVA.
SHE'S ALWAYS BEEN A BIT OF AN OVERACHIEVER. AND AN AVID READER. SHE'S ALREADY TAKING COLLEGE COURSES.
HOLA, PAPÁ VIC. HEY, BETO.
DEE-NO! YOU'RE HERE! I'M SO EXCITED!
PLEASE DON'T CALL ME THAT.
THAT'S JULIAN. EVA'S TWIN.
WE HAVEN'T SEEN YOU IN SO LONG!
JULIAN'S A VLOGGER. HE MAKES VIDEOS ABOUT FASHION AND POP CULTURE.
MY ONE RULE, BETITO. NO DINOSAUR TRANSFORMATIONS INSIDE THE HOUSE. THE LAST THING I NEED IS A LOT OF HOME-REPAIR PROJECTS.
YOU GOT IT, *TÍA*. WON'T BE A PROBLEM. I'VE PUT THAT ALL BEHIND ME NOW ANYWAY.
YEAH, SURE YOU HAVE.

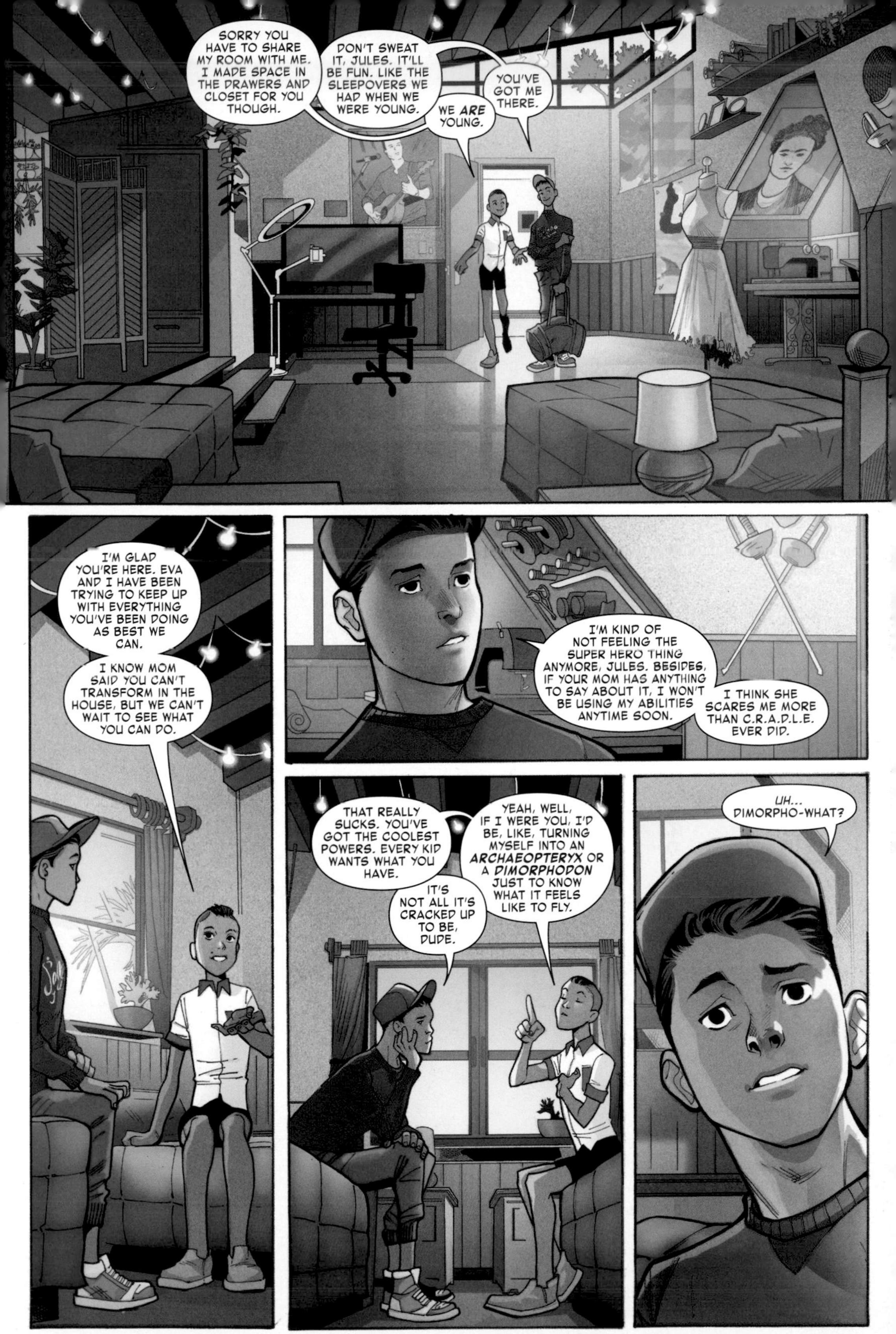
SORRY YOU HAVE TO SHARE MY ROOM WITH ME. I MADE SPACE IN THE DRAWERS AND CLOSET FOR YOU THOUGH.
DON'T SWEAT IT, JULES. IT'LL BE FUN. LIKE THE SLEEPOVERS WE HAD WHEN WE WERE YOUNG.
WE *ARE* YOUNG.
YOU'VE GOT ME THERE.
I'M GLAD YOU'RE HERE. EVA AND I HAVE BEEN TRYING TO KEEP UP WITH EVERYTHING YOU'VE BEEN DOING AS BEST WE CAN.
I KNOW MOM SAID YOU CAN'T TRANSFORM IN THE HOUSE, BUT WE CAN'T WAIT TO SEE WHAT YOU CAN DO.
I'M KIND OF NOT FEELING THE SUPER HERO THING ANYMORE, JULES. BESIDES, IF YOUR MOM HAS ANYTHING TO SAY ABOUT IT, I WON'T BE USING MY ABILITIES ANYTIME SOON.
I THINK SHE SCARES ME MORE THAN C.R.A.D.L.E. EVER DID.
THAT REALLY SUCKS. YOU'VE GOT THE COOLEST POWERS. EVERY KID WANTS WHAT YOU HAVE.
IT'S NOT ALL IT'S CRACKED UP TO BE, DUDE.
YEAH, WELL, IF I WERE YOU, I'D BE, LIKE, TURNING MYSELF INTO AN ***ARCHAEOPTERYX*** OR A ***DIMORPHODON*** JUST TO KNOW WHAT IT FEELS LIKE TO FLY.
UH... DIMORPHO-WHAT?

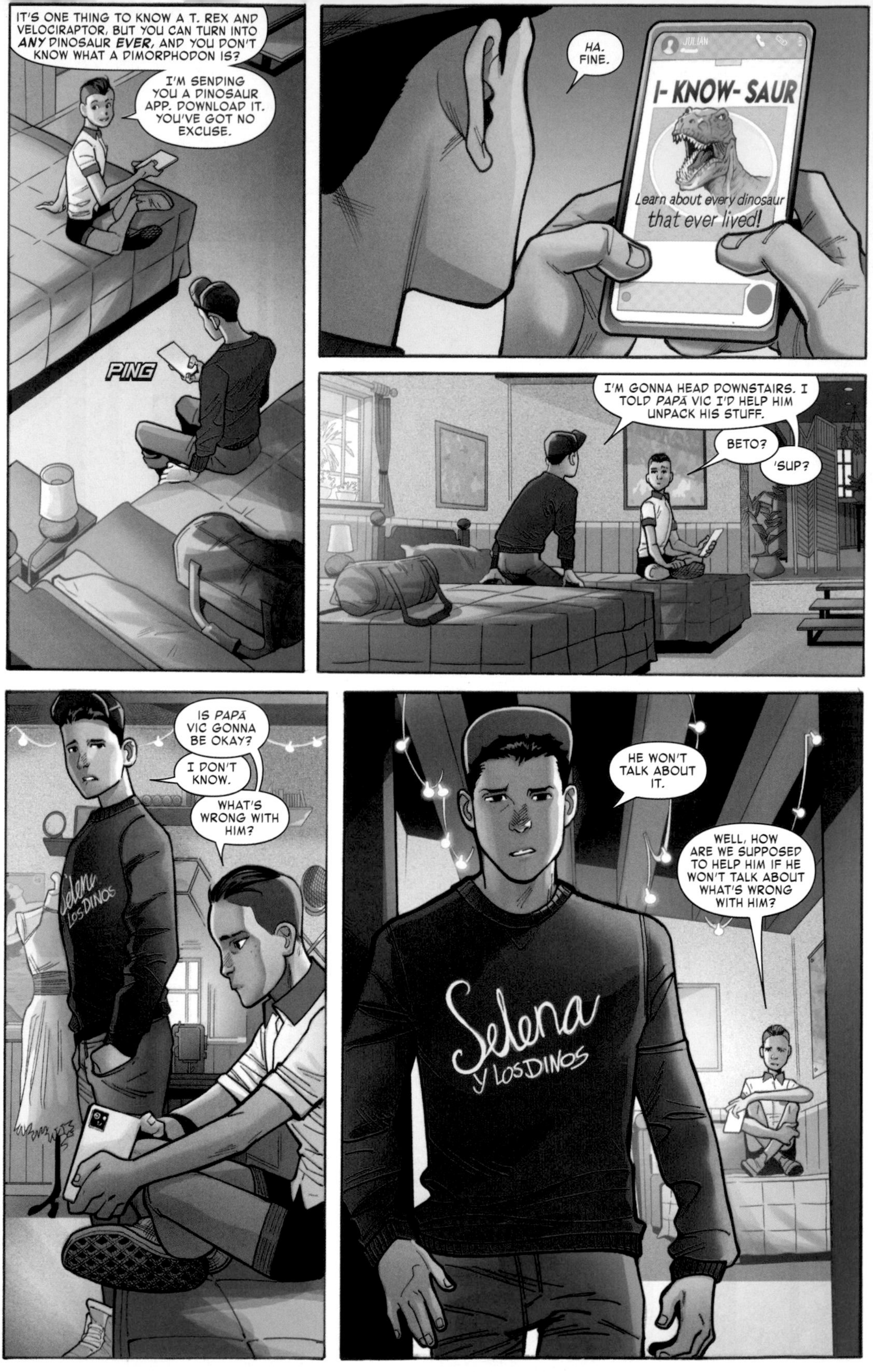

IT'S ONE THING TO KNOW A T. REX AND VELOCIRAPTOR, BUT YOU CAN TURN INTO *ANY* DINOSAUR *EVER*, AND YOU DON'T KNOW WHAT A DIMORPHODON IS?
I'M SENDING YOU A DINOSAUR APP. DOWNLOAD IT. YOU'VE GOT NO EXCUSE.
PING
HA. FINE.
JULIÁN
I- KNOW- SAUR
Learn about every dinosaur that ever lived!
I'M GONNA HEAD DOWNSTAIRS. I TOLD *PAPĀ* VIC I'D HELP HIM UNPACK HIS STUFF.
BETO?
'SUP?
IS *PAPĀ* VIC GONNA BE OKAY?
I DON'T KNOW.
WHAT'S WRONG WITH HIM?
Selena Los Dinos
HE WON'T TALK ABOUT IT.
WELL, HOW ARE WE SUPPOSED TO HELP HIM IF HE WON'T TALK ABOUT WHAT'S WRONG WITH HIM?
Selena y Los Dinos

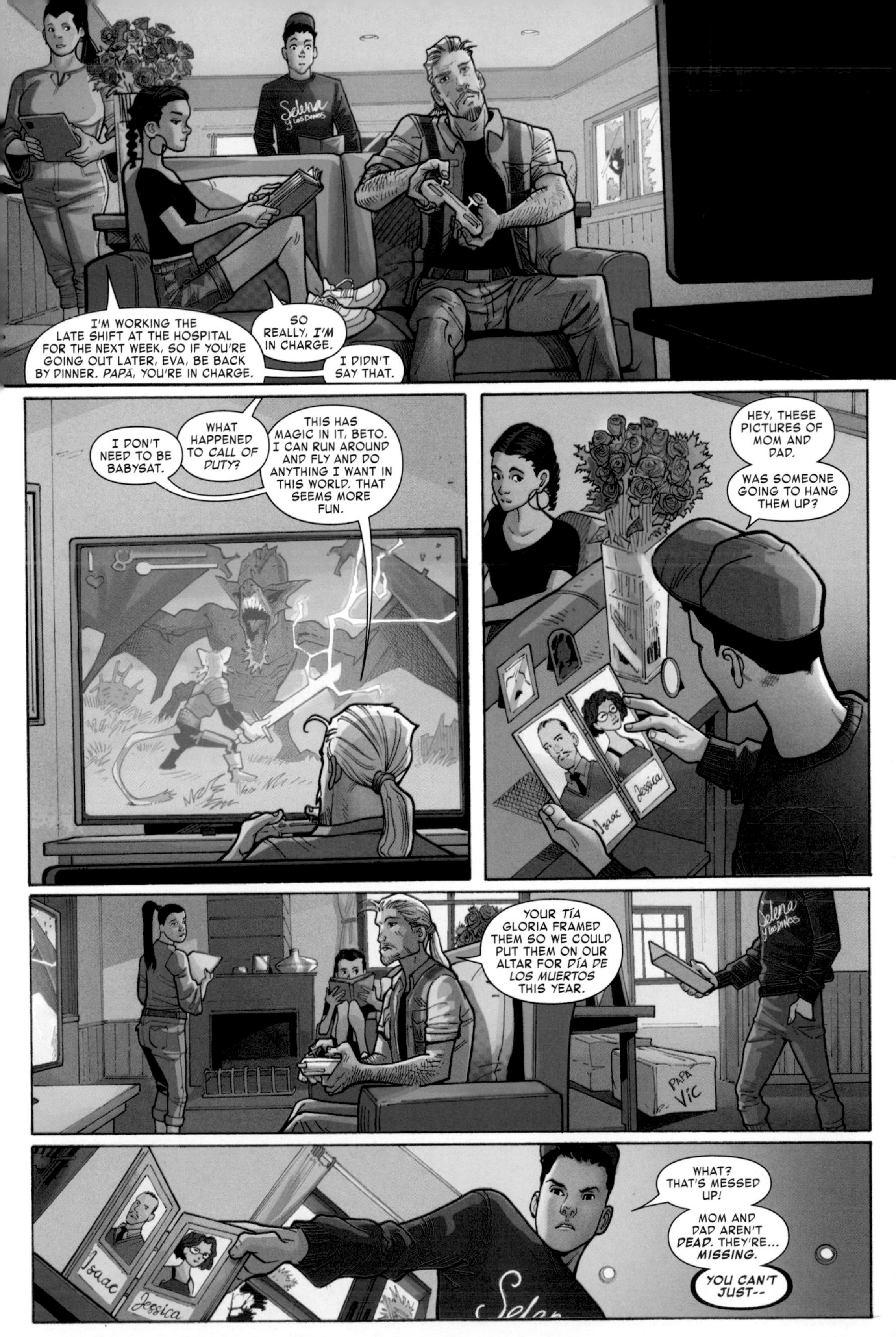
I'M WORKING THE LATE SHIFT AT THE HOSPITAL FOR THE NEXT WEEK, SO IF YOU'RE GOING OUT LATER, EVA, BE BACK BY DINNER. *PAPÁ*, YOU'RE IN CHARGE.
SO REALLY, *I'M* IN CHARGE.
I DIDN'T SAY THAT.
I DON'T NEED TO BE BABYSAT.
WHAT HAPPENED TO *CALL OF DUTY?*
THIS HAS MAGIC IN IT, BETO. I CAN RUN AROUND AND FLY AND DO ANYTHING I WANT IN THIS WORLD. THAT SEEMS MORE FUN.
HEY, THESE PICTURES OF MOM AND DAD.
WAS SOMEONE GOING TO HANG THEM UP?
Isaac
Jessica
YOUR *TÍA* GLORIA FRAMED THEM SO WE COULD PUT THEM ON OUR ALTAR FOR *DÍA DE LOS MUERTOS* THIS YEAR.
PAPA Vic
WHAT? THAT'S MESSED UP!
MOM AND DAD AREN'T *DEAD*. THEY'RE... *MISSING*.
YOU CAN'T JUST--

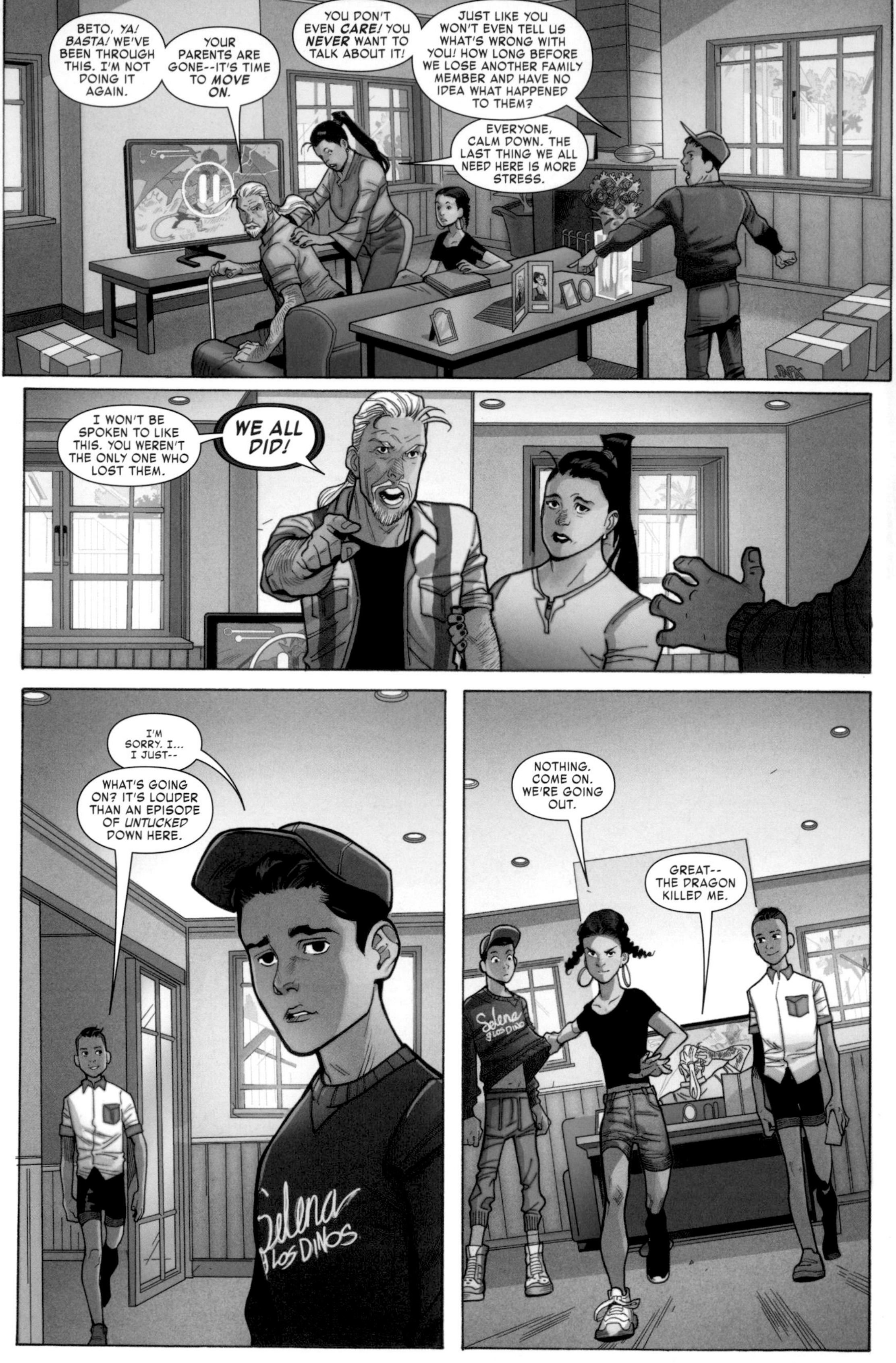
BETO, YA! BASTA! WE'VE BEEN THROUGH THIS. I'M NOT DOING IT AGAIN.
YOUR PARENTS ARE GONE--IT'S TIME TO MOVE ON.
YOU DON'T EVEN CARE! YOU NEVER WANT TO TALK ABOUT IT!
JUST LIKE YOU WON'T EVEN TELL US WHAT'S WRONG WITH YOU! HOW LONG BEFORE WE LOSE ANOTHER FAMILY MEMBER AND HAVE NO IDEA WHAT HAPPENED TO THEM?
EVERYONE, CALM DOWN. THE LAST THING WE ALL NEED HERE IS MORE STRESS.
I WON'T BE SPOKEN TO LIKE THIS. YOU WEREN'T THE ONLY ONE WHO LOST THEM.
WE ALL DID!
I'M SORRY. I... I JUST--
WHAT'S GOING ON? IT'S LOUDER THAN AN EPISODE OF UNTUCKED DOWN HERE.
NOTHING. COME ON. WE'RE GOING OUT.
GREAT-- THE DRAGON KILLED ME.
Selena y LOS DINOS

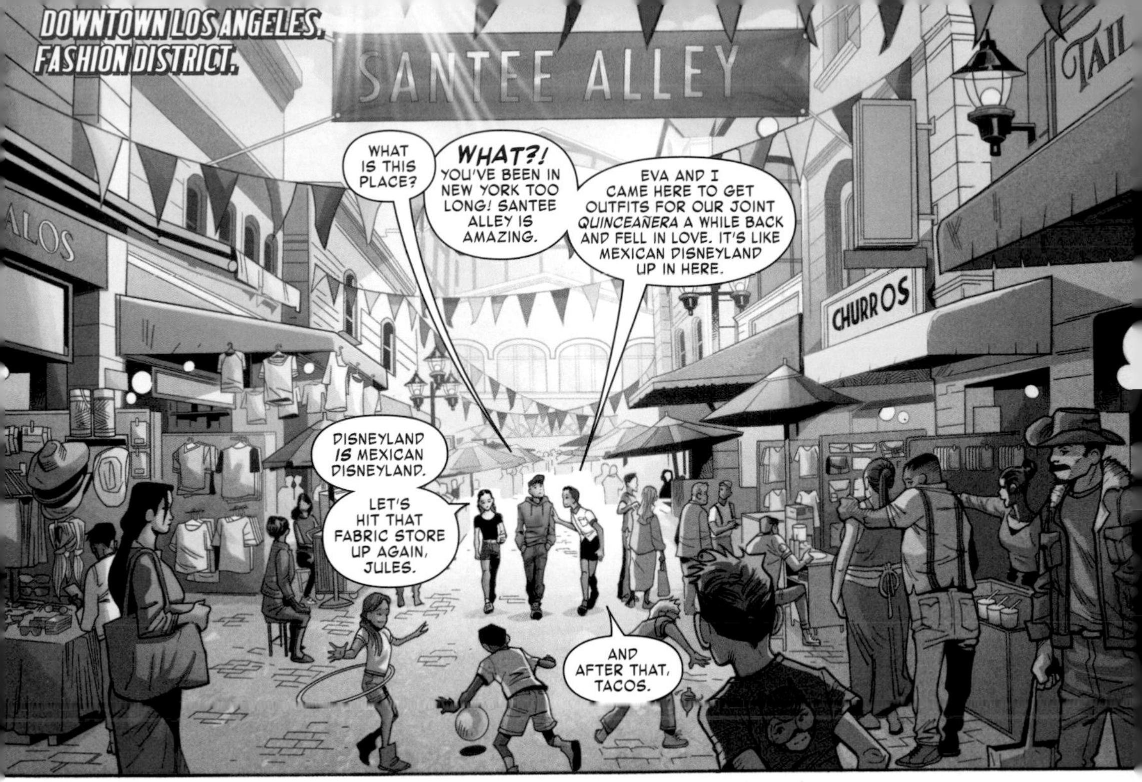
DOWNTOWN LOS ANGELES, FASHION DISTRICT.
SANTEE ALLEY
WHAT IS THIS PLACE?
WHAT?! YOU'VE BEEN IN NEW YORK TOO LONG! SANTEE ALLEY IS AMAZING.
EVA AND I CAME HERE TO GET OUTFITS FOR OUR JOINT *QUINCEAÑERA* A WHILE BACK AND FELL IN LOVE. IT'S LIKE MEXICAN DISNEYLAND UP IN HERE.
CHURROS
DISNEYLAND *IS* MEXICAN DISNEYLAND.
LET'S HIT THAT FABRIC STORE UP AGAIN, JULES.
AND AFTER THAT, TACOS.

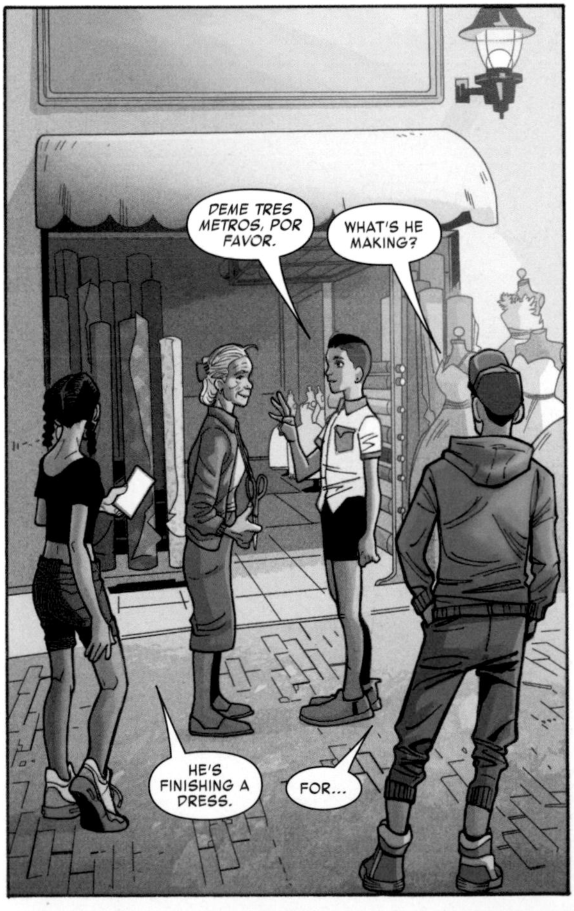
DEME TRES METROS, POR FAVOR.
WHAT'S HE MAKING?
HE'S FINISHING A DRESS.
FOR...

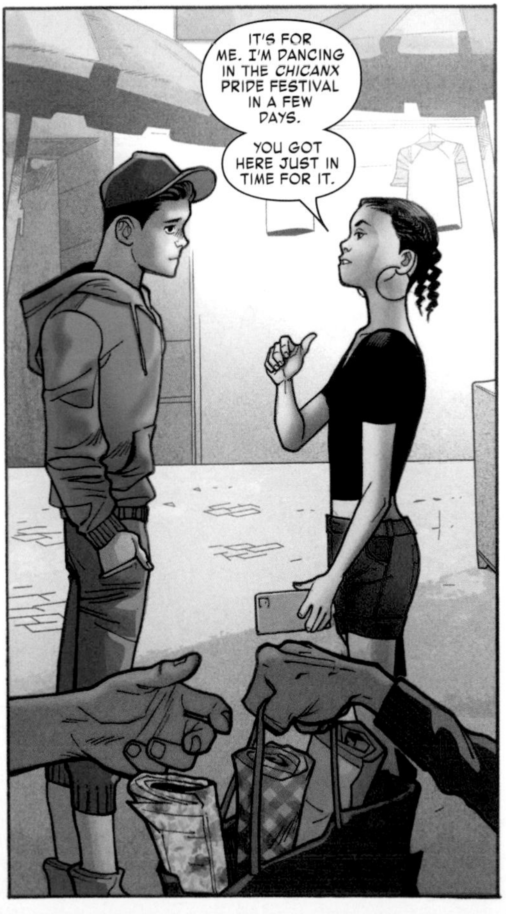
IT'S FOR ME. I'M DANCING IN THE *CHICANX* PRIDE FESTIVAL IN A FEW DAYS.
YOU GOT HERE JUST IN TIME FOR IT.

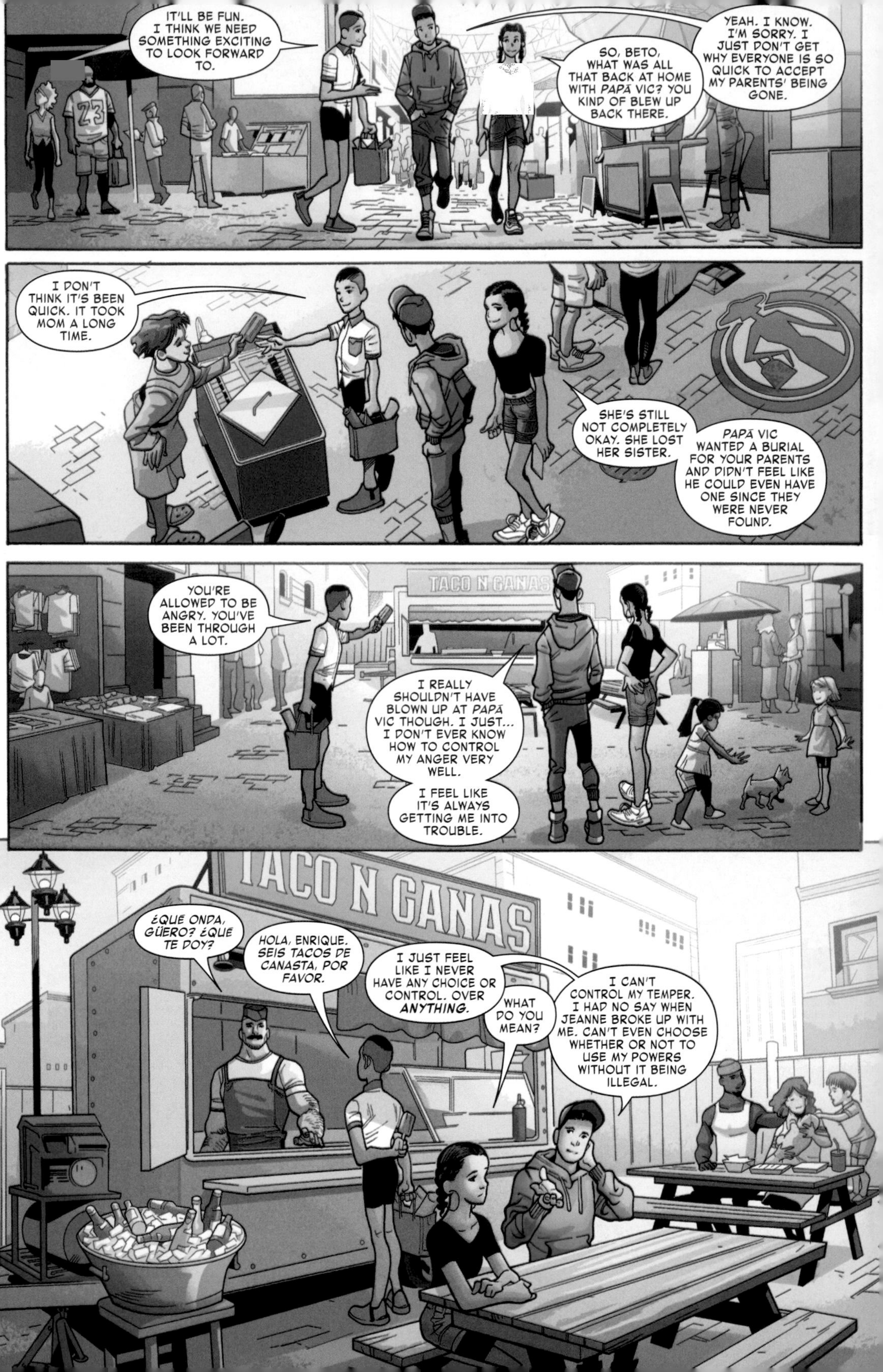
IT'LL BE FUN. I THINK WE NEED SOMETHING EXCITING TO LOOK FORWARD TO.
SO, BETO, WHAT WAS ALL THAT BACK AT HOME WITH *PAPÁ* VIC? YOU KIND OF BLEW UP BACK THERE.
YEAH. I KNOW. I'M SORRY. I JUST DON'T GET WHY EVERYONE IS SO QUICK TO ACCEPT MY PARENTS' BEING GONE.
I DON'T THINK IT'S BEEN QUICK. IT TOOK MOM A LONG TIME.
SHE'S STILL NOT COMPLETELY OKAY. SHE LOST HER SISTER.
PAPÁ VIC WANTED A BURIAL FOR YOUR PARENTS AND DIDN'T FEEL LIKE HE COULD EVEN HAVE ONE SINCE THEY WERE NEVER FOUND.
YOU'RE ALLOWED TO BE ANGRY. YOU'VE BEEN THROUGH A LOT.
TACO N GANAS
I REALLY SHOULDN'T HAVE BLOWN UP AT *PAPÁ* VIC THOUGH. I JUST... I DON'T EVER KNOW HOW TO CONTROL MY ANGER VERY WELL.
I FEEL LIKE IT'S ALWAYS GETTING ME INTO TROUBLE.
TACO N GANAS
¿QUÉ ONDA, GÜERO? ¿QUÉ TE DOY?
HOLA, ENRIQUE. SEIS TACOS DE CANASTA, POR FAVOR.
I JUST FEEL LIKE I NEVER HAVE ANY CHOICE OR CONTROL. OVER ***ANYTHING.***
WHAT DO YOU MEAN?
I CAN'T CONTROL MY TEMPER. I HAD NO SAY WHEN JEANNE BROKE UP WITH ME. CAN'T EVEN CHOOSE WHETHER OR NOT TO USE MY POWERS WITHOUT IT BEING ILLEGAL.

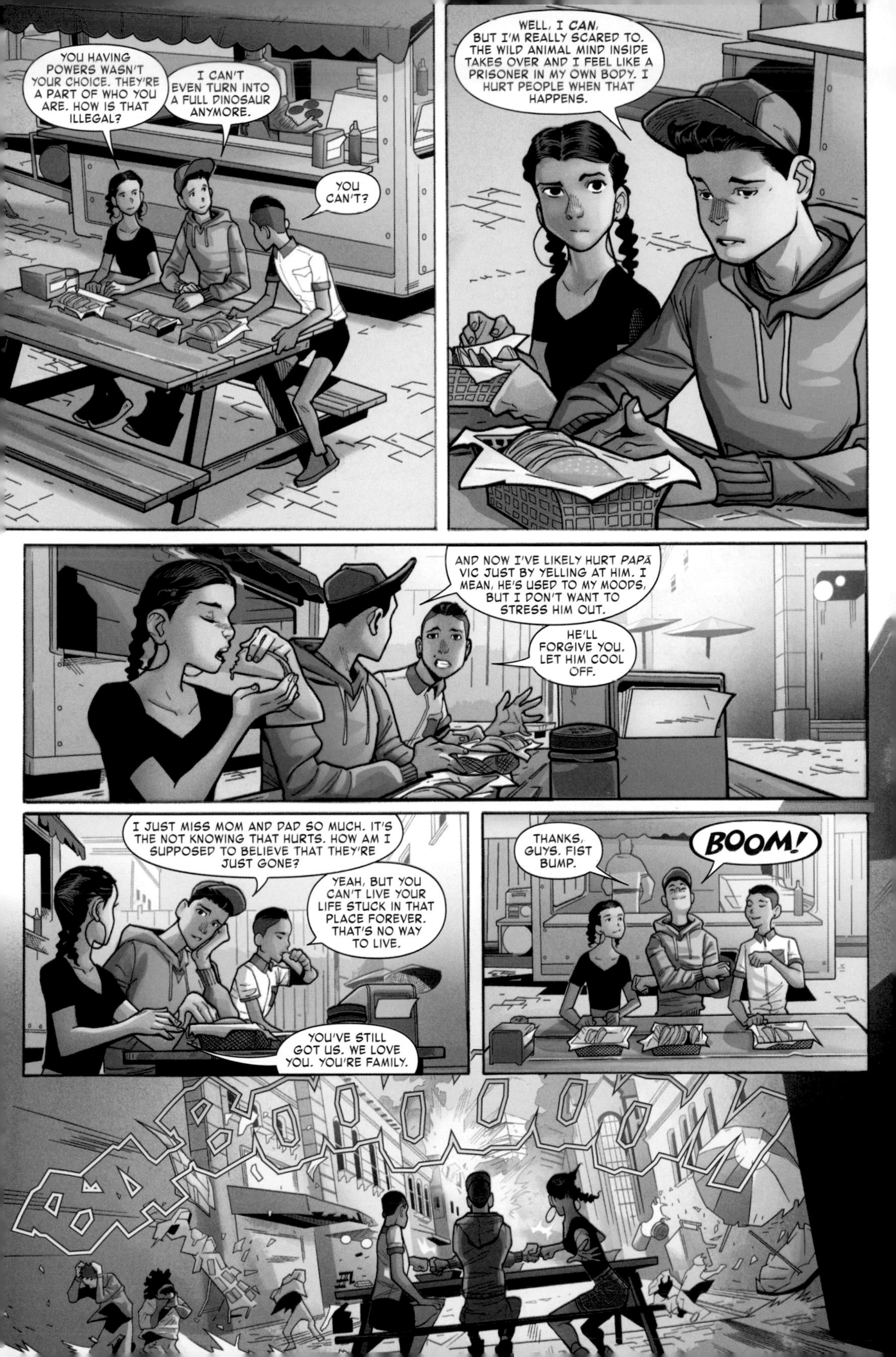
YOU HAVING POWERS WASN'T YOUR CHOICE. THEY'RE A PART OF WHO YOU ARE. HOW IS THAT ILLEGAL?
I CAN'T EVEN TURN INTO A FULL DINOSAUR ANYMORE.
YOU CAN'T?
WELL, I *CAN*, BUT I'M REALLY SCARED TO. THE WILD ANIMAL MIND INSIDE TAKES OVER AND I FEEL LIKE A PRISONER IN MY OWN BODY. I HURT PEOPLE WHEN THAT HAPPENS.
AND NOW I'VE LIKELY HURT *PAPĀ* VIC JUST BY YELLING AT HIM. I MEAN, HE'S USED TO MY MOODS, BUT I DON'T WANT TO STRESS HIM OUT.
HE'LL FORGIVE YOU. LET HIM COOL OFF.
I JUST MISS MOM AND DAD SO MUCH. IT'S THE NOT KNOWING THAT HURTS. HOW AM I SUPPOSED TO BELIEVE THAT THEY'RE JUST GONE?
YEAH, BUT YOU CAN'T LIVE YOUR LIFE STUCK IN THAT PLACE FOREVER. THAT'S NO WAY TO LIVE.
YOU'VE STILL GOT US. WE LOVE YOU. YOU'RE FAMILY.
THANKS, GUYS. FIST BUMP.
BOOM!

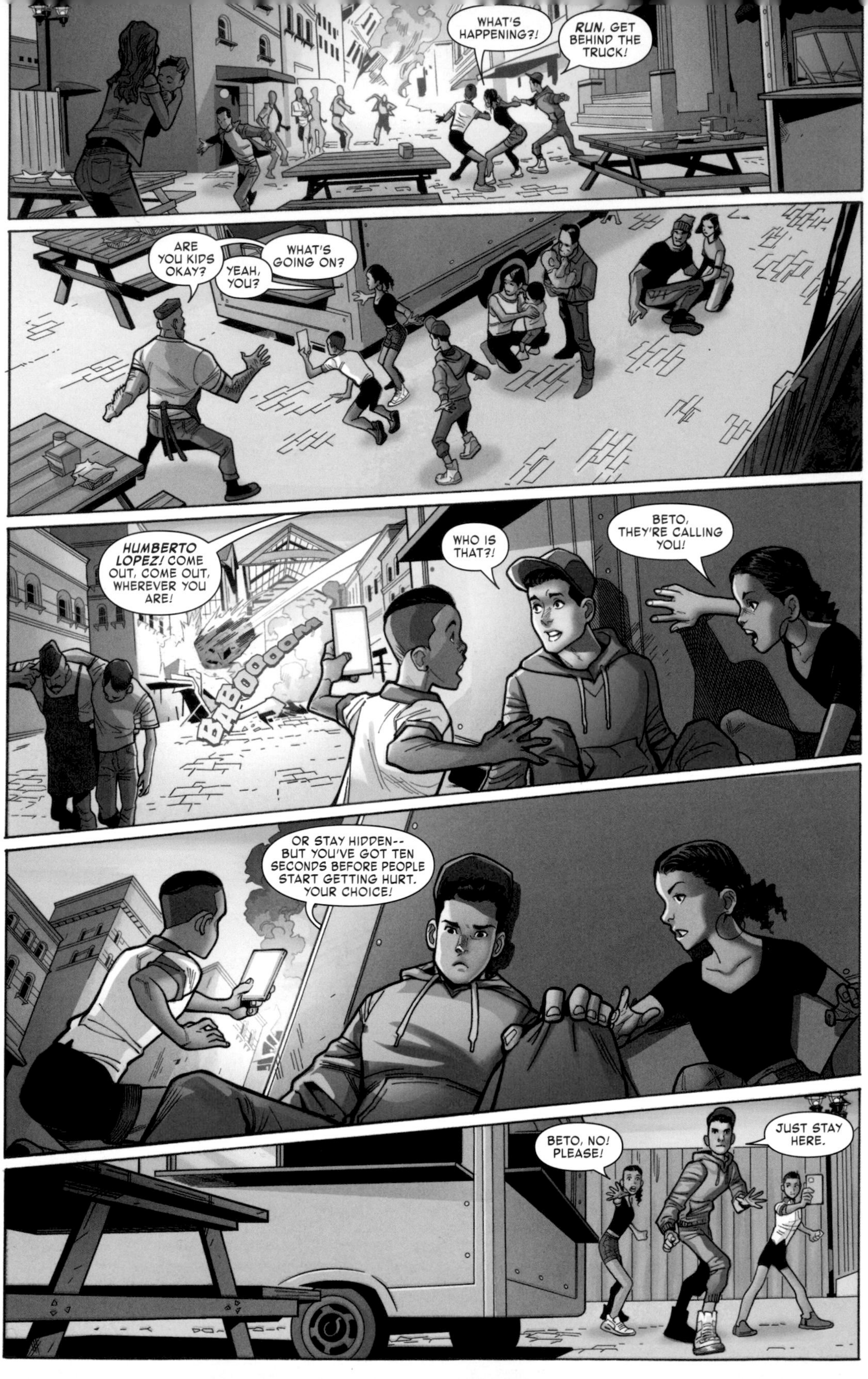
WHAT'S HAPPENING?!
RUN, GET BEHIND THE TRUCK!
ARE YOU KIDS OKAY?
YEAH, YOU?
WHAT'S GOING ON?
HUMBERTO LOPEZ! COME OUT, COME OUT, WHEREVER YOU ARE!
BABOOOOOM
WHO IS THAT?!
BETO, THEY'RE CALLING YOU!
OR STAY HIDDEN-- BUT YOU'VE GOT TEN SECONDS BEFORE PEOPLE START GETTING HURT. YOUR CHOICE!
BETO, NO! PLEASE!
JUST STAY HERE.

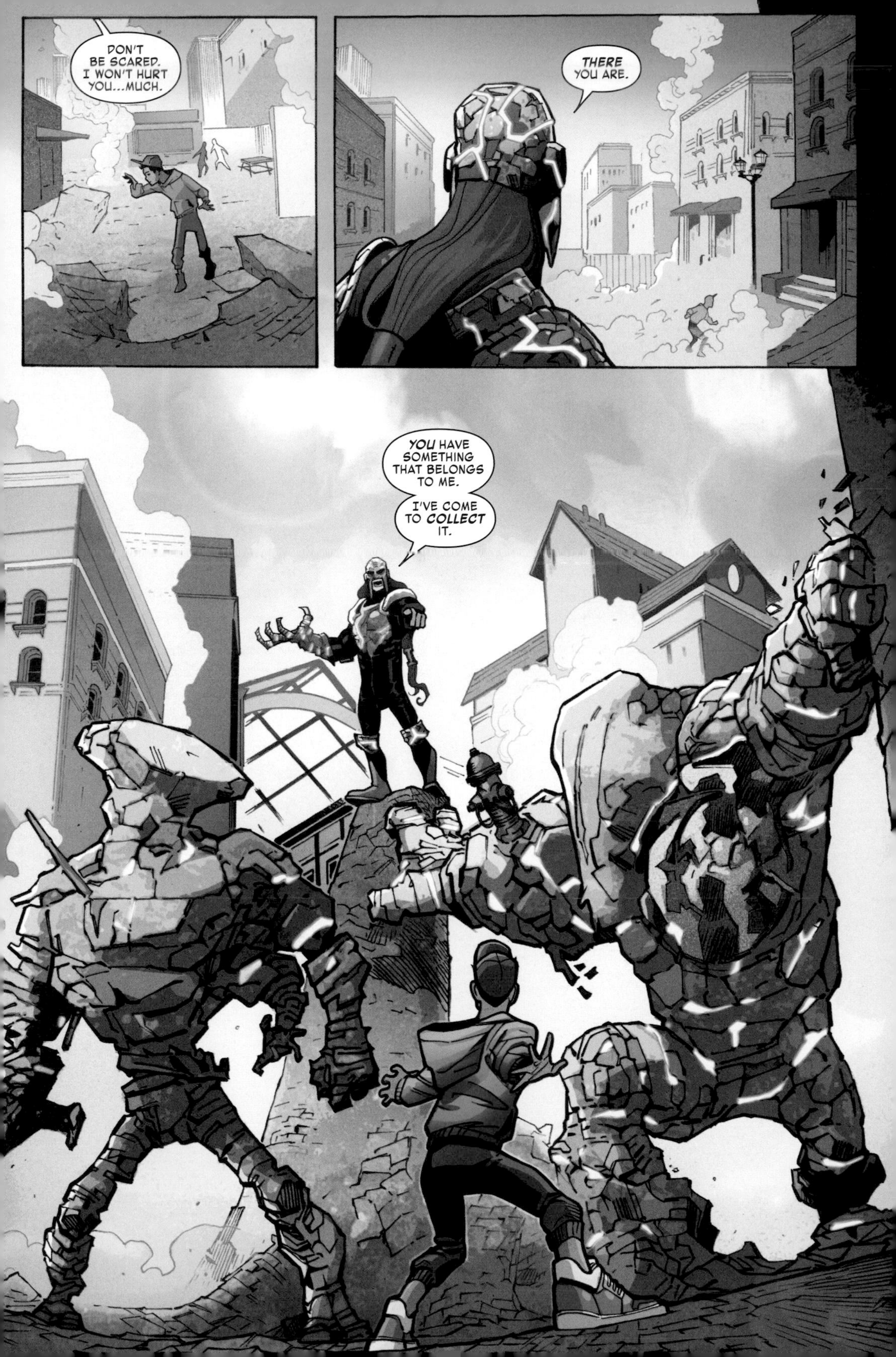
DON'T BE SCARED. I WON'T HURT YOU...MUCH.
THERE YOU ARE.
YOU HAVE SOMETHING THAT BELONGS TO ME.
I'VE COME TO COLLECT IT.

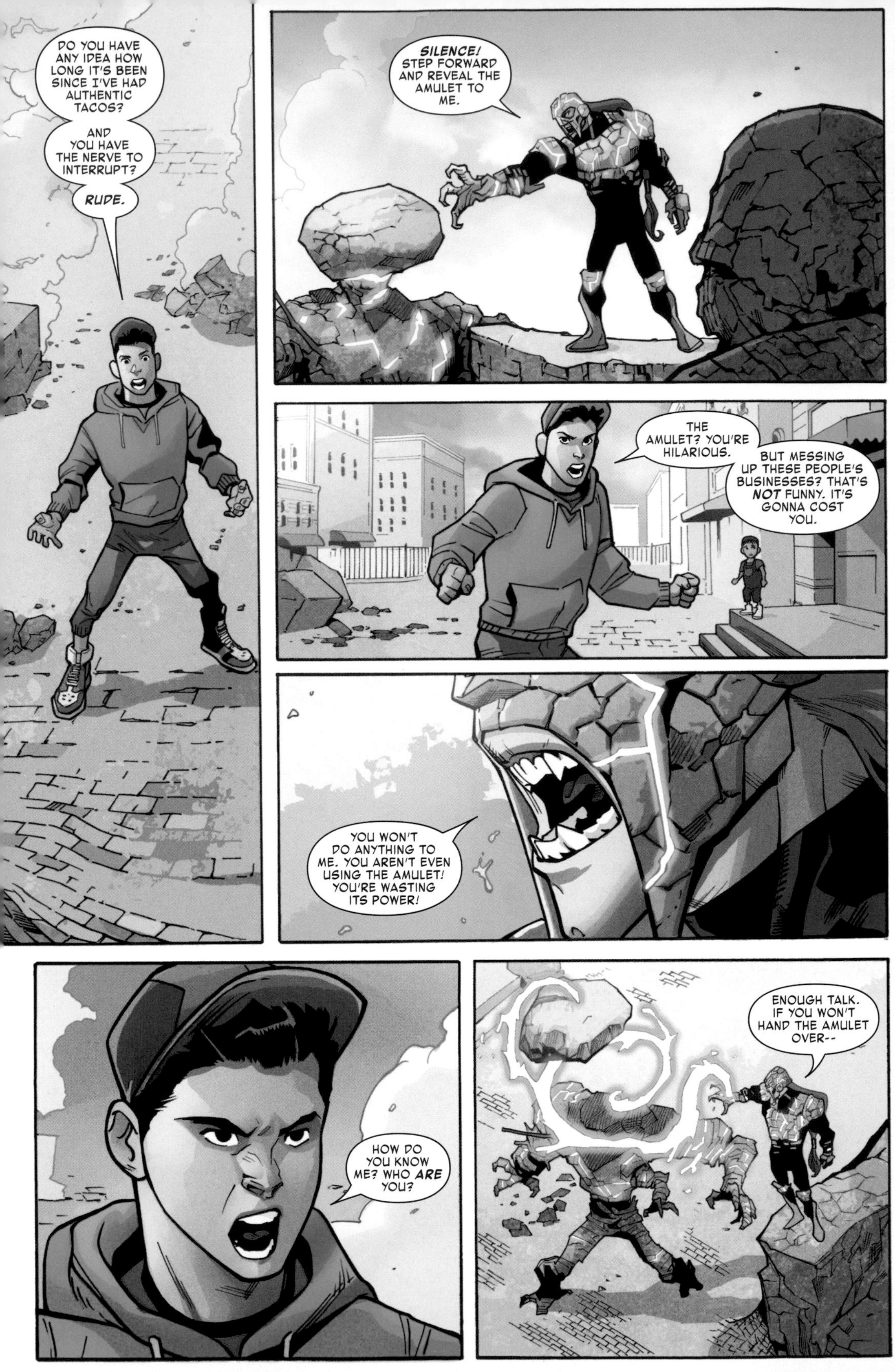
DO YOU HAVE ANY IDEA HOW LONG IT'S BEEN SINCE I'VE HAD AUTHENTIC TACOS?
AND YOU HAVE THE NERVE TO INTERRUPT?
RUDE.
SILENCE! STEP FORWARD AND REVEAL THE AMULET TO ME.
THE AMULET? YOU'RE HILARIOUS.
BUT MESSING UP THESE PEOPLE'S BUSINESSES? THAT'S *NOT* FUNNY. IT'S GONNA COST YOU.
YOU WON'T DO ANYTHING TO ME. YOU AREN'T EVEN USING THE AMULET! YOU'RE WASTING ITS POWER!
HOW DO YOU KNOW ME? WHO *ARE* YOU?
ENOUGH TALK. IF YOU WON'T HAND THE AMULET OVER--

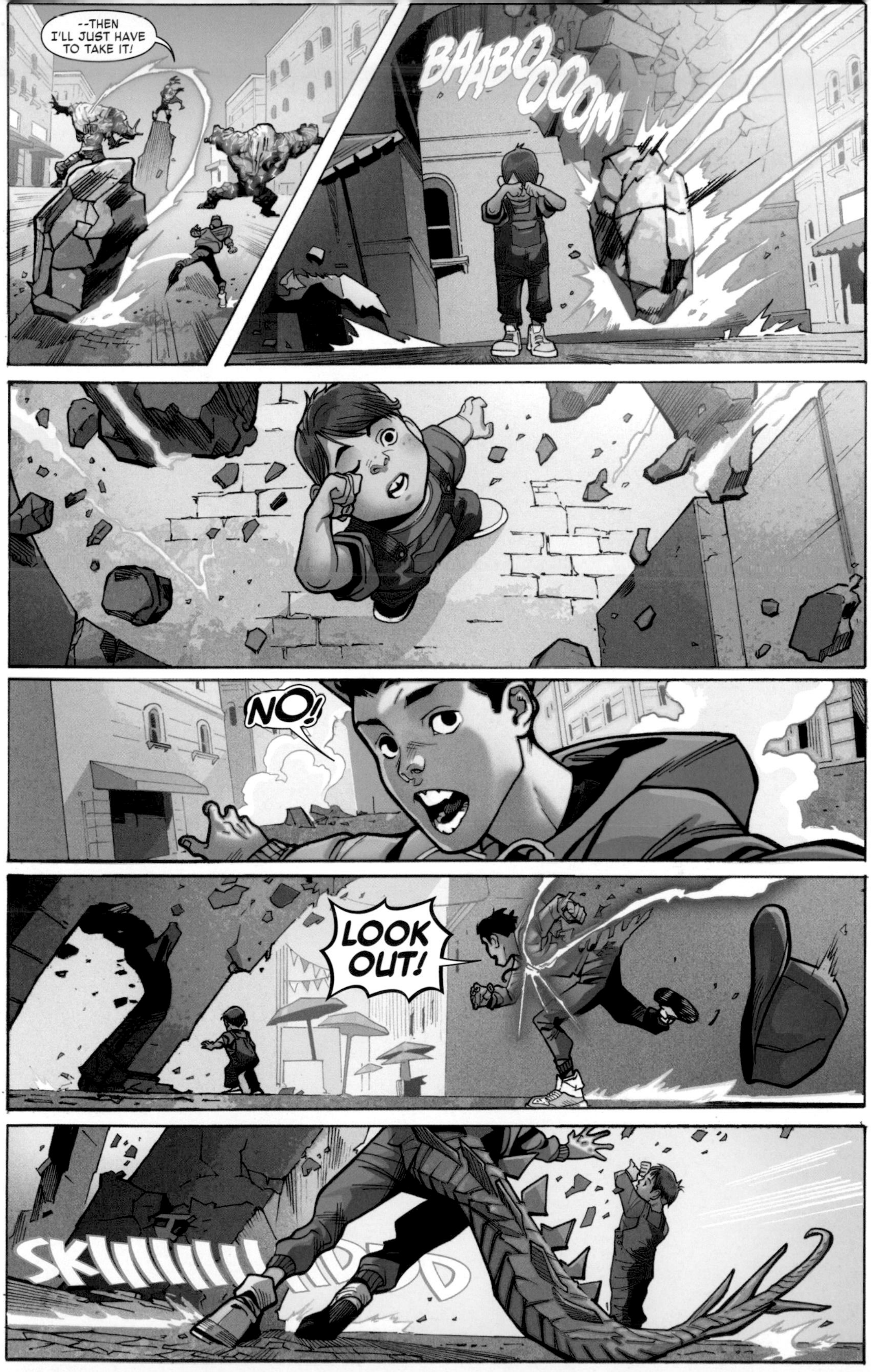
--THEN I'LL JUST HAVE TO TAKE IT!
BAABOOOOM
NO!
LOOK OUT!
SKIIIIIIIDDD

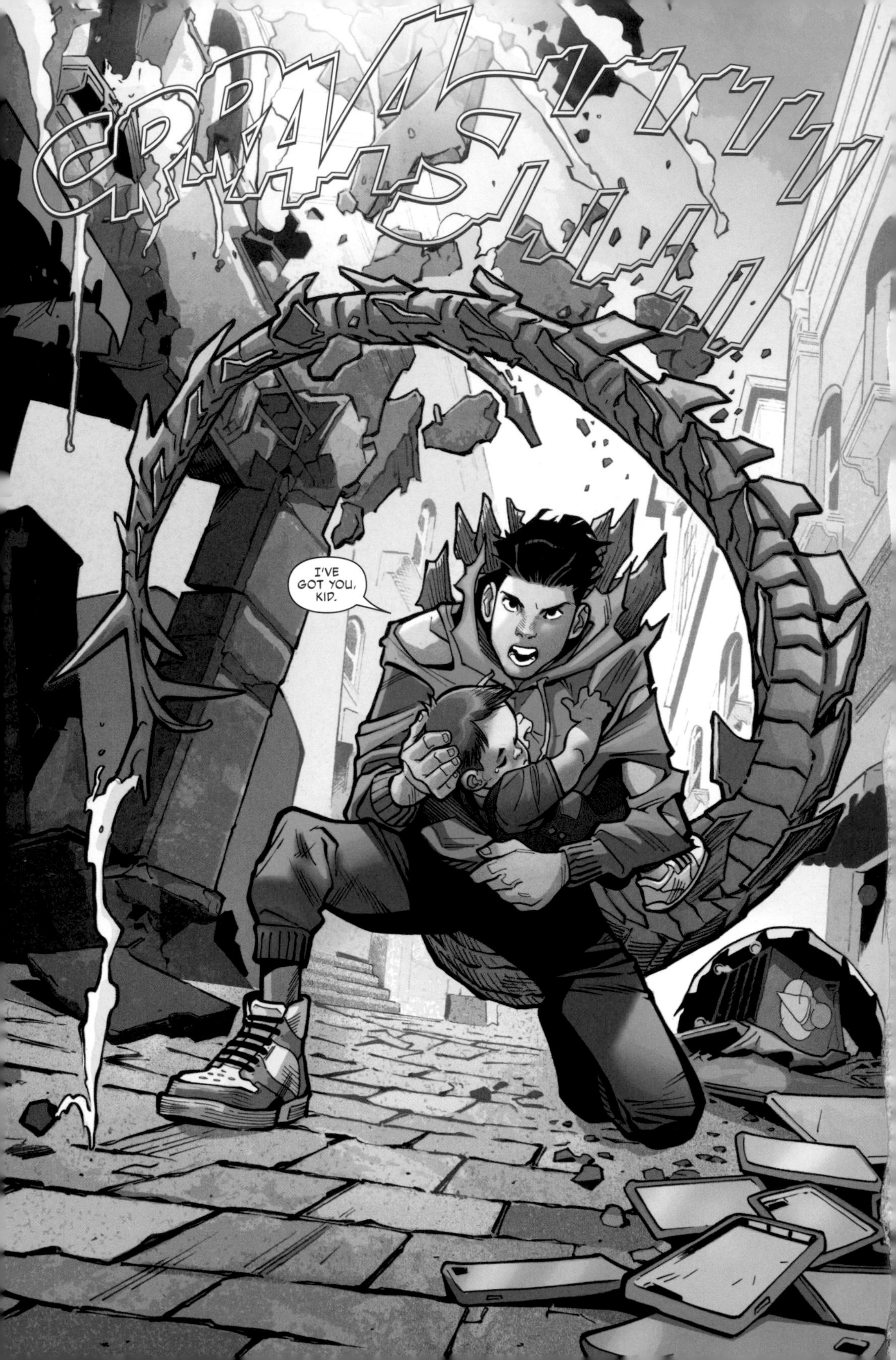
I'VE GOT YOU, KID.

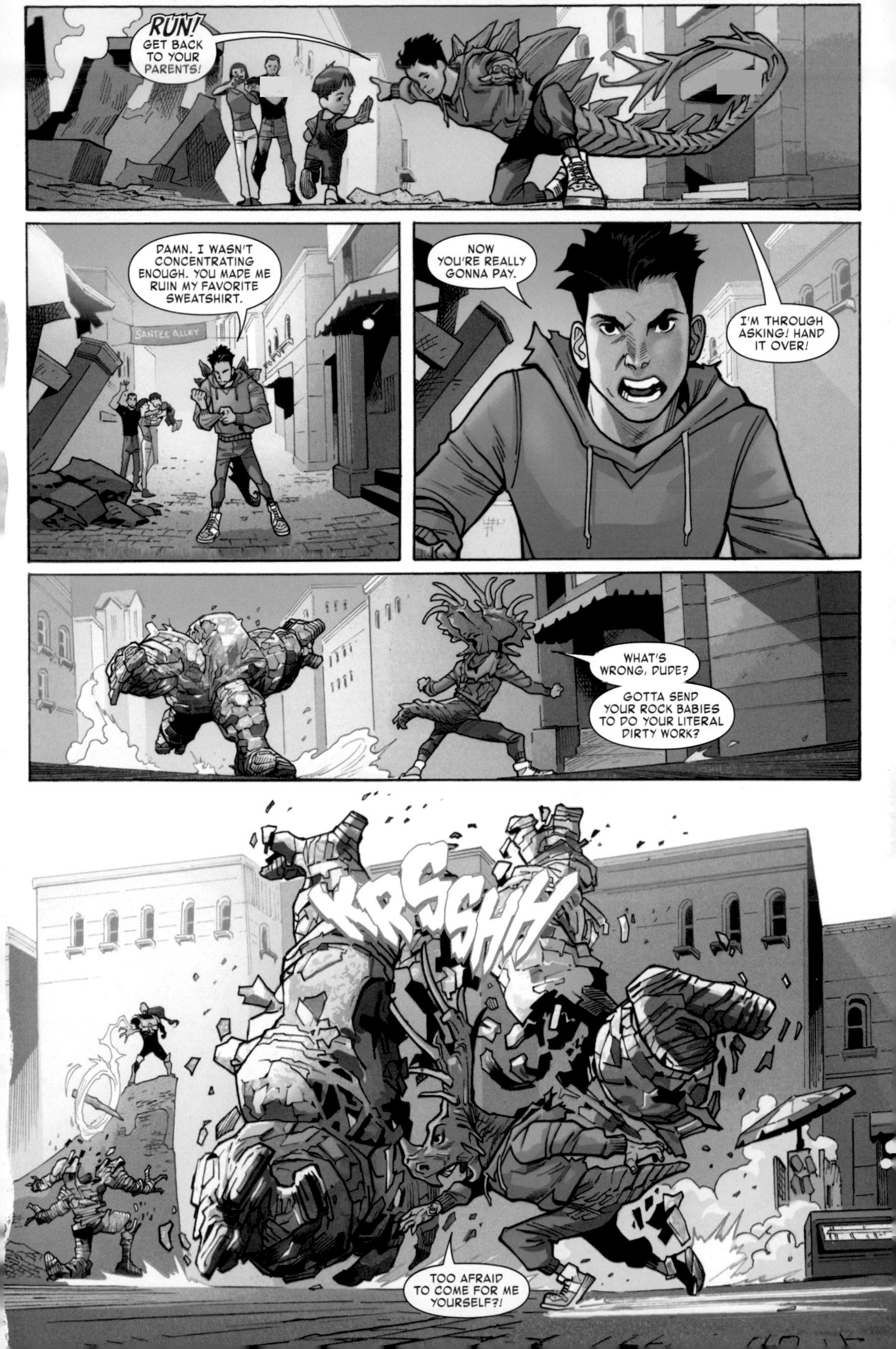
RUN! GET BACK TO YOUR PARENTS!
DAMN. I WASN'T CONCENTRATING ENOUGH. YOU MADE ME RUIN MY FAVORITE SWEATSHIRT.
SANTEE ALLEY
NOW YOU'RE REALLY GONNA PAY.
I'M THROUGH ASKING! HAND IT OVER!
WHAT'S WRONG, DUDE?
GOTTA SEND YOUR ROCK BABIES TO DO YOUR LITERAL DIRTY WORK?
KRSSHH
TOO AFRAID TO COME FOR ME YOURSELF?!

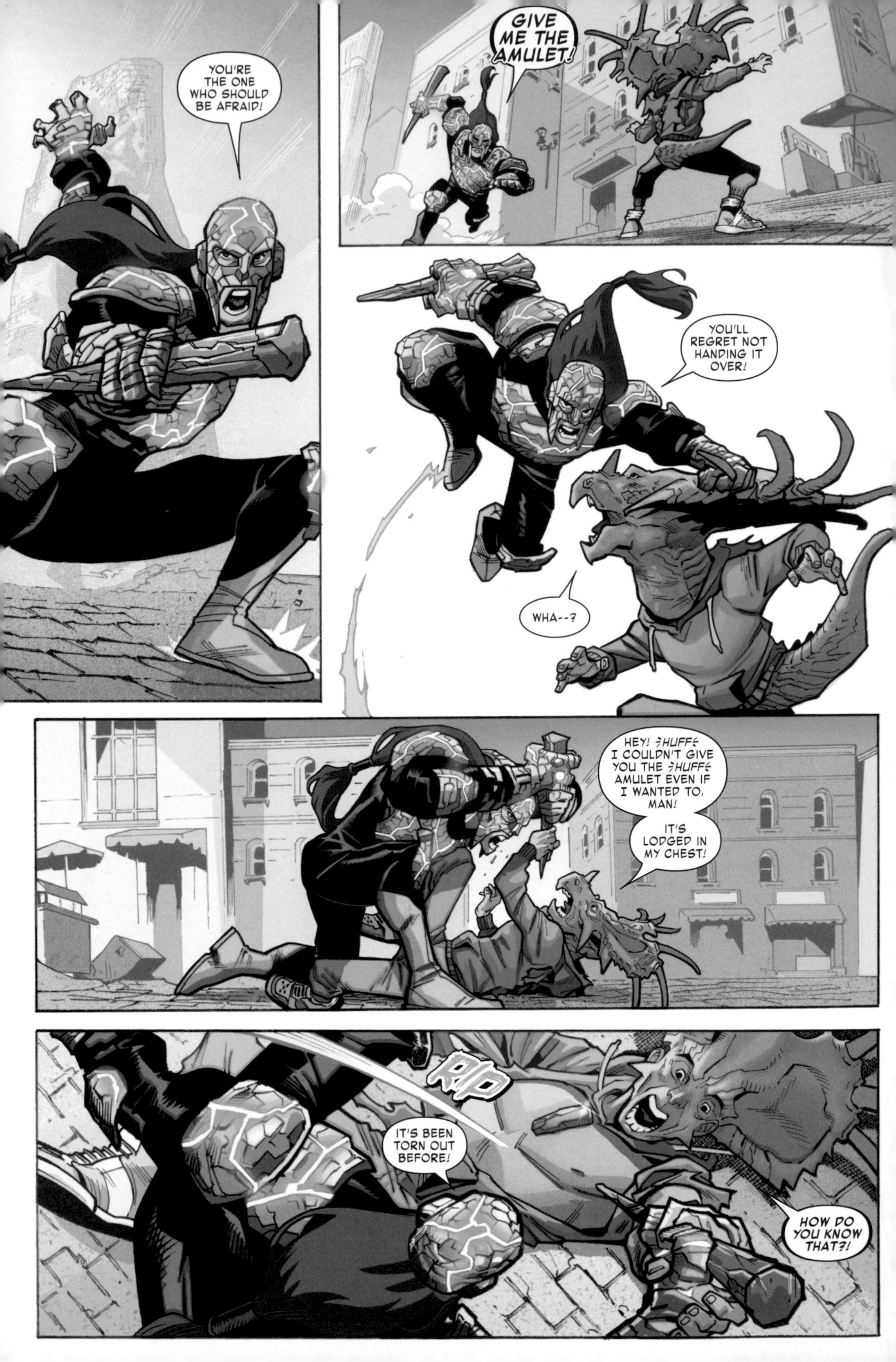

YOU'RE THE ONE WHO SHOULD BE AFRAID!
GIVE ME THE AMULET!
YOU'LL REGRET NOT HANDING IT OVER!
WHA--?
HEY! *HUFF* I COULDN'T GIVE YOU THE *HUFF* AMULET EVEN IF I WANTED TO, MAN!
IT'S LODGED IN MY CHEST!
RIP
IT'S BEEN TORN OUT BEFORE!
HOW DO YOU KNOW THAT?!

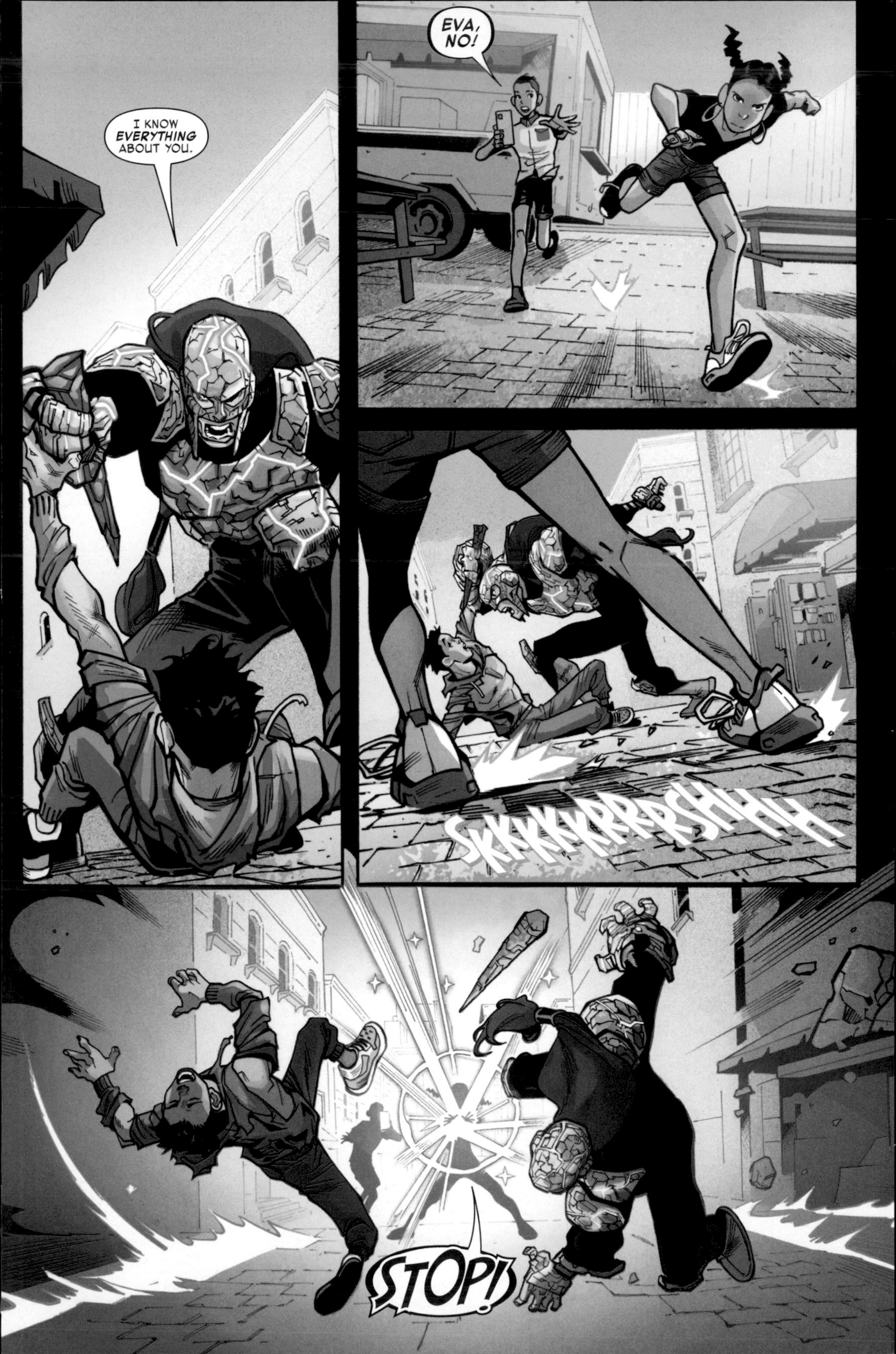
I KNOW EVERYTHING ABOUT YOU.
EVA, NO!
SKKKKRRRSHHH
STOP!

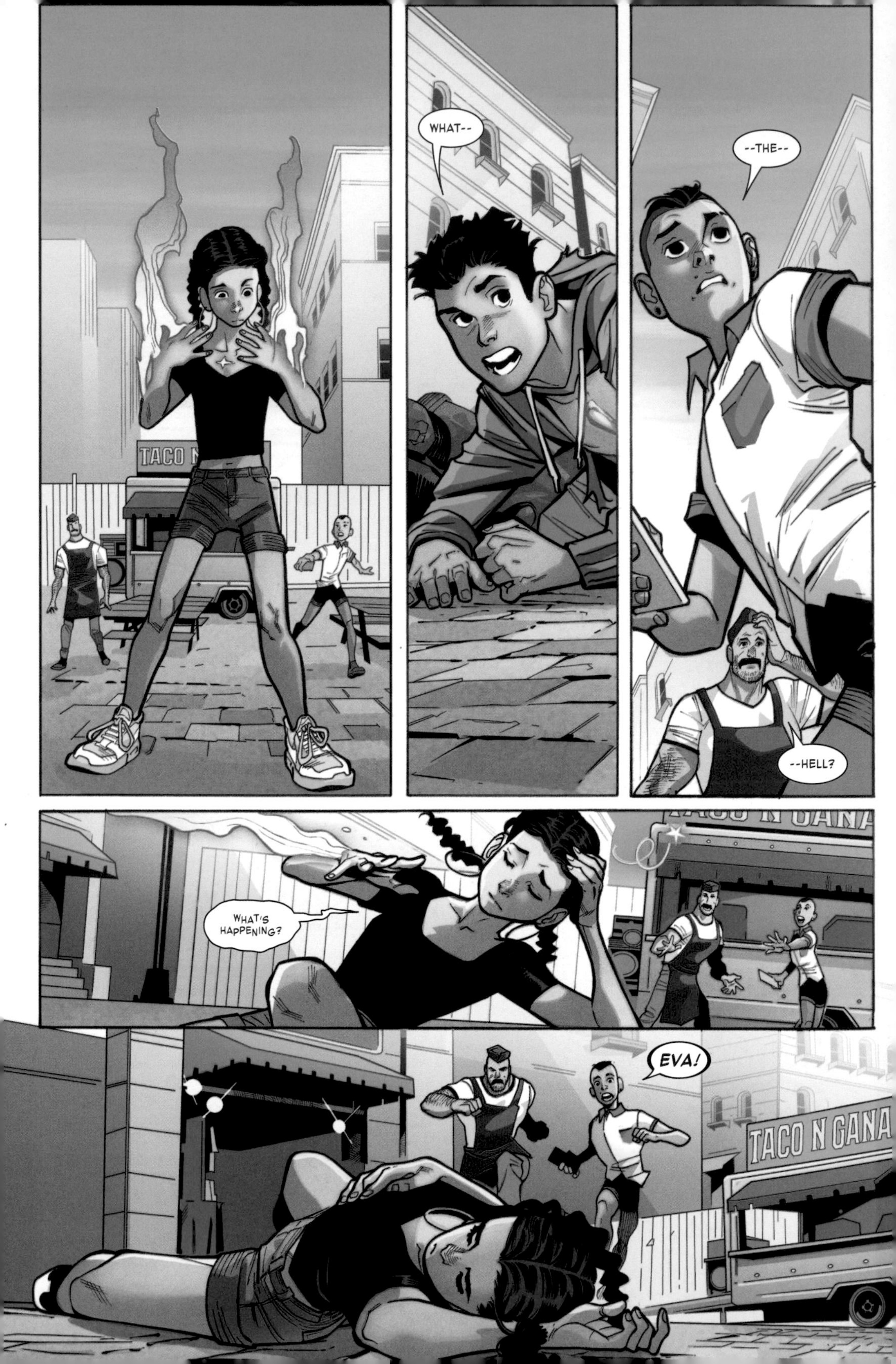
TACO N
WHAT--
--THE--
--HELL?
WHAT'S HAPPENING?
TACO N GANA
EVA!
TACO N GANA

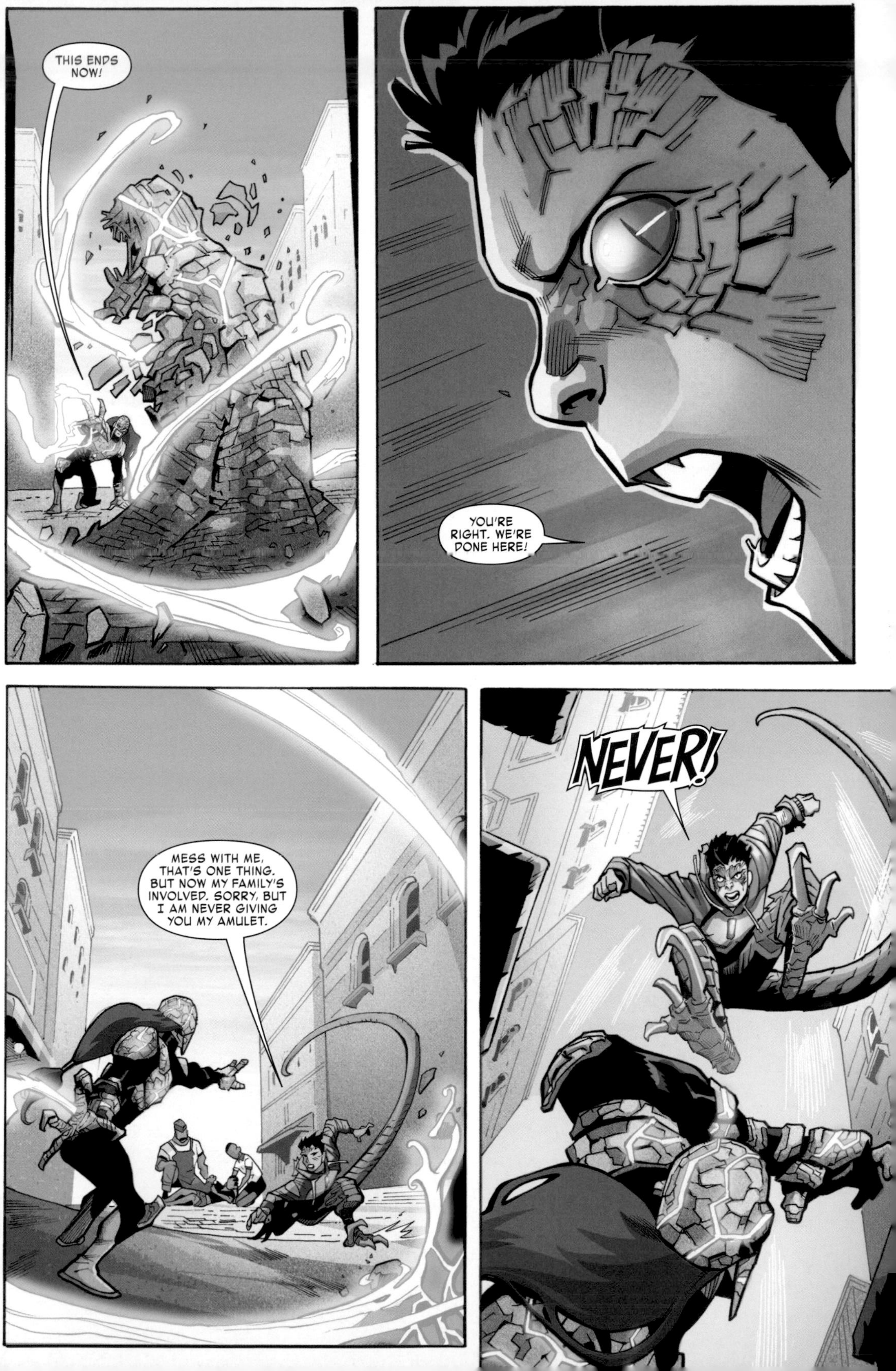
THIS ENDS NOW!
YOU'RE RIGHT. WE'RE DONE HERE!
MESS WITH ME, THAT'S ONE THING. BUT NOW MY FAMILY'S INVOLVED. SORRY, BUT I AM NEVER GIVING YOU MY AMULET.
NEVER!

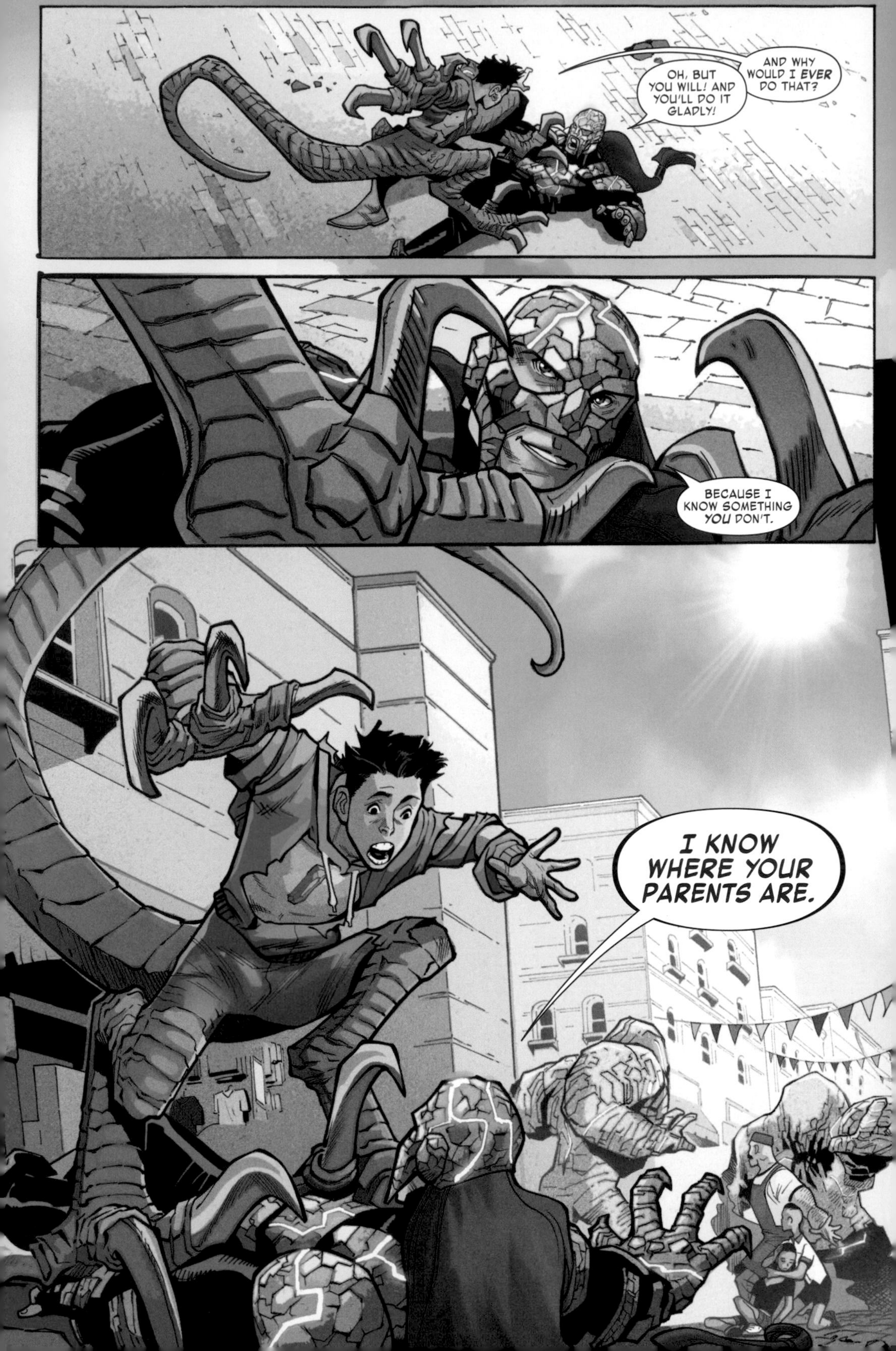
AND WHY WOULD I EVER DO THAT?
OH, BUT YOU WILL! AND YOU'LL DO IT GLADLY!
BECAUSE I KNOW SOMETHING YOU DON'T.
I KNOW WHERE YOUR PARENTS ARE.

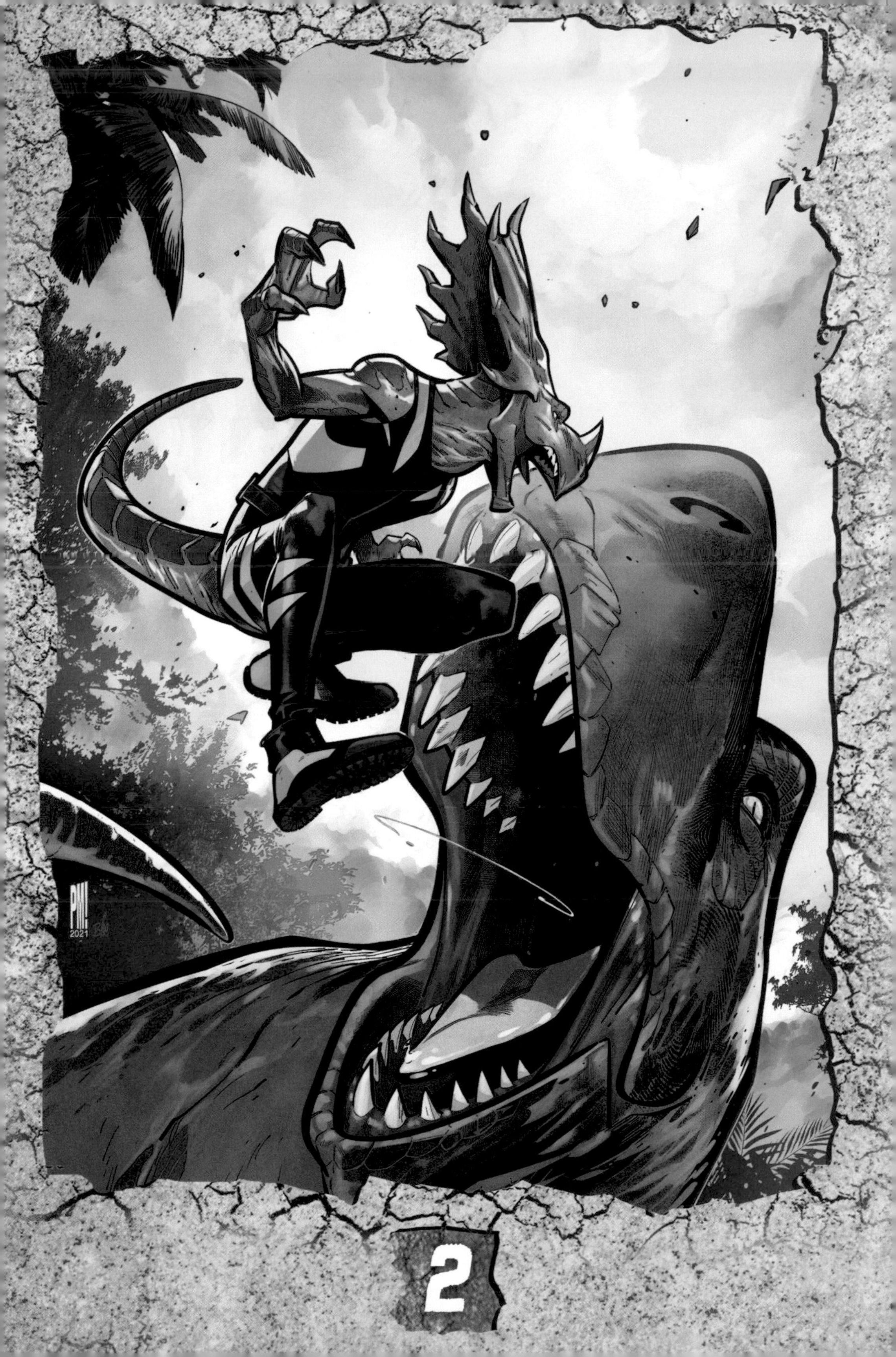
2

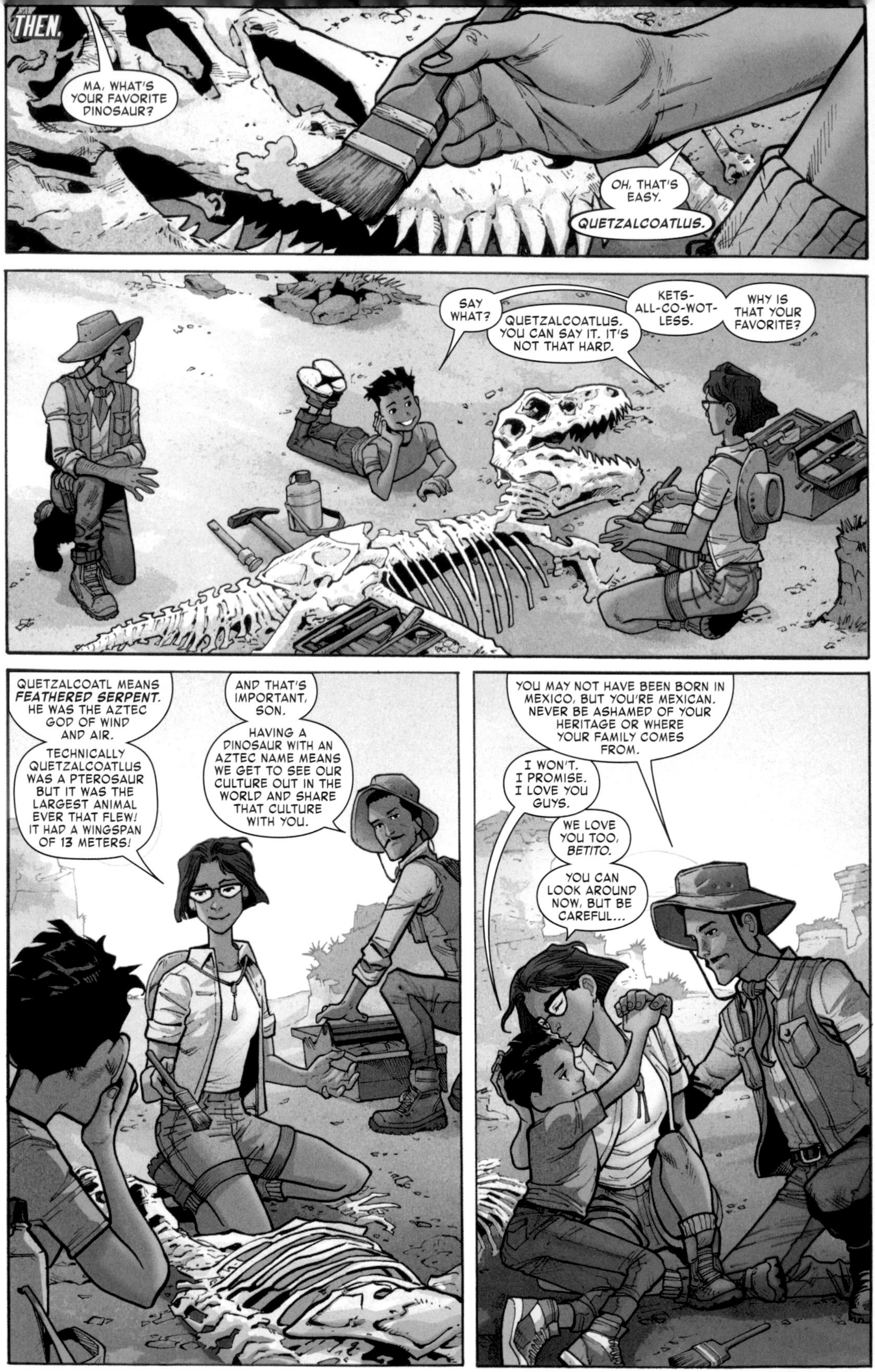
THEN.
MA, WHAT'S YOUR FAVORITE DINOSAUR?
OH, THAT'S EASY.
QUETZALCOATLUS.
SAY WHAT?
QUETZALCOATLUS. YOU CAN SAY IT. IT'S NOT THAT HARD.
KETS-ALL-CO-WOT-LESS.
WHY IS THAT YOUR FAVORITE?
QUETZALCOATL MEANS FEATHERED SERPENT. HE WAS THE AZTEC GOD OF WIND AND AIR.
TECHNICALLY QUETZALCOATLUS WAS A PTEROSAUR BUT IT WAS THE LARGEST ANIMAL EVER THAT FLEW! IT HAD A WINGSPAN OF 13 METERS!
AND THAT'S IMPORTANT, SON.
HAVING A DINOSAUR WITH AN AZTEC NAME MEANS WE GET TO SEE OUR CULTURE OUT IN THE WORLD AND SHARE THAT CULTURE WITH YOU.
YOU MAY NOT HAVE BEEN BORN IN MEXICO, BUT YOU'RE MEXICAN. NEVER BE ASHAMED OF YOUR HERITAGE OR WHERE YOUR FAMILY COMES FROM.
I WON'T. I PROMISE. I LOVE YOU GUYS.
WE LOVE YOU TOO, BETITO.
YOU CAN LOOK AROUND NOW, BUT BE CAREFUL...

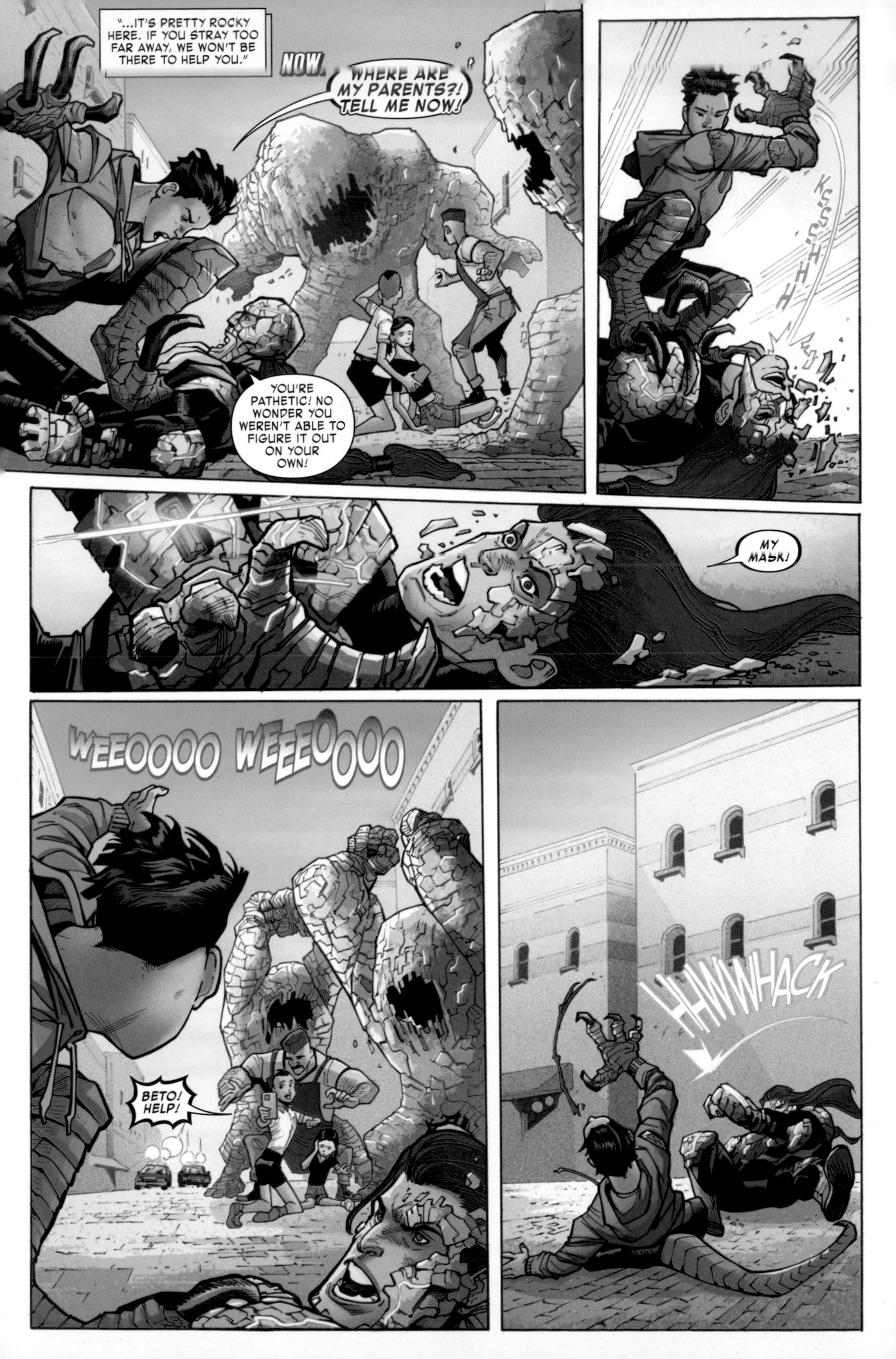
"...IT'S PRETTY ROCKY HERE. IF YOU STRAY TOO FAR AWAY, WE WON'T BE THERE TO HELP YOU."
NOW.
WHERE ARE MY PARENTS?! TELL ME NOW!
YOU'RE PATHETIC! NO WONDER YOU WEREN'T ABLE TO FIGURE IT OUT ON YOUR OWN!
KSSHHH
MY MASK!
WEEOOOO WEEEOOOO
BETO! HELP!
HHWWHACK

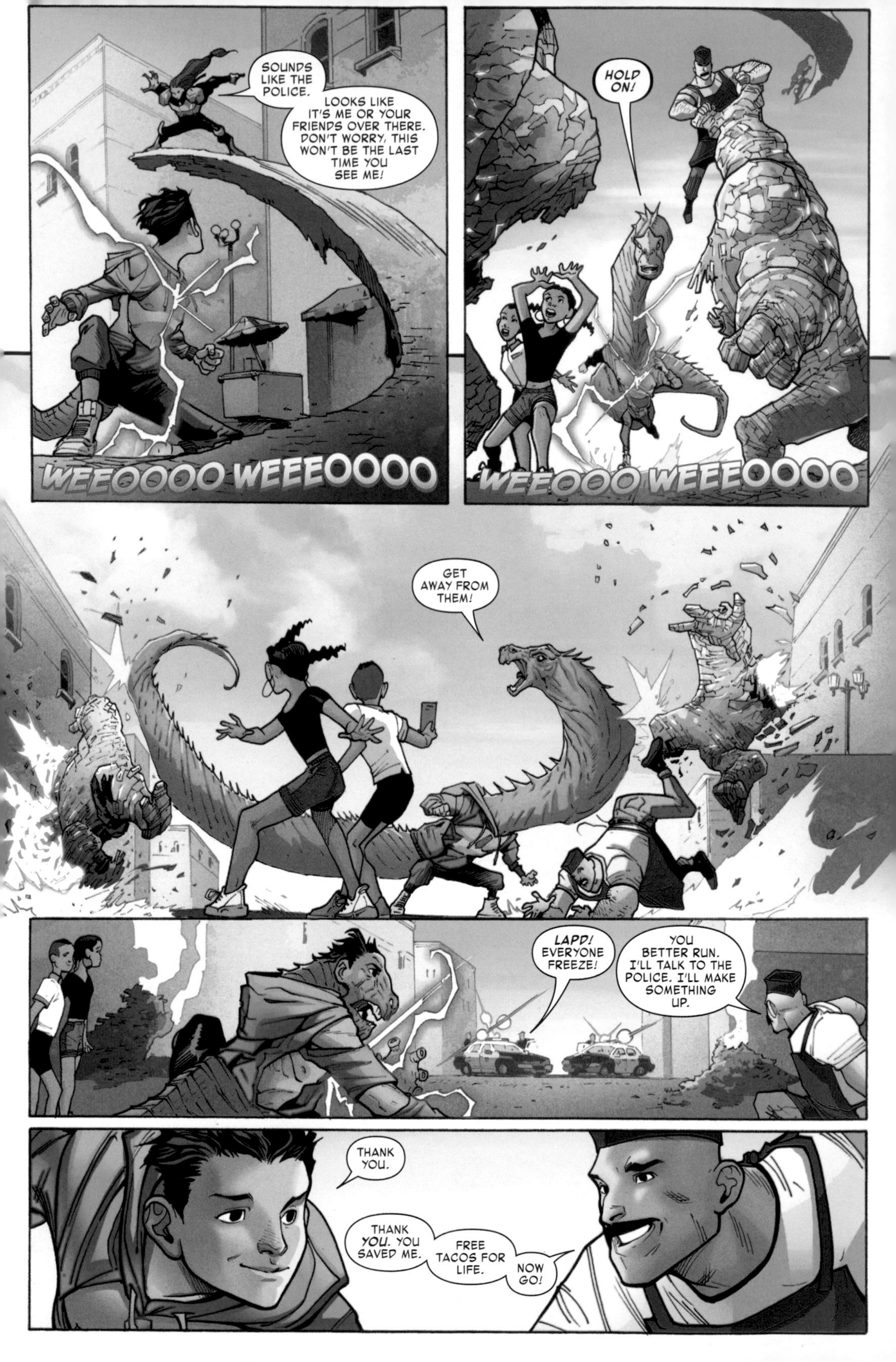
SOUNDS LIKE THE POLICE.
LOOKS LIKE IT'S ME OR YOUR FRIENDS OVER THERE. DON'T WORRY, THIS WON'T BE THE LAST TIME YOU SEE ME!
WEEOOOO WEEEOOOO
HOLD ON!
WEEOOO WEEEOOOO
GET AWAY FROM THEM!
LAPD! EVERYONE FREEZE!
YOU BETTER RUN. I'LL TALK TO THE POLICE. I'LL MAKE SOMETHING UP.
THANK YOU.
THANK YOU. YOU SAVED ME.
FREE TACOS FOR LIFE.
NOW GO!

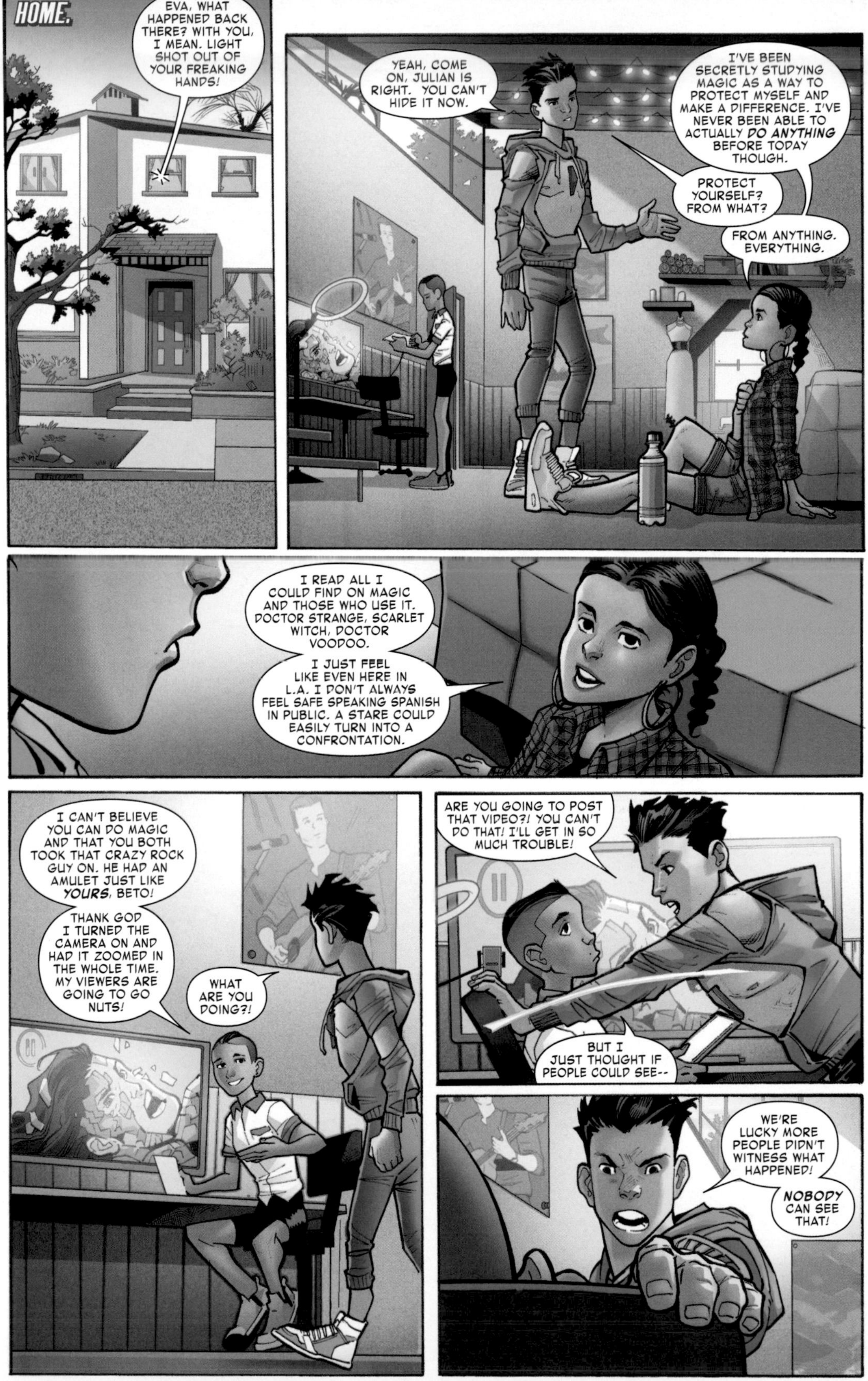
HOME.
EVA, WHAT HAPPENED BACK THERE? WITH YOU, I MEAN. LIGHT SHOT OUT OF YOUR FREAKING HANDS!
YEAH, COME ON, JULIAN IS RIGHT. YOU CAN'T HIDE IT NOW.
I'VE BEEN SECRETLY STUDYING MAGIC AS A WAY TO PROTECT MYSELF AND MAKE A DIFFERENCE. I'VE NEVER BEEN ABLE TO ACTUALLY DO ANYTHING BEFORE TODAY THOUGH.
PROTECT YOURSELF? FROM WHAT?
FROM ANYTHING. EVERYTHING.
I READ ALL I COULD FIND ON MAGIC AND THOSE WHO USE IT. DOCTOR STRANGE, SCARLET WITCH, DOCTOR VOODOO.
I JUST FEEL LIKE EVEN HERE IN L.A. I DON'T ALWAYS FEEL SAFE SPEAKING SPANISH IN PUBLIC. A STARE COULD EASILY TURN INTO A CONFRONTATION.
I CAN'T BELIEVE YOU CAN DO MAGIC AND THAT YOU BOTH TOOK THAT CRAZY ROCK GUY ON. HE HAD AN AMULET JUST LIKE YOURS, BETO!
THANK GOD I TURNED THE CAMERA ON AND HAD IT ZOOMED IN THE WHOLE TIME. MY VIEWERS ARE GOING TO GO NUTS!
WHAT ARE YOU DOING?!
ARE YOU GOING TO POST THAT VIDEO?! YOU CAN'T DO THAT! I'LL GET IN SO MUCH TROUBLE!
BUT I JUST THOUGHT IF PEOPLE COULD SEE--
WE'RE LUCKY MORE PEOPLE DIDN'T WITNESS WHAT HAPPENED!
NOBODY CAN SEE THAT!

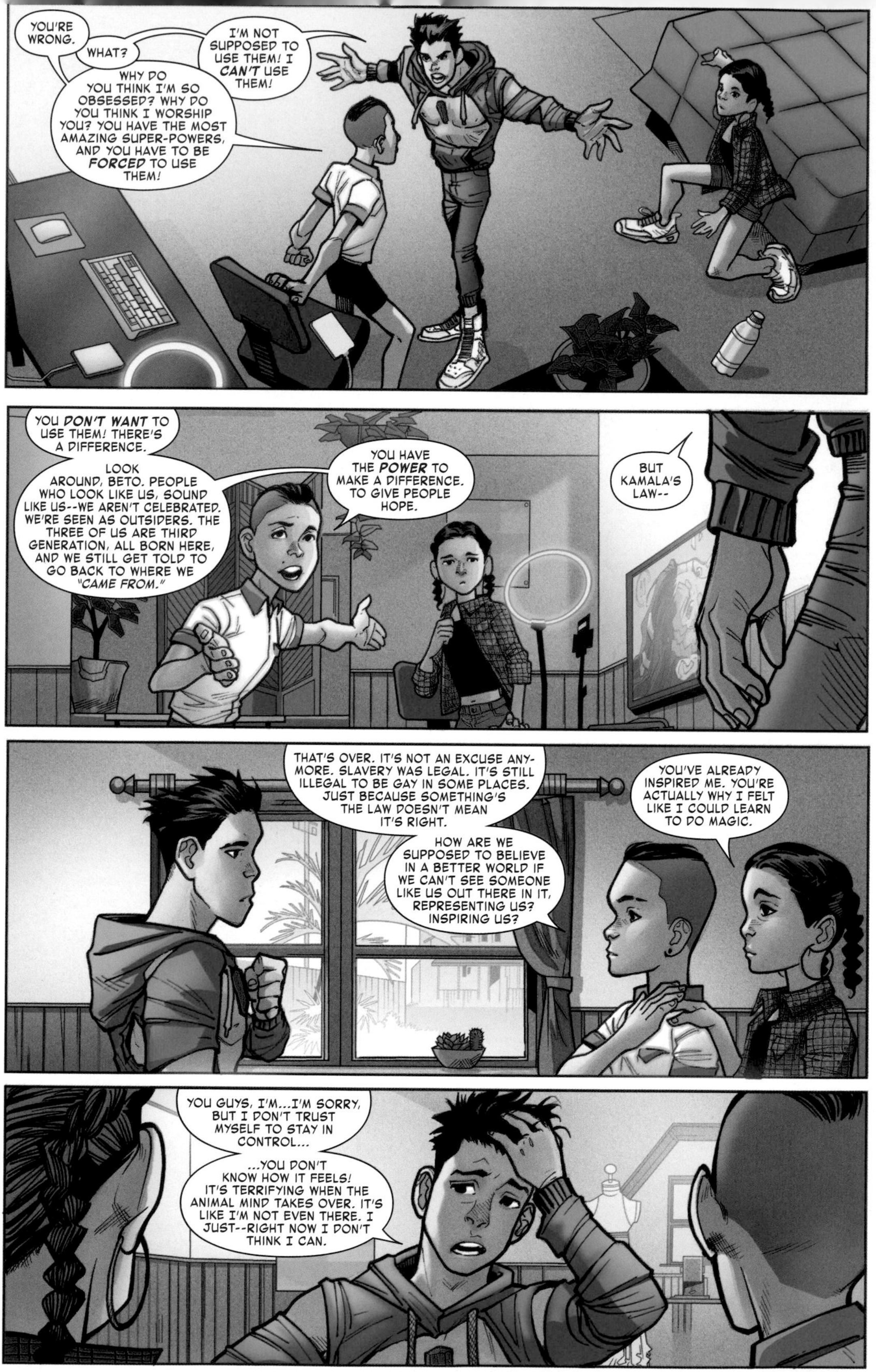
YOU'RE WRONG.
WHAT?
I'M NOT SUPPOSED TO USE THEM! I CAN'T USE THEM!
WHY DO YOU THINK I'M SO OBSESSED? WHY DO YOU THINK I WORSHIP YOU? YOU HAVE THE MOST AMAZING SUPER-POWERS, AND YOU HAVE TO BE FORCED TO USE THEM!
YOU DON'T WANT TO USE THEM! THERE'S A DIFFERENCE.
LOOK AROUND, BETO. PEOPLE WHO LOOK LIKE US, SOUND LIKE US--WE AREN'T CELEBRATED. WE'RE SEEN AS OUTSIDERS. THE THREE OF US ARE THIRD GENERATION, ALL BORN HERE, AND WE STILL GET TOLD TO GO BACK TO WHERE WE "CAME FROM."
YOU HAVE THE POWER TO MAKE A DIFFERENCE. TO GIVE PEOPLE HOPE.
BUT KAMALA'S LAW--
THAT'S OVER. IT'S NOT AN EXCUSE ANYMORE. SLAVERY WAS LEGAL. IT'S STILL ILLEGAL TO BE GAY IN SOME PLACES. JUST BECAUSE SOMETHING'S THE LAW DOESN'T MEAN IT'S RIGHT.
HOW ARE WE SUPPOSED TO BELIEVE IN A BETTER WORLD IF WE CAN'T SEE SOMEONE LIKE US OUT THERE IN IT, REPRESENTING US? INSPIRING US?
YOU'VE ALREADY INSPIRED ME. YOU'RE ACTUALLY WHY I FELT LIKE I COULD LEARN TO DO MAGIC.
YOU GUYS, I'M...I'M SORRY, BUT I DON'T TRUST MYSELF TO STAY IN CONTROL...
...YOU DON'T KNOW HOW IT FEELS! IT'S TERRIFYING WHEN THE ANIMAL MIND TAKES OVER. IT'S LIKE I'M NOT EVEN THERE. I JUST--RIGHT NOW I DON'T THINK I CAN.

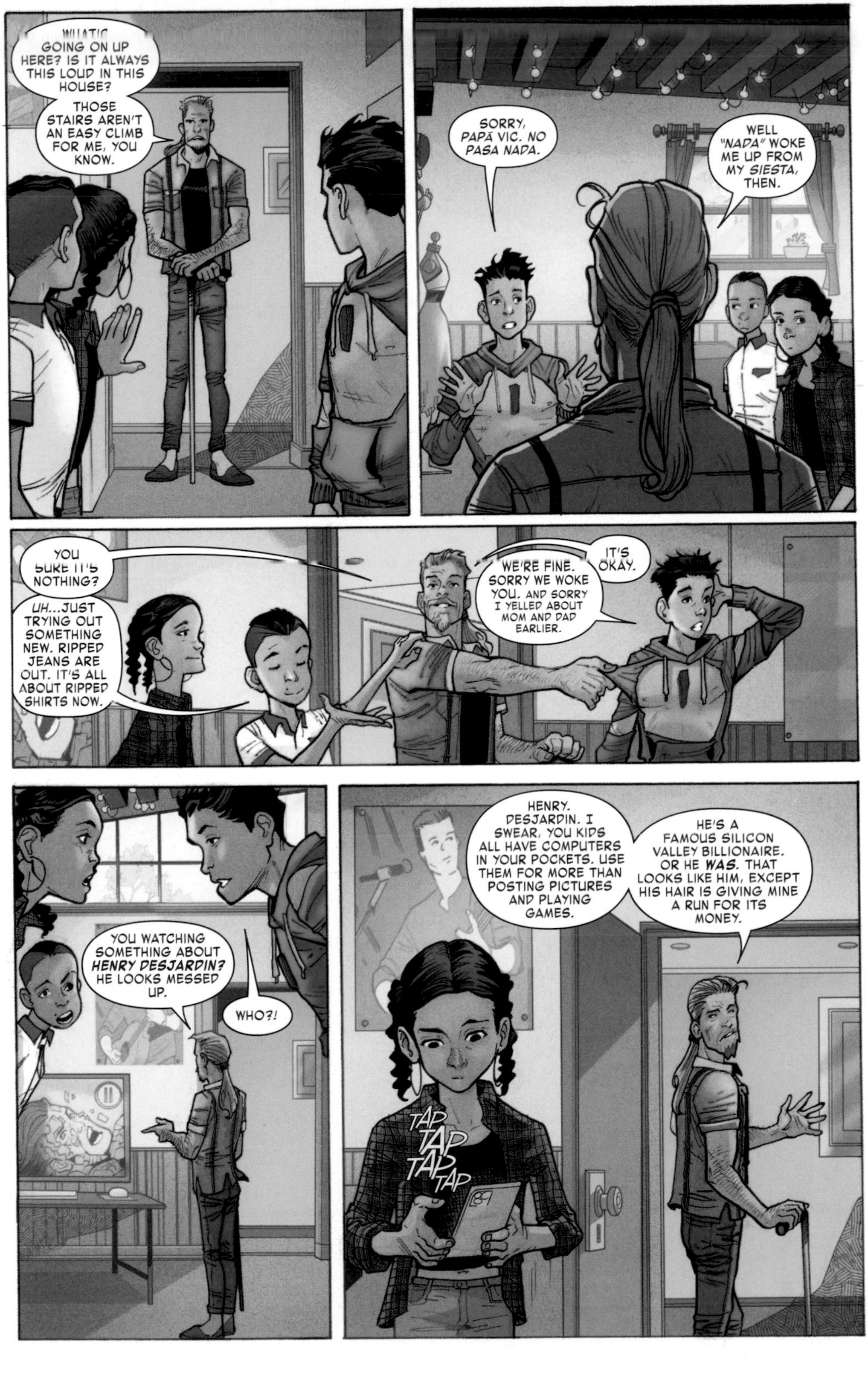

WHAT'S GOING ON UP HERE? IS IT ALWAYS THIS LOUD IN THIS HOUSE?
THOSE STAIRS AREN'T AN EASY CLIMB FOR ME, YOU KNOW.
SORRY, PAPÁ VIC. NO PASA NADA.
WELL "NADA" WOKE ME UP FROM MY SIESTA, THEN.
YOU SURE IT'S NOTHING?
UH...JUST TRYING OUT SOMETHING NEW. RIPPED JEANS ARE OUT. IT'S ALL ABOUT RIPPED SHIRTS NOW.
IT'S OKAY.
WE'RE FINE. SORRY WE WOKE YOU. AND SORRY I YELLED ABOUT MOM AND DAD EARLIER.
YOU WATCHING SOMETHING ABOUT HENRY DESJARDIN? HE LOOKS MESSED UP.
WHO?!
HENRY. DESJARDIN. I SWEAR, YOU KIDS ALL HAVE COMPUTERS IN YOUR POCKETS. USE THEM FOR MORE THAN POSTING PICTURES AND PLAYING GAMES.
HE'S A FAMOUS SILICON VALLEY BILLIONAIRE. OR HE WAS. THAT LOOKS LIKE HIM, EXCEPT HIS HAIR IS GIVING MINE A RUN FOR ITS MONEY.
TAP TAP TAP TAP

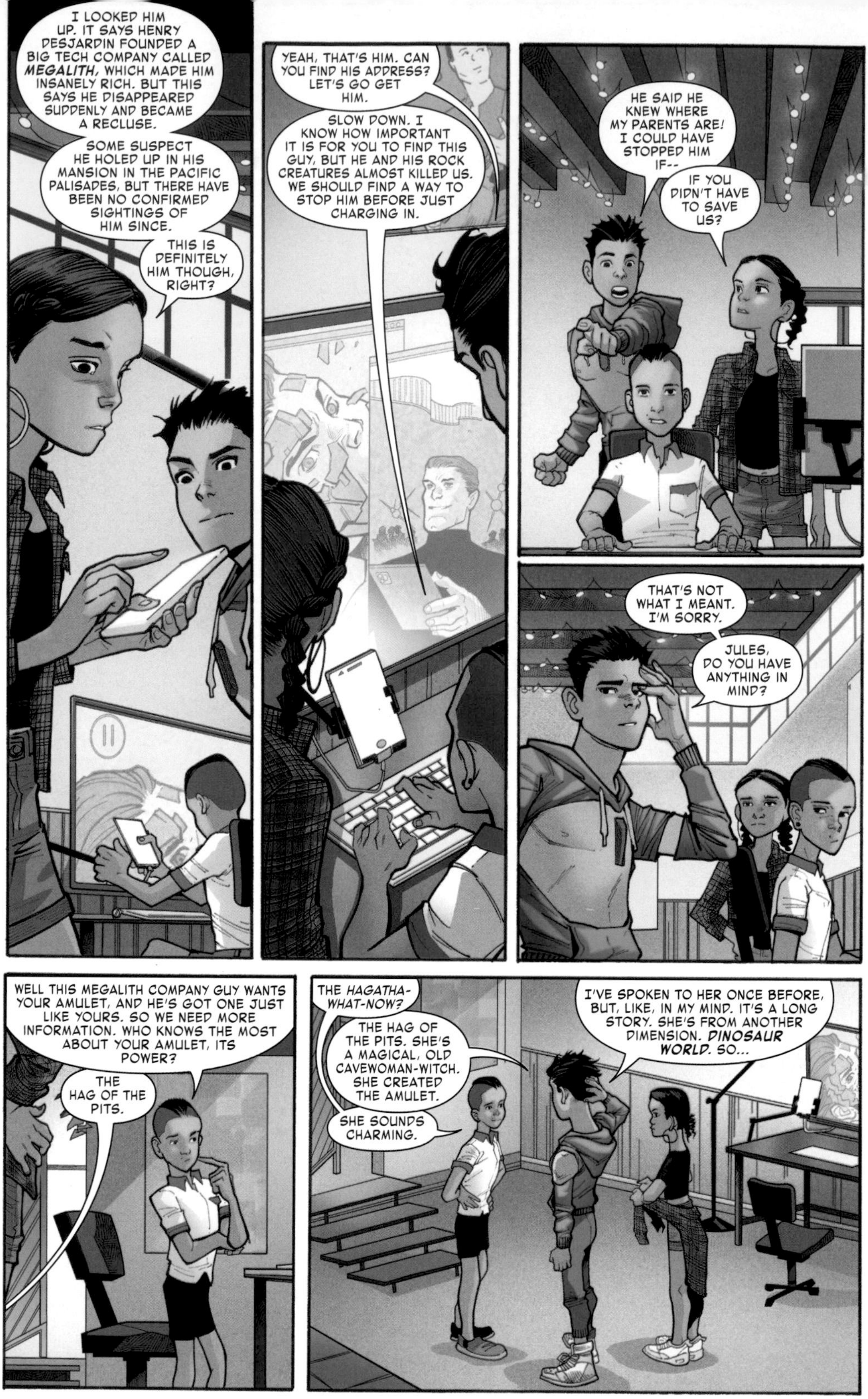
I LOOKED HIM UP. IT SAYS HENRY DESJARDIN FOUNDED A BIG TECH COMPANY CALLED MEGALITH, WHICH MADE HIM INSANELY RICH. BUT THIS SAYS HE DISAPPEARED SUDDENLY AND BECAME A RECLUSE.
SOME SUSPECT HE HOLED UP IN HIS MANSION IN THE PACIFIC PALISADES, BUT THERE HAVE BEEN NO CONFIRMED SIGHTINGS OF HIM SINCE.
THIS IS DEFINITELY HIM THOUGH, RIGHT?
YEAH, THAT'S HIM. CAN YOU FIND HIS ADDRESS? LET'S GO GET HIM.
SLOW DOWN. I KNOW HOW IMPORTANT IT IS FOR YOU TO FIND THIS GUY, BUT HE AND HIS ROCK CREATURES ALMOST KILLED US. WE SHOULD FIND A WAY TO STOP HIM BEFORE JUST CHARGING IN.
HE SAID HE KNEW WHERE MY PARENTS ARE! I COULD HAVE STOPPED HIM IF--
IF YOU DIDN'T HAVE TO SAVE US?
THAT'S NOT WHAT I MEANT. I'M SORRY.
JULES, DO YOU HAVE ANYTHING IN MIND?
WELL THIS MEGALITH COMPANY GUY WANTS YOUR AMULET, AND HE'S GOT ONE JUST LIKE YOURS. SO WE NEED MORE INFORMATION. WHO KNOWS THE MOST ABOUT YOUR AMULET, ITS POWER?
THE HAG OF THE PITS.
THE HAGATHA-WHAT-NOW?
THE HAG OF THE PITS. SHE'S A MAGICAL, OLD CAVEWOMAN-WITCH. SHE CREATED THE AMULET.
SHE SOUNDS CHARMING.
I'VE SPOKEN TO HER ONCE BEFORE, BUT, LIKE, IN MY MIND. IT'S A LONG STORY. SHE'S FROM ANOTHER DIMENSION. DINOSAUR WORLD. SO...

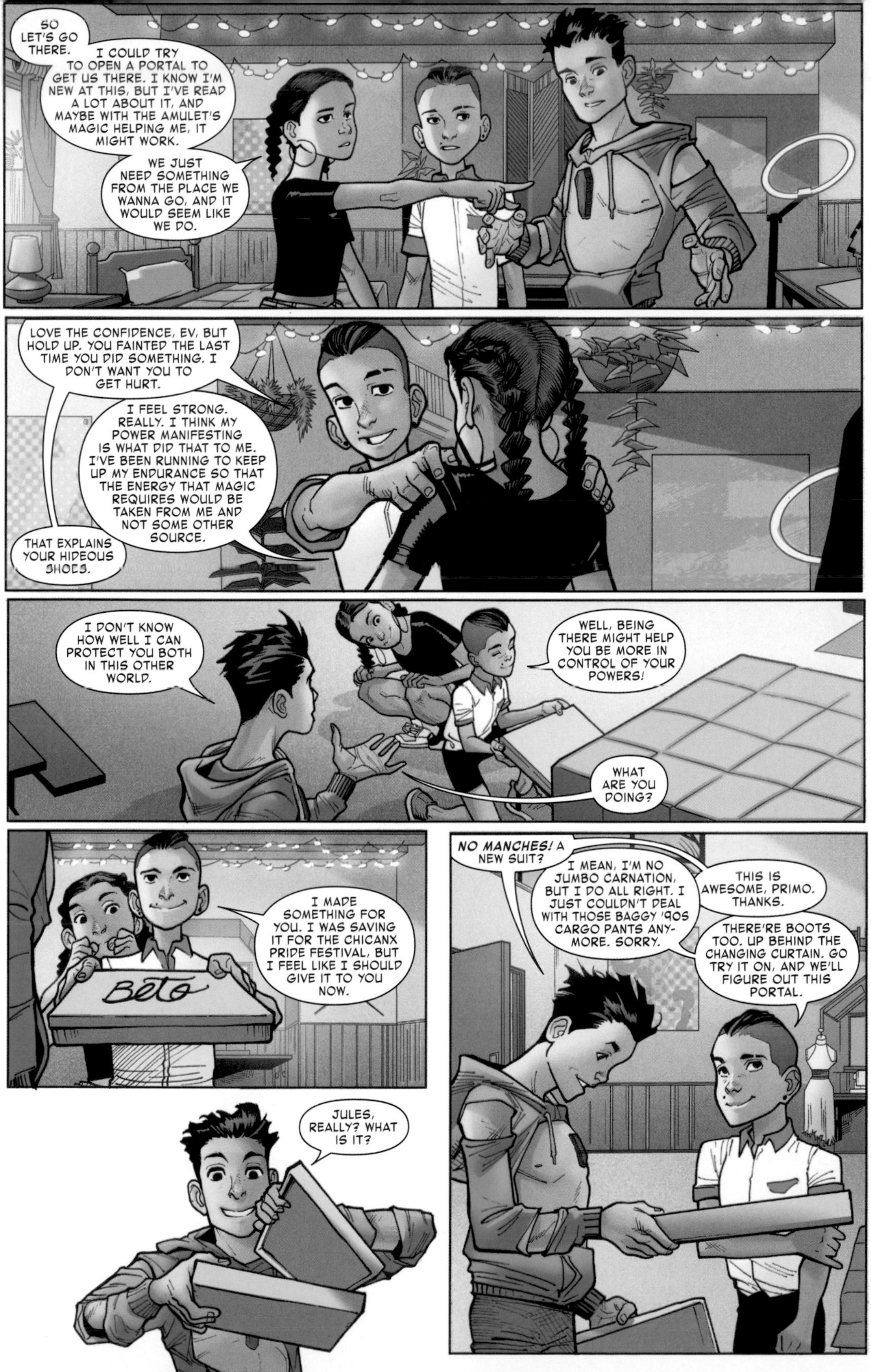
SO LET'S GO THERE.
I COULD TRY TO OPEN A PORTAL TO GET US THERE. I KNOW I'M NEW AT THIS, BUT I'VE READ A LOT ABOUT IT, AND MAYBE WITH THE AMULET'S MAGIC HELPING ME, IT MIGHT WORK.
WE JUST NEED SOMETHING FROM THE PLACE WE WANNA GO, AND IT WOULD SEEM LIKE WE DO.
LOVE THE CONFIDENCE, EV, BUT HOLD UP. YOU FAINTED THE LAST TIME YOU DID SOMETHING. I DON'T WANT YOU TO GET HURT.
I FEEL STRONG. REALLY. I THINK MY POWER MANIFESTING IS WHAT DID THAT TO ME. I'VE BEEN RUNNING TO KEEP UP MY ENDURANCE SO THAT THE ENERGY THAT MAGIC REQUIRES WOULD BE TAKEN FROM ME AND NOT SOME OTHER SOURCE.
THAT EXPLAINS YOUR HIDEOUS SHOES.
I DON'T KNOW HOW WELL I CAN PROTECT YOU BOTH IN THIS OTHER WORLD.
WELL, BEING THERE MIGHT HELP YOU BE MORE IN CONTROL OF YOUR POWERS!
WHAT ARE YOU DOING?
Beto
I MADE SOMETHING FOR YOU. I WAS SAVING IT FOR THE CHICANX PRIDE FESTIVAL, BUT I FEEL LIKE I SHOULD GIVE IT TO YOU NOW.
JULES, REALLY? WHAT IS IT?
NO MANCHES! A NEW SUIT?
I MEAN, I'M NO JUMBO CARNATION, BUT I DO ALL RIGHT. I JUST COULDN'T DEAL WITH THOSE BAGGY '90S CARGO PANTS ANY-MORE. SORRY.
THIS IS AWESOME, PRIMO. THANKS.
THERE'RE BOOTS TOO. UP BEHIND THE CHANGING CURTAIN. GO TRY IT ON, AND WE'LL FIGURE OUT THIS PORTAL.

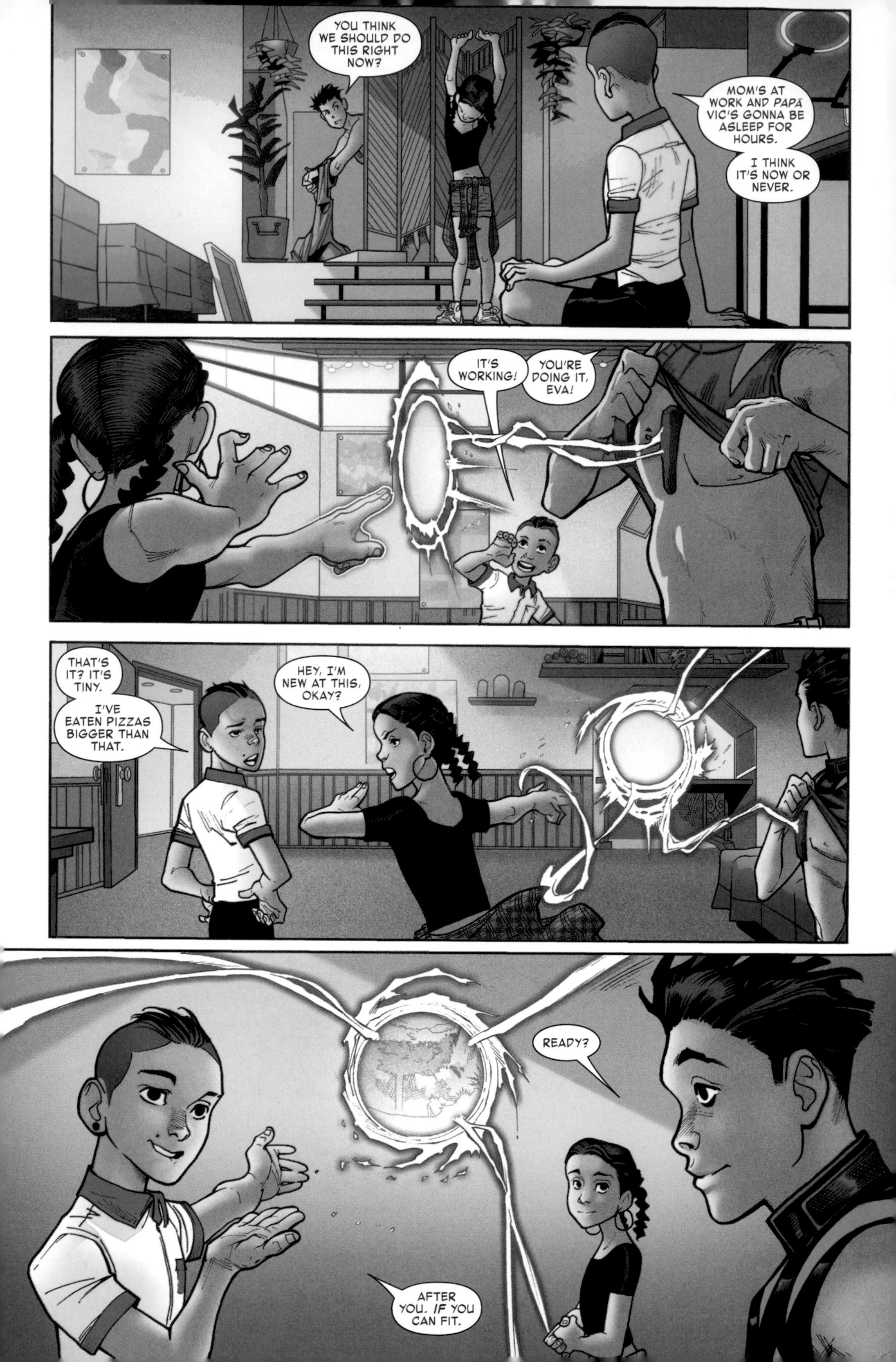
YOU THINK WE SHOULD DO THIS RIGHT NOW?
MOM'S AT WORK AND PAPĀ VIC'S GONNA BE ASLEEP FOR HOURS.
I THINK IT'S NOW OR NEVER.
IT'S WORKING!
YOU'RE DOING IT, EVA!
THAT'S IT? IT'S TINY.
I'VE EATEN PIZZAS BIGGER THAN THAT.
HEY, I'M NEW AT THIS, OKAY?
READY?
AFTER YOU. IF YOU CAN FIT.

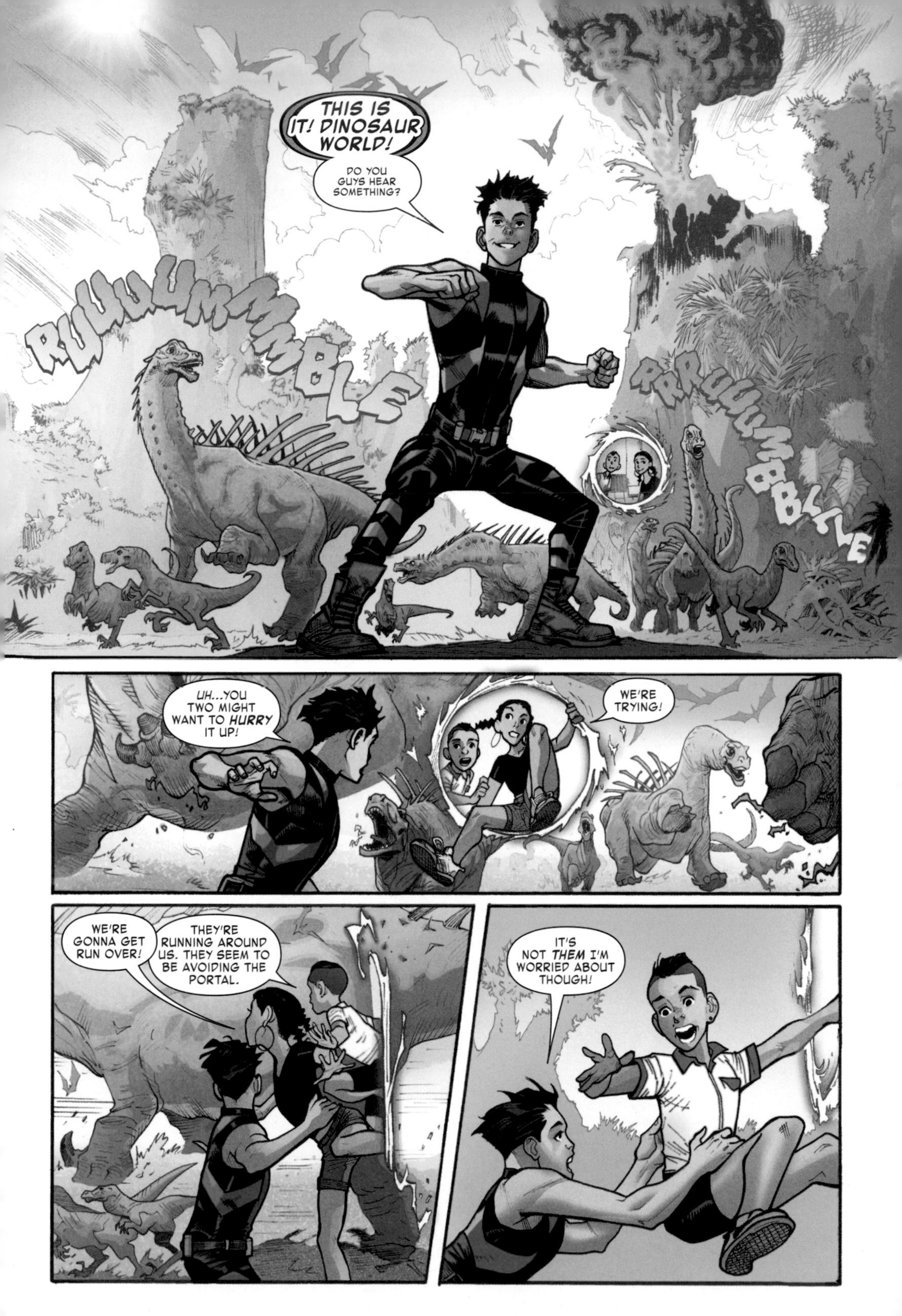

THIS IS IT! DINOSAUR WORLD!
DO YOU GUYS HEAR SOMETHING?
RUUUUMMMBLE
RRRUUUMBBLLE
UH...YOU TWO MIGHT WANT TO HURRY IT UP!
WE'RE TRYING!
WE'RE GONNA GET RUN OVER!
THEY'RE RUNNING AROUND US. THEY SEEM TO BE AVOIDING THE PORTAL.
IT'S NOT THEM I'M WORRIED ABOUT THOUGH!

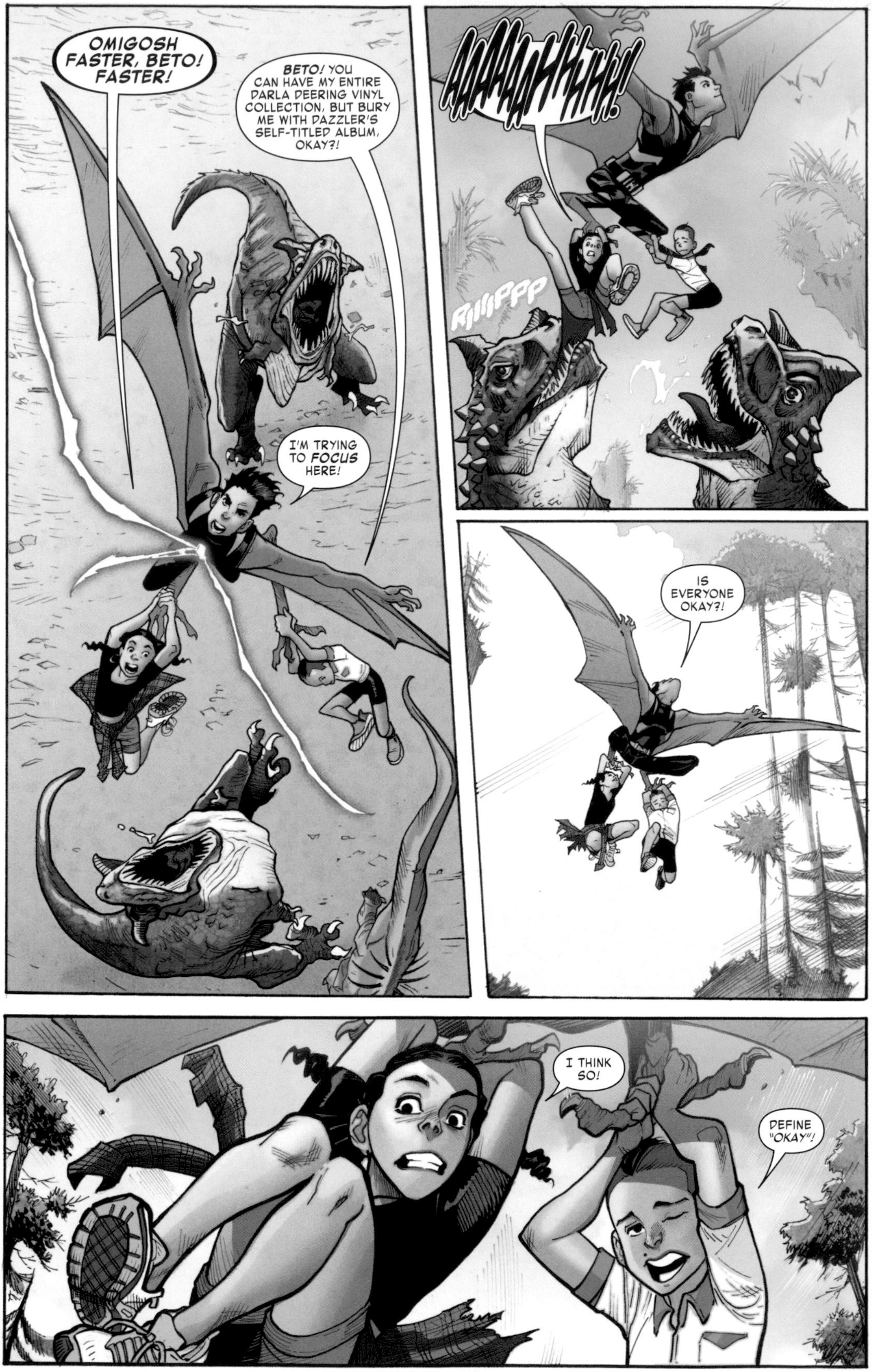
OMIGOSH FASTER, BETO! FASTER!
BETO! YOU CAN HAVE MY ENTIRE DARLA DEERING VINYL COLLECTION, BUT BURY ME WITH DAZZLER'S SELF-TITLED ALBUM, OKAY?!
I'M TRYING TO FOCUS HERE!
RIIIPPP
IS EVERYONE OKAY?!
I THINK SO!
DEFINE "OKAY"!

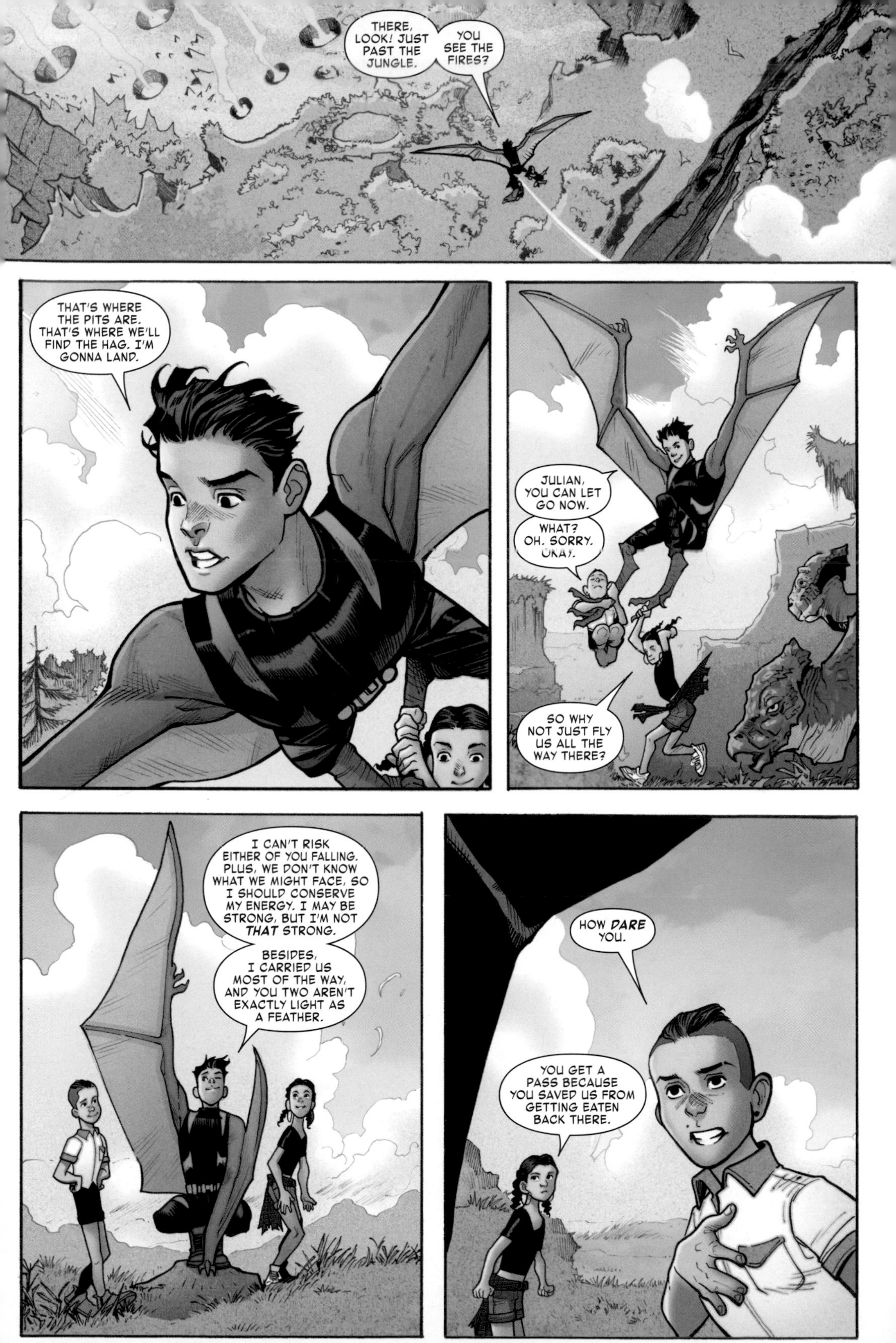
THERE, LOOK! JUST PAST THE JUNGLE.
YOU SEE THE FIRES?
THAT'S WHERE THE PITS ARE. THAT'S WHERE WE'LL FIND THE HAG. I'M GONNA LAND.
JULIAN, YOU CAN LET GO NOW.
WHAT? OH. SORRY. OKAY.
SO WHY NOT JUST FLY US ALL THE WAY THERE?
I CAN'T RISK EITHER OF YOU FALLING. PLUS, WE DON'T KNOW WHAT WE MIGHT FACE, SO I SHOULD CONSERVE MY ENERGY. I MAY BE STRONG, BUT I'M NOT THAT STRONG.
BESIDES, I CARRIED US MOST OF THE WAY, AND YOU TWO AREN'T EXACTLY LIGHT AS A FEATHER.
HOW DARE YOU.
YOU GET A PASS BECAUSE YOU SAVED US FROM GETTING EATEN BACK THERE.

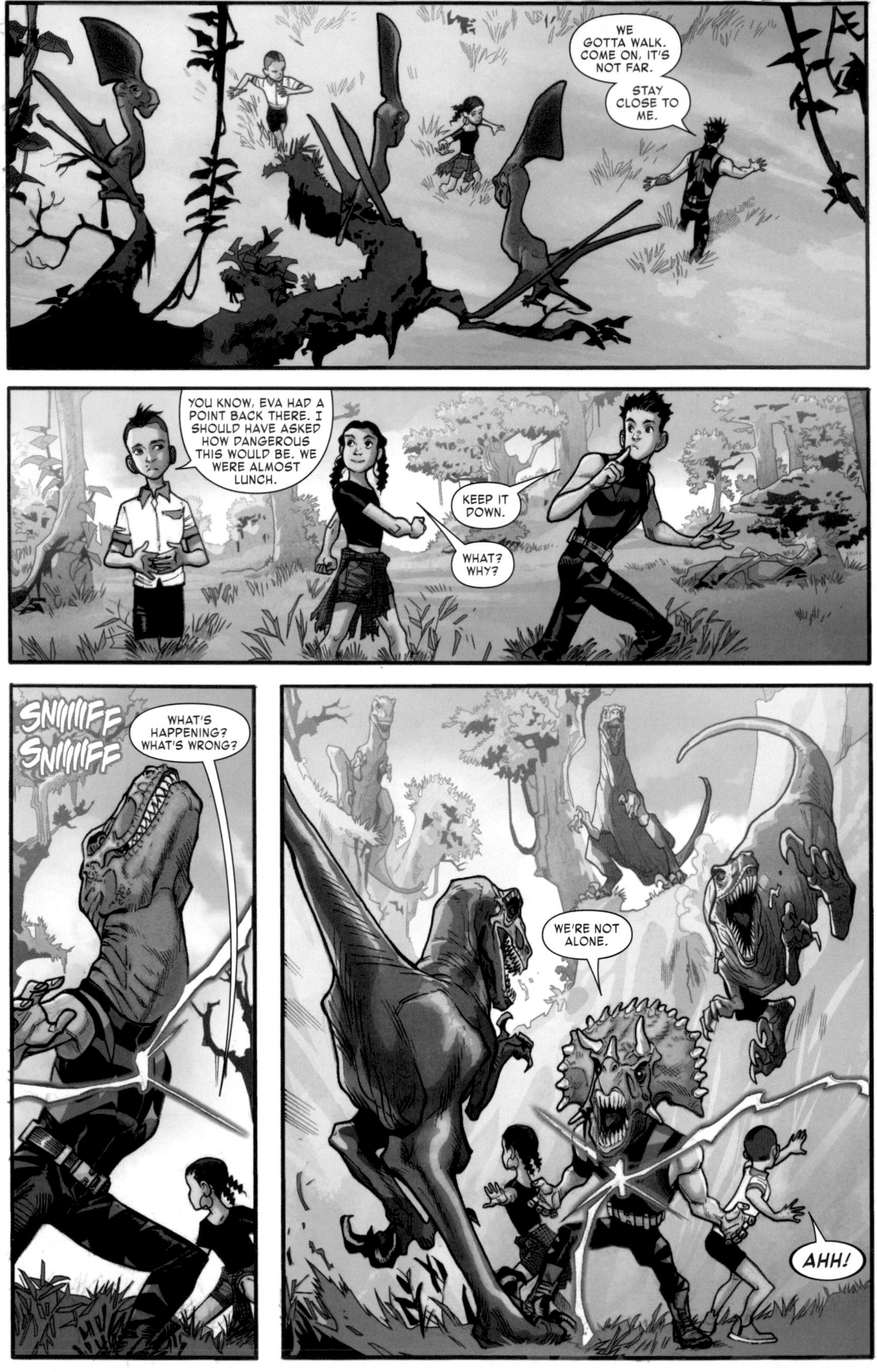
WE GOTTA WALK. COME ON, IT'S NOT FAR.
STAY CLOSE TO ME.
YOU KNOW, EVA HAD A POINT BACK THERE. I SHOULD HAVE ASKED HOW DANGEROUS THIS WOULD BE. WE WERE ALMOST LUNCH.
KEEP IT DOWN.
WHAT? WHY?
SNIIIIFF
SNIIIIFF
WHAT'S HAPPENING? WHAT'S WRONG?
WE'RE NOT ALONE.
AHH!

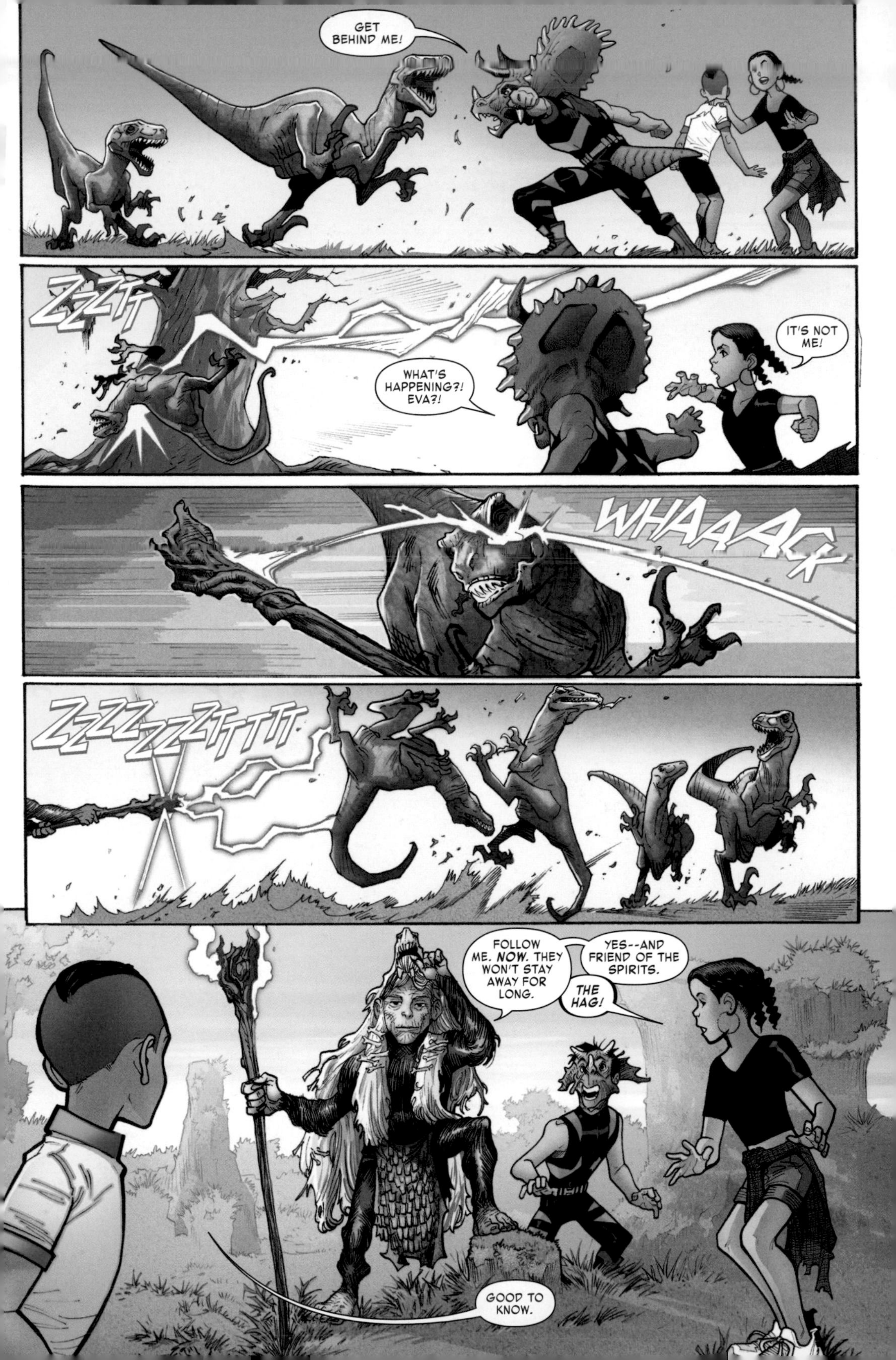
GET BEHIND ME!
ZZZTTT
WHAT'S HAPPENING?! EVA?!
IT'S NOT ME!
WHAAAACK
ZZZZZZZTTTTT
FOLLOW ME. NOW. THEY WON'T STAY AWAY FOR LONG.
THE HAG!
YES--AND FRIEND OF THE SPIRITS.
GOOD TO KNOW.

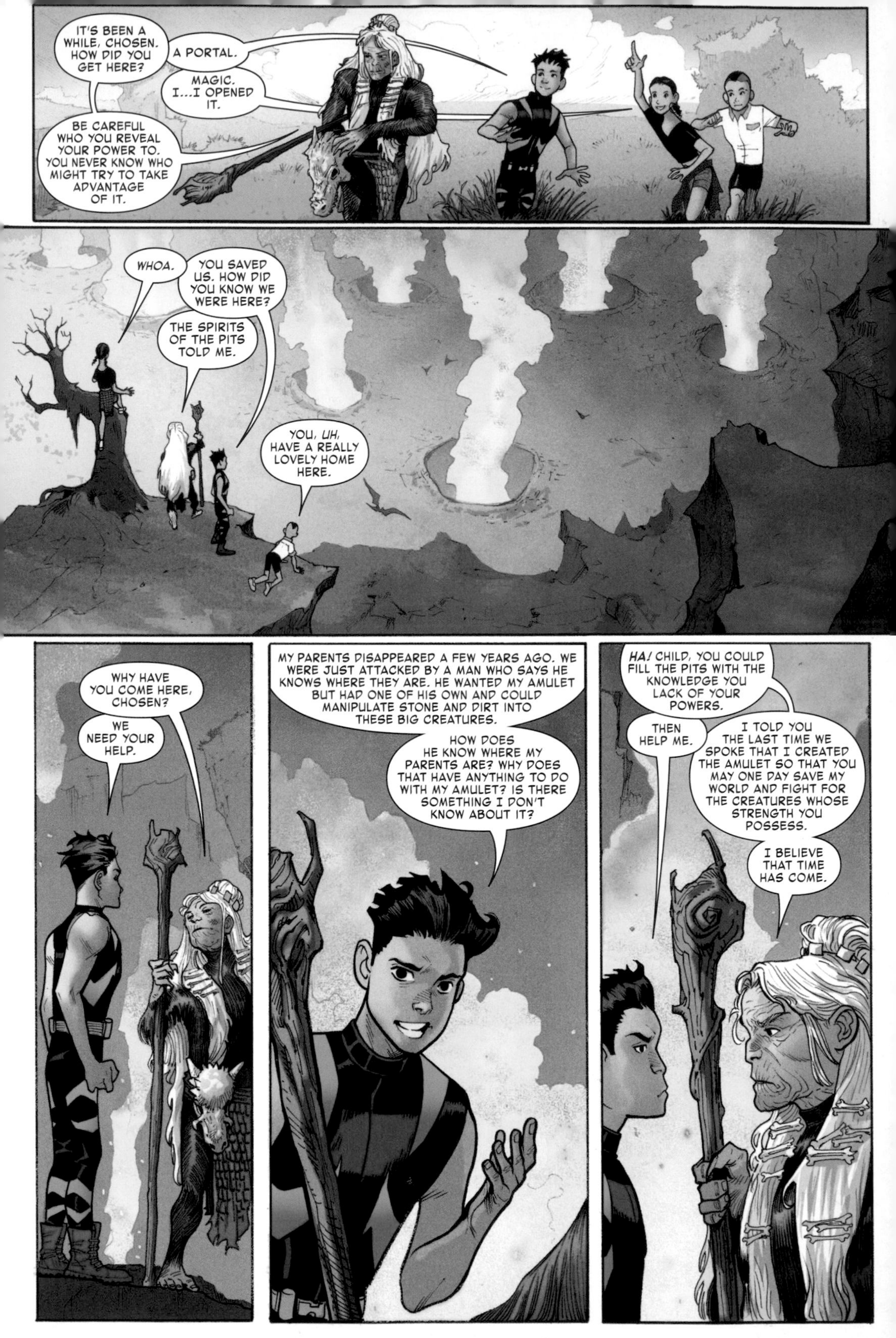
IT'S BEEN A WHILE, CHOSEN. HOW DID YOU GET HERE?
A PORTAL.
MAGIC. I...I OPENED IT.
BE CAREFUL WHO YOU REVEAL YOUR POWER TO. YOU NEVER KNOW WHO MIGHT TRY TO TAKE ADVANTAGE OF IT.
WHOA.
YOU SAVED US. HOW DID YOU KNOW WE WERE HERE?
THE SPIRITS OF THE PITS TOLD ME.
YOU, UH, HAVE A REALLY LOVELY HOME HERE.
WHY HAVE YOU COME HERE, CHOSEN?
WE NEED YOUR HELP.
MY PARENTS DISAPPEARED A FEW YEARS AGO. WE WERE JUST ATTACKED BY A MAN WHO SAYS HE KNOWS WHERE THEY ARE. HE WANTED MY AMULET BUT HAD ONE OF HIS OWN AND COULD MANIPULATE STONE AND DIRT INTO THESE BIG CREATURES.
HOW DOES HE KNOW WHERE MY PARENTS ARE? WHY DOES THAT HAVE ANYTHING TO DO WITH MY AMULET? IS THERE SOMETHING I DON'T KNOW ABOUT IT?
HA! CHILD, YOU COULD FILL THE PITS WITH THE KNOWLEDGE YOU LACK OF YOUR POWERS.
THEN HELP ME.
I TOLD YOU THE LAST TIME WE SPOKE THAT I CREATED THE AMULET SO THAT YOU MAY ONE DAY SAVE MY WORLD AND FIGHT FOR THE CREATURES WHOSE STRENGTH YOU POSSESS.
I BELIEVE THAT TIME HAS COME.

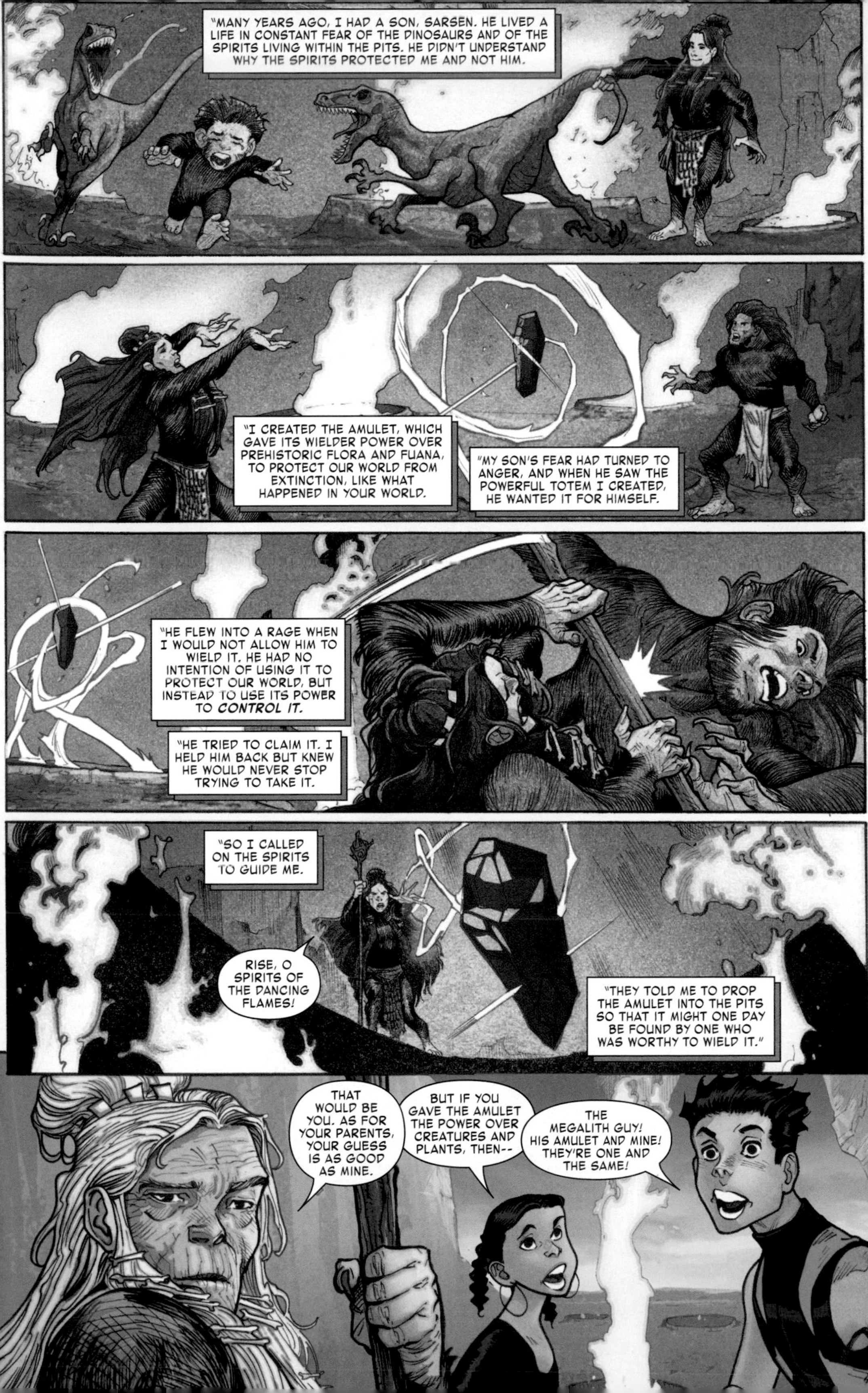
"MANY YEARS AGO, I HAD A SON, SARSEN. HE LIVED A LIFE IN CONSTANT FEAR OF THE DINOSAURS AND OF THE SPIRITS LIVING WITHIN THE PITS. HE DIDN'T UNDERSTAND WHY THE SPIRITS PROTECTED ME AND NOT HIM.
"I CREATED THE AMULET, WHICH GAVE ITS WIELDER POWER OVER PREHISTORIC FLORA AND FUANA, TO PROTECT OUR WORLD FROM EXTINCTION, LIKE WHAT HAPPENED IN YOUR WORLD.
"MY SON'S FEAR HAD TURNED TO ANGER, AND WHEN HE SAW THE POWERFUL TOTEM I CREATED, HE WANTED IT FOR HIMSELF.
"HE FLEW INTO A RAGE WHEN I WOULD NOT ALLOW HIM TO WIELD IT. HE HAD NO INTENTION OF USING IT TO PROTECT OUR WORLD, BUT INSTEAD TO USE ITS POWER TO *CONTROL IT.*
"HE TRIED TO CLAIM IT. I HELD HIM BACK BUT KNEW HE WOULD NEVER STOP TRYING TO TAKE IT.
"SO I CALLED ON THE SPIRITS TO GUIDE ME.
RISE, O SPIRITS OF THE DANCING FLAMES!
"THEY TOLD ME TO DROP THE AMULET INTO THE PITS SO THAT IT MIGHT ONE DAY BE FOUND BY ONE WHO WAS WORTHY TO WIELD IT."
THAT WOULD BE YOU. AS FOR YOUR PARENTS, YOUR GUESS IS AS GOOD AS MINE.
BUT IF YOU GAVE THE AMULET THE POWER OVER CREATURES AND PLANTS, THEN--
THE MEGALITH GUY! HIS AMULET AND MINE! THEY'RE ONE AND THE SAME!

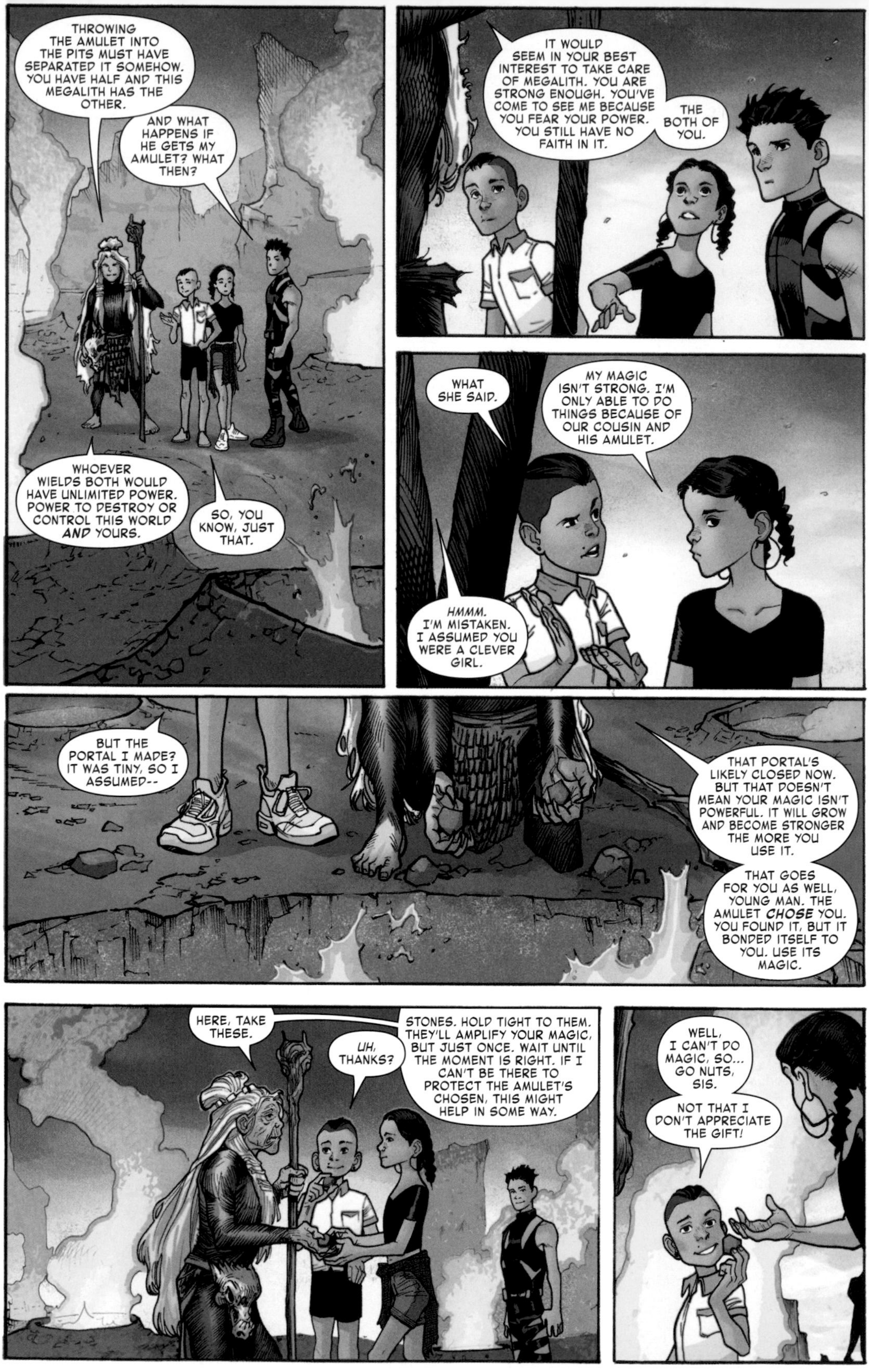
THROWING THE AMULET INTO THE PITS MUST HAVE SEPARATED IT SOMEHOW. YOU HAVE HALF AND THIS MEGALITH HAS THE OTHER.
AND WHAT HAPPENS IF HE GETS MY AMULET? WHAT THEN?
WHOEVER WIELDS BOTH WOULD HAVE UNLIMITED POWER. POWER TO DESTROY OR CONTROL THIS WORLD AND YOURS.
SO, YOU KNOW, JUST THAT.
IT WOULD SEEM IN YOUR BEST INTEREST TO TAKE CARE OF MEGALITH. YOU ARE STRONG ENOUGH. YOU'VE COME TO SEE ME BECAUSE YOU FEAR YOUR POWER. YOU STILL HAVE NO FAITH IN IT.
THE BOTH OF YOU.
WHAT SHE SAID.
MY MAGIC ISN'T STRONG. I'M ONLY ABLE TO DO THINGS BECAUSE OF OUR COUSIN AND HIS AMULET.
HMMM. I'M MISTAKEN. I ASSUMED YOU WERE A CLEVER GIRL.
BUT THE PORTAL I MADE? IT WAS TINY, SO I ASSUMED--
THAT PORTAL'S LIKELY CLOSED NOW. BUT THAT DOESN'T MEAN YOUR MAGIC ISN'T POWERFUL. IT WILL GROW AND BECOME STRONGER THE MORE YOU USE IT.
THAT GOES FOR YOU AS WELL, YOUNG MAN. THE AMULET CHOSE YOU. YOU FOUND IT, BUT IT BONDED ITSELF TO YOU. USE ITS MAGIC.
HERE, TAKE THESE.
STONES. HOLD TIGHT TO THEM. THEY'LL AMPLIFY YOUR MAGIC, BUT JUST ONCE. WAIT UNTIL THE MOMENT IS RIGHT. IF I CAN'T BE THERE TO PROTECT THE AMULET'S CHOSEN, THIS MIGHT HELP IN SOME WAY.
UH, THANKS?
WELL, I CAN'T DO MAGIC, SO... GO NUTS, SIS.
NOT THAT I DON'T APPRECIATE THE GIFT!

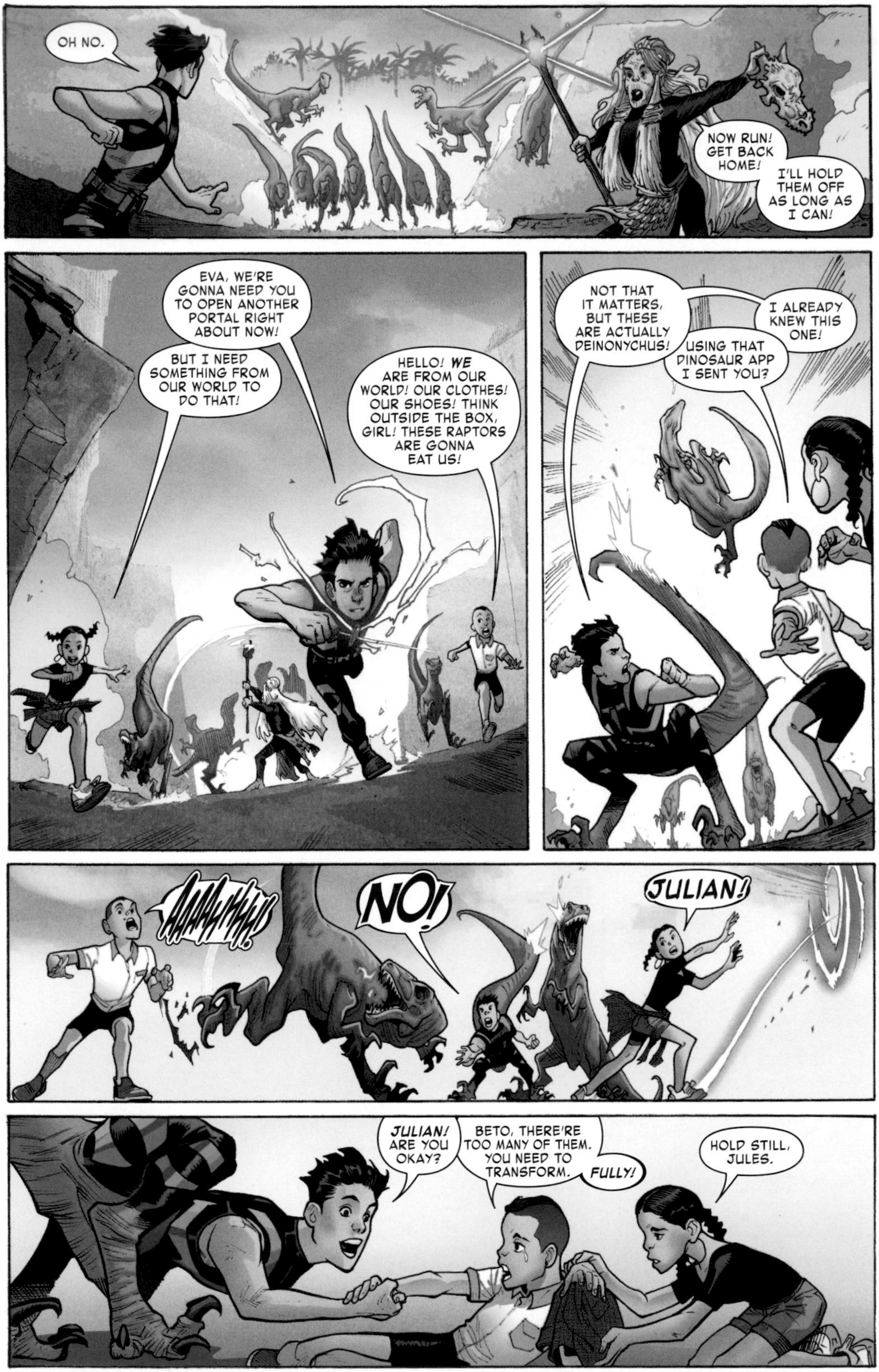
OH NO.
NOW RUN! GET BACK HOME!
I'LL HOLD THEM OFF AS LONG AS I CAN!
EVA, WE'RE GONNA NEED YOU TO OPEN ANOTHER PORTAL RIGHT ABOUT NOW!
BUT I NEED SOMETHING FROM OUR WORLD TO DO THAT!
HELLO! WE ARE FROM OUR WORLD! OUR CLOTHES! OUR SHOES! THINK OUTSIDE THE BOX, GIRL! THESE RAPTORS ARE GONNA EAT US!
NOT THAT IT MATTERS, BUT THESE ARE ACTUALLY DEINONYCHUS!
USING THAT DINOSAUR APP I SENT YOU?
I ALREADY KNEW THIS ONE!
AAAAHHHH!
NO!
JULIAN!
JULIAN! ARE YOU OKAY?
BETO, THERE'RE TOO MANY OF THEM. YOU NEED TO TRANSFORM.
FULLY!
HOLD STILL, JULES.

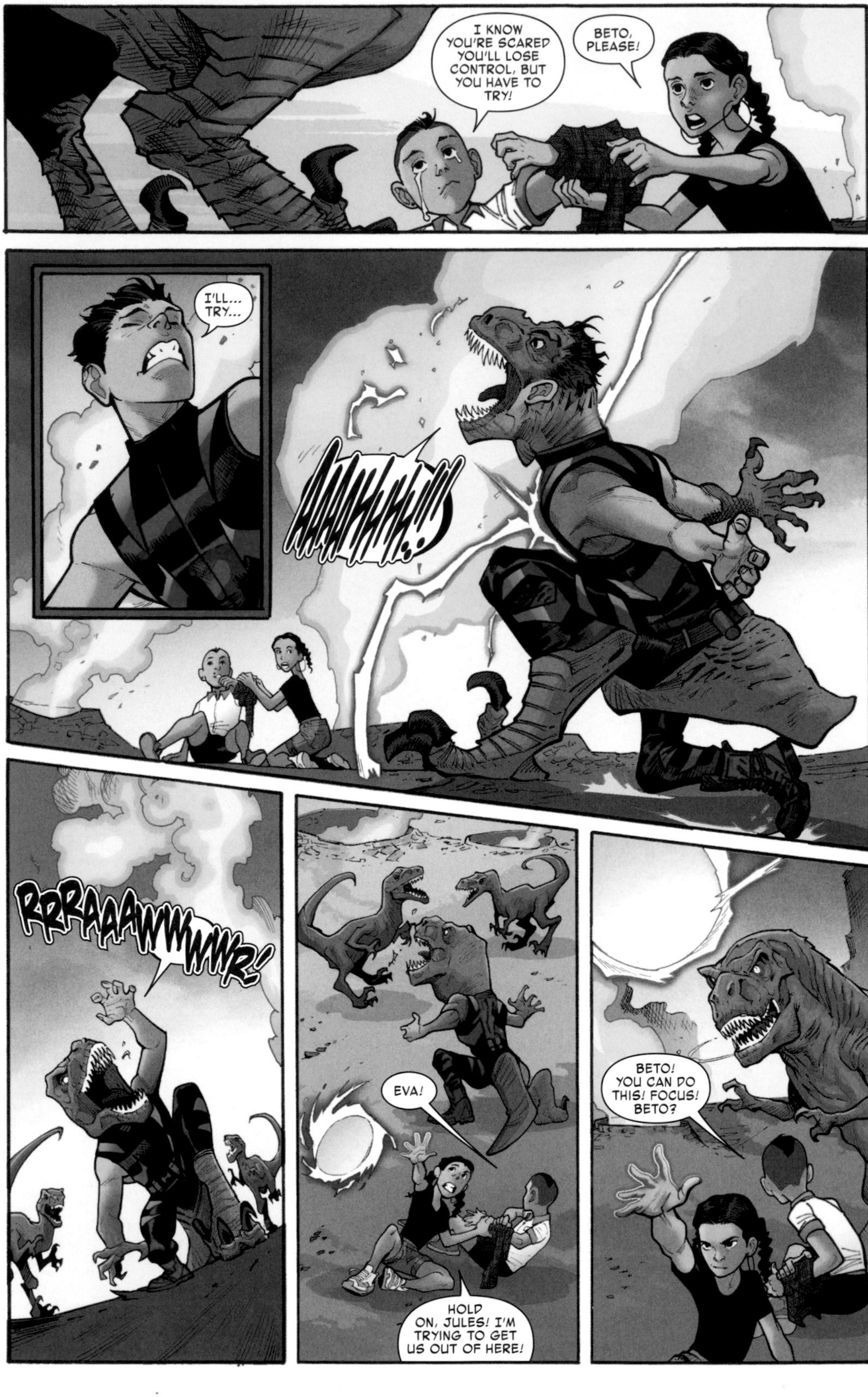
I KNOW YOU'RE SCARED YOU'LL LOSE CONTROL, BUT YOU HAVE TO TRY!
BETO, PLEASE!
I'LL... TRY...
AAAHHHH!!!
RRRAAAWWWWR!
EVA!
HOLD ON, JULES! I'M TRYING TO GET US OUT OF HERE!
BETO! YOU CAN DO THIS! FOCUS! BETO?

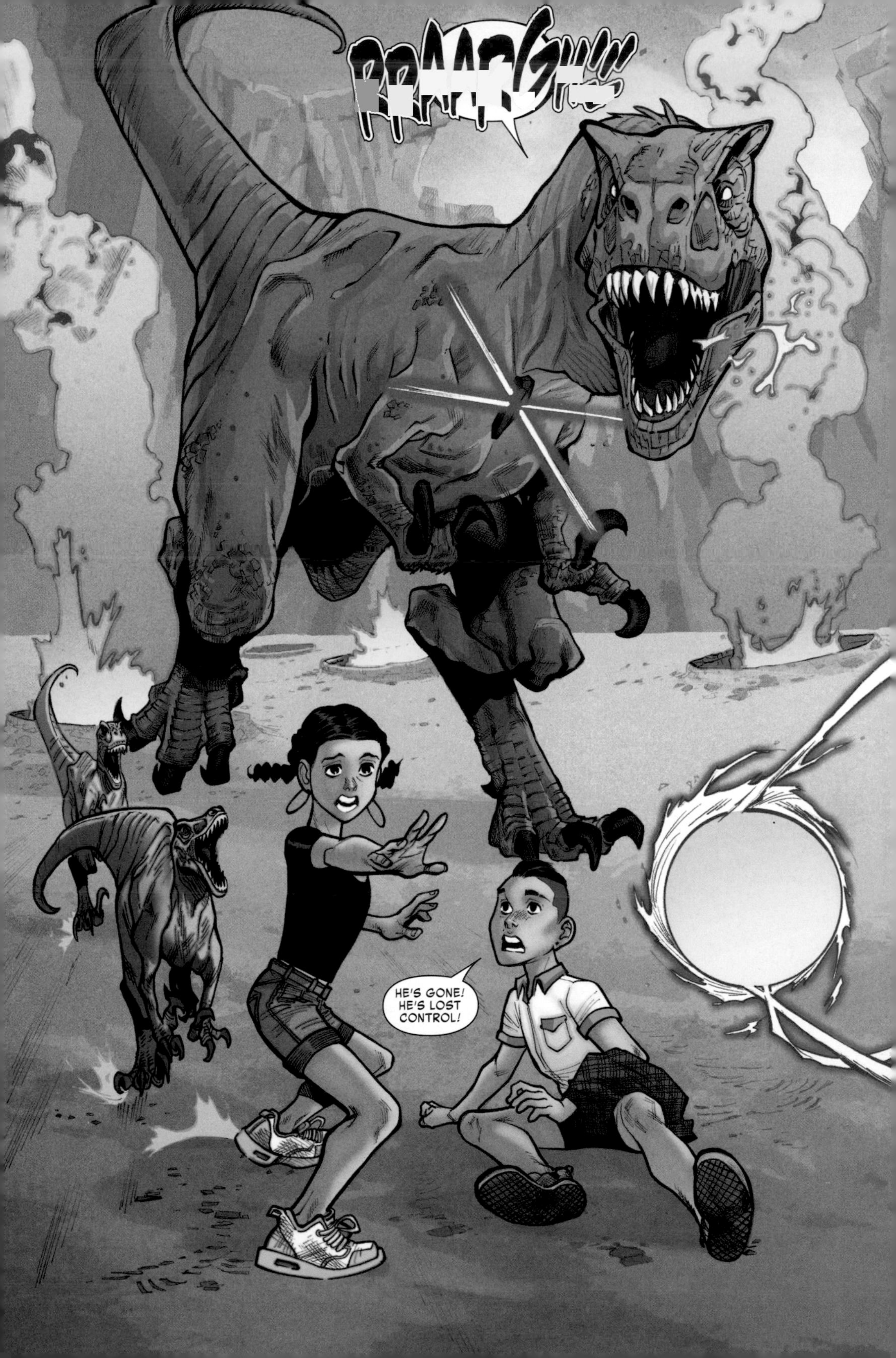
HE'S GONE! HE'S LOST CONTROL!

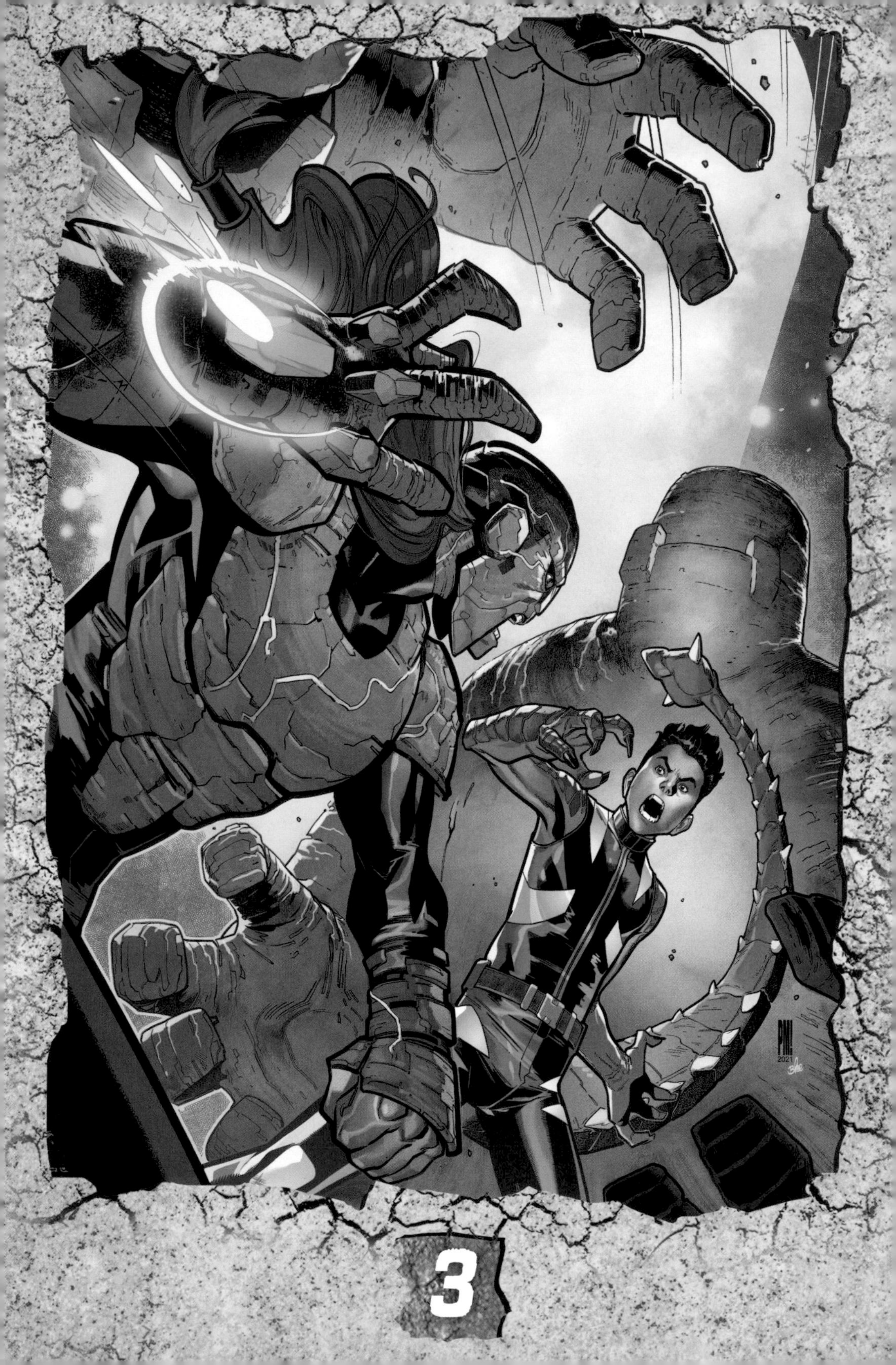

3

ROOOOAAAARR!!!

JULIAN, GO! *NOW!* BETO'S NOT IN CONTROL OF HIMSELF!

AAAHHHHHHH!!!

ZZZMMMTTT

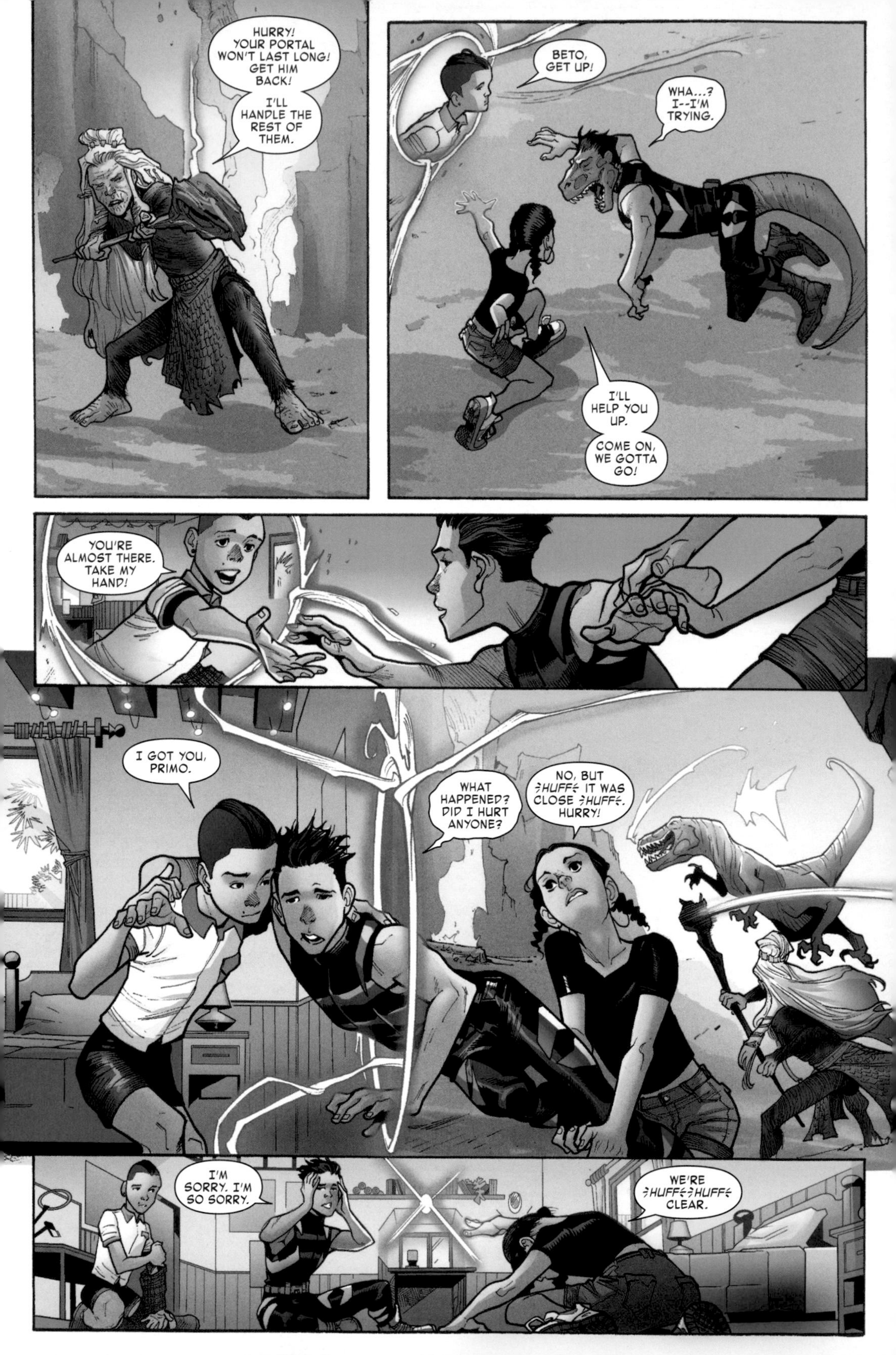
HURRY! YOUR PORTAL WON'T LAST LONG! GET HIM BACK!
I'LL HANDLE THE REST OF THEM.
BETO, GET UP!
WHA...? I--I'M TRYING.
I'LL HELP YOU UP.
COME ON, WE GOTTA GO!
YOU'RE ALMOST THERE. TAKE MY HAND!
I GOT YOU, PRIMO.
WHAT HAPPENED? DID I HURT ANYONE?
NO, BUT *HUFF* IT WAS CLOSE *HUFF*. HURRY!
I'M SORRY. I'M SO SORRY.
WE'RE *HUFF* *HUFF* CLEAR.

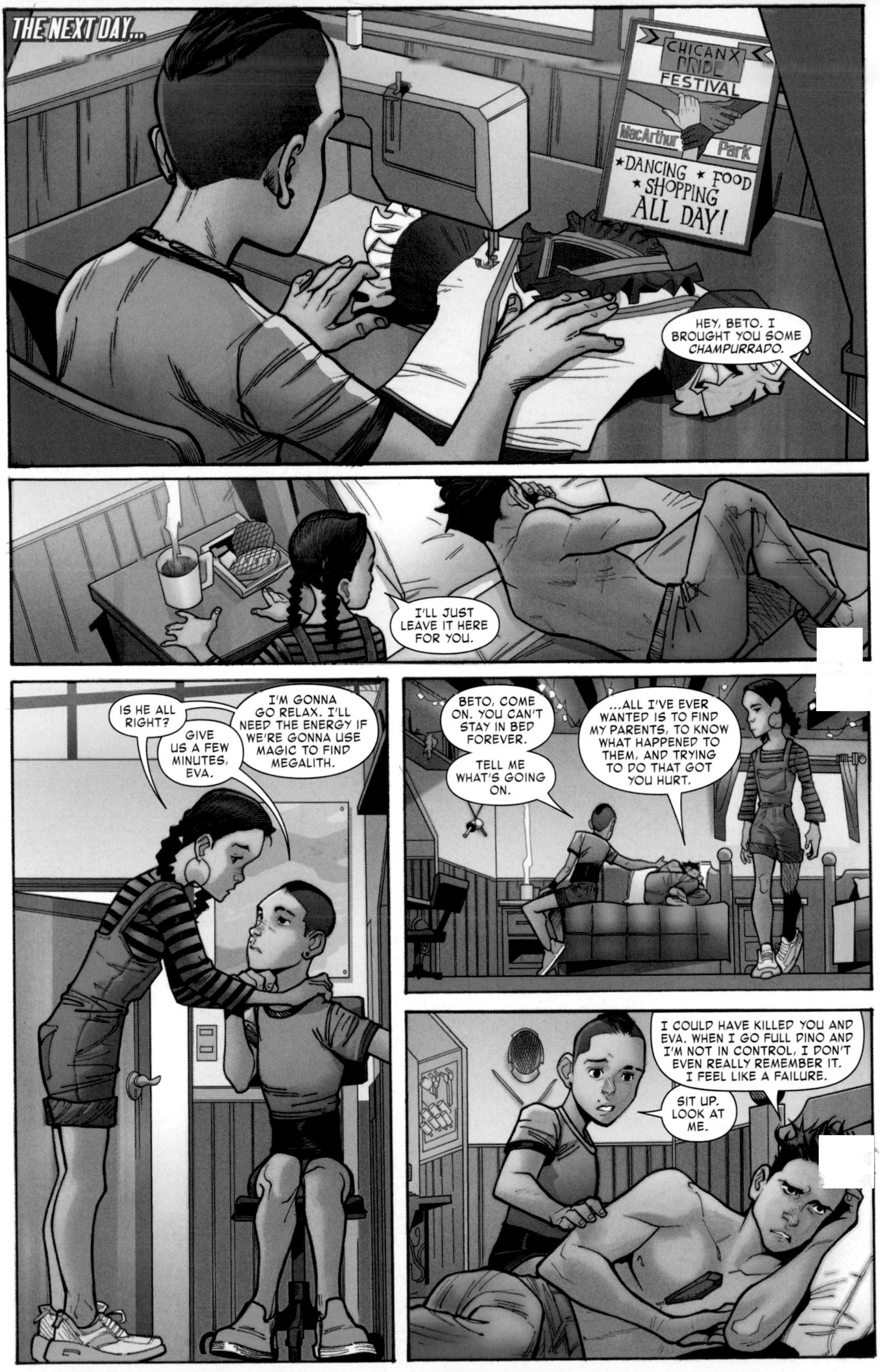
THE NEXT DAY...
CHICANX PRIDE FESTIVAL
MacArthur Park
★DANCING ★FOOD ★SHOPPING ALL DAY!
HEY, BETO. I BROUGHT YOU SOME CHAMPURRADO.
I'LL JUST LEAVE IT HERE FOR YOU.
IS HE ALL RIGHT?
GIVE US A FEW MINUTES, EVA.
I'M GONNA GO RELAX. I'LL NEED THE ENERGY IF WE'RE GONNA USE MAGIC TO FIND MEGALITH.
BETO, COME ON. YOU CAN'T STAY IN BED FOREVER.
TELL ME WHAT'S GOING ON.
...ALL I'VE EVER WANTED IS TO FIND MY PARENTS, TO KNOW WHAT HAPPENED TO THEM, AND TRYING TO DO THAT GOT YOU HURT.
I COULD HAVE KILLED YOU AND EVA. WHEN I GO FULL DINO AND I'M NOT IN CONTROL, I DON'T EVEN REALLY REMEMBER IT. I FEEL LIKE A FAILURE.
SIT UP. LOOK AT ME.

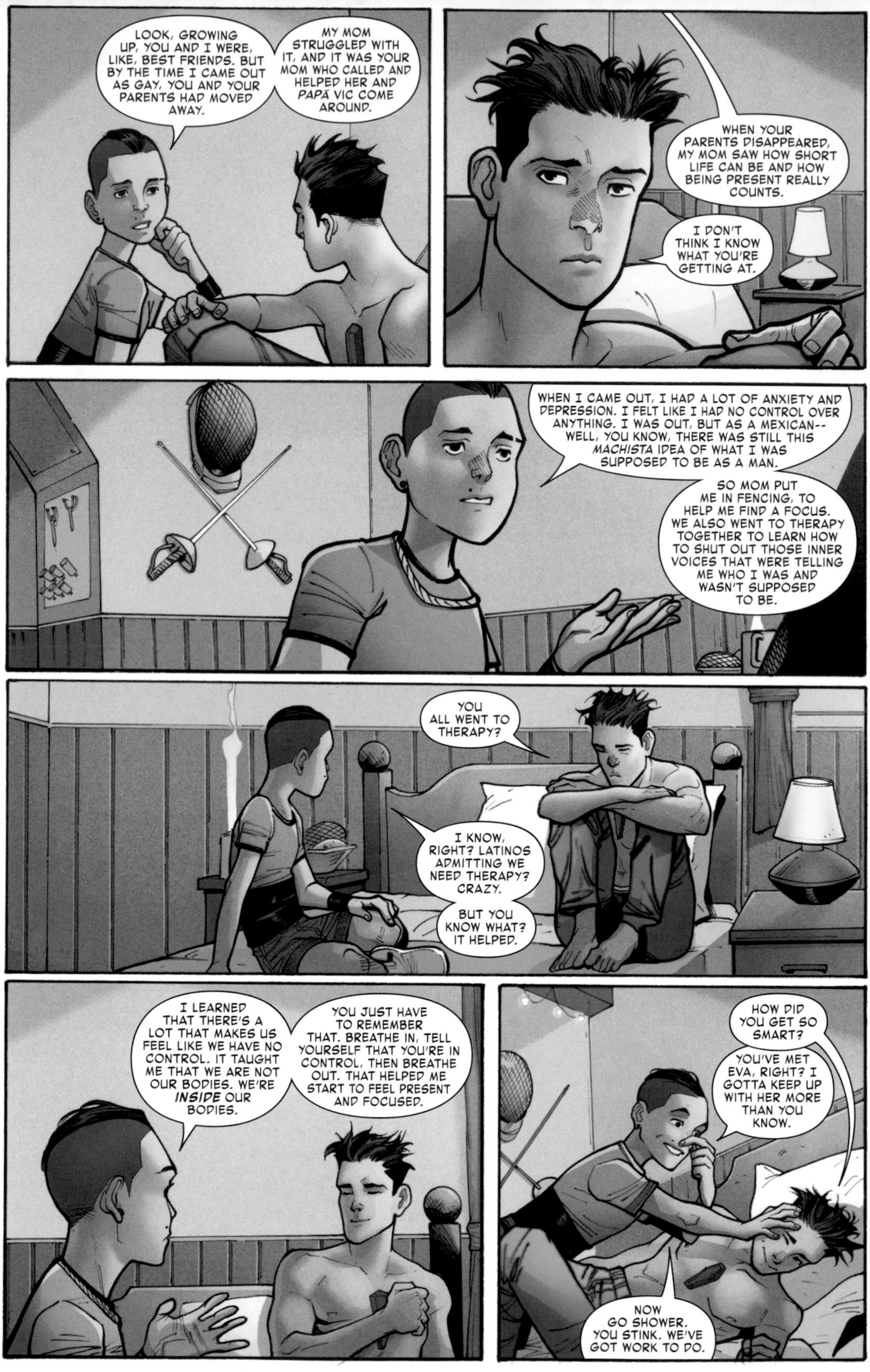
LOOK, GROWING UP, YOU AND I WERE, LIKE, BEST FRIENDS. BUT BY THE TIME I CAME OUT AS GAY, YOU AND YOUR PARENTS HAD MOVED AWAY.
MY MOM STRUGGLED WITH IT, AND IT WAS YOUR MOM WHO CALLED AND HELPED HER AND *PAPÁ* VIC COME AROUND.
WHEN YOUR PARENTS DISAPPEARED, MY MOM SAW HOW SHORT LIFE CAN BE AND HOW BEING PRESENT REALLY COUNTS.
I DON'T THINK I KNOW WHAT YOU'RE GETTING AT.
WHEN I CAME OUT, I HAD A LOT OF ANXIETY AND DEPRESSION. I FELT LIKE I HAD NO CONTROL OVER ANYTHING. I WAS OUT, BUT AS A MEXICAN-- WELL, YOU KNOW, THERE WAS STILL THIS *MACHISTA* IDEA OF WHAT I WAS SUPPOSED TO BE AS A MAN.
SO MOM PUT ME IN FENCING, TO HELP ME FIND A FOCUS. WE ALSO WENT TO THERAPY TOGETHER TO LEARN HOW TO SHUT OUT THOSE INNER VOICES THAT WERE TELLING ME WHO I WAS AND WASN'T SUPPOSED TO BE.
YOU ALL WENT TO THERAPY?
I KNOW, RIGHT? LATINOS ADMITTING WE NEED THERAPY? CRAZY.
BUT YOU KNOW WHAT? IT HELPED.
I LEARNED THAT THERE'S A LOT THAT MAKES US FEEL LIKE WE HAVE NO CONTROL. IT TAUGHT ME THAT WE ARE NOT OUR BODIES. WE'RE ***INSIDE*** OUR BODIES.
YOU JUST HAVE TO REMEMBER THAT. BREATHE IN, TELL YOURSELF THAT YOU'RE IN CONTROL, THEN BREATHE OUT. THAT HELPED ME START TO FEEL PRESENT AND FOCUSED.
HOW DID YOU GET SO SMART?
YOU'VE MET EVA, RIGHT? I GOTTA KEEP UP WITH HER MORE THAN YOU KNOW.
NOW GO SHOWER. YOU STINK. WE'VE GOT WORK TO DO.

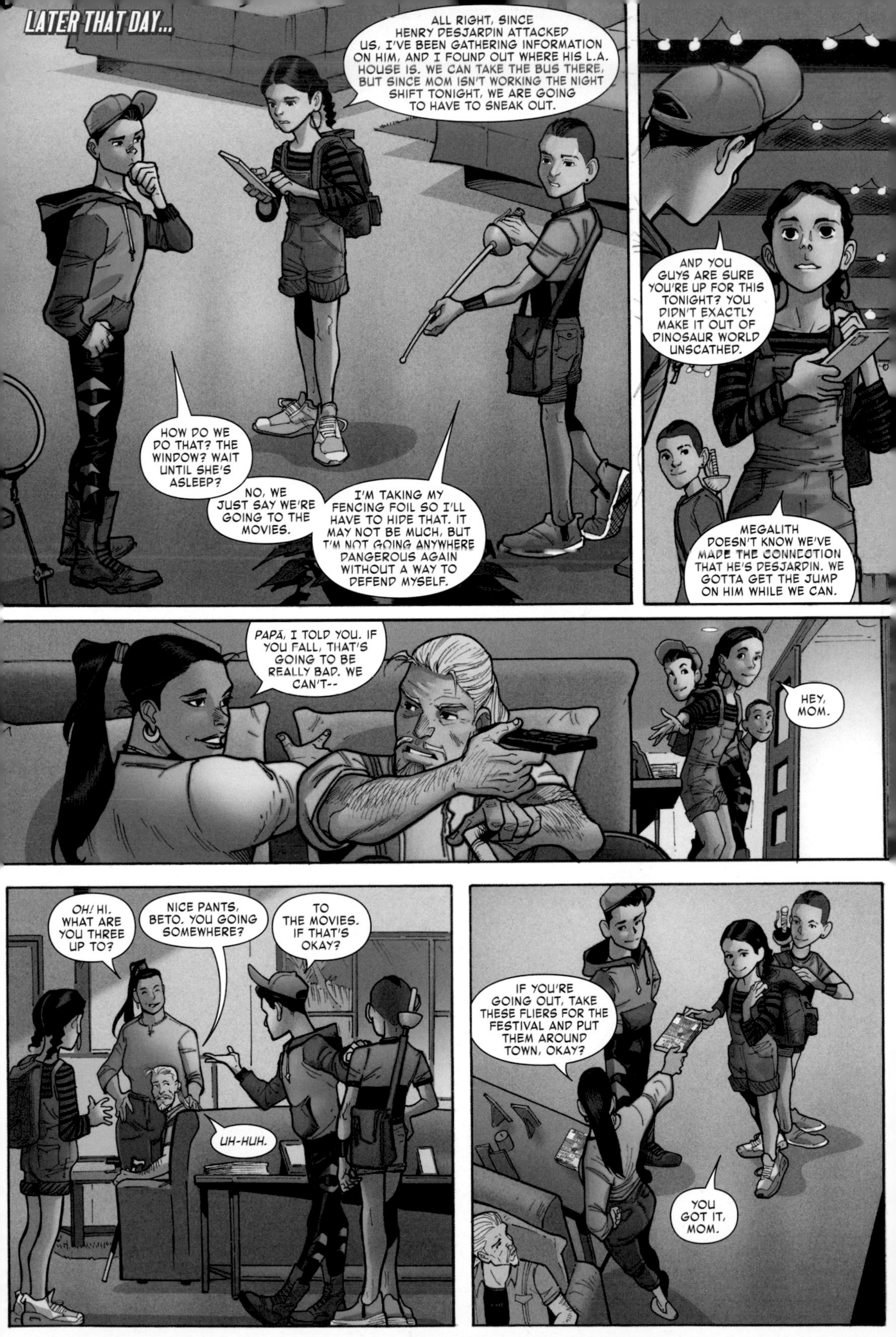
LATER THAT DAY...
ALL RIGHT, SINCE HENRY DESJARDIN ATTACKED US, I'VE BEEN GATHERING INFORMATION ON HIM, AND I FOUND OUT WHERE HIS L.A. HOUSE IS. WE CAN TAKE THE BUS THERE, BUT SINCE MOM ISN'T WORKING THE NIGHT SHIFT TONIGHT, WE ARE GOING TO HAVE TO SNEAK OUT.
HOW DO WE DO THAT? THE WINDOW? WAIT UNTIL SHE'S ASLEEP?
NO, WE JUST SAY WE'RE GOING TO THE MOVIES.
I'M TAKING MY FENCING FOIL SO I'LL HAVE TO HIDE THAT. IT MAY NOT BE MUCH, BUT I'M NOT GOING ANYWHERE DANGEROUS AGAIN WITHOUT A WAY TO DEFEND MYSELF.
AND YOU GUYS ARE SURE YOU'RE UP FOR THIS TONIGHT? YOU DIDN'T EXACTLY MAKE IT OUT OF DINOSAUR WORLD UNSCATHED.
MEGALITH DOESN'T KNOW WE'VE MADE THE CONNECTION THAT HE'S DESJARDIN. WE GOTTA GET THE JUMP ON HIM WHILE WE CAN.
PAPÁ, I TOLD YOU. IF YOU FALL, THAT'S GOING TO BE REALLY BAD. WE CAN'T--
HEY, MOM.
OH! HI. WHAT ARE YOU THREE UP TO?
NICE PANTS, BETO. YOU GOING SOMEWHERE?
TO THE MOVIES. IF THAT'S OKAY?
UH-HUH.
IF YOU'RE GOING OUT, TAKE THESE FLIERS FOR THE FESTIVAL AND PUT THEM AROUND TOWN, OKAY?
YOU GOT IT, MOM.

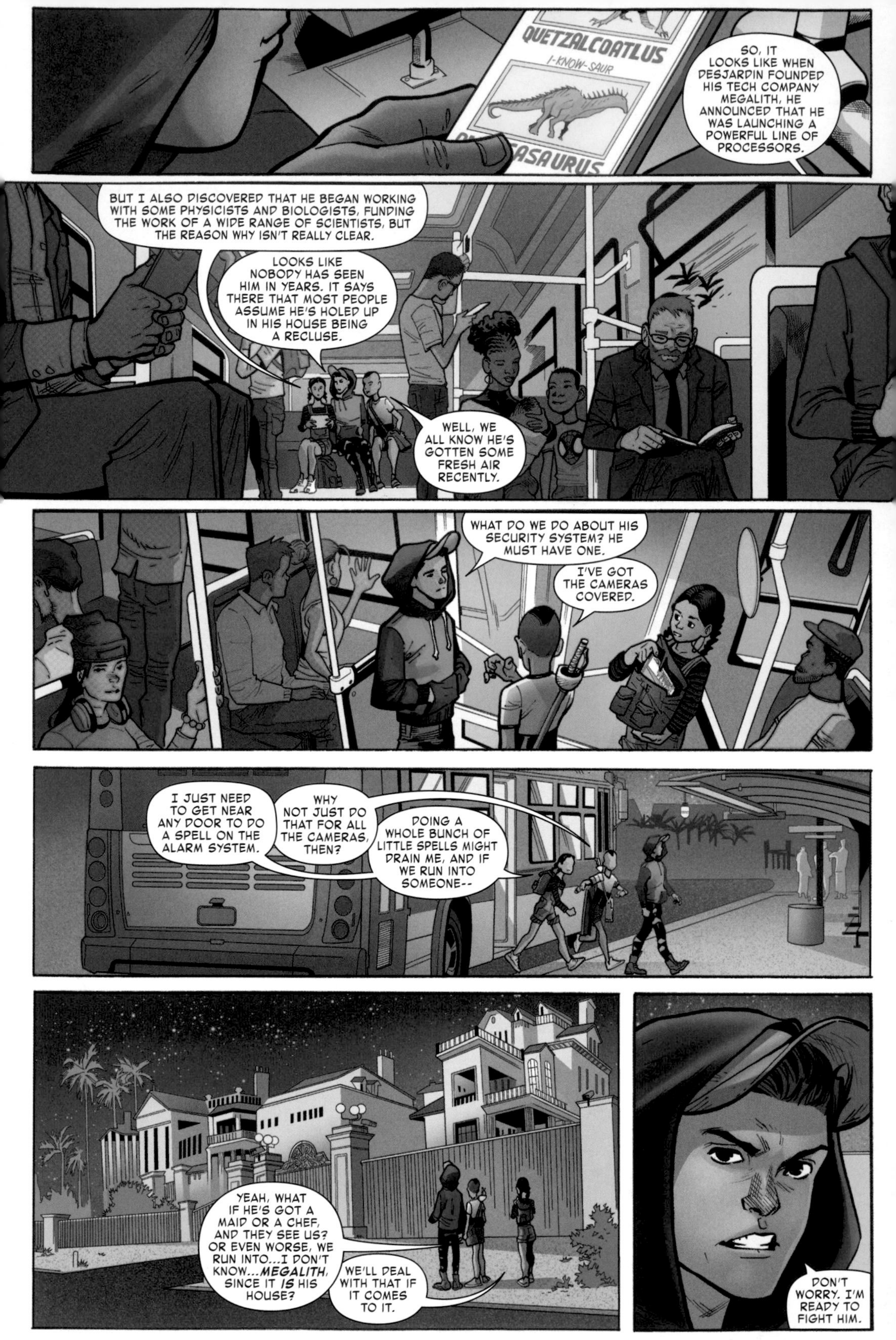
QUETZALCOATLUS
I-KNOW-SAUR
SO, IT LOOKS LIKE WHEN DESJARDIN FOUNDED HIS TECH COMPANY MEGALITH, HE ANNOUNCED THAT HE WAS LAUNCHING A POWERFUL LINE OF PROCESSORS.
BUT I ALSO DISCOVERED THAT HE BEGAN WORKING WITH SOME PHYSICISTS AND BIOLOGISTS, FUNDING THE WORK OF A WIDE RANGE OF SCIENTISTS, BUT THE REASON WHY ISN'T REALLY CLEAR.
LOOKS LIKE NOBODY HAS SEEN HIM IN YEARS. IT SAYS THERE THAT MOST PEOPLE ASSUME HE'S HOLED UP IN HIS HOUSE BEING A RECLUSE.
WELL, WE ALL KNOW HE'S GOTTEN SOME FRESH AIR RECENTLY.
WHAT DO WE DO ABOUT HIS SECURITY SYSTEM? HE MUST HAVE ONE.
I'VE GOT THE CAMERAS COVERED.
I JUST NEED TO GET NEAR ANY DOOR TO DO A SPELL ON THE ALARM SYSTEM.
WHY NOT JUST DO THAT FOR ALL THE CAMERAS, THEN?
DOING A WHOLE BUNCH OF LITTLE SPELLS MIGHT DRAIN ME, AND IF WE RUN INTO SOMEONE--
YEAH, WHAT IF HE'S GOT A MAID OR A CHEF, AND THEY SEE US? OR EVEN WORSE, WE RUN INTO...I DON'T KNOW...*MEGALITH*, SINCE IT *IS* HIS HOUSE?
WE'LL DEAL WITH THAT IF IT COMES TO IT.
DON'T WORRY. I'M READY TO FIGHT HIM.

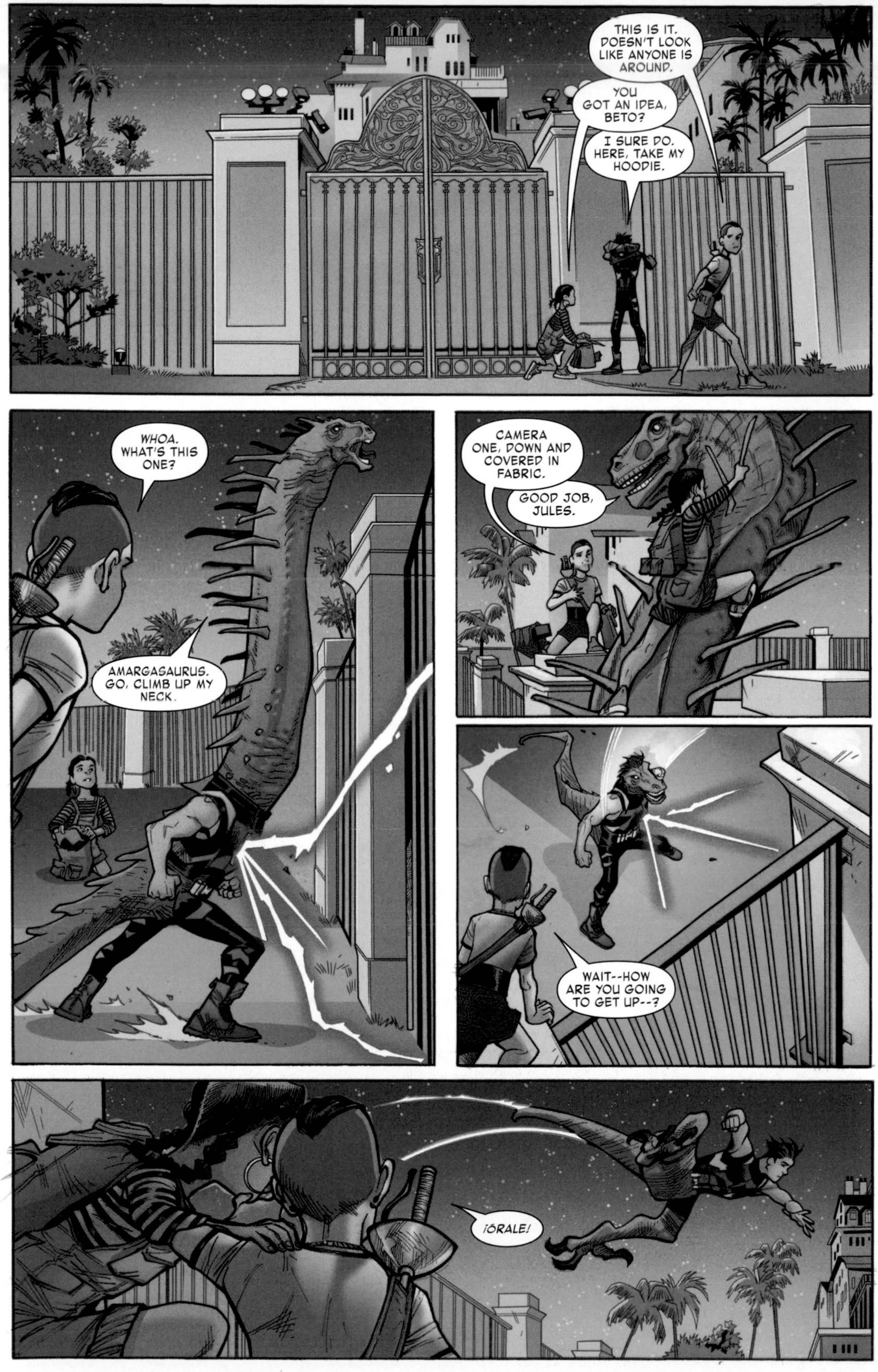
THIS IS IT. DOESN'T LOOK LIKE ANYONE IS AROUND.
YOU GOT AN IDEA, BETO?
I SURE DO. HERE, TAKE MY HOODIE.
WHOA. WHAT'S THIS ONE?
AMARGASAURUS. GO, CLIMB UP MY NECK.
CAMERA ONE, DOWN AND COVERED IN FABRIC.
GOOD JOB, JULES.
WAIT--HOW ARE YOU GOING TO GET UP--?
¡ÓRALE!

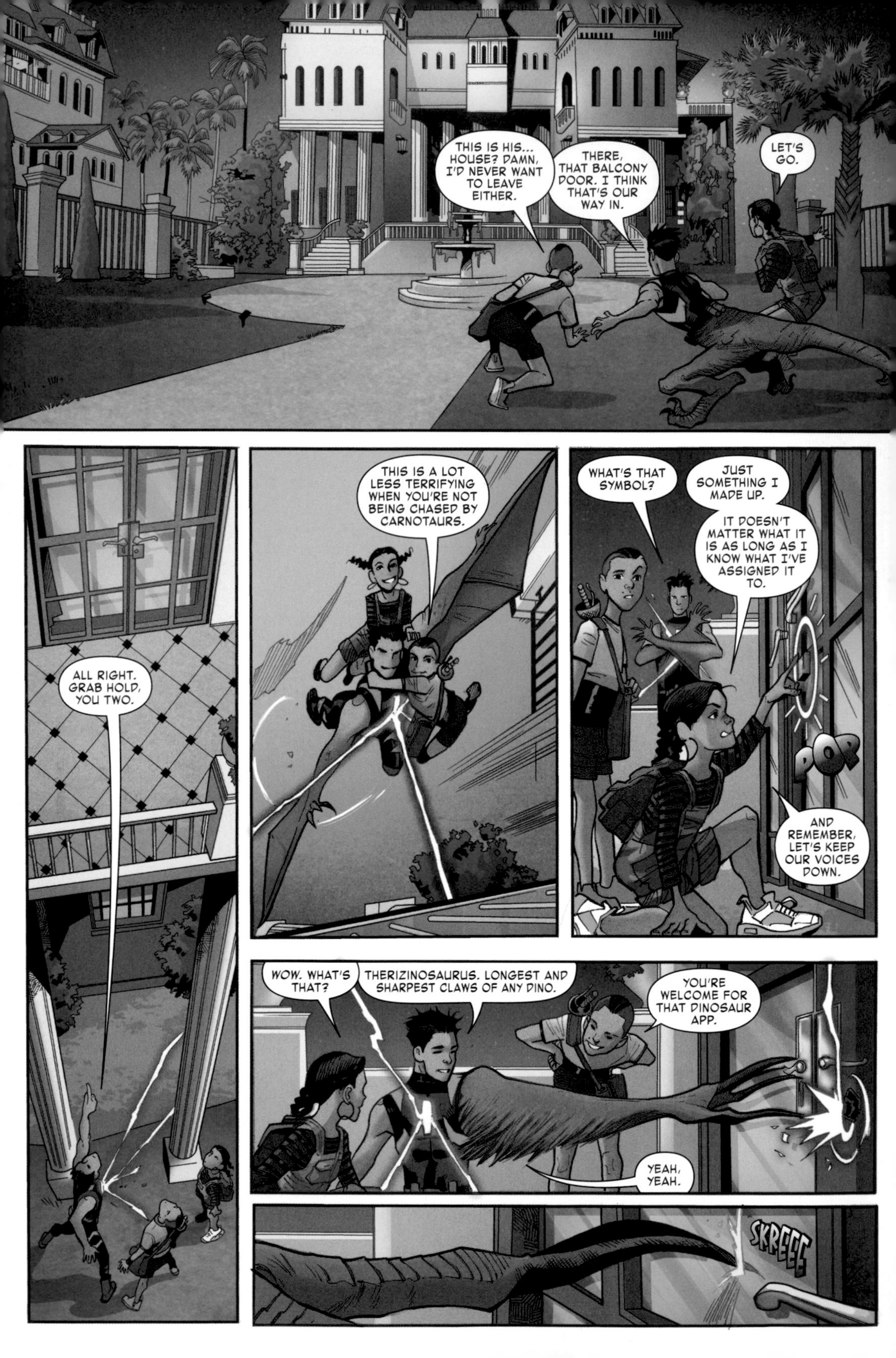

THIS IS HIS... HOUSE? DAMN, I'D NEVER WANT TO LEAVE EITHER.
THERE, THAT BALCONY DOOR. I THINK THAT'S OUR WAY IN.
LET'S GO.
ALL RIGHT. GRAB HOLD, YOU TWO.
THIS IS A LOT LESS TERRIFYING WHEN YOU'RE NOT BEING CHASED BY CARNOTAURS.
WHAT'S THAT SYMBOL?
JUST SOMETHING I MADE UP.
IT DOESN'T MATTER WHAT IT IS AS LONG AS I KNOW WHAT I'VE ASSIGNED IT TO.
POP
AND REMEMBER, LET'S KEEP OUR VOICES DOWN.
WOW. WHAT'S THAT?
THERIZINOSAURUS. LONGEST AND SHARPEST CLAWS OF ANY DINO.
YOU'RE WELCOME FOR THAT DINOSAUR APP.
YEAH, YEAH.
SKREEE

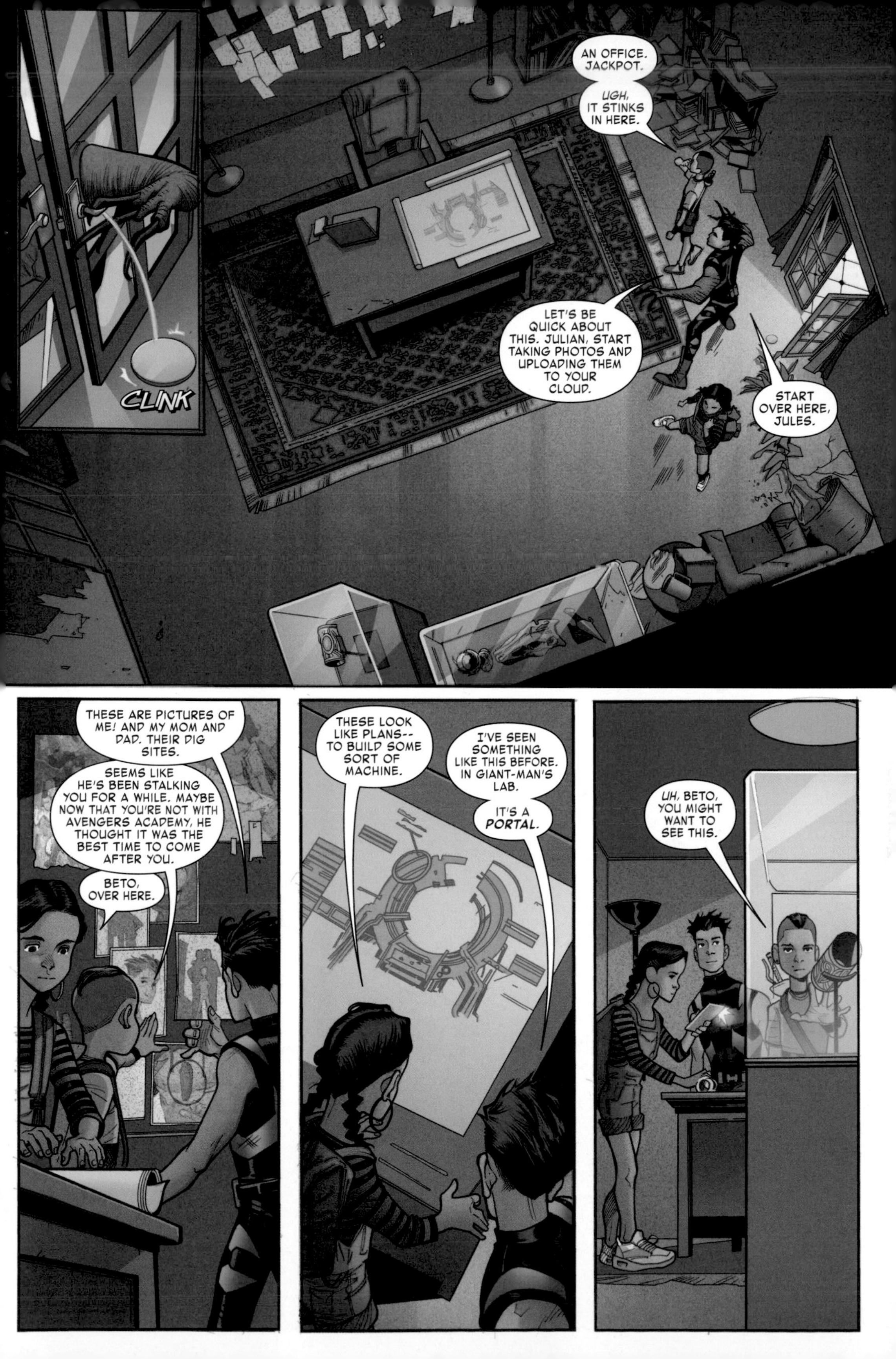
CLINK
AN OFFICE. JACKPOT.
UGH, IT STINKS IN HERE.
LET'S BE QUICK ABOUT THIS. JULIAN, START TAKING PHOTOS AND UPLOADING THEM TO YOUR CLOUD.
START OVER HERE, JULES.
THESE ARE PICTURES OF ME! AND MY MOM AND DAD. THEIR DIG SITES.
SEEMS LIKE HE'S BEEN STALKING YOU FOR A WHILE. MAYBE NOW THAT YOU'RE NOT WITH AVENGERS ACADEMY, HE THOUGHT IT WAS THE BEST TIME TO COME AFTER YOU.
BETO, OVER HERE.
THESE LOOK LIKE PLANS-- TO BUILD SOME SORT OF MACHINE.
I'VE SEEN SOMETHING LIKE THIS BEFORE. IN GIANT-MAN'S LAB.
IT'S A PORTAL.
UH, BETO, YOU MIGHT WANT TO SEE THIS.

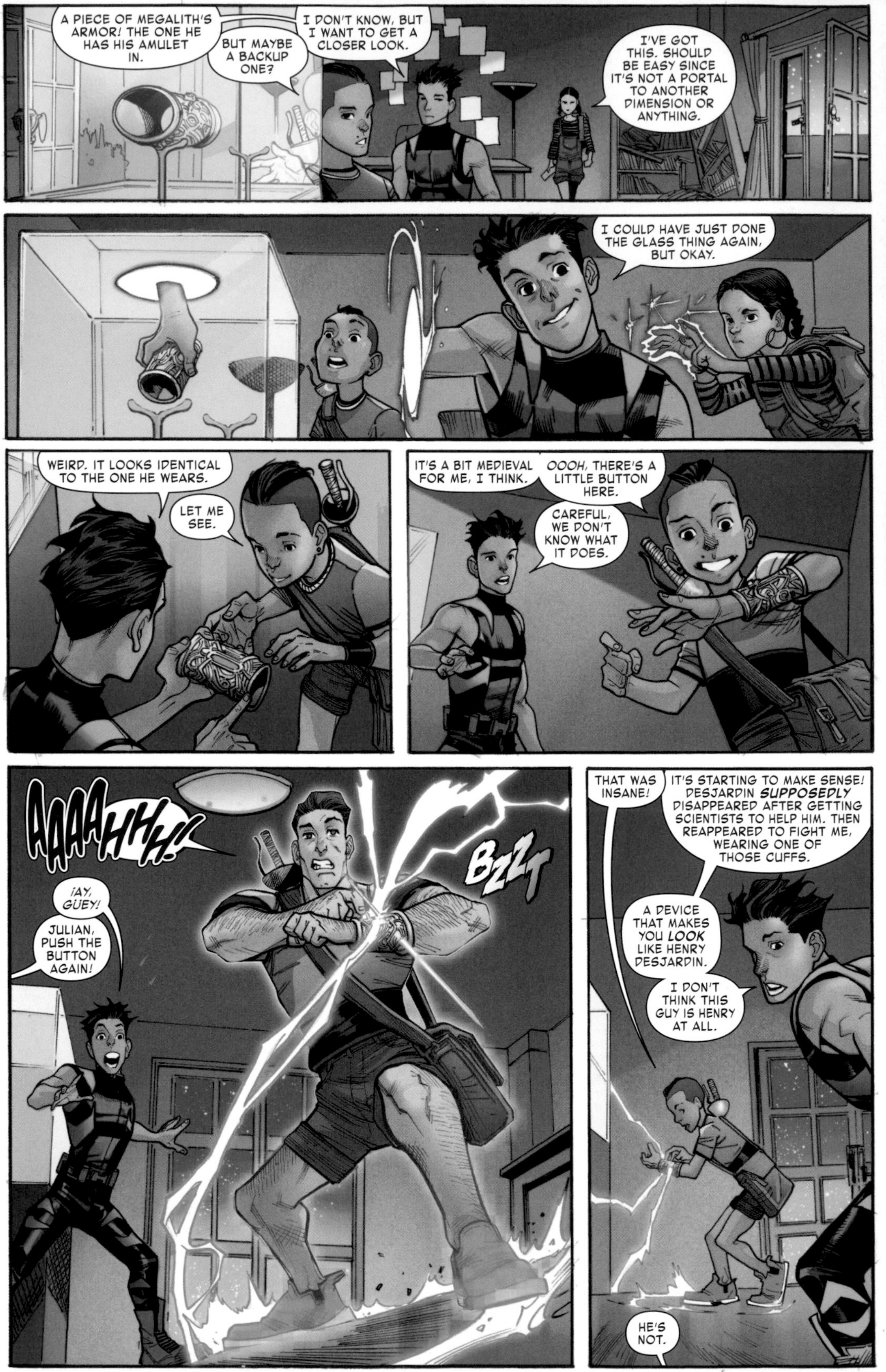
A PIECE OF MEGALITH'S ARMOR! THE ONE HE HAS HIS AMULET IN.
BUT MAYBE A BACKUP ONE?
I DON'T KNOW, BUT I WANT TO GET A CLOSER LOOK.
I'VE GOT THIS. SHOULD BE EASY SINCE IT'S NOT A PORTAL TO ANOTHER DIMENSION OR ANYTHING.
I COULD HAVE JUST DONE THE GLASS THING AGAIN, BUT OKAY.
WEIRD. IT LOOKS IDENTICAL TO THE ONE HE WEARS.
LET ME SEE.
IT'S A BIT MEDIEVAL FOR ME, I THINK.
OOOH, THERE'S A LITTLE BUTTON HERE.
CAREFUL, WE DON'T KNOW WHAT IT DOES.
AAAAHHH!
BZZT
¡AY, GÜEY!
JULIAN, PUSH THE BUTTON AGAIN!
THAT WAS INSANE!
IT'S STARTING TO MAKE SENSE! DESJARDIN SUPPOSEDLY DISAPPEARED AFTER GETTING SCIENTISTS TO HELP HIM. THEN REAPPEARED TO FIGHT ME, WEARING ONE OF THOSE CUFFS.
A DEVICE THAT MAKES YOU LOOK LIKE HENRY DESJARDIN.
I DON'T THINK THIS GUY IS HENRY AT ALL.
HE'S NOT.

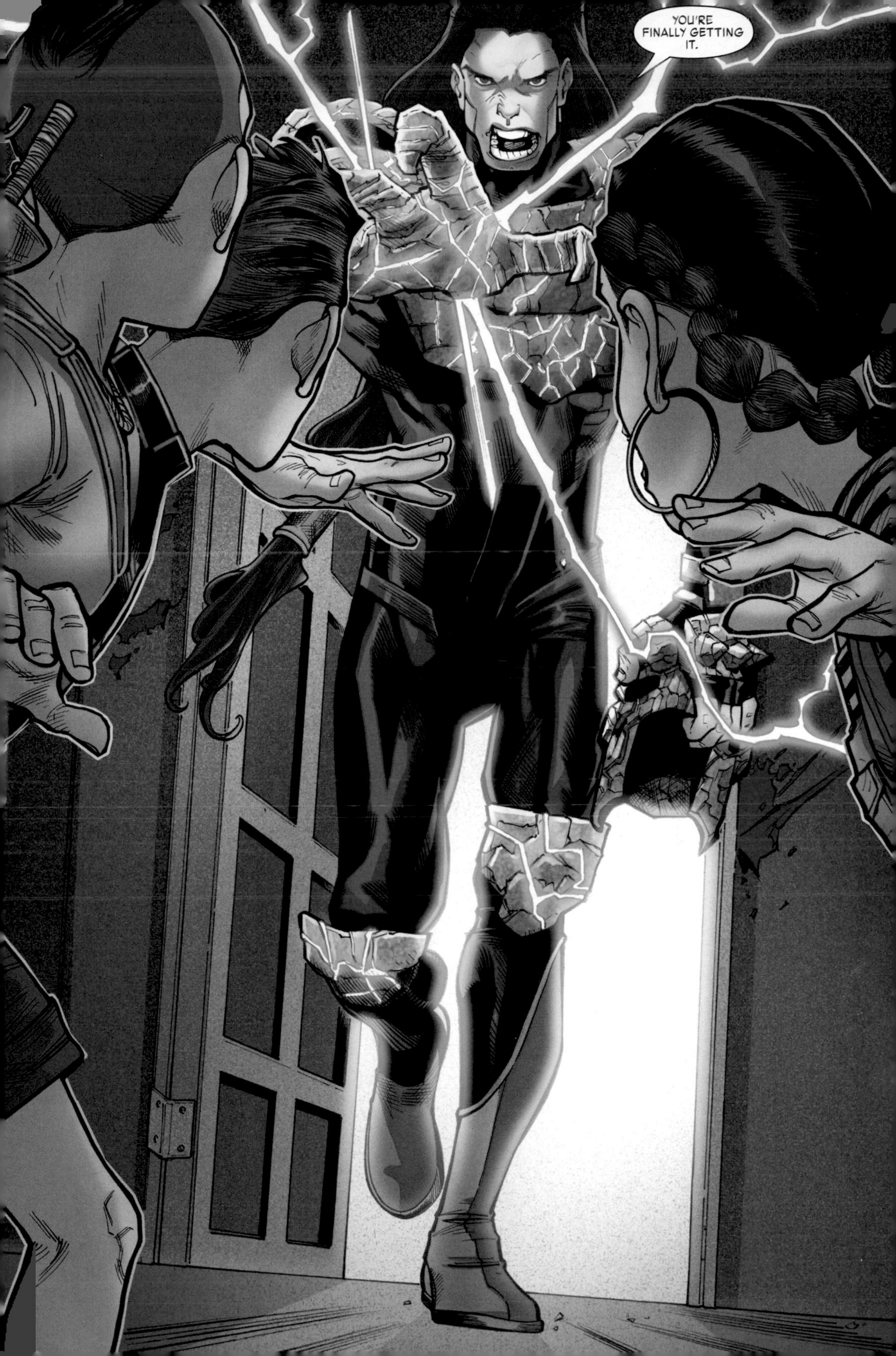
YOU'RE FINALLY GETTING IT.

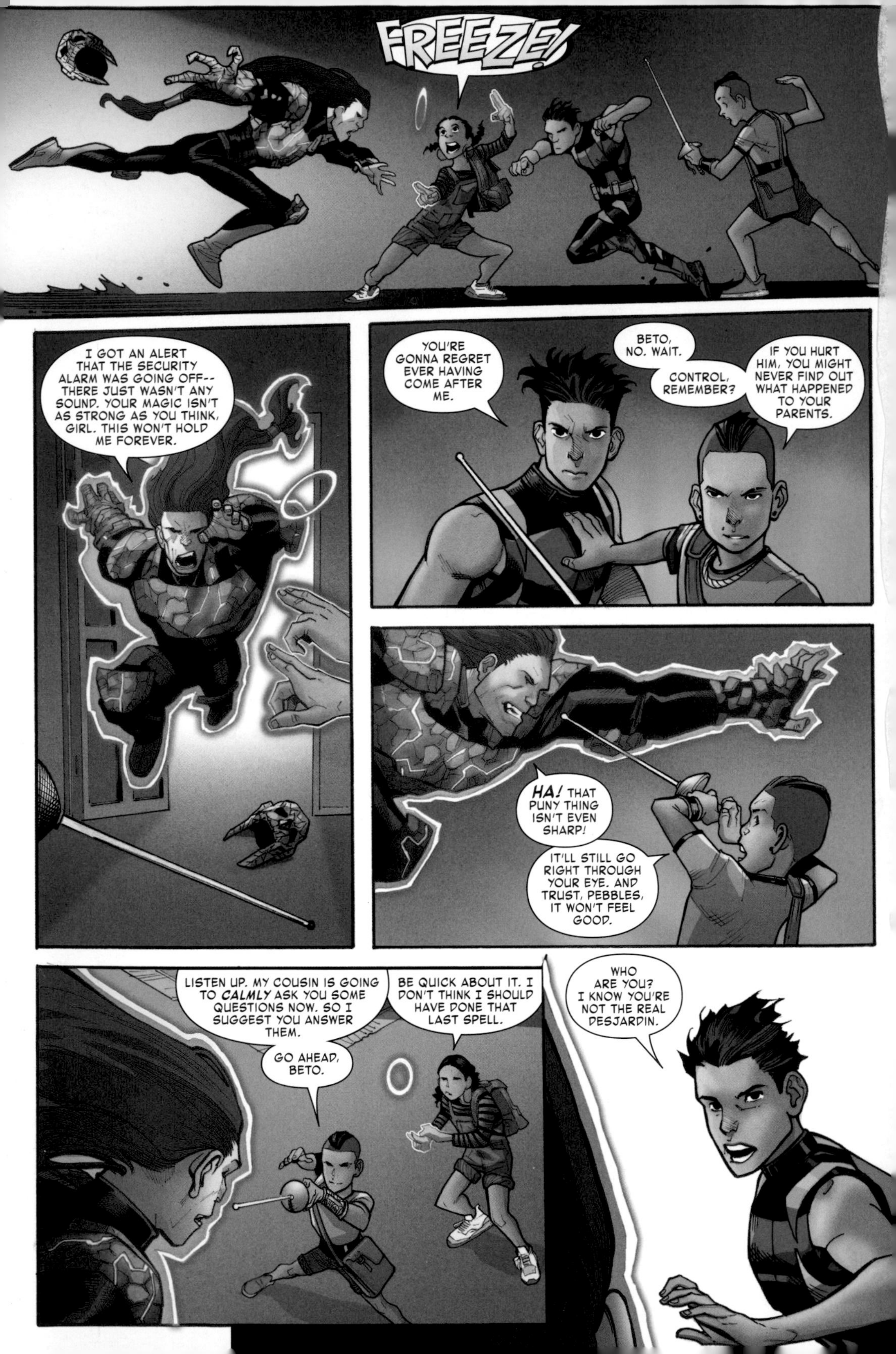
FREEZE!
I GOT AN ALERT THAT THE SECURITY ALARM WAS GOING OFF-- THERE JUST WASN'T ANY SOUND. YOUR MAGIC ISN'T AS STRONG AS YOU THINK, GIRL. THIS WON'T HOLD ME FOREVER.
YOU'RE GONNA REGRET EVER HAVING COME AFTER ME.
BETO, NO. WAIT.
CONTROL, REMEMBER?
IF YOU HURT HIM, YOU MIGHT NEVER FIND OUT WHAT HAPPENED TO YOUR PARENTS.
HA! THAT PUNY THING ISN'T EVEN SHARP!
IT'LL STILL GO RIGHT THROUGH YOUR EYE. AND TRUST, PEBBLES, IT WON'T FEEL GOOD.
LISTEN UP. MY COUSIN IS GOING TO CALMLY ASK YOU SOME QUESTIONS NOW. SO I SUGGEST YOU ANSWER THEM.
GO AHEAD, BETO.
BE QUICK ABOUT IT. I DON'T THINK I SHOULD HAVE DONE THAT LAST SPELL.
WHO ARE YOU? I KNOW YOU'RE NOT THE REAL DESJARDIN.

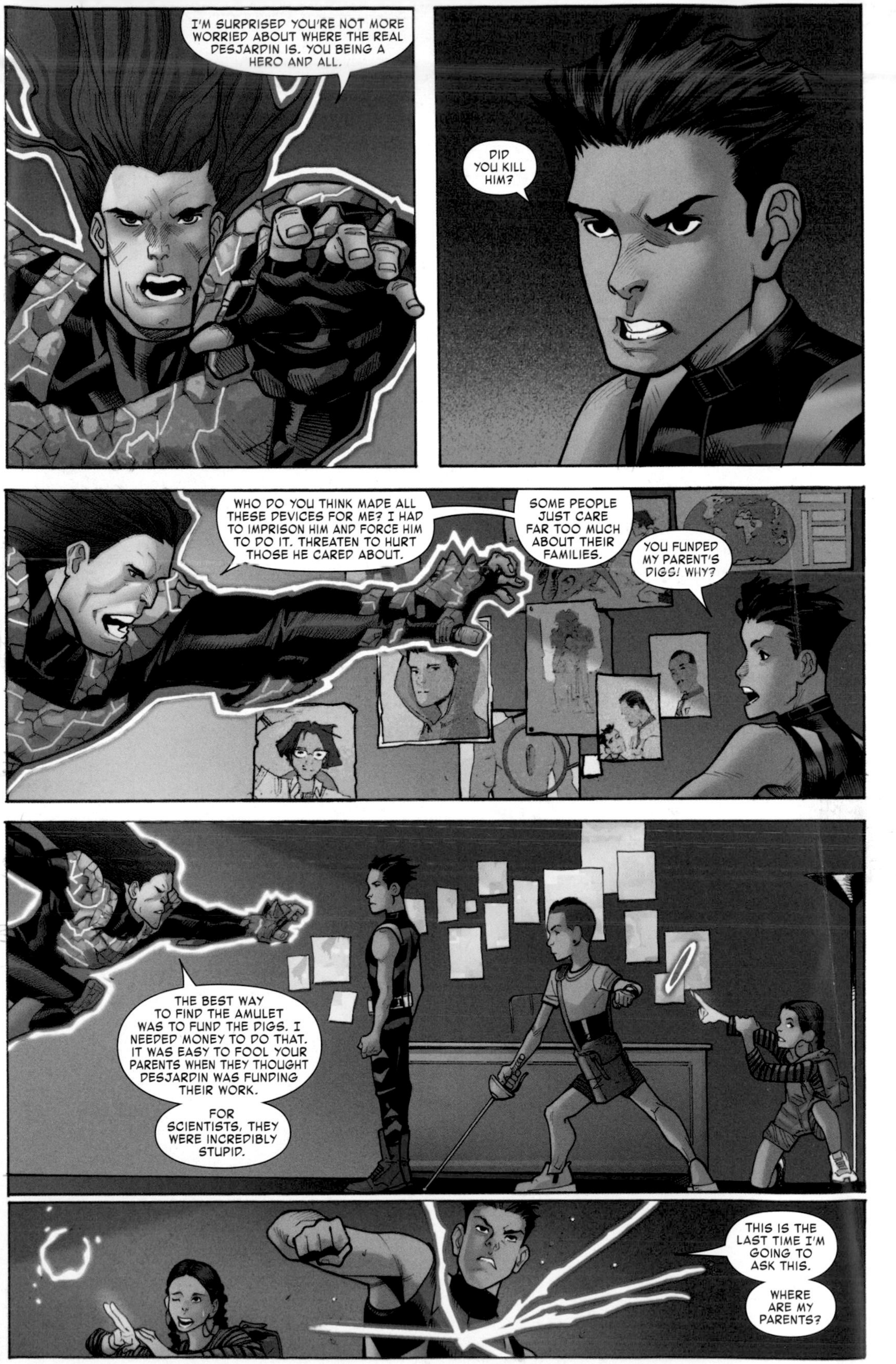
I'M SURPRISED YOU'RE NOT MORE WORRIED ABOUT WHERE THE REAL DESJARDIN IS. YOU BEING A HERO AND ALL.
DID YOU KILL HIM?
WHO DO YOU THINK MADE ALL THESE DEVICES FOR ME? I HAD TO IMPRISON HIM AND FORCE HIM TO DO IT. THREATEN TO HURT THOSE HE CARED ABOUT.
SOME PEOPLE JUST CARE FAR TOO MUCH ABOUT THEIR FAMILIES.
YOU FUNDED MY PARENT'S DIGS! WHY?
THE BEST WAY TO FIND THE AMULET WAS TO FUND THE DIGS. I NEEDED MONEY TO DO THAT. IT WAS EASY TO FOOL YOUR PARENTS WHEN THEY THOUGHT DESJARDIN WAS FUNDING THEIR WORK.
FOR SCIENTISTS, THEY WERE INCREDIBLY STUPID.
THIS IS THE LAST TIME I'M GOING TO ASK THIS.
WHERE ARE MY PARENTS?

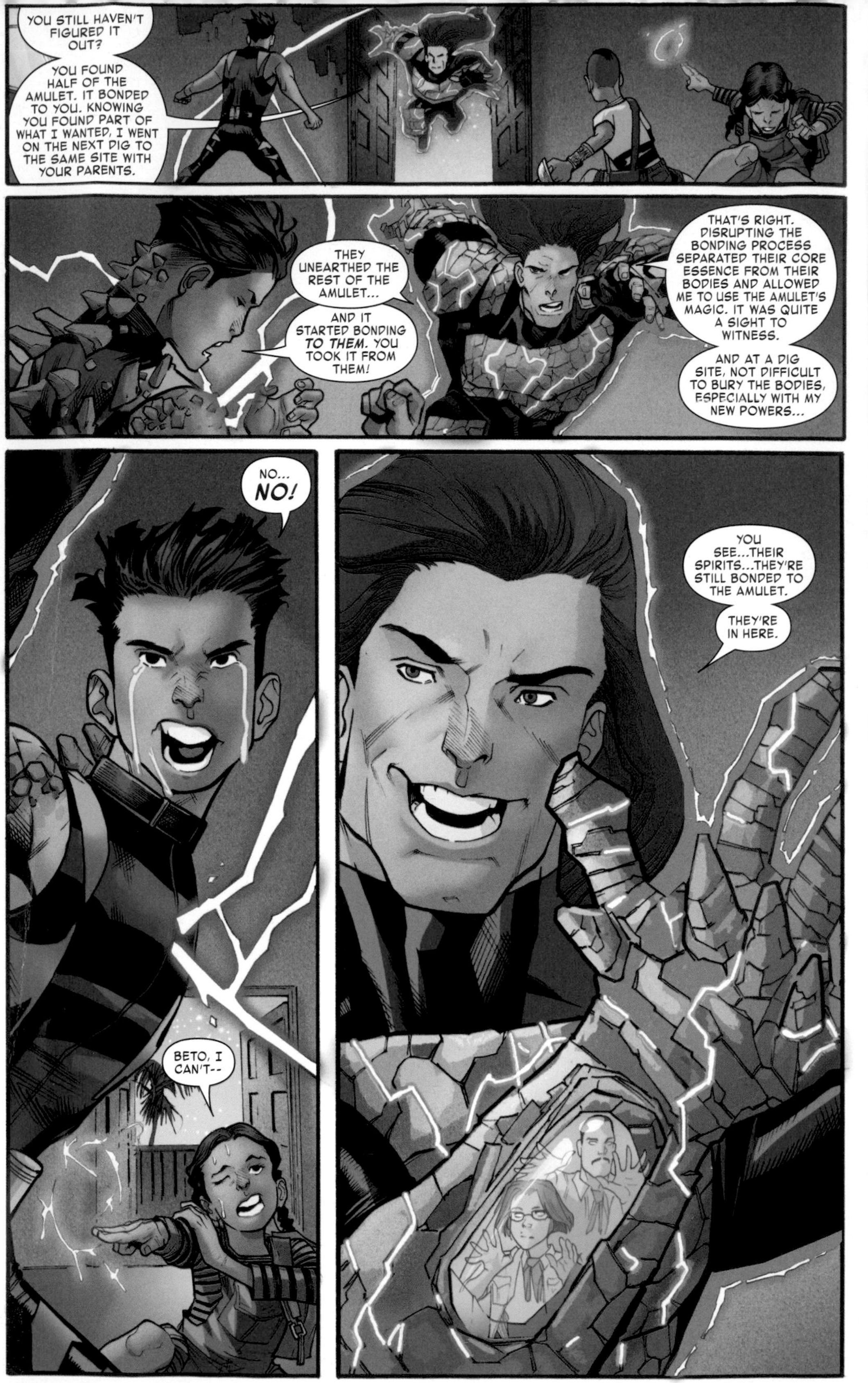
YOU STILL HAVEN'T FIGURED IT OUT?
YOU FOUND HALF OF THE AMULET. IT BONDED TO YOU. KNOWING YOU FOUND PART OF WHAT I WANTED, I WENT ON THE NEXT DIG TO THE SAME SITE WITH YOUR PARENTS.
THEY UNEARTHED THE REST OF THE AMULET...
AND IT STARTED BONDING TO THEM. YOU TOOK IT FROM THEM!
THAT'S RIGHT. DISRUPTING THE BONDING PROCESS SEPARATED THEIR CORE ESSENCE FROM THEIR BODIES AND ALLOWED ME TO USE THE AMULET'S MAGIC. IT WAS QUITE A SIGHT TO WITNESS.
AND AT A DIG SITE, NOT DIFFICULT TO BURY THE BODIES, ESPECIALLY WITH MY NEW POWERS...
NO... NO!
BETO, I CAN'T--
YOU SEE...THEIR SPIRITS...THEY'RE STILL BONDED TO THE AMULET.
THEY'RE IN HERE.

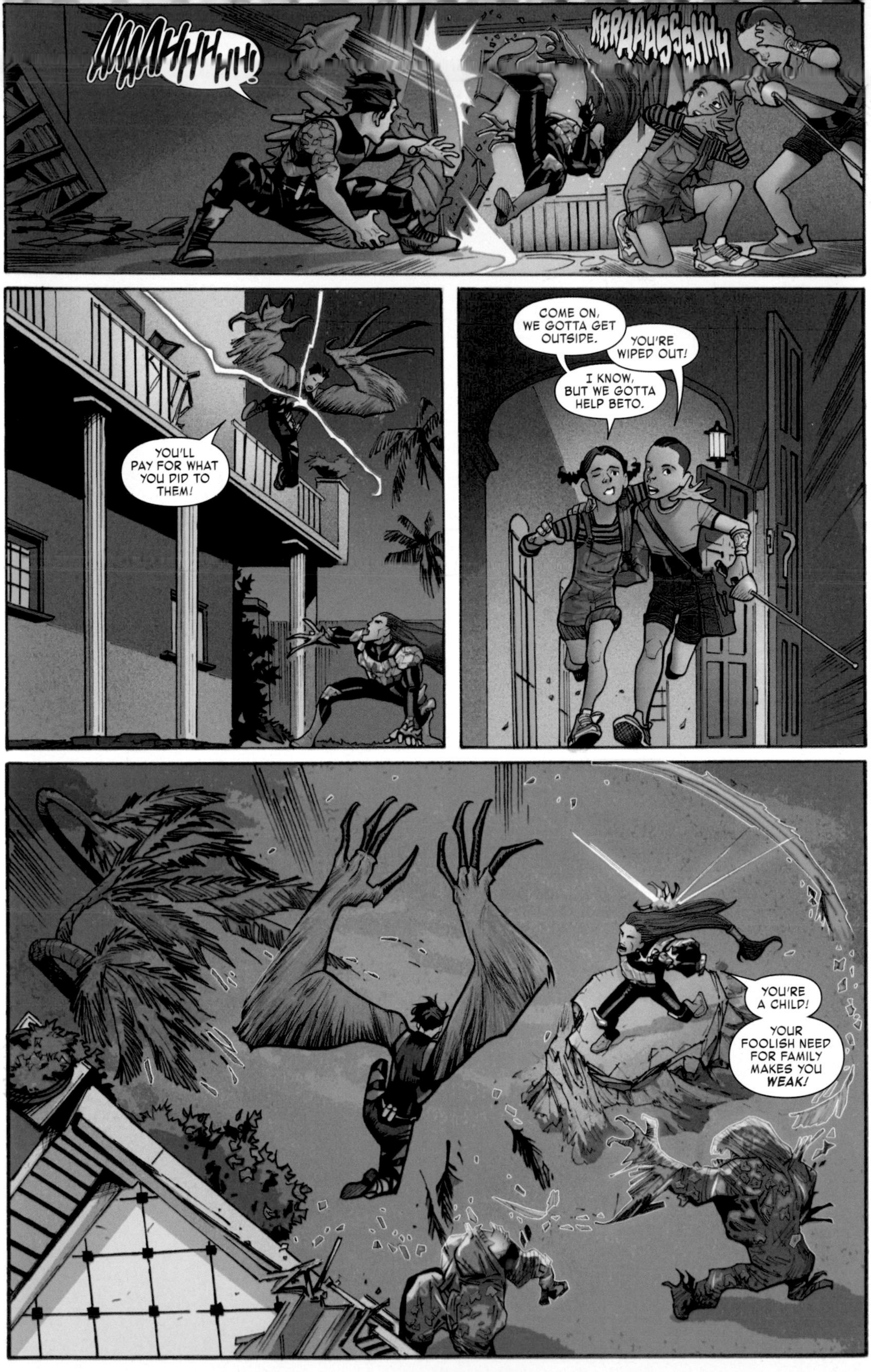

AAAAHHHHH!
KRRAAASSHHH
YOU'LL PAY FOR WHAT YOU DID TO THEM!
COME ON, WE GOTTA GET OUTSIDE.
YOU'RE WIPED OUT!
I KNOW, BUT WE GOTTA HELP BETO.
YOU'RE A CHILD!
YOUR FOOLISH NEED FOR FAMILY MAKES YOU *WEAK!*

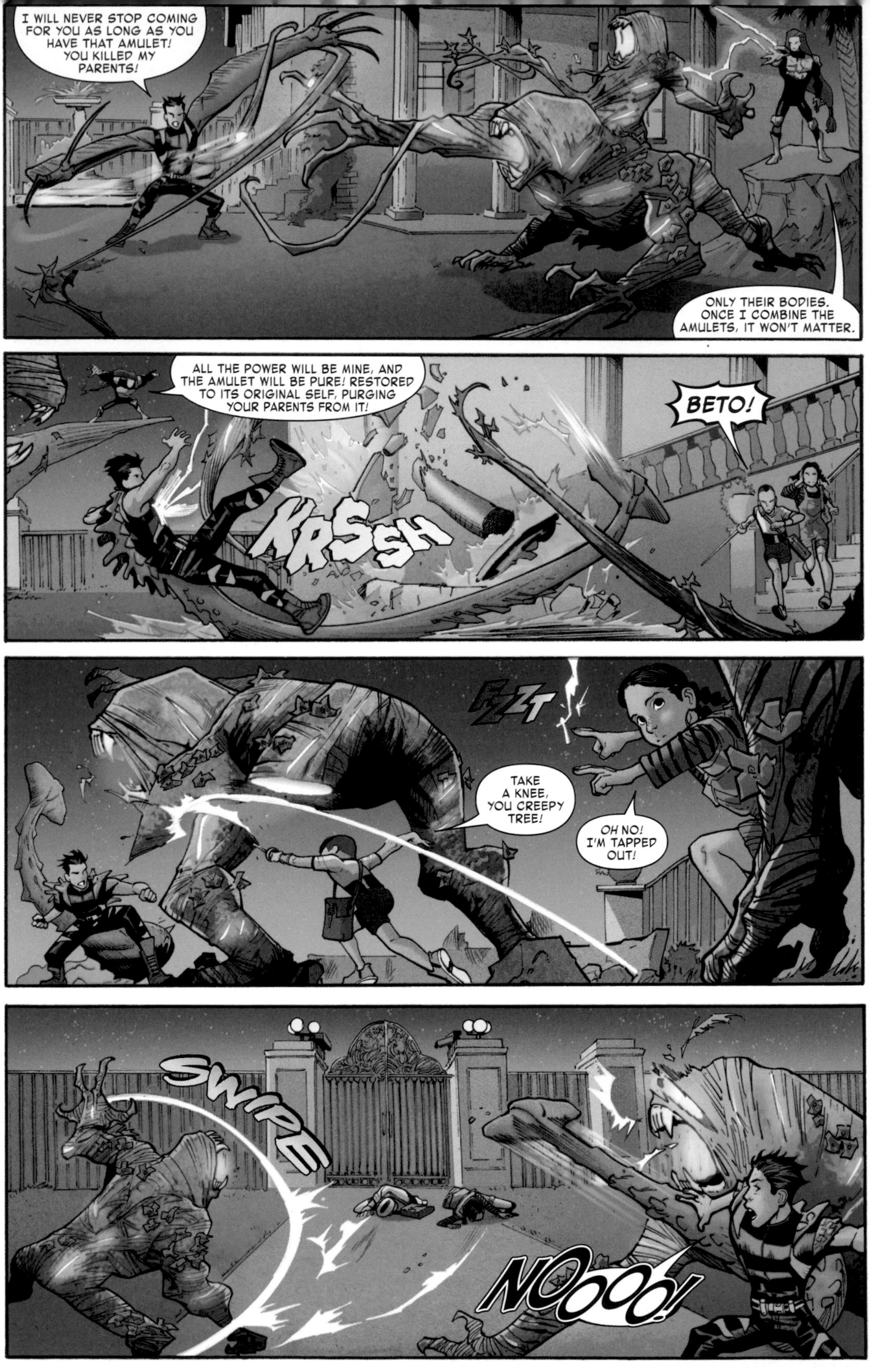

I WILL NEVER STOP COMING FOR YOU AS LONG AS YOU HAVE THAT AMULET! YOU KILLED MY PARENTS!
ONLY THEIR BODIES. ONCE I COMBINE THE AMULETS, IT WON'T MATTER.
ALL THE POWER WILL BE MINE, AND THE AMULET WILL BE PURE! RESTORED TO ITS ORIGINAL SELF, PURGING YOUR PARENTS FROM IT!
KRSSH
BETO!
FZZT
TAKE A KNEE, YOU CREEPY TREE!
OH NO! I'M TAPPED OUT!
SWIPE
NOOOO!

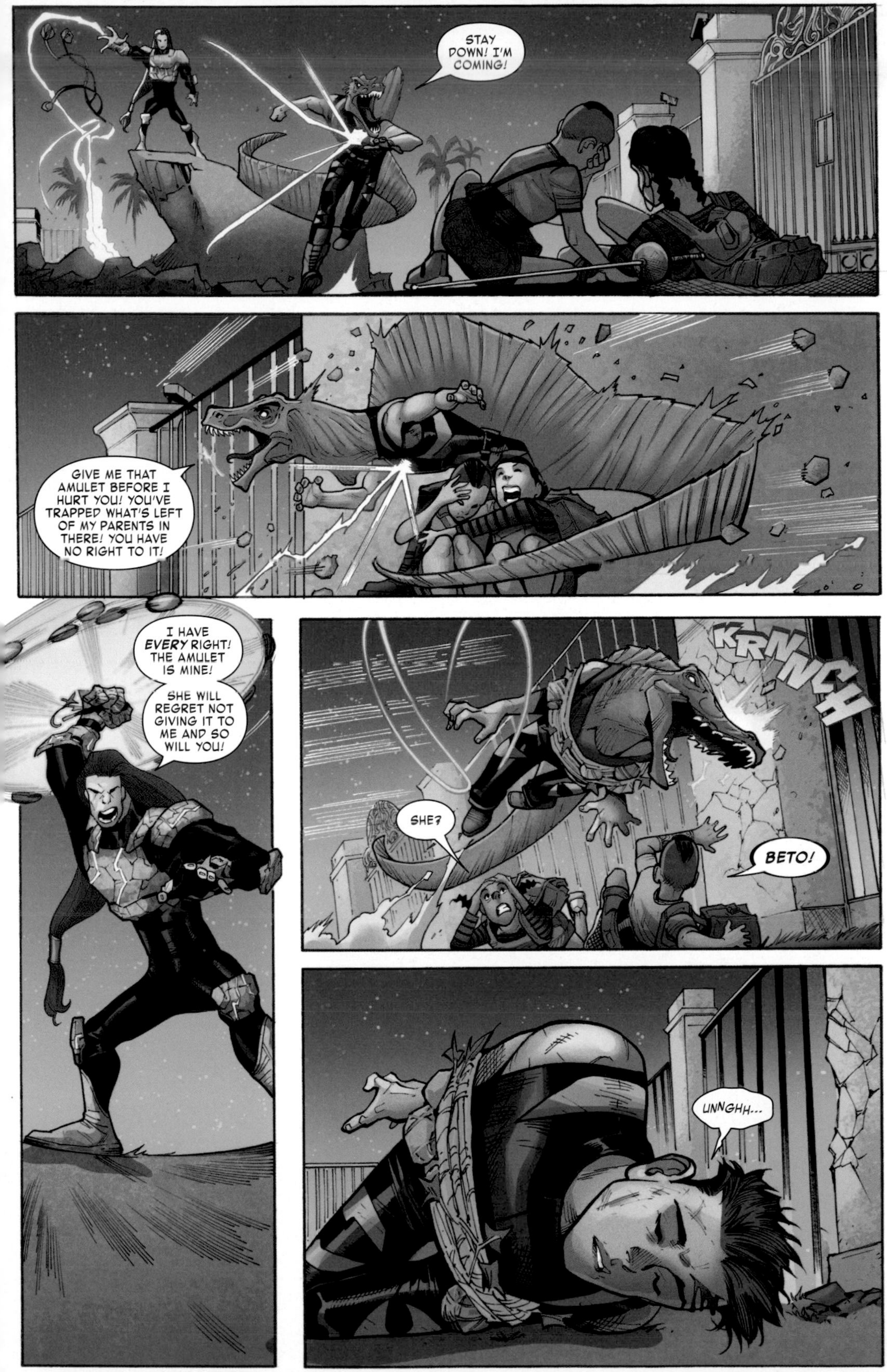
STAY DOWN! I'M COMING!
GIVE ME THAT AMULET BEFORE I HURT YOU! YOU'VE TRAPPED WHAT'S LEFT OF MY PARENTS IN THERE! YOU HAVE NO RIGHT TO IT!
I HAVE *EVERY* RIGHT! THE AMULET IS MINE!
SHE WILL REGRET NOT GIVING IT TO ME AND SO WILL YOU!
KRNNCH
SHE?
BETO!
UNNGHH...

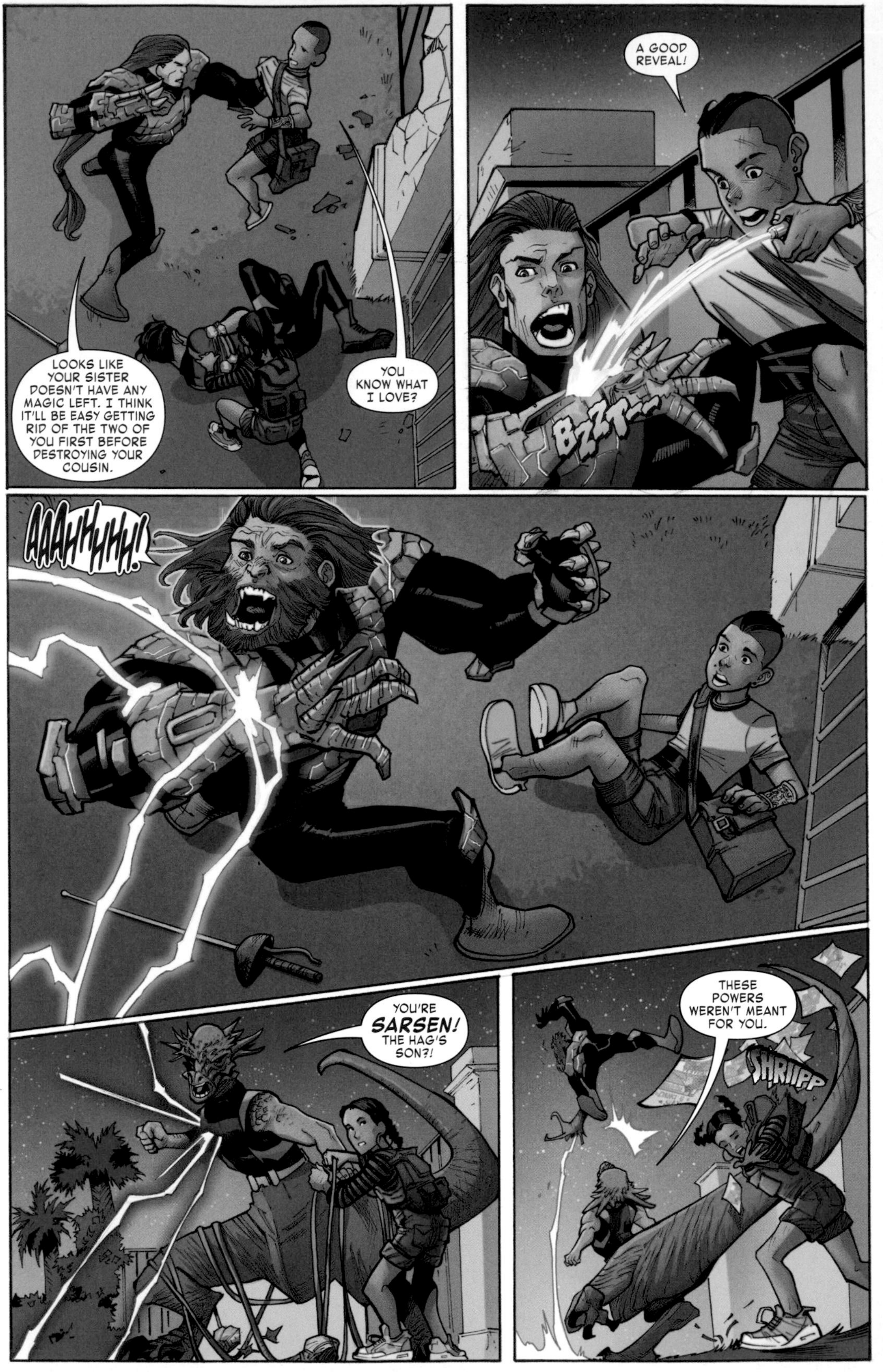

LOOKS LIKE YOUR SISTER DOESN'T HAVE ANY MAGIC LEFT. I THINK IT'LL BE EASY GETTING RID OF THE TWO OF YOU FIRST BEFORE DESTROYING YOUR COUSIN.
YOU KNOW WHAT I LOVE?
A GOOD REVEAL!
BZZT--
AAAHHHHH!
YOU'RE SARSEN! THE HAG'S SON?!
THESE POWERS WEREN'T MEANT FOR YOU.
SHRIIPP

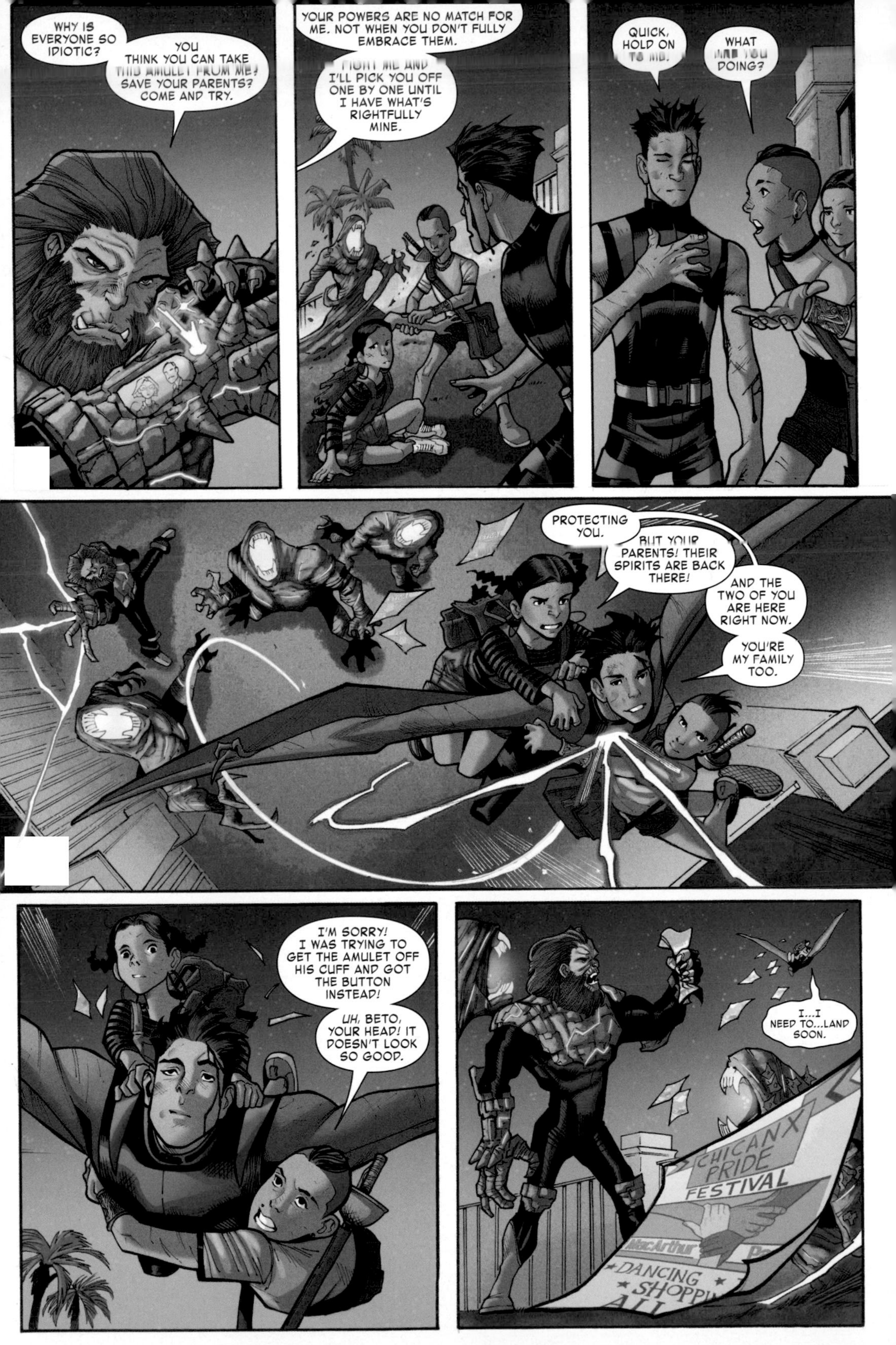
WHY IS EVERYONE SO IDIOTIC?
YOU THINK YOU CAN TAKE THIS AMULET FROM ME? SAVE YOUR PARENTS? COME AND TRY.
YOUR POWERS ARE NO MATCH FOR ME. NOT WHEN YOU DON'T FULLY EMBRACE THEM.
FIGHT ME AND I'LL PICK YOU OFF ONE BY ONE UNTIL I HAVE WHAT'S RIGHTFULLY MINE.
QUICK, HOLD ON TO ME.
WHAT ARE YOU DOING?
PROTECTING YOU.
BUT YOUR PARENTS! THEIR SPIRITS ARE BACK THERE!
AND THE TWO OF YOU ARE HERE RIGHT NOW.
YOU'RE MY FAMILY TOO.
I'M SORRY! I WAS TRYING TO GET THE AMULET OFF HIS CUFF AND GOT THE BUTTON INSTEAD!
UH, BETO, YOUR HEAD! IT DOESN'T LOOK SO GOOD.
I...I NEED TO...LAND SOON.
CHICANX PRIDE FESTIVAL
MacArthur
DANCING
SHOPP
ALL

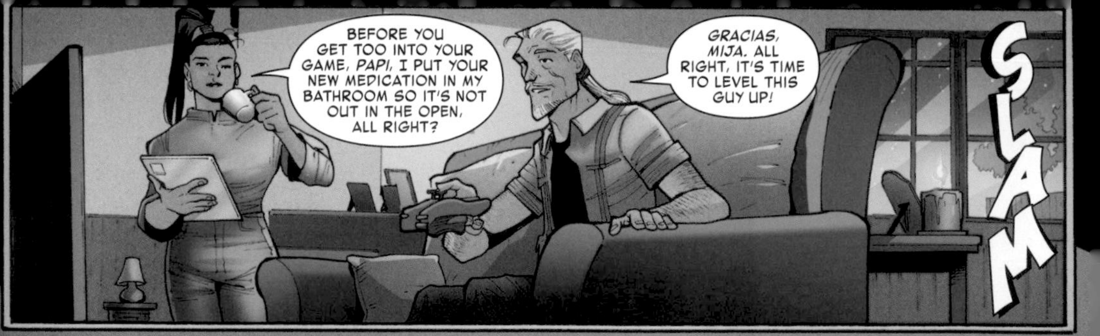
BEFORE YOU GET TOO INTO YOUR GAME, *PAPI*, I PUT YOUR NEW MEDICATION IN MY BATHROOM SO IT'S NOT OUT IN THE OPEN, ALL RIGHT?
GRACIAS, MIJA. ALL RIGHT, IT'S TIME TO LEVEL THIS GUY UP!
SLAM

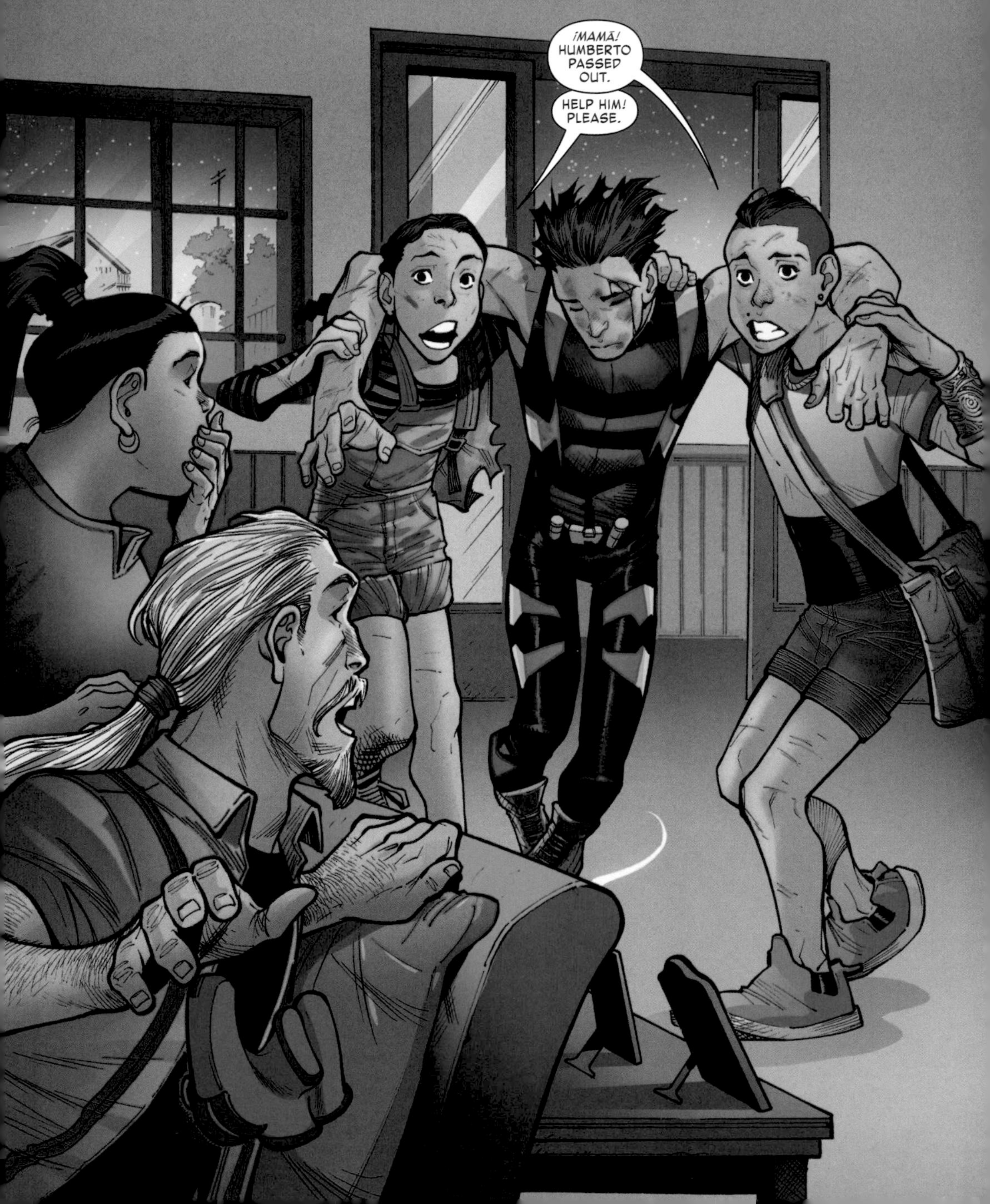
¡MAMÁ! HUMBERTO PASSED OUT.
HELP HIM! PLEASE.

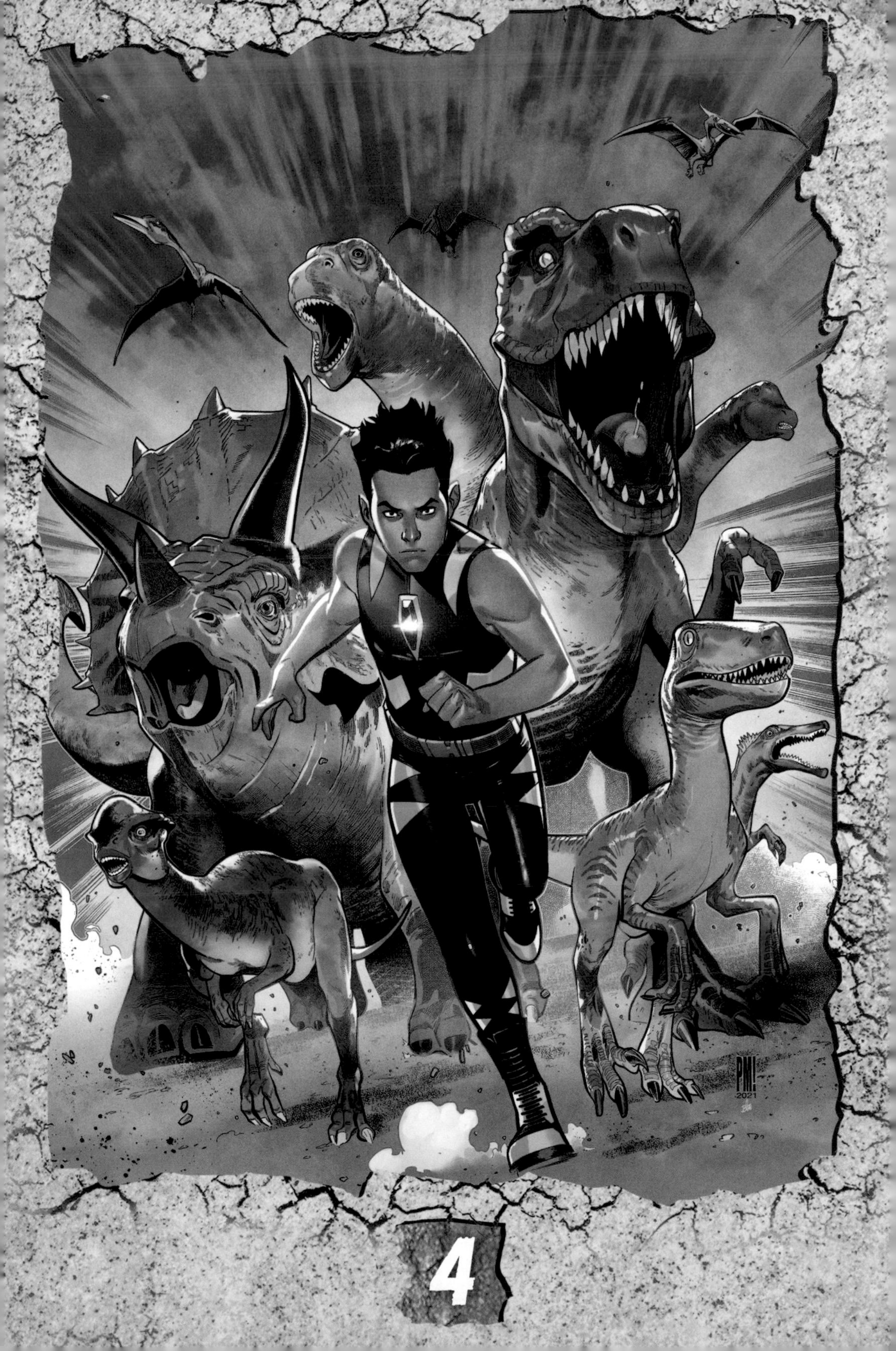

4

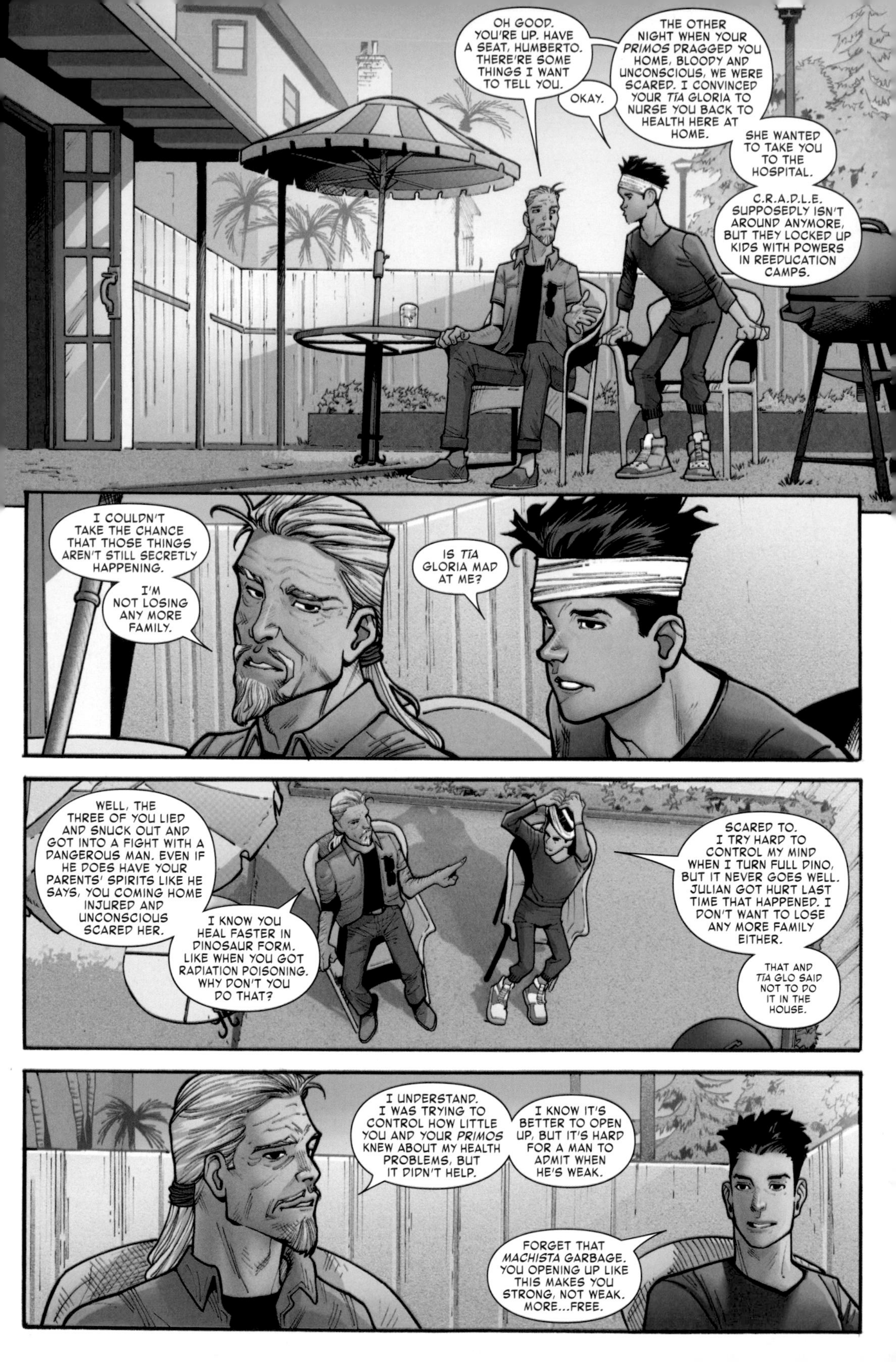
OH GOOD. YOU'RE UP. HAVE A SEAT, HUMBERTO. THERE'RE SOME THINGS I WANT TO TELL YOU.
OKAY.
THE OTHER NIGHT WHEN YOUR *PRIMOS* DRAGGED YOU HOME, BLOODY AND UNCONSCIOUS, WE WERE SCARED. I CONVINCED YOUR *TÍA* GLORIA TO NURSE YOU BACK TO HEALTH HERE AT HOME.
SHE WANTED TO TAKE YOU TO THE HOSPITAL.
C.R.A.D.L.E. SUPPOSEDLY ISN'T AROUND ANYMORE, BUT THEY LOCKED UP KIDS WITH POWERS IN REEDUCATION CAMPS.
I COULDN'T TAKE THE CHANCE THAT THOSE THINGS AREN'T STILL SECRETLY HAPPENING.
I'M NOT LOSING ANY MORE FAMILY.
IS *TÍA* GLORIA MAD AT ME?
WELL, THE THREE OF YOU LIED AND SNUCK OUT AND GOT INTO A FIGHT WITH A DANGEROUS MAN. EVEN IF HE DOES HAVE YOUR PARENTS' SPIRITS LIKE HE SAYS, YOU COMING HOME INJURED AND UNCONSCIOUS SCARED HER.
I KNOW YOU HEAL FASTER IN DINOSAUR FORM. LIKE WHEN YOU GOT RADIATION POISONING. WHY DON'T YOU DO THAT?
SCARED TO. I TRY HARD TO CONTROL MY MIND WHEN I TURN FULL DINO, BUT IT NEVER GOES WELL. JULIAN GOT HURT LAST TIME THAT HAPPENED. I DON'T WANT TO LOSE ANY MORE FAMILY EITHER.
THAT AND *TÍA GLO* SAID NOT TO DO IT IN THE HOUSE.
I UNDERSTAND. I WAS TRYING TO CONTROL HOW LITTLE YOU AND YOUR *PRIMOS* KNEW ABOUT MY HEALTH PROBLEMS, BUT IT DIDN'T HELP.
I KNOW IT'S BETTER TO OPEN UP, BUT IT'S HARD FOR A MAN TO ADMIT WHEN HE'S WEAK.
FORGET THAT *MACHISTA* GARBAGE. YOU OPENING UP LIKE THIS MAKES YOU STRONG, NOT WEAK. MORE...FREE.

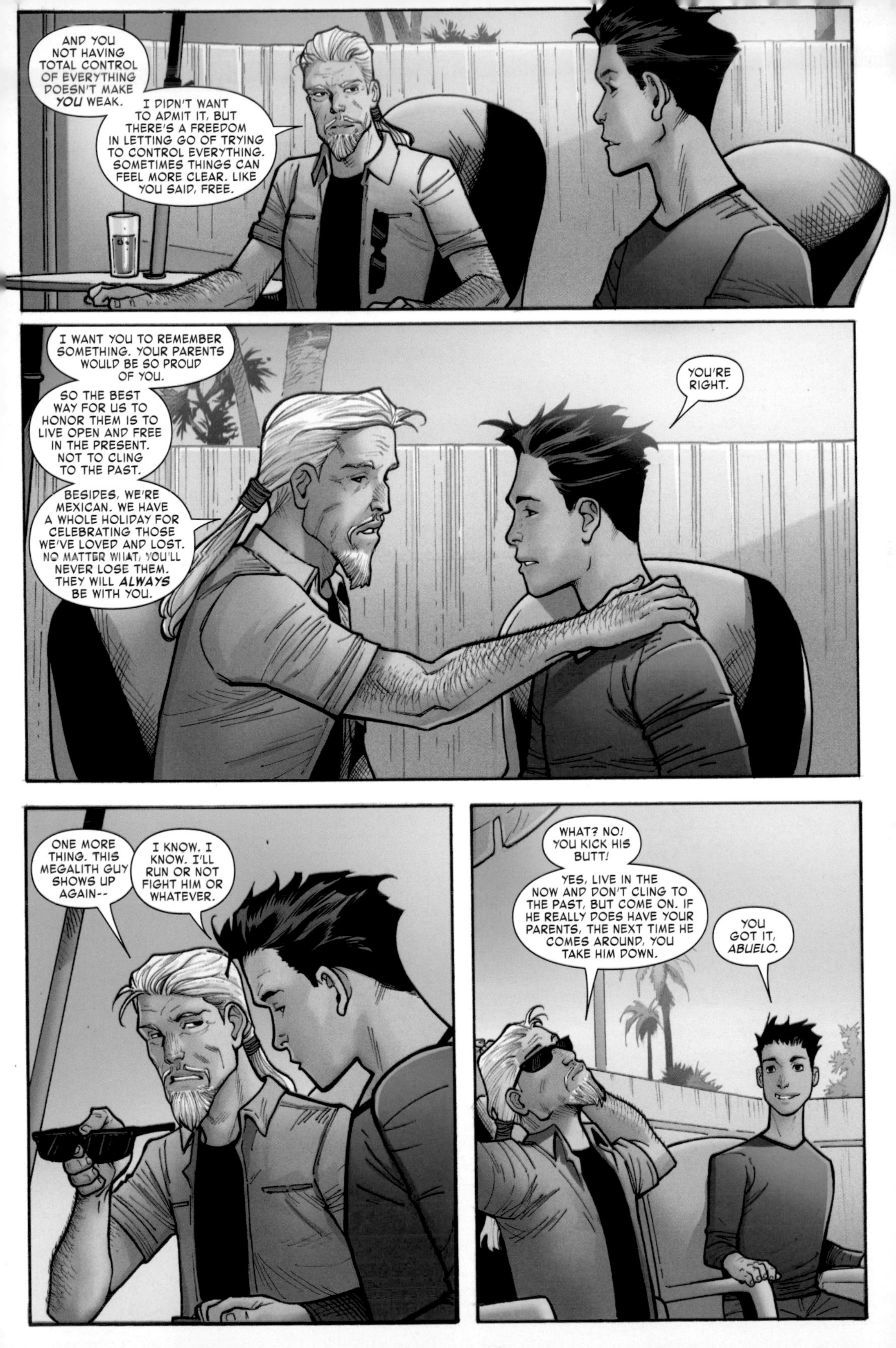
AND YOU NOT HAVING TOTAL CONTROL OF EVERYTHING DOESN'T MAKE *YOU* WEAK.
I DIDN'T WANT TO ADMIT IT, BUT THERE'S A FREEDOM IN LETTING GO OF TRYING TO CONTROL EVERYTHING. SOMETIMES THINGS CAN FEEL MORE CLEAR. LIKE YOU SAID, FREE.
I WANT YOU TO REMEMBER SOMETHING. YOUR PARENTS WOULD BE SO PROUD OF YOU.
SO THE BEST WAY FOR US TO HONOR THEM IS TO LIVE OPEN AND FREE IN THE PRESENT. NOT TO CLING TO THE PAST.
BESIDES, WE'RE MEXICAN. WE HAVE A WHOLE HOLIDAY FOR CELEBRATING THOSE WE'VE LOVED AND LOST. NO MATTER WHAT, YOU'LL NEVER LOSE THEM. THEY WILL *ALWAYS* BE WITH YOU.
YOU'RE RIGHT.
ONE MORE THING. THIS MEGALITH GUY SHOWS UP AGAIN--
I KNOW. I KNOW. I'LL RUN OR NOT FIGHT HIM OR WHATEVER.
WHAT? NO! YOU KICK HIS BUTT!
YES, LIVE IN THE NOW AND DON'T CLING TO THE PAST, BUT COME ON. IF HE REALLY DOES HAVE YOUR PARENTS, THE NEXT TIME HE COMES AROUND, YOU TAKE HIM DOWN.
YOU GOT IT, *ABUELO*.

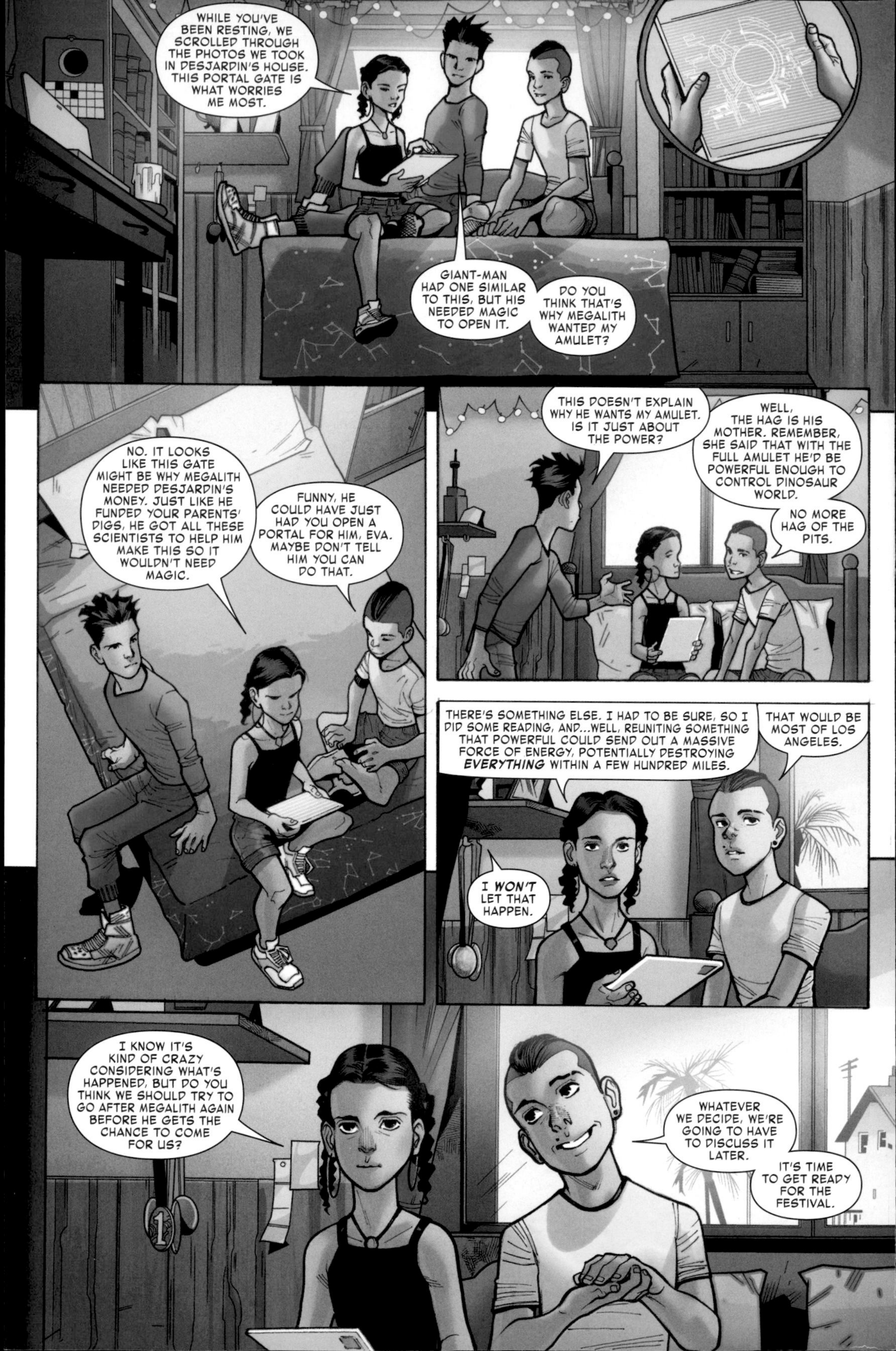

WHILE YOU'VE BEEN RESTING, WE SCROLLED THROUGH THE PHOTOS WE TOOK IN DESJARDIN'S HOUSE. THIS PORTAL GATE IS WHAT WORRIES ME MOST.
GIANT-MAN HAD ONE SIMILAR TO THIS, BUT HIS NEEDED MAGIC TO OPEN IT.
DO YOU THINK THAT'S WHY MEGALITH WANTED MY AMULET?
NO. IT LOOKS LIKE THIS GATE MIGHT BE WHY MEGALITH NEEDED DESJARDIN'S MONEY. JUST LIKE HE FUNDED YOUR PARENTS' DIGS, HE GOT ALL THESE SCIENTISTS TO HELP HIM MAKE THIS SO IT WOULDN'T NEED MAGIC.
FUNNY, HE COULD HAVE JUST HAD YOU OPEN A PORTAL FOR HIM, EVA. MAYBE DON'T TELL HIM YOU CAN DO THAT.
THIS DOESN'T EXPLAIN WHY HE WANTS MY AMULET. IS IT JUST ABOUT THE POWER?
WELL, THE HAG IS HIS MOTHER. REMEMBER, SHE SAID THAT WITH THE FULL AMULET HE'D BE POWERFUL ENOUGH TO CONTROL DINOSAUR WORLD.
NO MORE HAG OF THE PITS.
THERE'S SOMETHING ELSE. I HAD TO BE SURE, SO I DID SOME READING, AND...WELL, REUNITING SOMETHING THAT POWERFUL COULD SEND OUT A MASSIVE FORCE OF ENERGY, POTENTIALLY DESTROYING *EVERYTHING* WITHIN A FEW HUNDRED MILES.
THAT WOULD BE MOST OF LOS ANGELES.
I *WON'T* LET THAT HAPPEN.
I KNOW IT'S KIND OF CRAZY CONSIDERING WHAT'S HAPPENED, BUT DO YOU THINK WE SHOULD TRY TO GO AFTER MEGALITH AGAIN BEFORE HE GETS THE CHANCE TO COME FOR US?
WHATEVER WE DECIDE, WE'RE GOING TO HAVE TO DISCUSS IT LATER.
IT'S TIME TO GET READY FOR THE FESTIVAL.

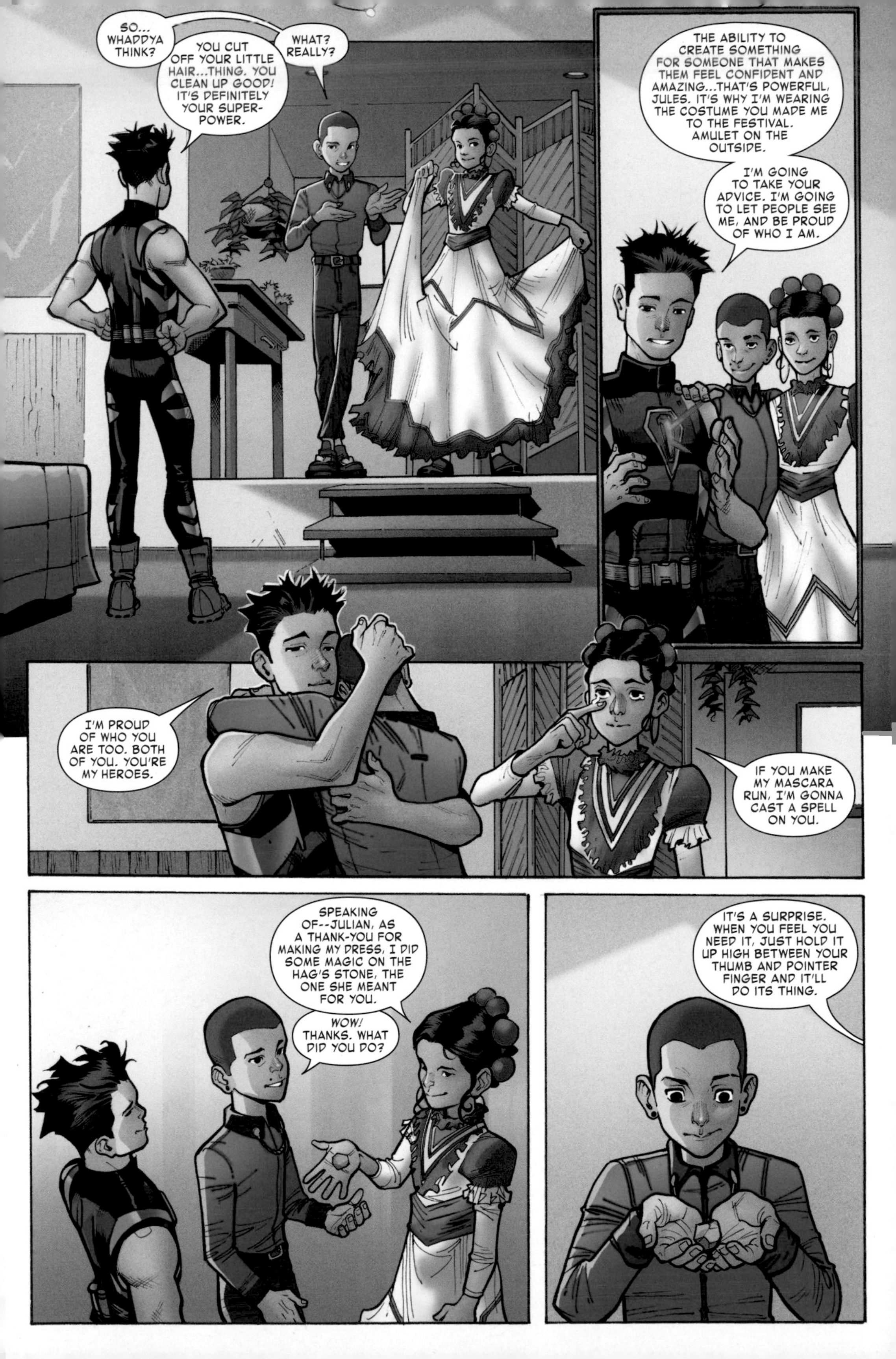
SO... WHADDYA THINK?
YOU CUT OFF YOUR LITTLE HAIR...THING. YOU CLEAN UP GOOD! IT'S DEFINITELY YOUR SUPER-POWER.
WHAT? REALLY?
THE ABILITY TO CREATE SOMETHING FOR SOMEONE THAT MAKES THEM FEEL CONFIDENT AND AMAZING...THAT'S POWERFUL, JULES. IT'S WHY I'M WEARING THE COSTUME YOU MADE ME TO THE FESTIVAL. AMULET ON THE OUTSIDE.
I'M GOING TO TAKE YOUR ADVICE. I'M GOING TO LET PEOPLE SEE ME, AND BE PROUD OF WHO I AM.
I'M PROUD OF WHO YOU ARE TOO. BOTH OF YOU. YOU'RE MY HEROES.
IF YOU MAKE MY MASCARA RUN, I'M GONNA CAST A SPELL ON YOU.
SPEAKING OF--JULIAN, AS A THANK-YOU FOR MAKING MY DRESS, I DID SOME MAGIC ON THE HAG'S STONE, THE ONE SHE MEANT FOR YOU.
WOW! THANKS. WHAT DID YOU DO?
IT'S A SURPRISE. WHEN YOU FEEL YOU NEED IT, JUST HOLD IT UP HIGH BETWEEN YOUR THUMB AND POINTER FINGER AND IT'LL DO ITS THING.

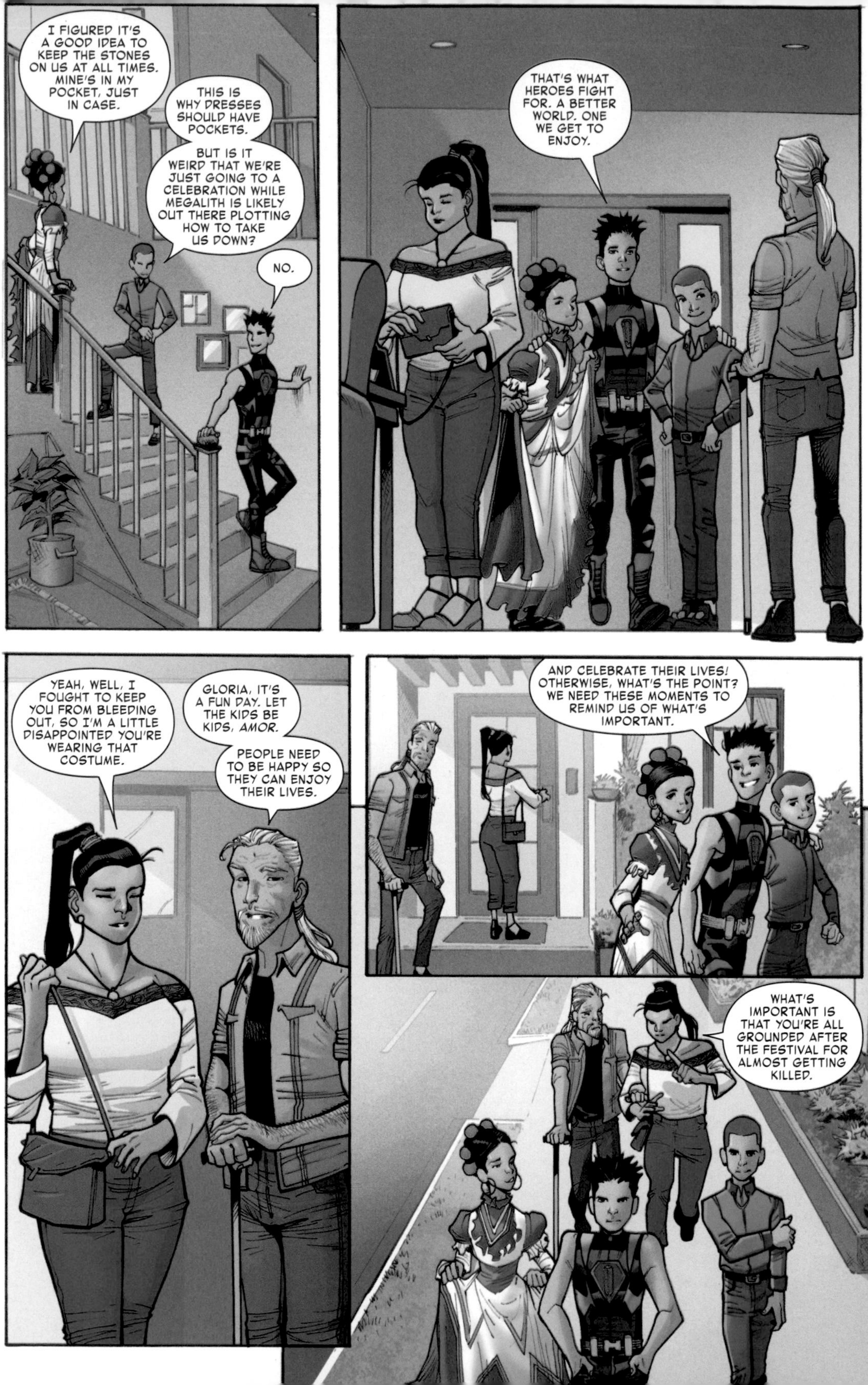
I FIGURED IT'S A GOOD IDEA TO KEEP THE STONES ON US AT ALL TIMES. MINE'S IN MY POCKET, JUST IN CASE.
THIS IS WHY DRESSES SHOULD HAVE POCKETS.
BUT IS IT WEIRD THAT WE'RE JUST GOING TO A CELEBRATION WHILE MEGALITH IS LIKELY OUT THERE PLOTTING HOW TO TAKE US DOWN?
NO.
THAT'S WHAT HEROES FIGHT FOR. A BETTER WORLD. ONE WE GET TO ENJOY.
YEAH, WELL, I FOUGHT TO KEEP YOU FROM BLEEDING OUT, SO I'M A LITTLE DISAPPOINTED YOU'RE WEARING THAT COSTUME.
GLORIA, IT'S A FUN DAY. LET THE KIDS BE KIDS, *AMOR*.
PEOPLE NEED TO BE HAPPY SO THEY CAN ENJOY THEIR LIVES.
AND CELEBRATE THEIR LIVES! OTHERWISE, WHAT'S THE POINT? WE NEED THESE MOMENTS TO REMIND US OF WHAT'S IMPORTANT.
WHAT'S IMPORTANT IS THAT YOU'RE ALL GROUNDED AFTER THE FESTIVAL FOR ALMOST GETTING KILLED.

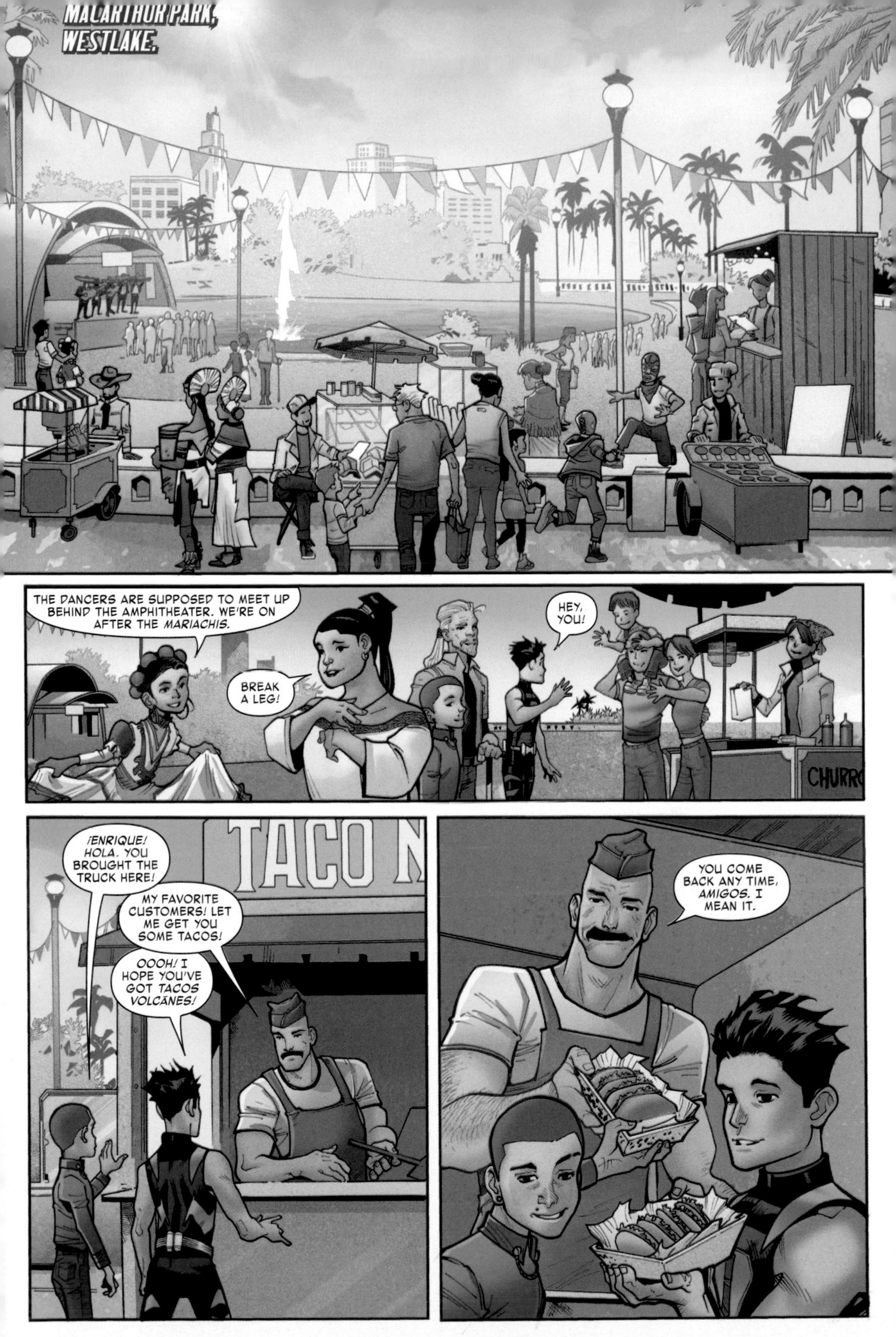
MACARTHUR PARK, WESTLAKE.
THE DANCERS ARE SUPPOSED TO MEET UP BEHIND THE AMPHITHEATER. WE'RE ON AFTER THE MARIACHIS.
BREAK A LEG!
HEY, YOU!
CHURRO
TACO N
¡ENRIQUE! HOLA. YOU BROUGHT THE TRUCK HERE!
MY FAVORITE CUSTOMERS! LET ME GET YOU SOME TACOS!
OOOH! I HOPE YOU'VE GOT TACOS VOLCÁNES!
YOU COME BACK ANY TIME, AMIGOS. I MEAN IT.

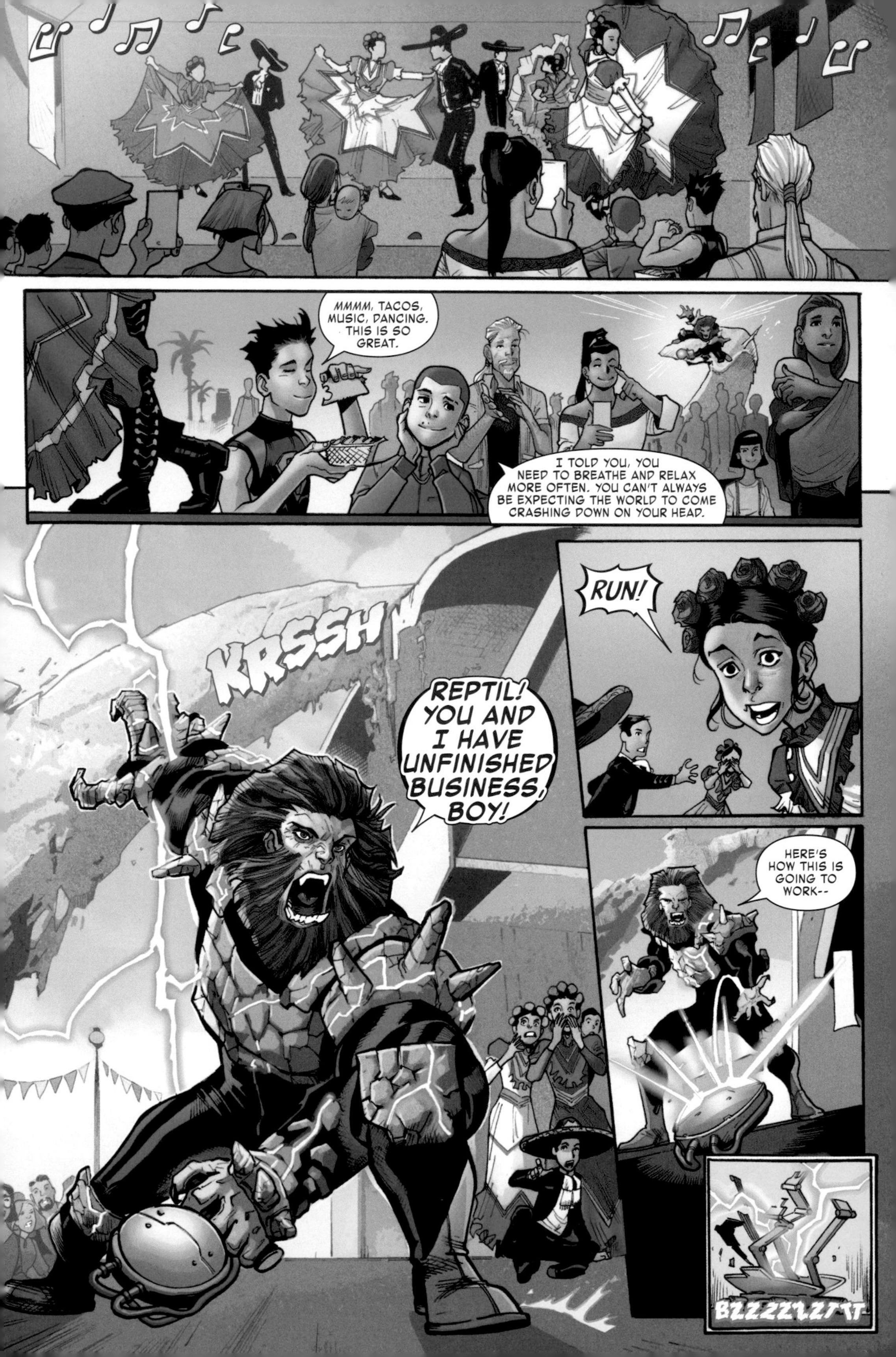

MMMM, TACOS, MUSIC, DANCING. THIS IS SO GREAT.
I TOLD YOU, YOU NEED TO BREATHE AND RELAX MORE OFTEN. YOU CAN'T ALWAYS BE EXPECTING THE WORLD TO COME CRASHING DOWN ON YOUR HEAD.
KRSSH
REPTIL! YOU AND I HAVE UNFINISHED BUSINESS, BOY!
RUN!
HERE'S HOW THIS IS GOING TO WORK--
BZZZZZZTTT

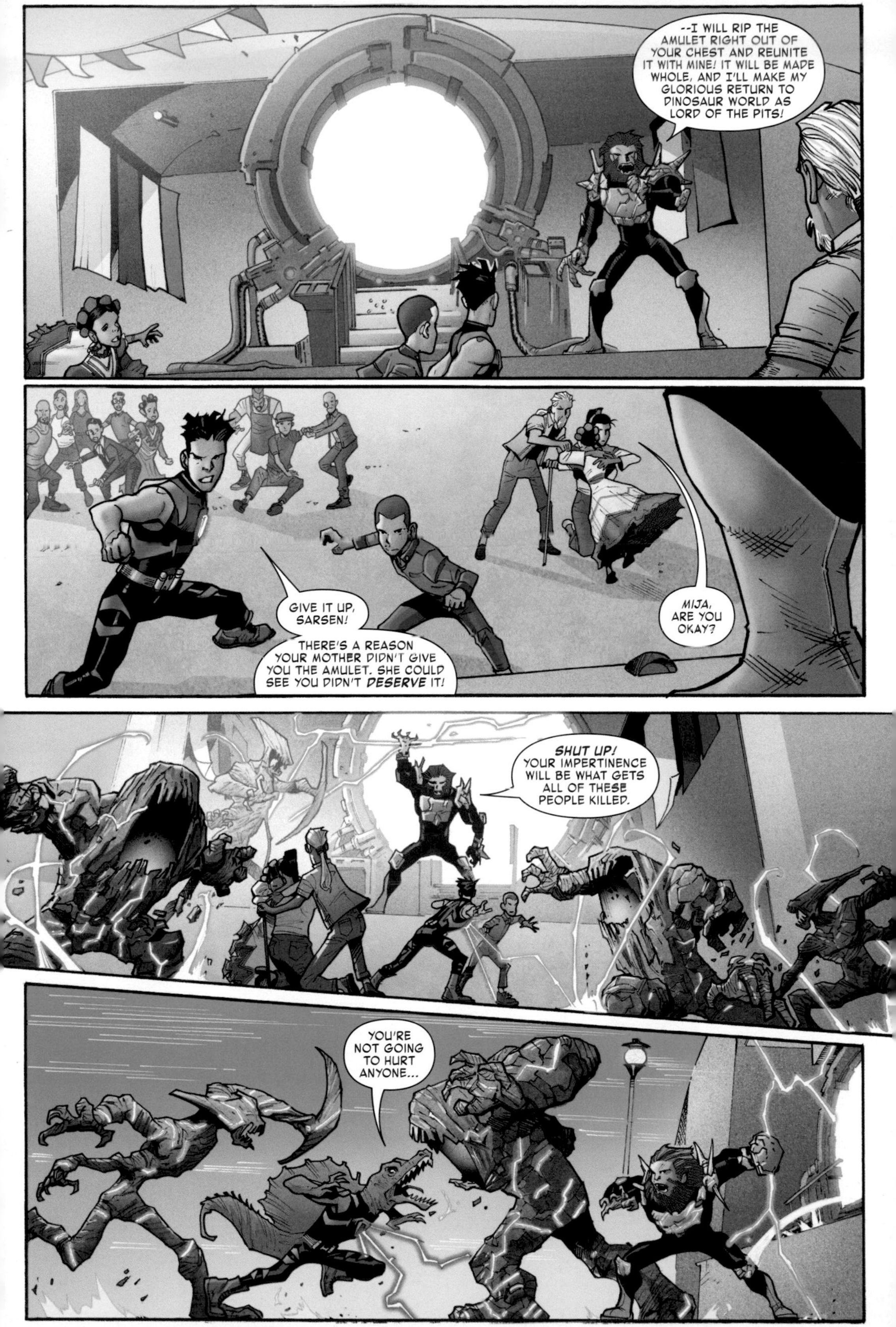
--I WILL RIP THE AMULET RIGHT OUT OF YOUR CHEST AND REUNITE IT WITH MINE! IT WILL BE MADE WHOLE, AND I'LL MAKE MY GLORIOUS RETURN TO DINOSAUR WORLD AS LORD OF THE PITS!
GIVE IT UP, SARSEN!
THERE'S A REASON YOUR MOTHER DIDN'T GIVE YOU THE AMULET. SHE COULD SEE YOU DIDN'T DESERVE IT!
MIJA, ARE YOU OKAY?
SHUT UP! YOUR IMPERTINENCE WILL BE WHAT GETS ALL OF THESE PEOPLE KILLED.
YOU'RE NOT GOING TO HURT ANYONE...

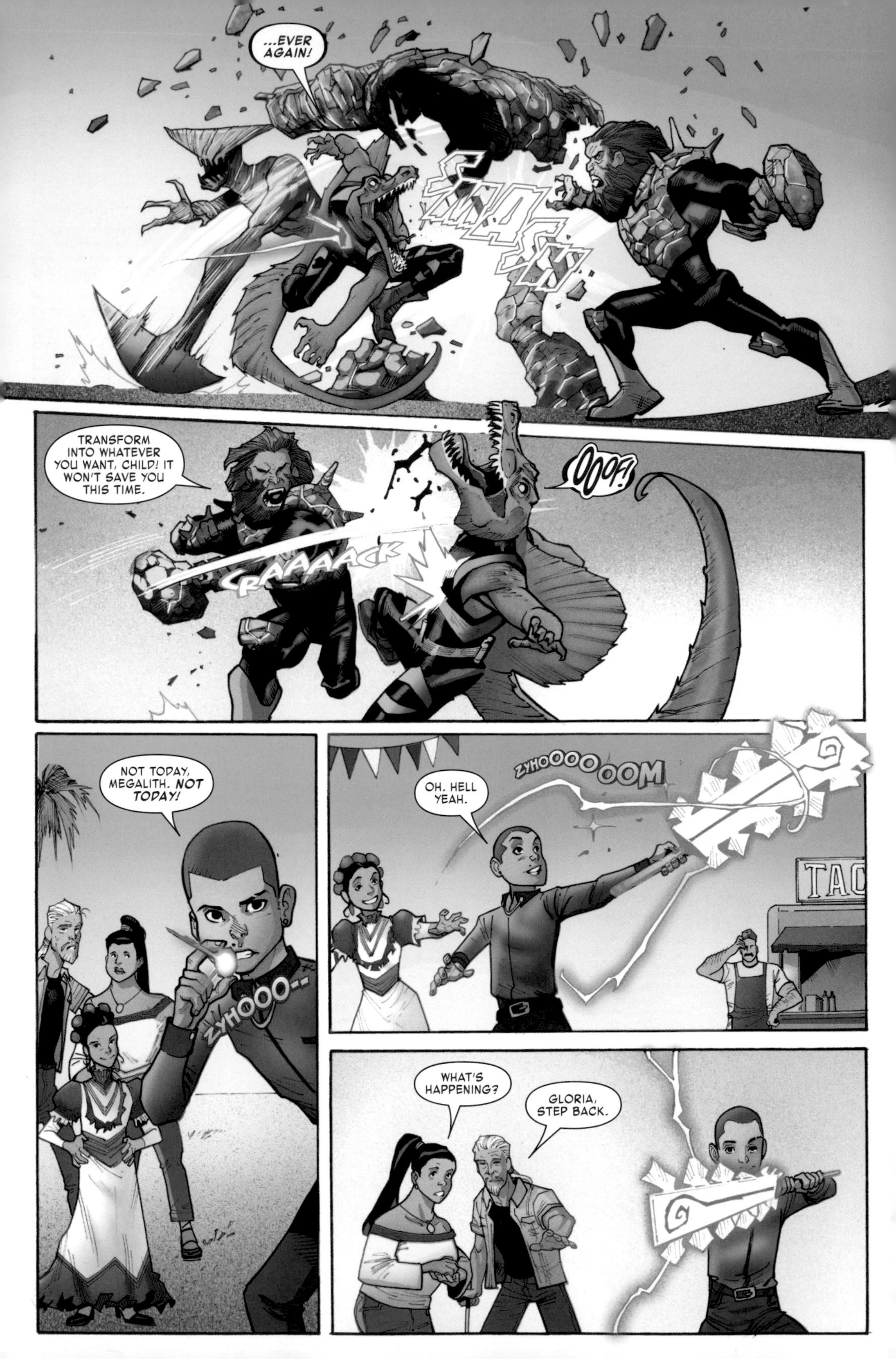
...EVER AGAIN!
TRANSFORM INTO WHATEVER YOU WANT, CHILD! IT WON'T SAVE YOU THIS TIME.
OOOF!
CRAAAACK
NOT TODAY, MEGALITH. NOT TODAY!
ZYHOOO--
ZYHOOOOOOM
OH. HELL YEAH.
TAC
WHAT'S HAPPENING?
GLORIA, STEP BACK.

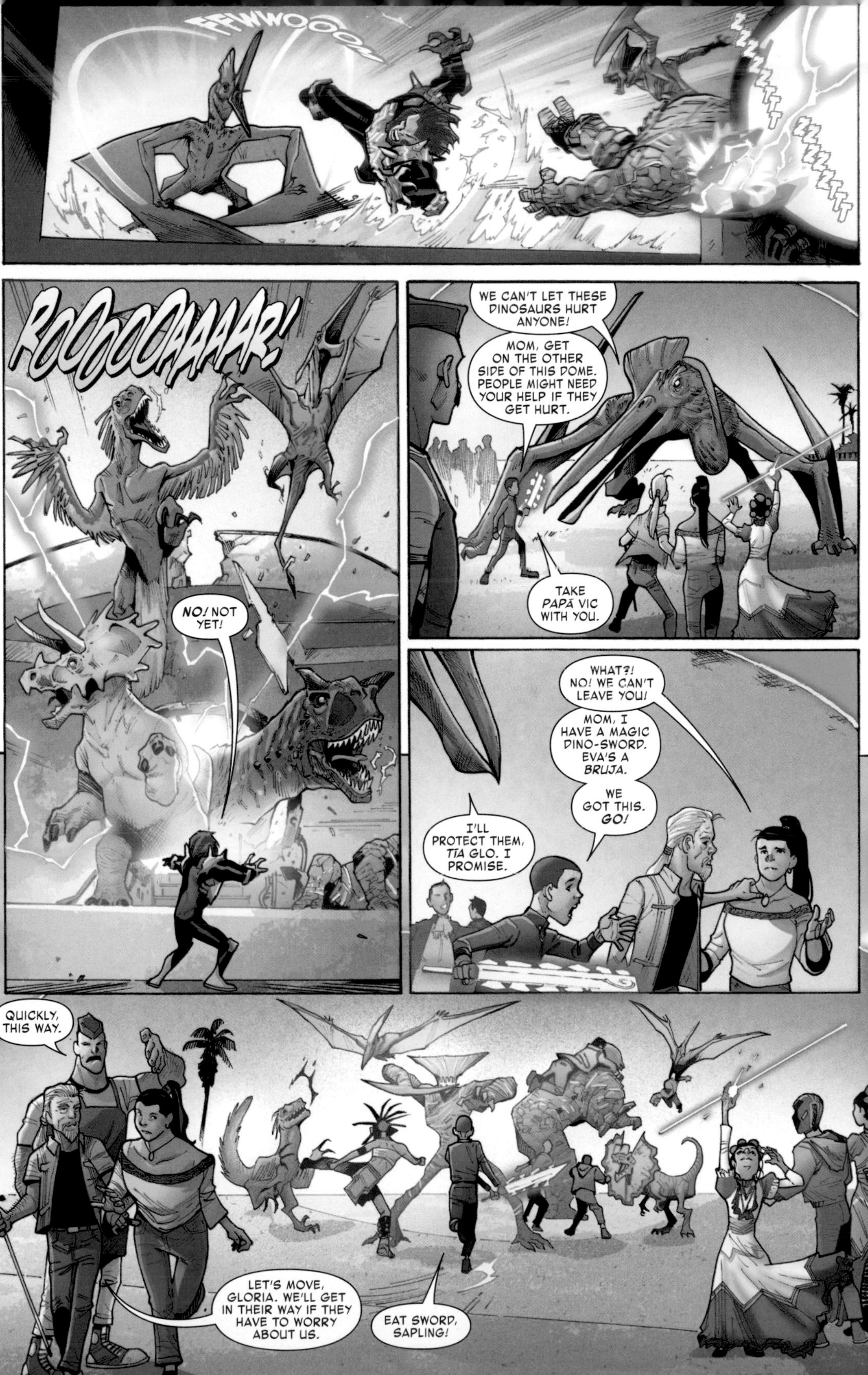
FFWWOOOM
ZZZZZTTT
ZZZZZZTTT
ROOOOOAAAAR!
NO! NOT YET!
WE CAN'T LET THESE DINOSAURS HURT ANYONE!
MOM, GET ON THE OTHER SIDE OF THIS DOME. PEOPLE MIGHT NEED YOUR HELP IF THEY GET HURT.
TAKE PAPÁ VIC WITH YOU.
WHAT?! NO! WE CAN'T LEAVE YOU!
MOM, I HAVE A MAGIC DINO-SWORD. EVA'S A BRUJA.
WE GOT THIS. GO!
I'LL PROTECT THEM, TÍA GLO. I PROMISE.
QUICKLY, THIS WAY.
LET'S MOVE, GLORIA. WE'LL GET IN THEIR WAY IF THEY HAVE TO WORRY ABOUT US.
EAT SWORD, SAPLING!

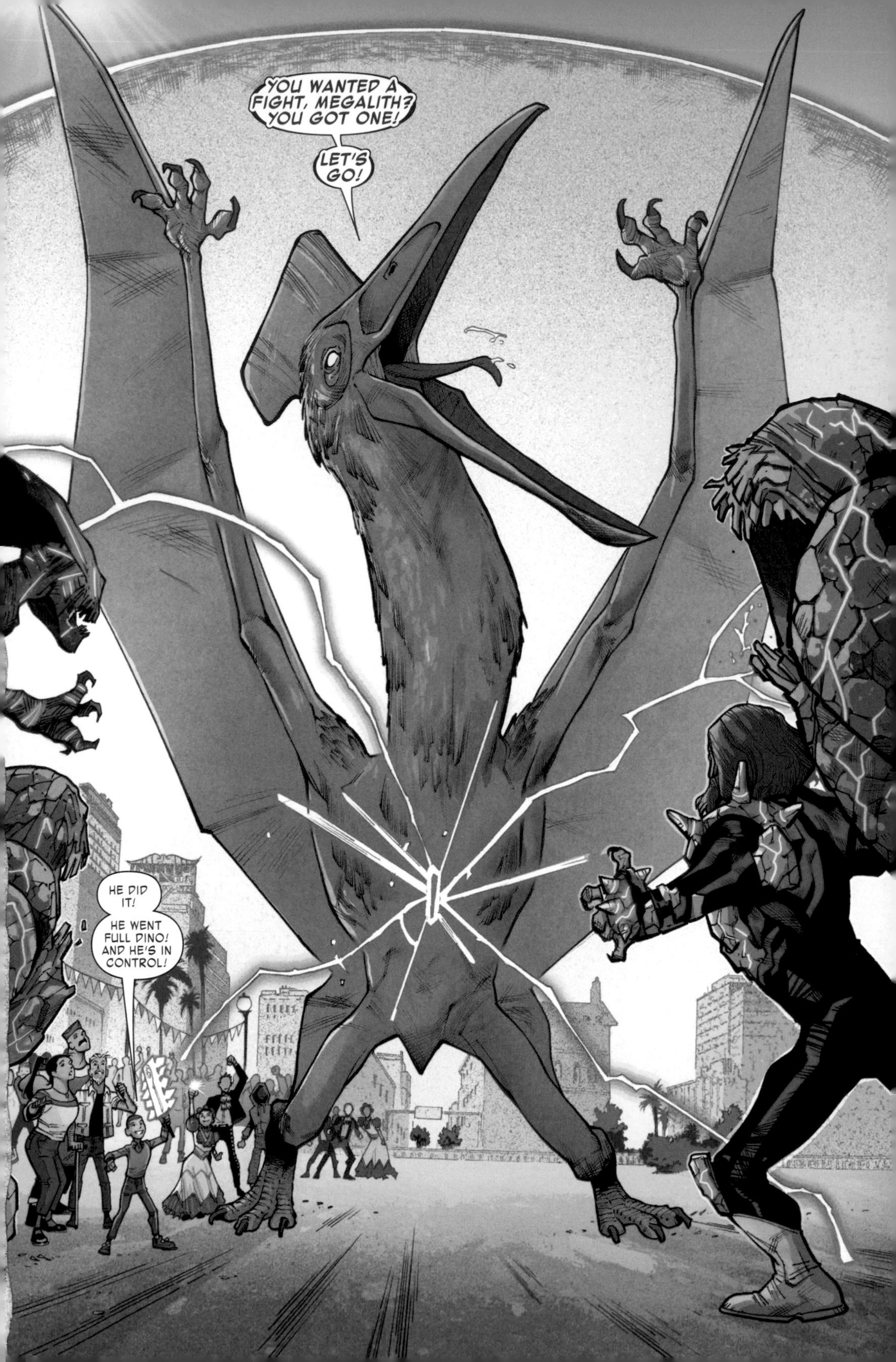
YOU WANTED A FIGHT, MEGALITH? YOU GOT ONE!
LET'S GO!
HE DID IT!
HE WENT FULL DINO! AND HE'S IN CONTROL!

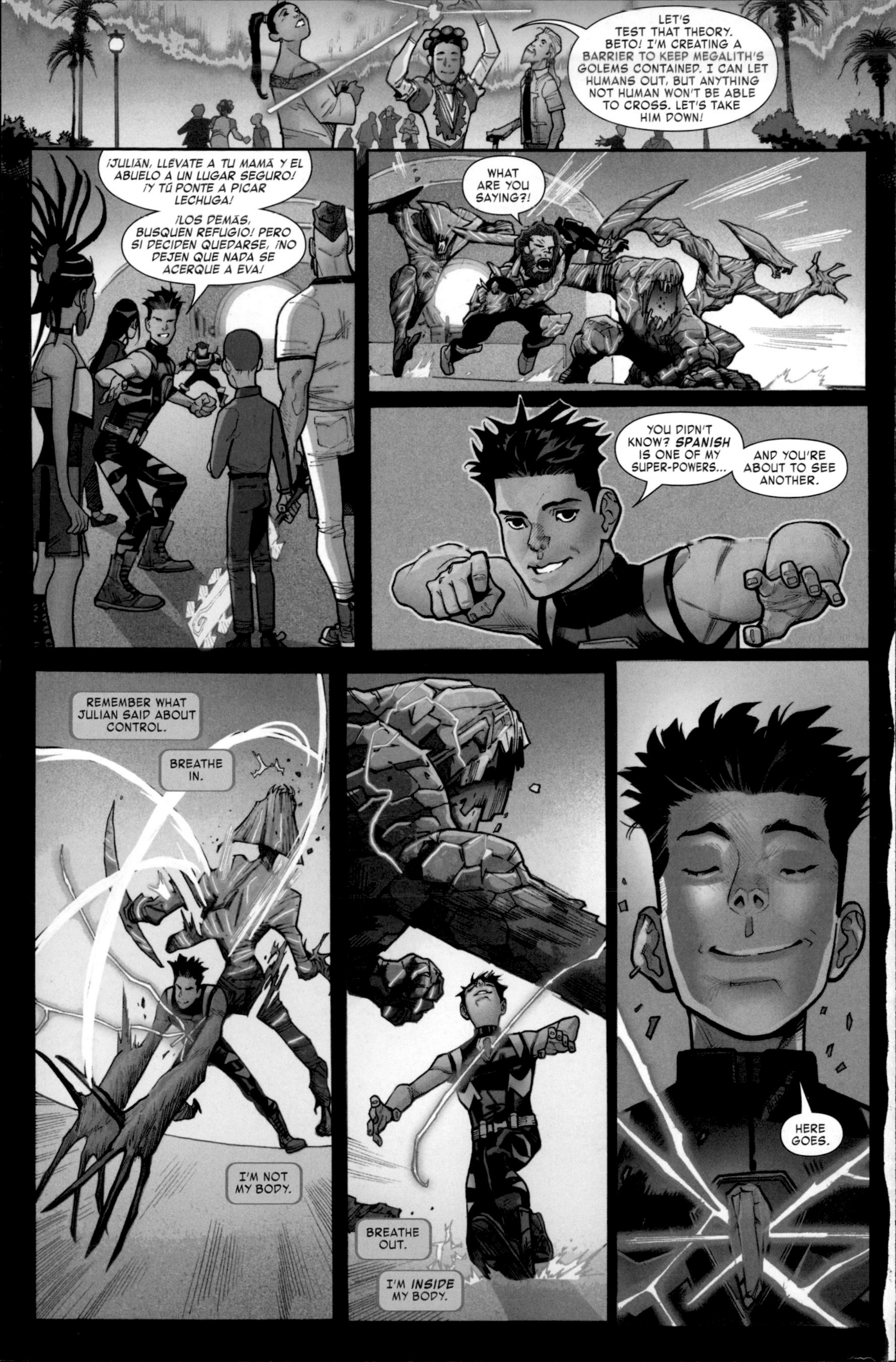
LET'S TEST THAT THEORY. BETO! I'M CREATING A BARRIER TO KEEP MEGALITH'S GOLEMS CONTAINED. I CAN LET HUMANS OUT, BUT ANYTHING NOT HUMAN WON'T BE ABLE TO CROSS. LET'S TAKE HIM DOWN!
¡JULIÁN, LLÉVATE A TU MAMÁ Y EL ABUELO A UN LUGAR SEGURO! ¡Y TÚ PONTE A PICAR LECHUGA!
¡LOS DEMÁS, BUSQUEN REFUGIO! PERO SI DECIDEN QUEDARSE, ¡NO DEJEN QUE NADA SE ACERQUE A EVA!
WHAT ARE YOU SAYING?!
YOU DIDN'T KNOW? SPANISH IS ONE OF MY SUPER-POWERS...
AND YOU'RE ABOUT TO SEE ANOTHER.
REMEMBER WHAT JULIAN SAID ABOUT CONTROL.
BREATHE IN.
I'M NOT MY BODY.
BREATHE OUT.
I'M INSIDE MY BODY.
HERE GOES.

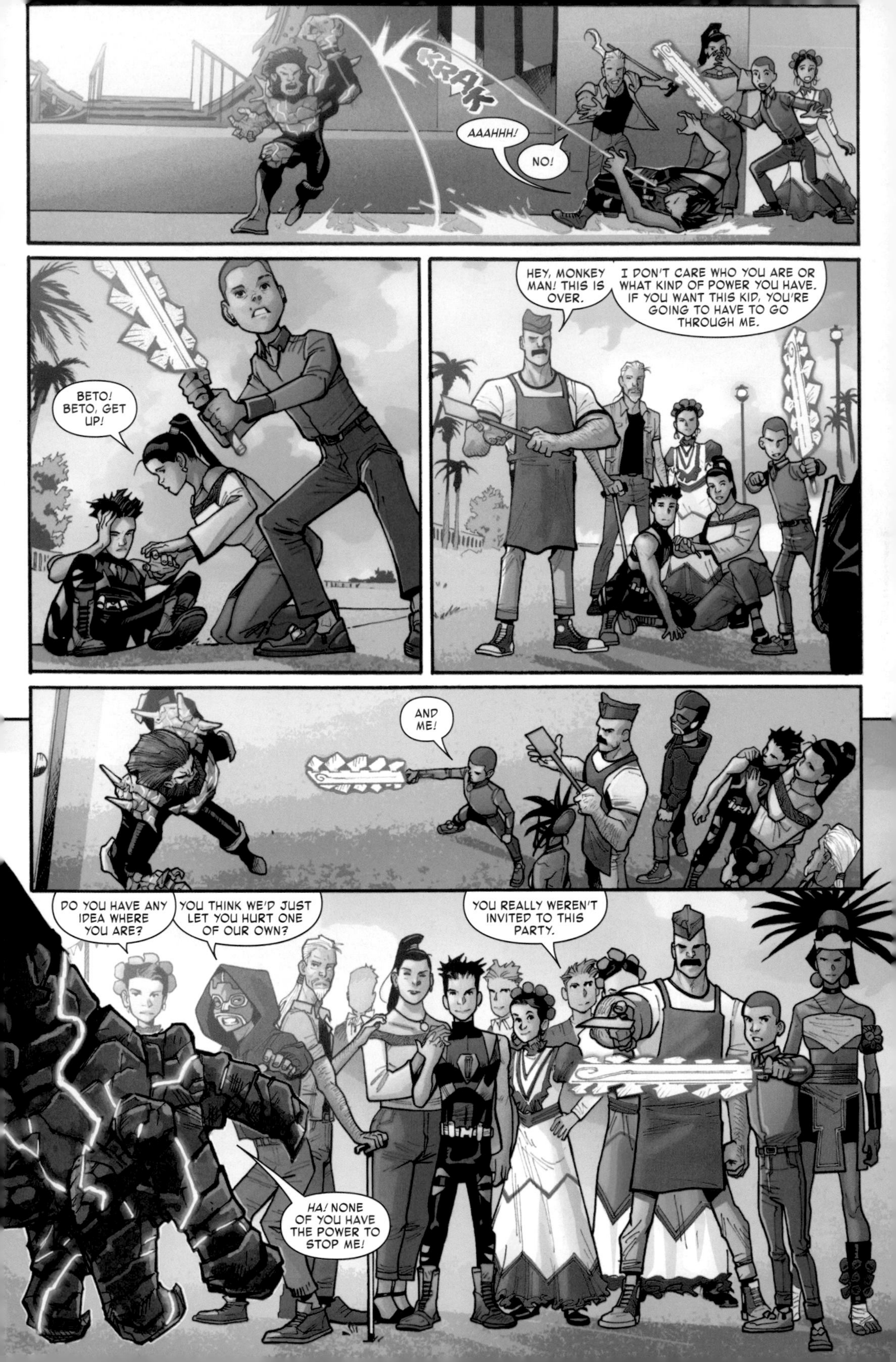
KRAK
AAAHHH!
NO!
BETO! BETO, GET UP!
HEY, MONKEY MAN! THIS IS OVER.
I DON'T CARE WHO YOU ARE OR WHAT KIND OF POWER YOU HAVE. IF YOU WANT THIS KID, YOU'RE GOING TO HAVE TO GO THROUGH ME.
AND ME!
DO YOU HAVE ANY IDEA WHERE YOU ARE?
YOU THINK WE'D JUST LET YOU HURT ONE OF OUR OWN?
YOU REALLY WEREN'T INVITED TO THIS PARTY.
HA! NONE OF YOU HAVE THE POWER TO STOP ME!

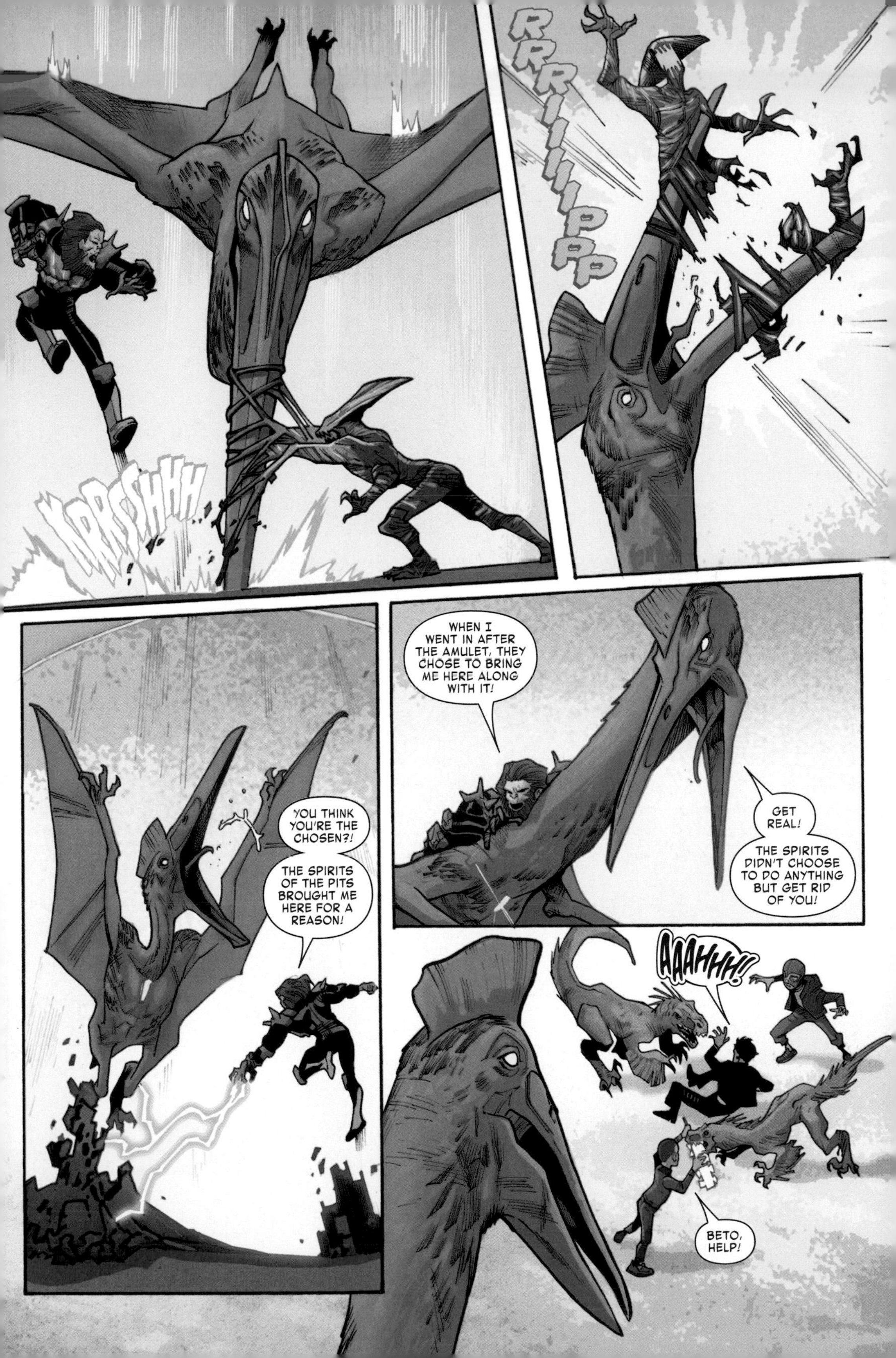
KRRSSHHH
RRRIIIIIPPP
YOU THINK YOU'RE THE CHOSEN?!
THE SPIRITS OF THE PITS BROUGHT ME HERE FOR A REASON!
WHEN I WENT IN AFTER THE AMULET, THEY CHOSE TO BRING ME HERE ALONG WITH IT!
GET REAL!
THE SPIRITS DIDN'T CHOOSE TO DO ANYTHING BUT GET RID OF YOU!
AAAHHH!!
BETO, HELP!

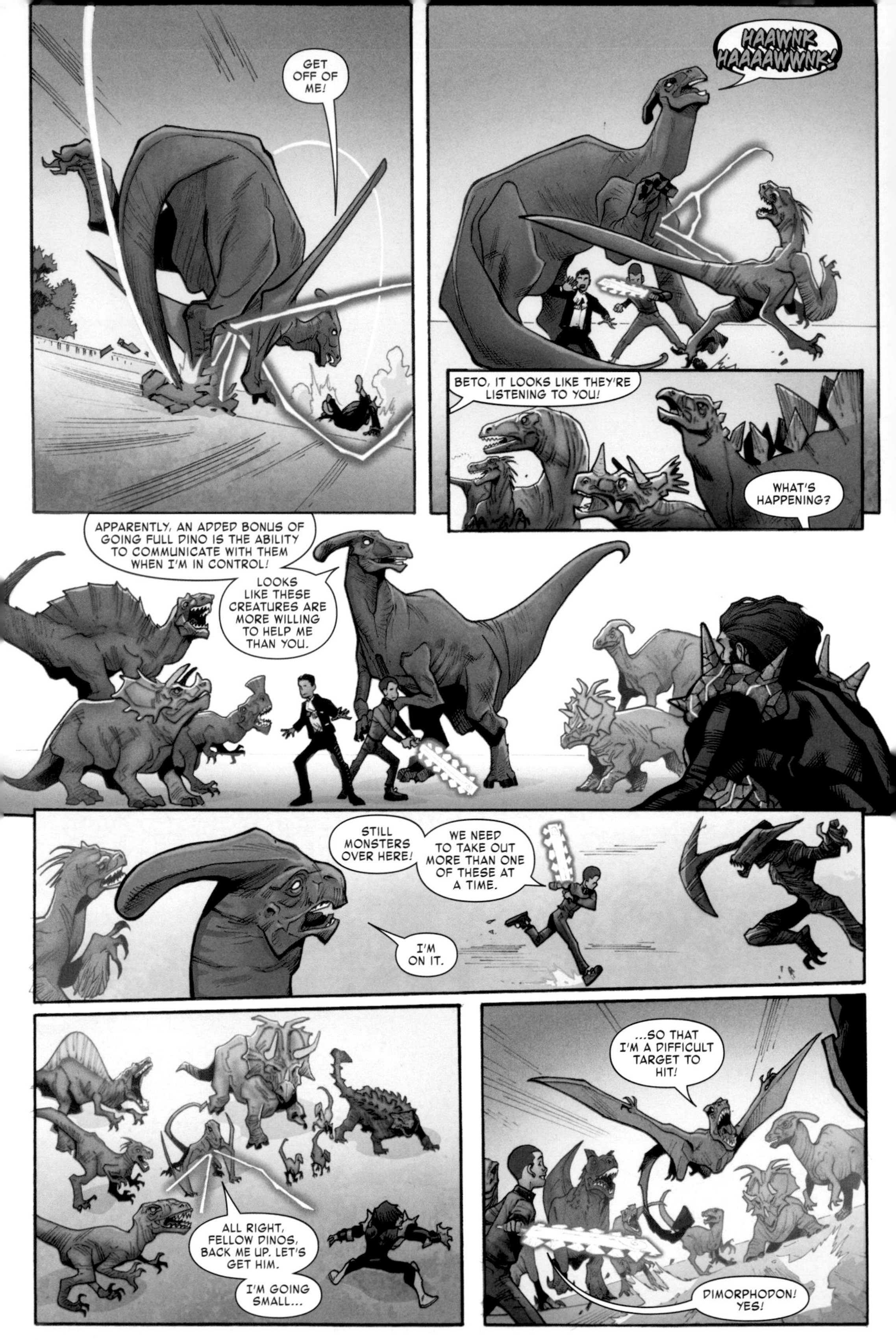
GET OFF OF ME!
HAAWNK HAAAAWWNK!
BETO, IT LOOKS LIKE THEY'RE LISTENING TO YOU!
WHAT'S HAPPENING?
APPARENTLY, AN ADDED BONUS OF GOING FULL DINO IS THE ABILITY TO COMMUNICATE WITH THEM WHEN I'M IN CONTROL!
LOOKS LIKE THESE CREATURES ARE MORE WILLING TO HELP ME THAN YOU.
STILL MONSTERS OVER HERE!
WE NEED TO TAKE OUT MORE THAN ONE OF THESE AT A TIME.
I'M ON IT.
ALL RIGHT, FELLOW DINOS, BACK ME UP. LET'S GET HIM.
I'M GOING SMALL...
...SO THAT I'M A DIFFICULT TARGET TO HIT!
DIMORPHODON! YES!

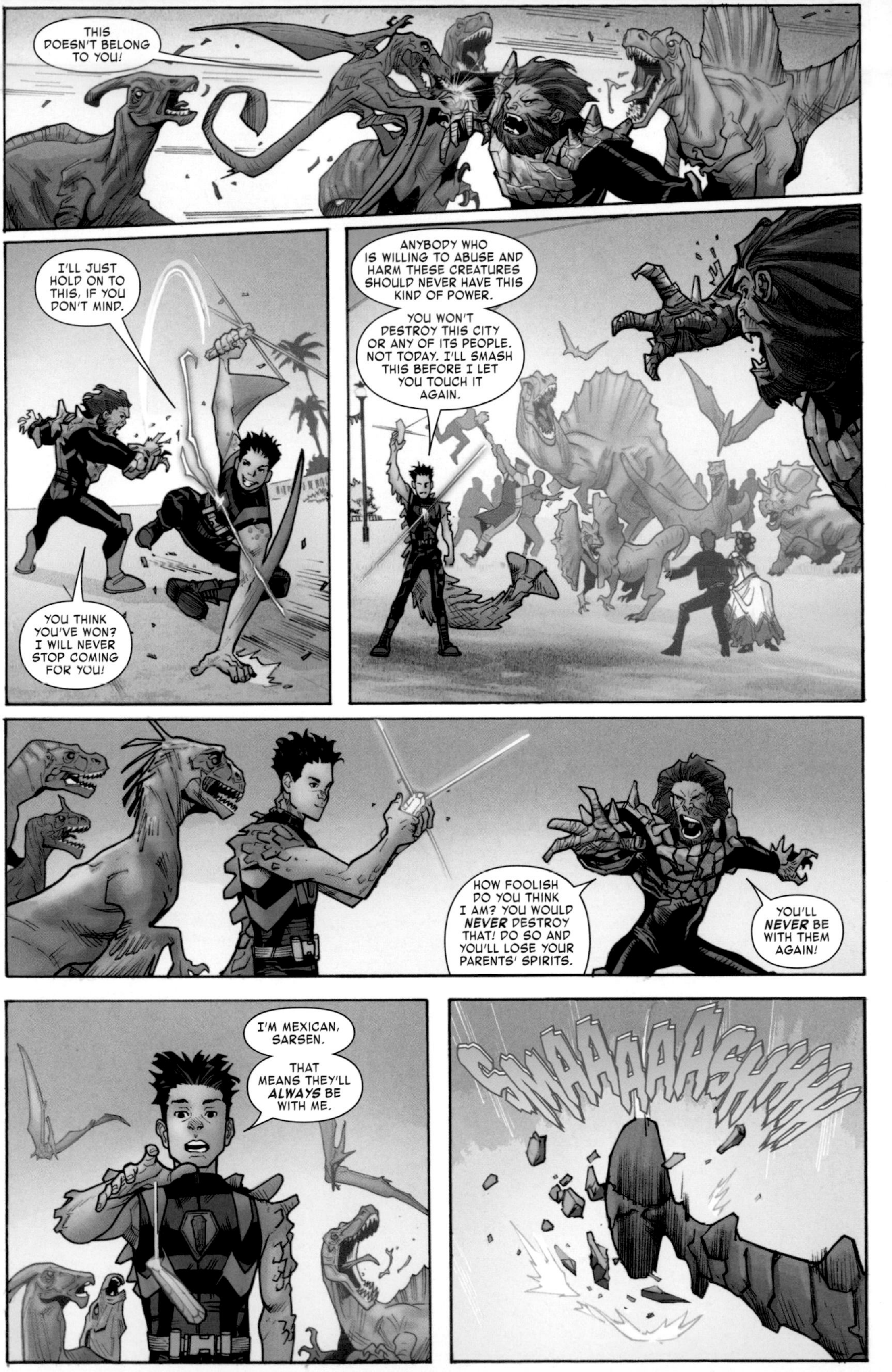

THIS DOESN'T BELONG TO YOU!
I'LL JUST HOLD ON TO THIS, IF YOU DON'T MIND.
YOU THINK YOU'VE WON? I WILL NEVER STOP COMING FOR YOU!
ANYBODY WHO IS WILLING TO ABUSE AND HARM THESE CREATURES SHOULD NEVER HAVE THIS KIND OF POWER.
YOU WON'T DESTROY THIS CITY OR ANY OF ITS PEOPLE. NOT TODAY. I'LL SMASH THIS BEFORE I LET YOU TOUCH IT AGAIN.
HOW FOOLISH DO YOU THINK I AM? YOU WOULD *NEVER* DESTROY THAT! DO SO AND YOU'LL LOSE YOUR PARENTS' SPIRITS.
YOU'LL *NEVER* BE WITH THEM AGAIN!
I'M MEXICAN, SARSEN.
THAT MEANS THEY'LL *ALWAYS* BE WITH ME.
SMAAAASHH!

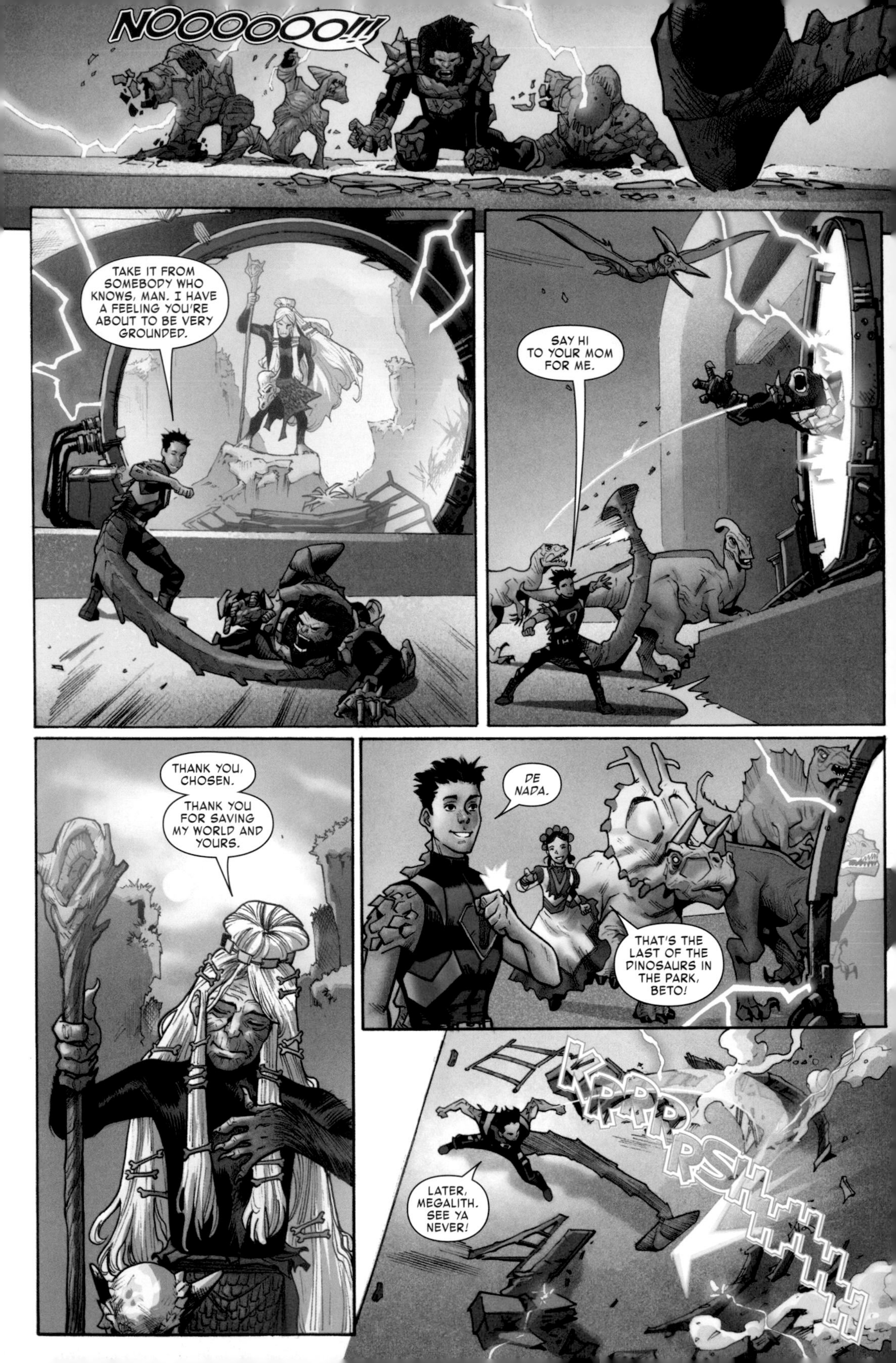
NOOOOOO!!!
TAKE IT FROM SOMEBODY WHO KNOWS, MAN. I HAVE A FEELING YOU'RE ABOUT TO BE VERY GROUNDED.
SAY HI TO YOUR MOM FOR ME.
THANK YOU, CHOSEN.
THANK YOU FOR SAVING MY WORLD AND YOURS.
DE NADA.
THAT'S THE LAST OF THE DINOSAURS IN THE PARK, BETO!
KRRRPSHHHHH
LATER, MEGALITH. SEE YA NEVER!

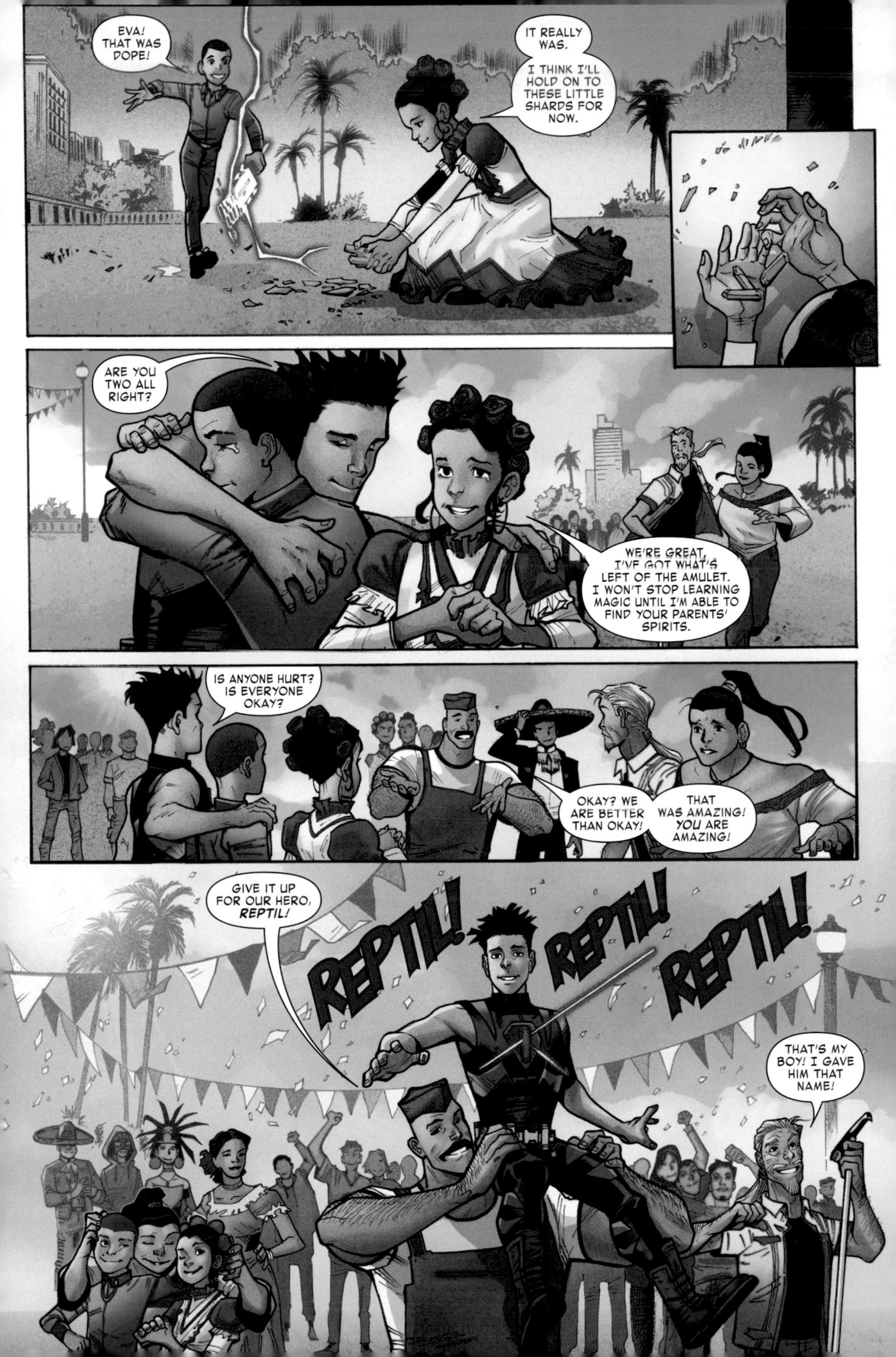
EVA! THAT WAS DOPE!
IT REALLY WAS.
I THINK I'LL HOLD ON TO THESE LITTLE SHARDS FOR NOW.
ARE YOU TWO ALL RIGHT?
WE'RE GREAT. I'VE GOT WHAT'S LEFT OF THE AMULET. I WON'T STOP LEARNING MAGIC UNTIL I'M ABLE TO FIND YOUR PARENTS' SPIRITS.
IS ANYONE HURT? IS EVERYONE OKAY?
OKAY? WE ARE BETTER THAN OKAY!
THAT WAS AMAZING! YOU ARE AMAZING!
GIVE IT UP FOR OUR HERO, REPTIL!
REPTIL! REPTIL! REPTIL!
THAT'S MY BOY! I GAVE HIM THAT NAME!

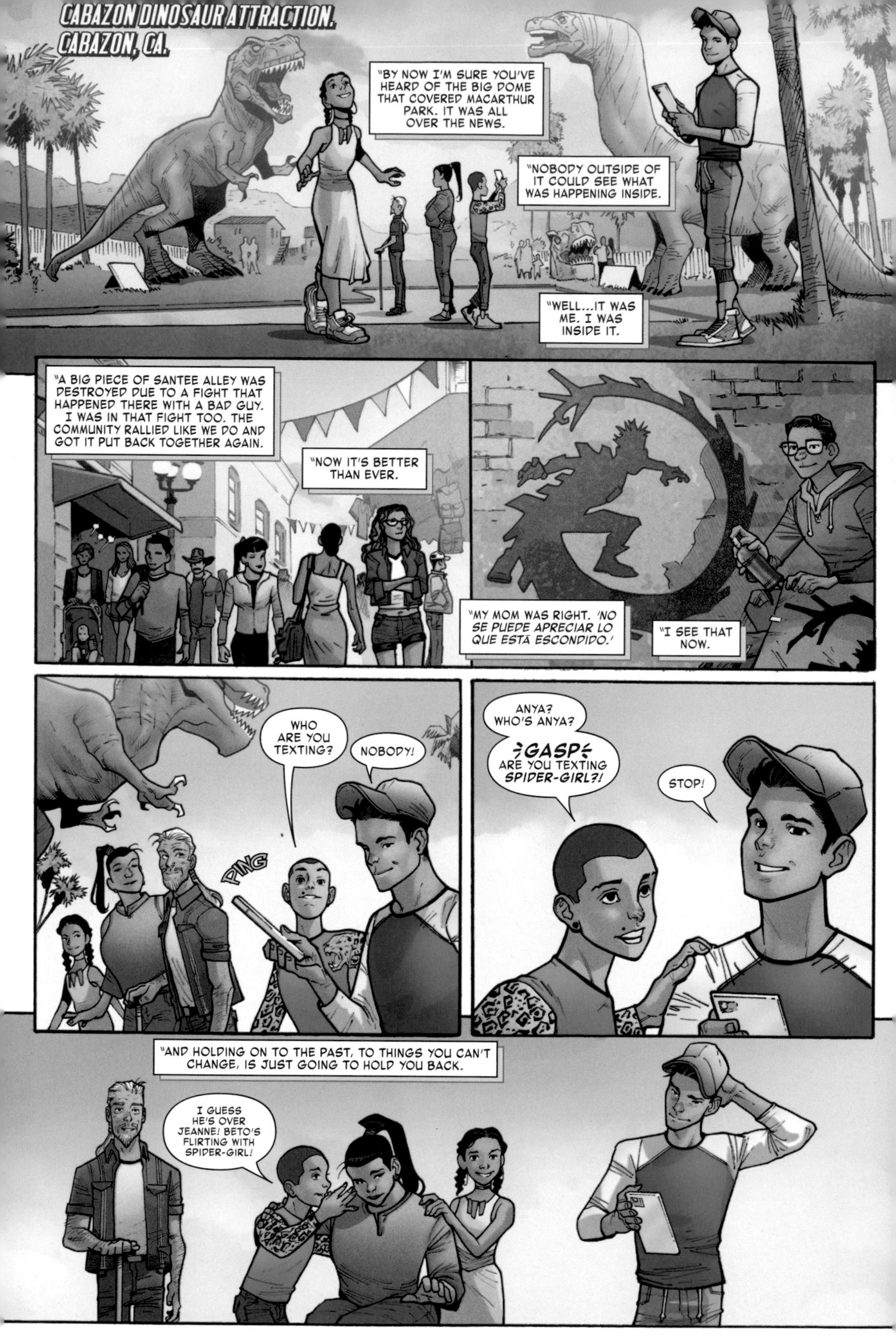
CABAZON DINOSAUR ATTRACTION. CABAZON, CA.
"BY NOW I'M SURE YOU'VE HEARD OF THE BIG DOME THAT COVERED MACARTHUR PARK. IT WAS ALL OVER THE NEWS.
"NOBODY OUTSIDE OF IT COULD SEE WHAT WAS HAPPENING INSIDE.
"WELL...IT WAS ME. I WAS INSIDE IT.
"A BIG PIECE OF SANTEE ALLEY WAS DESTROYED DUE TO A FIGHT THAT HAPPENED THERE WITH A BAD GUY. I WAS IN THAT FIGHT TOO. THE COMMUNITY RALLIED LIKE WE DO AND GOT IT PUT BACK TOGETHER AGAIN.
"NOW IT'S BETTER THAN EVER.
"MY MOM WAS RIGHT. 'NO SE PUEDE APRECIAR LO QUE ESTÁ ESCONDIDO.'
"I SEE THAT NOW.
WHO ARE YOU TEXTING?
NOBODY!
PING
ANYA? WHO'S ANYA?
GASP ARE YOU TEXTING SPIDER-GIRL?!
STOP!
"AND HOLDING ON TO THE PAST, TO THINGS YOU CAN'T CHANGE, IS JUST GOING TO HOLD YOU BACK.
I GUESS HE'S OVER JEANNE! BETO'S FLIRTING WITH SPIDER-GIRL!

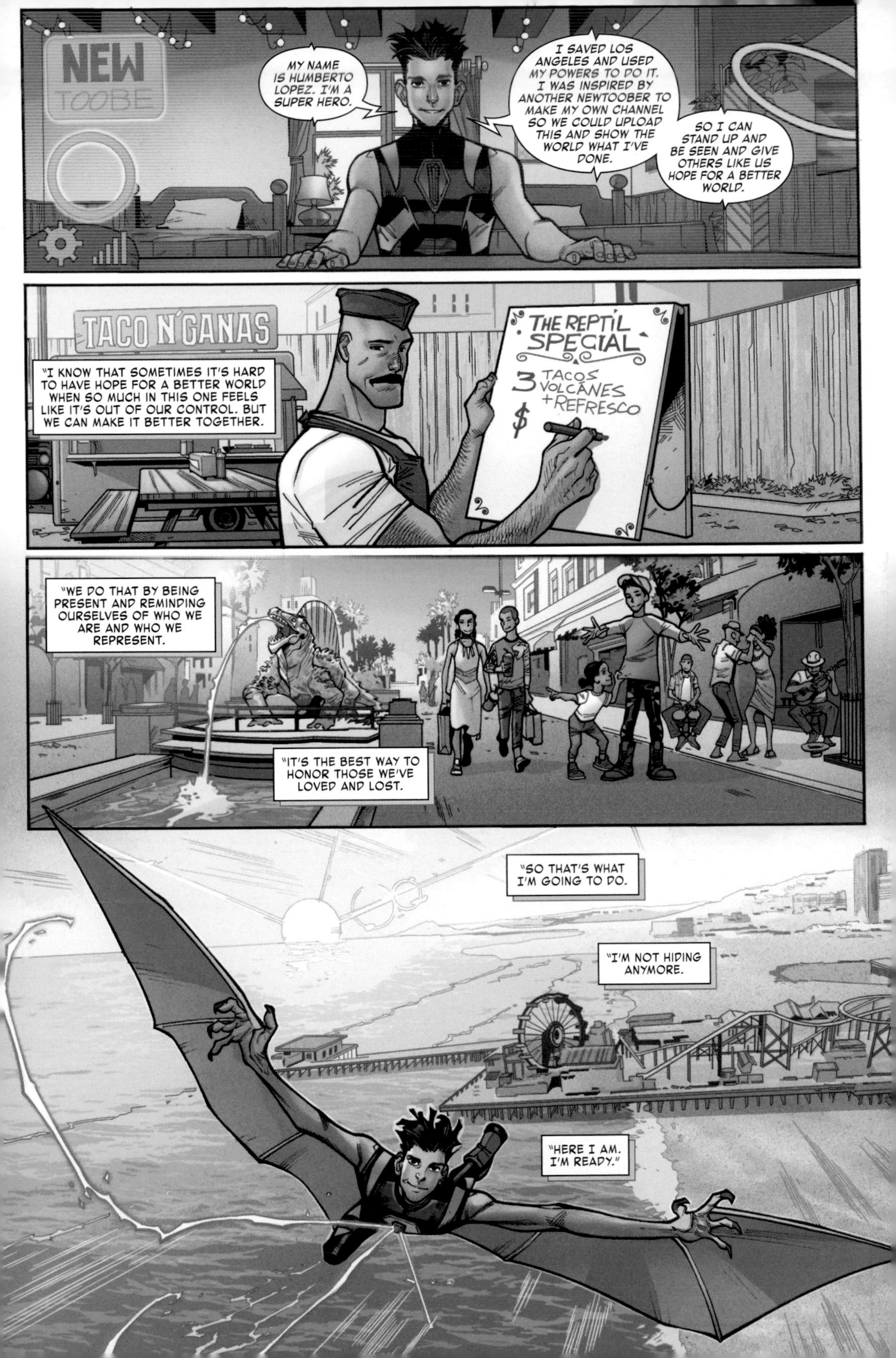
NEW TOOBE
MY NAME IS HUMBERTO LOPEZ. I'M A SUPER HERO.
I SAVED LOS ANGELES AND USED MY POWERS TO DO IT. I WAS INSPIRED BY ANOTHER NEWTOOBER TO MAKE MY OWN CHANNEL SO WE COULD UPLOAD THIS AND SHOW THE WORLD WHAT I'VE DONE.
SO I CAN STAND UP AND BE SEEN AND GIVE OTHERS LIKE US HOPE FOR A BETTER WORLD.
TACO N'GANAS
"I KNOW THAT SOMETIMES IT'S HARD TO HAVE HOPE FOR A BETTER WORLD WHEN SO MUCH IN THIS ONE FEELS LIKE IT'S OUT OF OUR CONTROL. BUT WE CAN MAKE IT BETTER TOGETHER.
THE REPTIL SPECIAL
3 TACOS VOLCÁNES +REFRESCO
$
"WE DO THAT BY BEING PRESENT AND REMINDING OURSELVES OF WHO WE ARE AND WHO WE REPRESENT.
"IT'S THE BEST WAY TO HONOR THOSE WE'VE LOVED AND LOST.
"SO THAT'S WHAT I'M GOING TO DO.
"I'M NOT HIDING ANYMORE.
"HERE I AM. I'M READY."

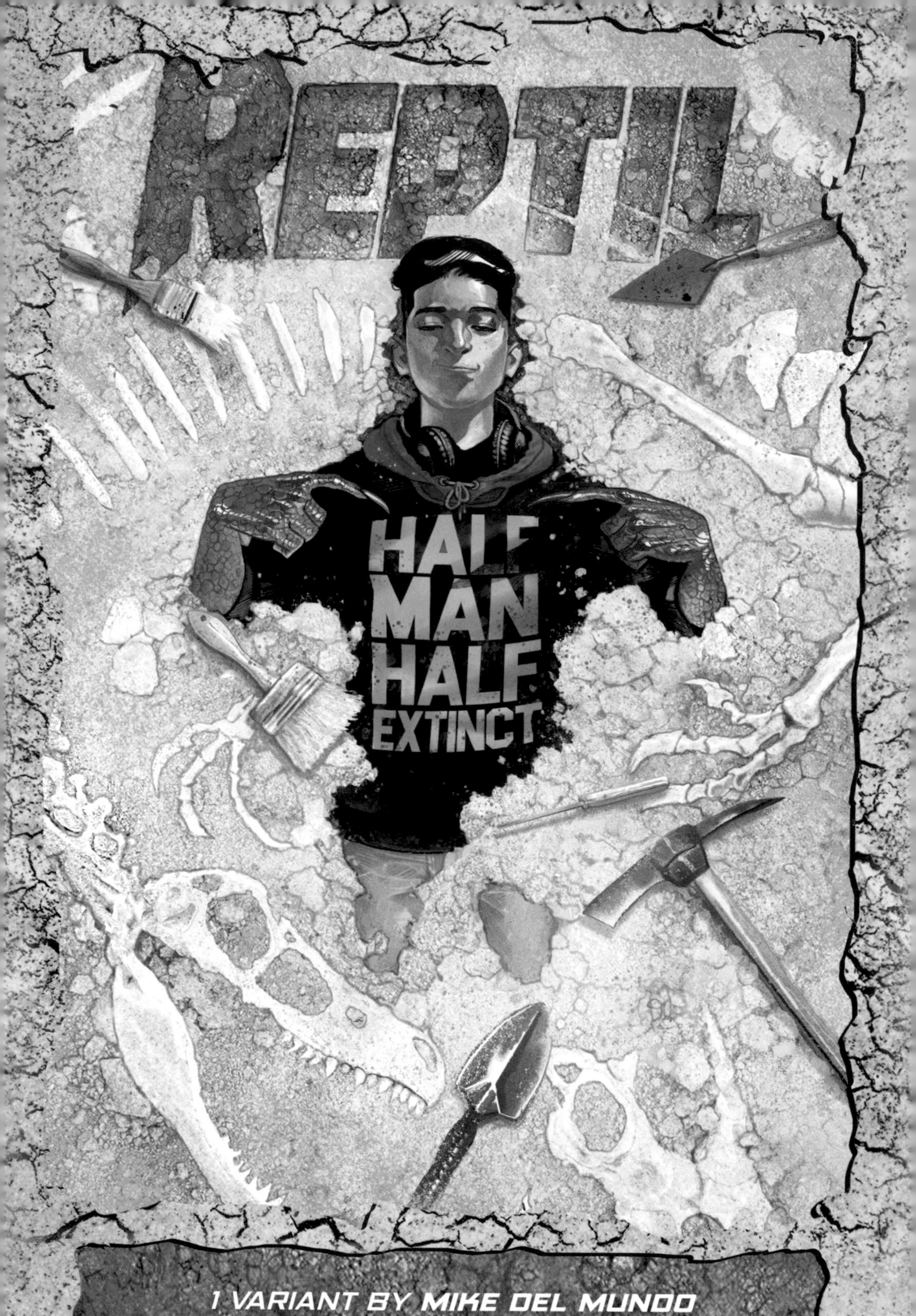
REPTIL
HALF
MAN
HALF
EXTINCT

1 VARIANT BY MIKE DEL MUNDO

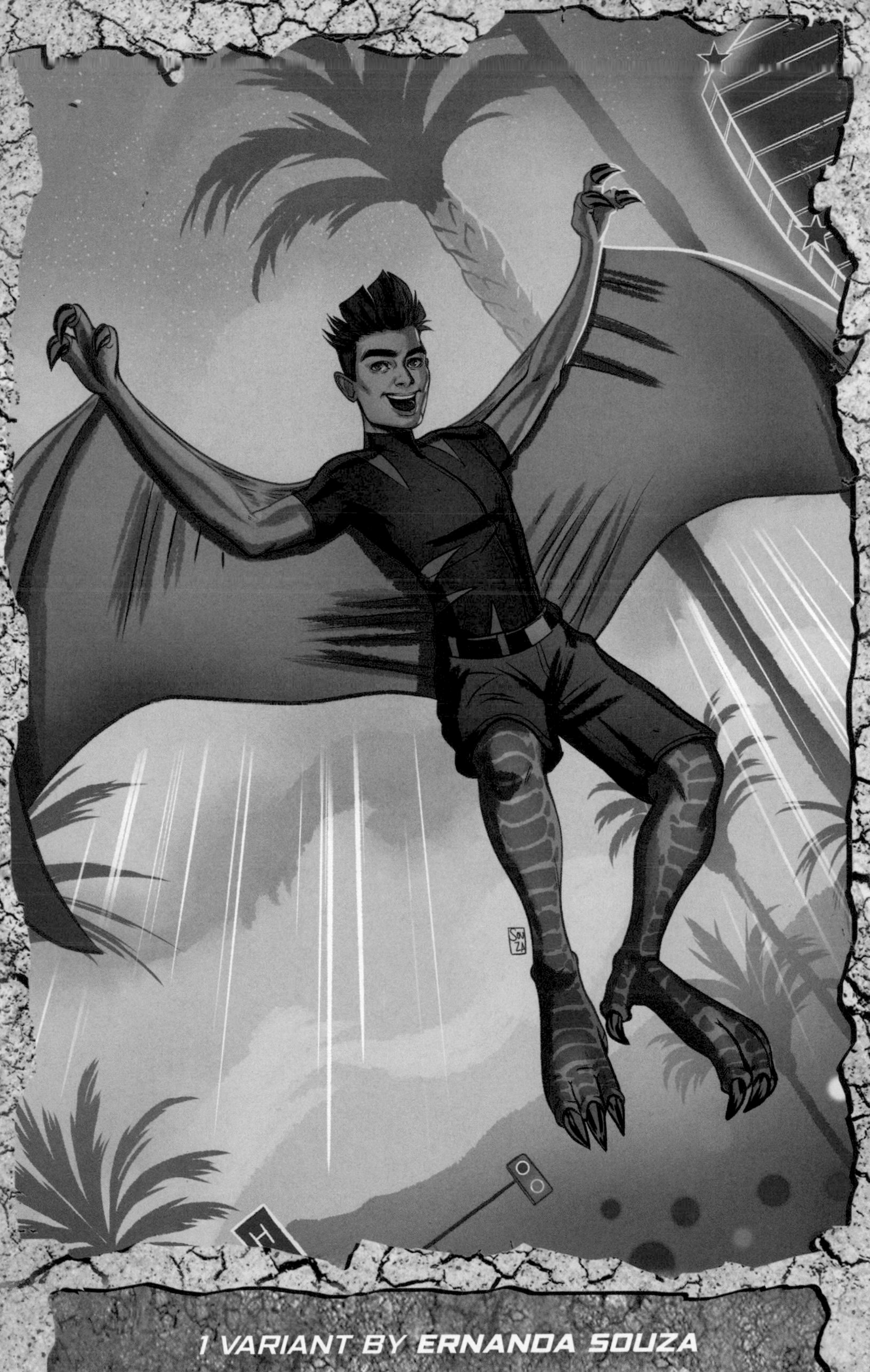

1 VARIANT BY ERNANDA SOUZA

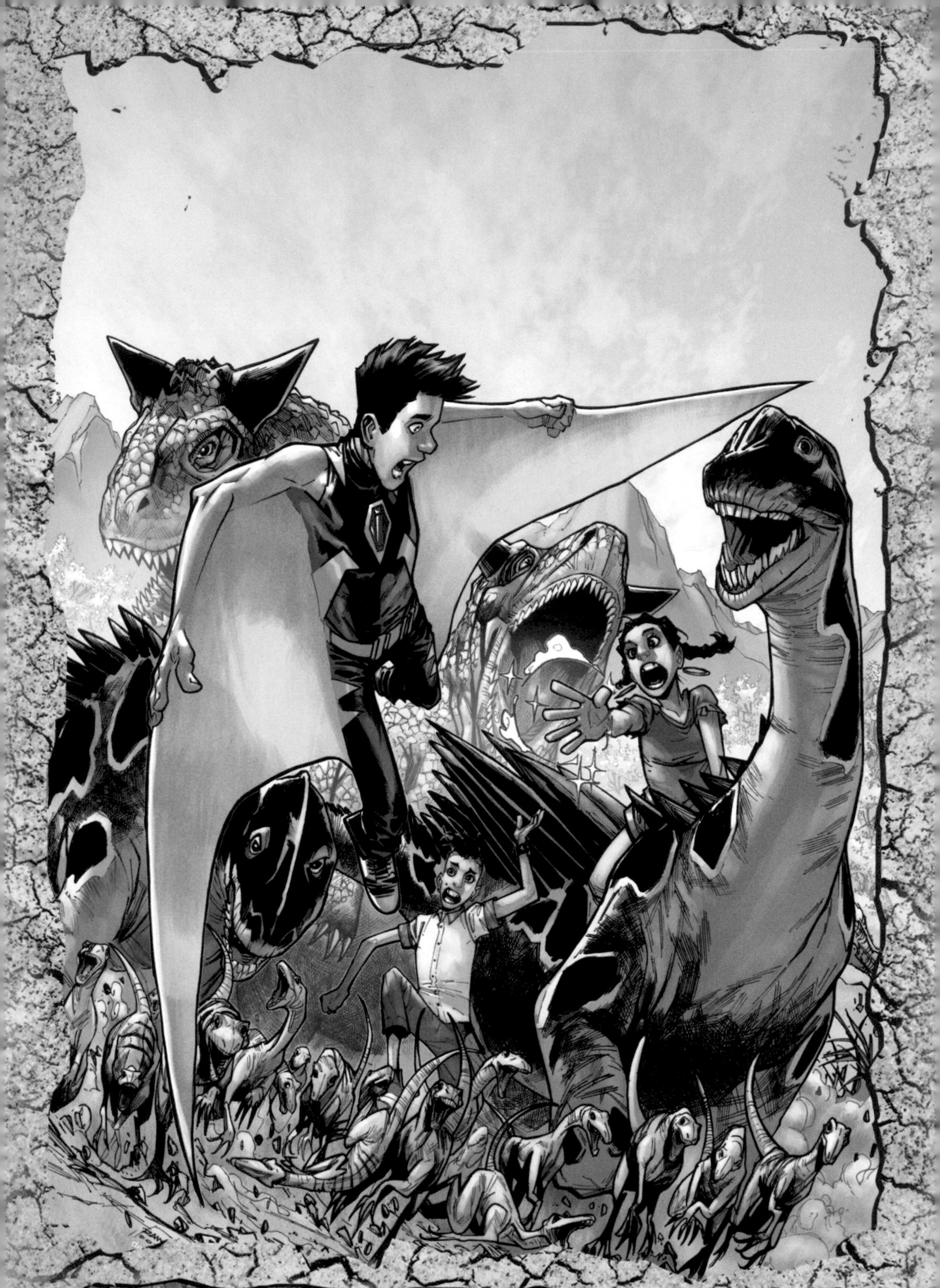

2 VARIANT BY
HUMBERTO RAMOS & EDGAR DELGADO

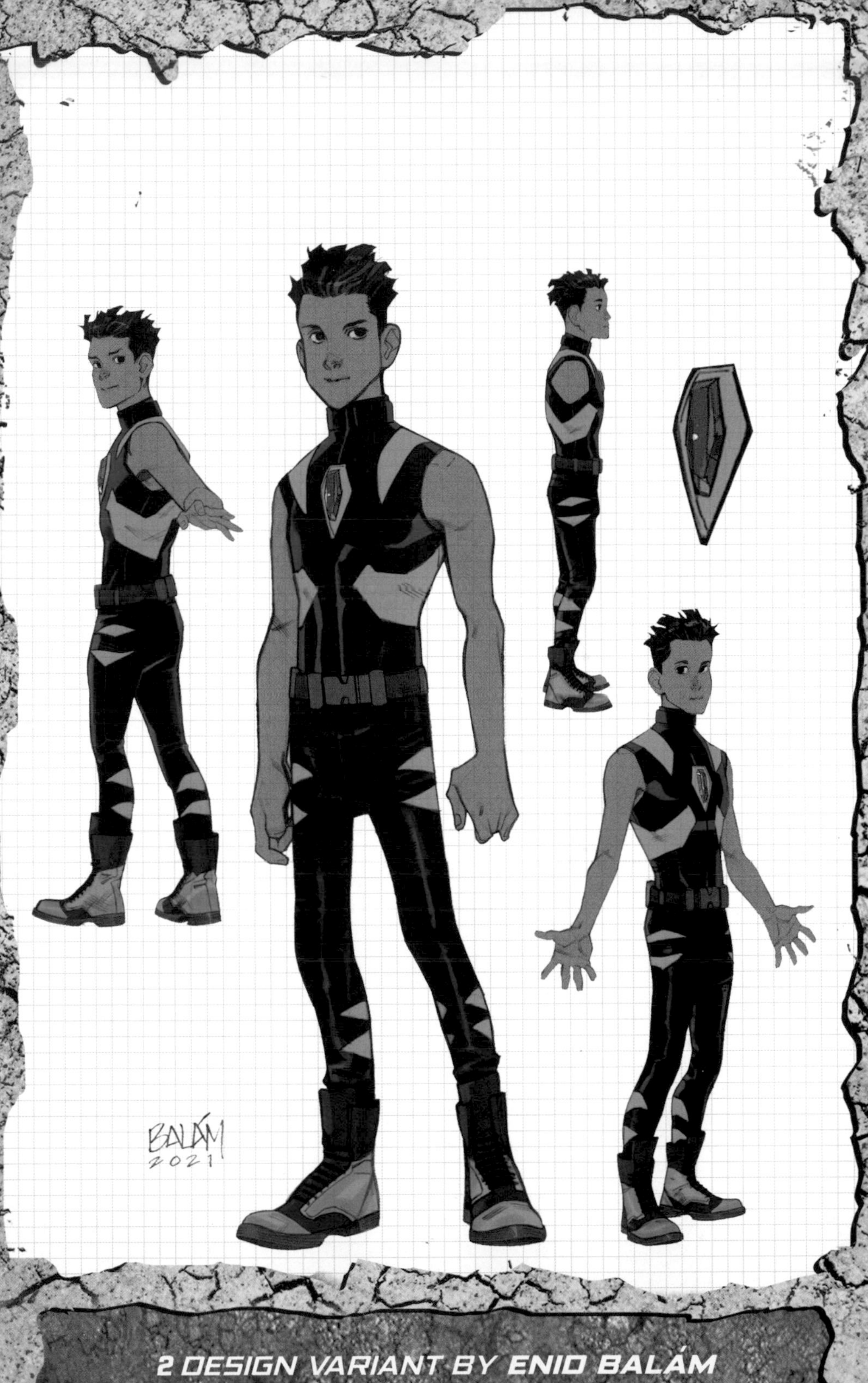
BALÁM
2021

2 DESIGN VARIANT BY ENID BALÁM

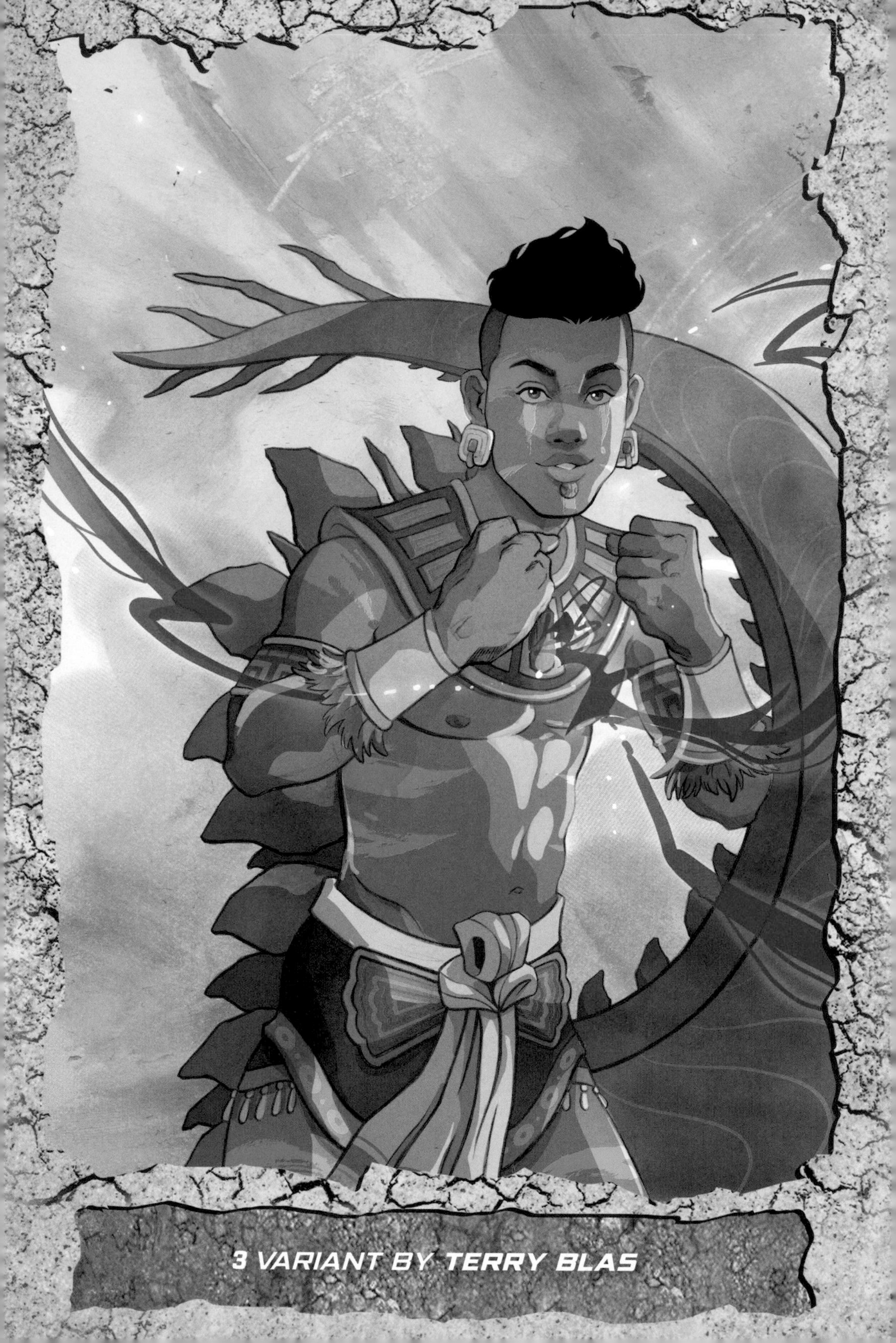

3 VARIANT BY TERRY BLAS

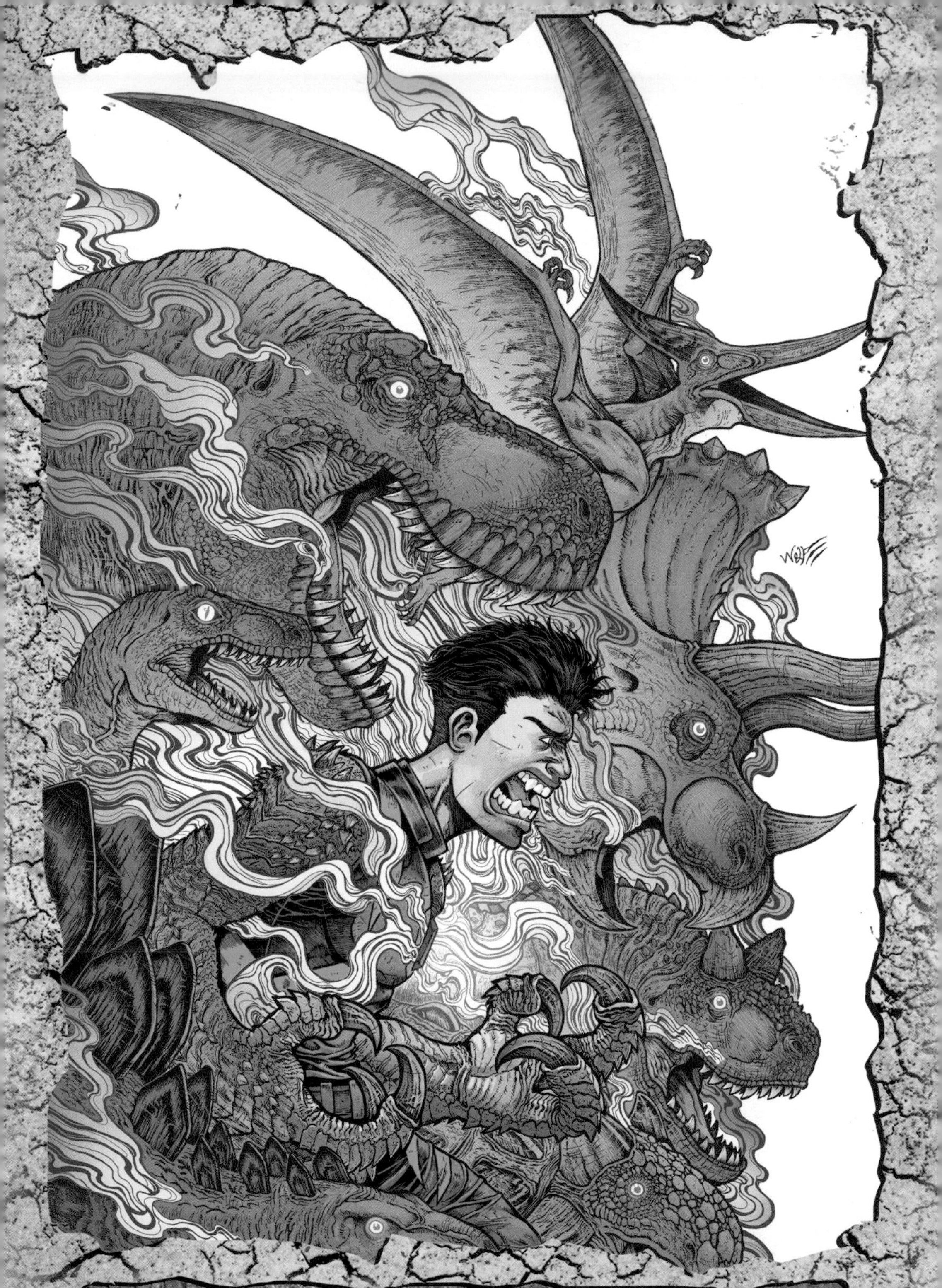

4 VARIANT BY
MARIA WOLF & MIKE SPICER

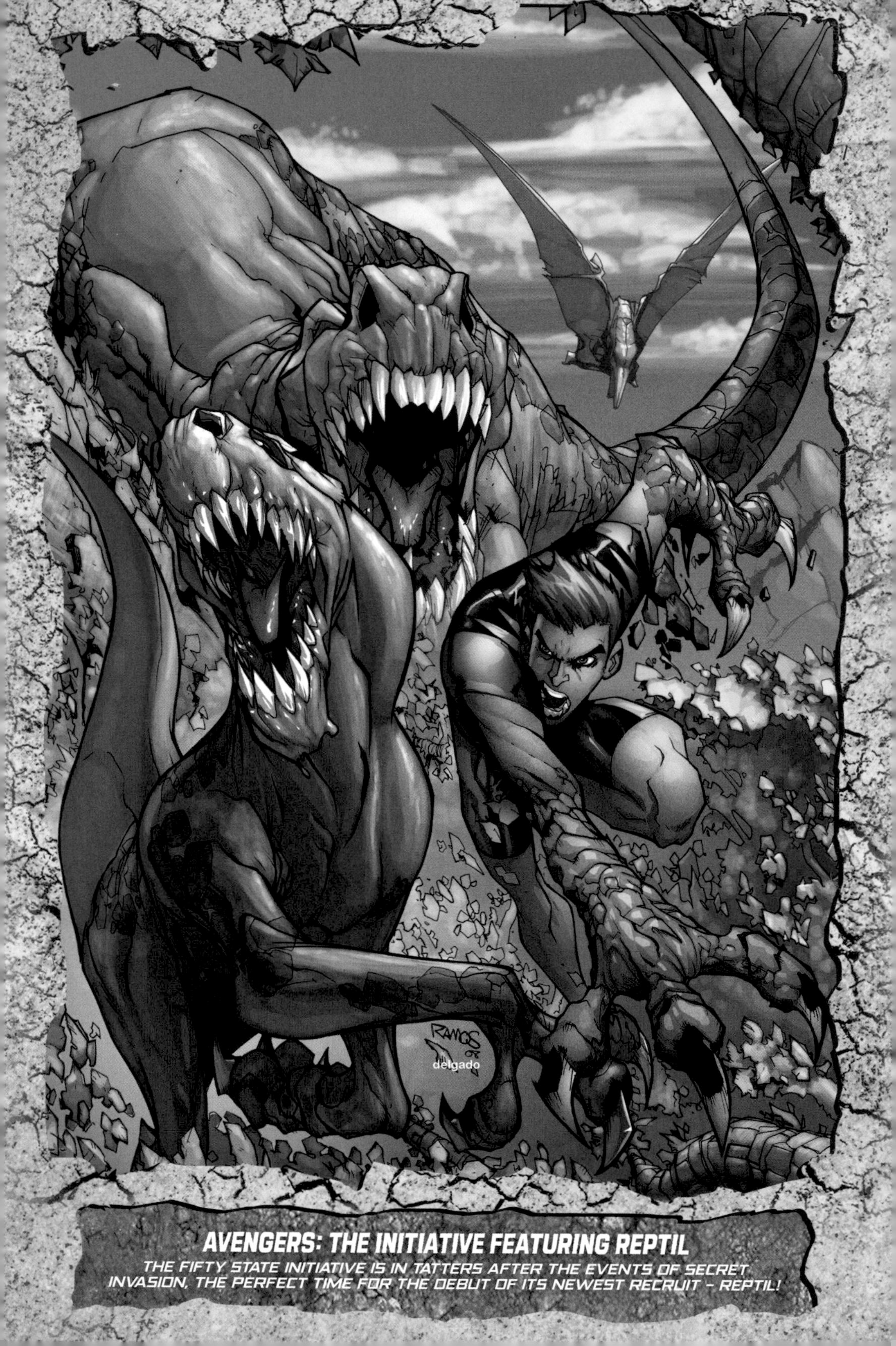
RAMOS 08
delgado

AVENGERS: THE INITIATIVE FEATURING REPTIL

THE FIFTY STATE INITIATIVE IS IN TATTERS AFTER THE EVENTS OF SECRET INVASION, THE PERFECT TIME FOR THE DEBUT OF ITS NEWEST RECRUIT – REPTIL!

AVENGERS
THE INITIATIVE

After Stamford, Connecticut was destroyed during a televised fight between the New Warriors and a group of dangerous villains, a federal Superhuman Registration Act was passed. All individuals possessing paranormal abilities must now register with the government. Tony Stark – a.k.a. Iron Man – was appointed director of S.H.I.E.L.D., the international peacekeeping force and has set into motion The Initiative, a plan for training and policing super heroes in this brave new world, intended to position a local super hero team in each of America's fifty states.

Most graduates have been assigned to teams and work with their home states to keep the peace, but the staff of Camp Hammond is always on call.

TIGRA

DR. VAL COOPER

PRODIGY

BATWING

KOMODO

SUNSTREAK

CLOUD 9

BARON VON BLITZSCHLAG

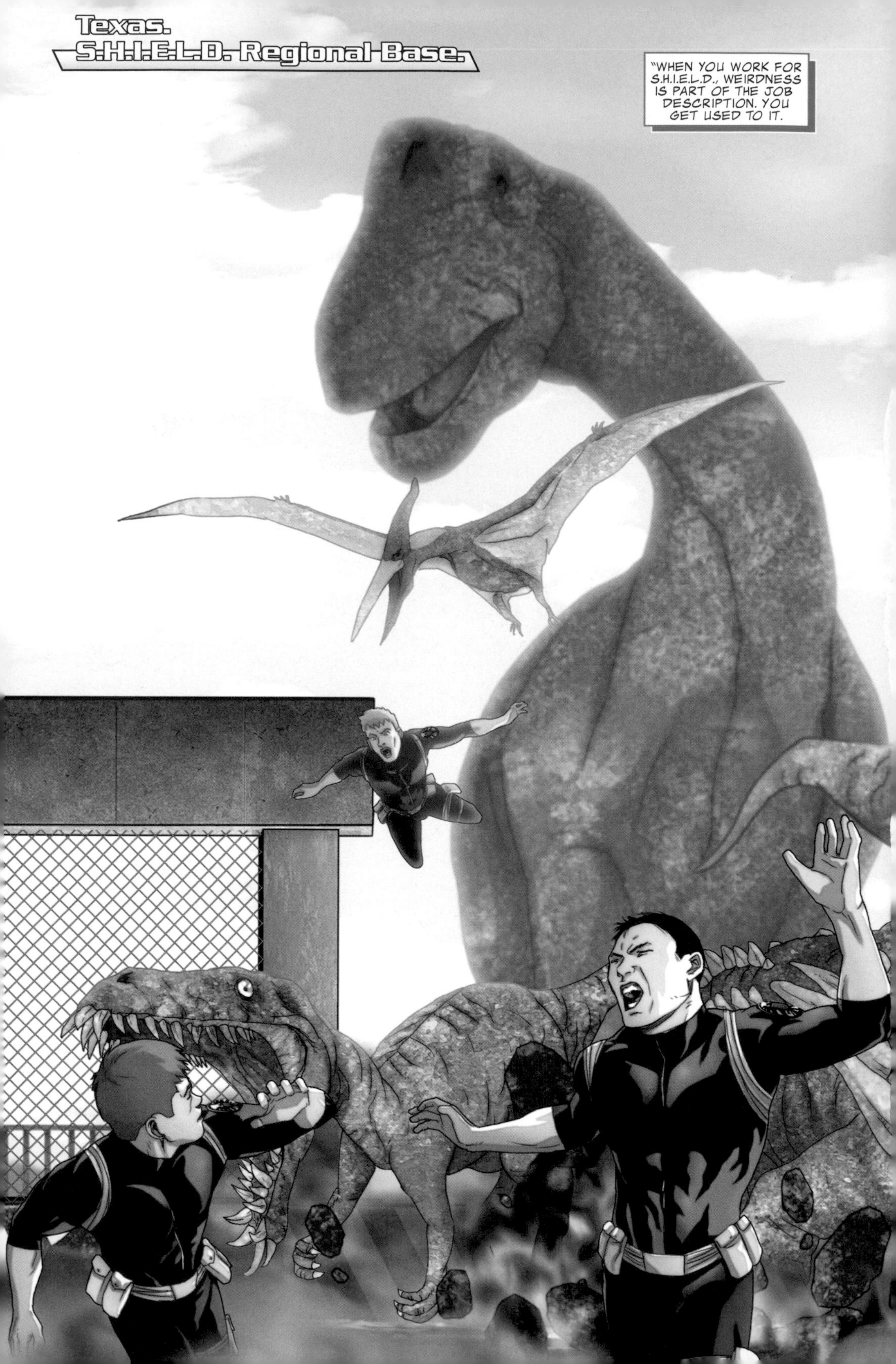
Texas.
S.H.I.E.L.D. Regional Base.
"WHEN YOU WORK FOR S.H.I.E.L.D., WEIRDNESS IS PART OF THE JOB DESCRIPTION. YOU GET USED TO IT.

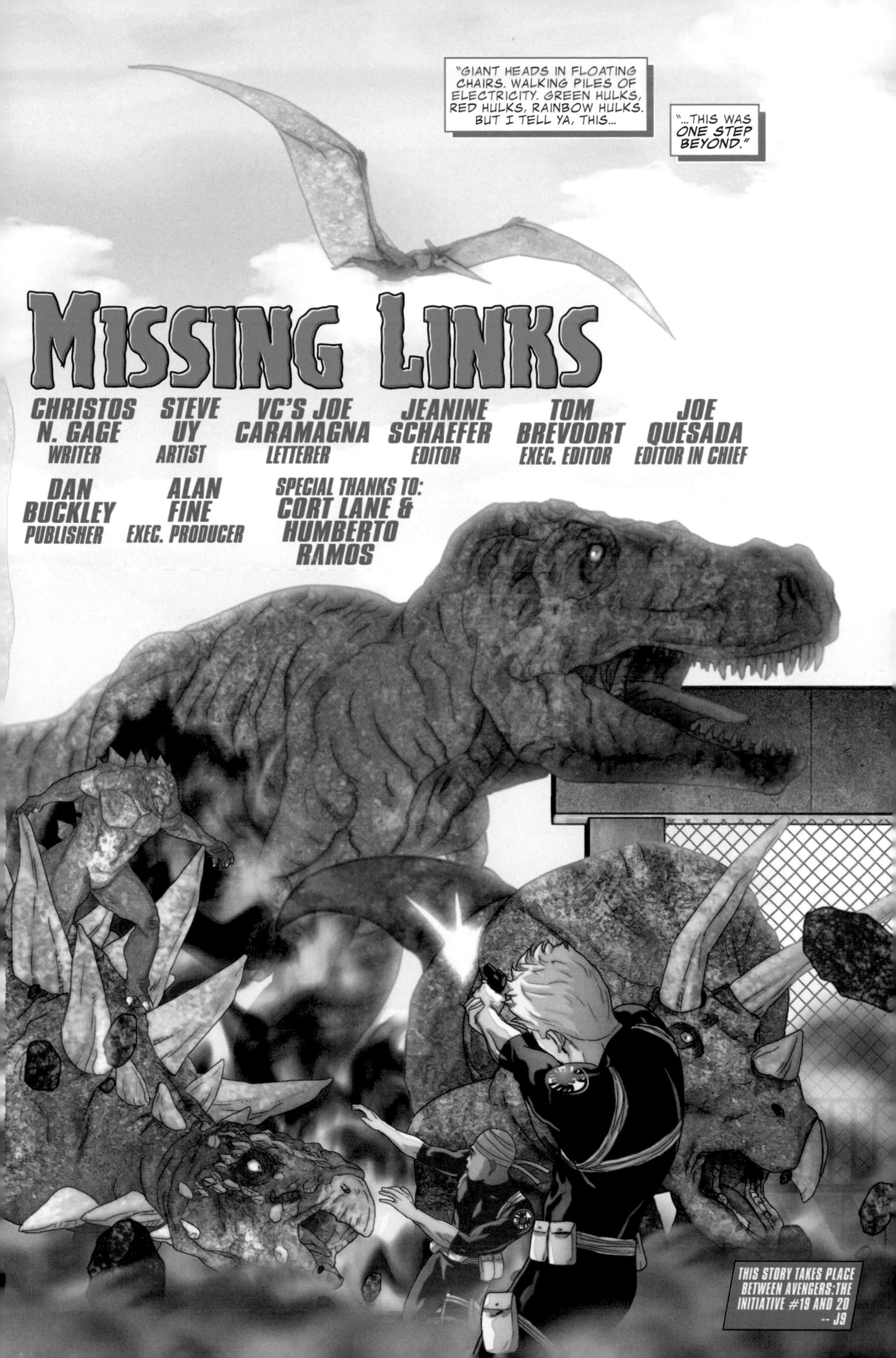
"GIANT HEADS IN FLOATING CHAIRS. WALKING PILES OF ELECTRICITY. GREEN HULKS, RED HULKS, RAINBOW HULKS. BUT I TELL YA, THIS...
"...THIS WAS ONE STEP BEYOND."
MISSING LINKS
CHRISTOS N. GAGE WRITER
STEVE UY ARTIST
VC'S JOE CARAMAGNA LETTERER
JEANINE SCHAEFER EDITOR
TOM BREVOORT EXEC. EDITOR
JOE QUESADA EDITOR IN CHIEF
DAN BUCKLEY PUBLISHER
ALAN FINE EXEC. PRODUCER
SPECIAL THANKS TO: CORT LANE & HUMBERTO RAMOS
THIS STORY TAKES PLACE BETWEEN AVENGERS: THE INITIATIVE #19 AND 20 -- J9

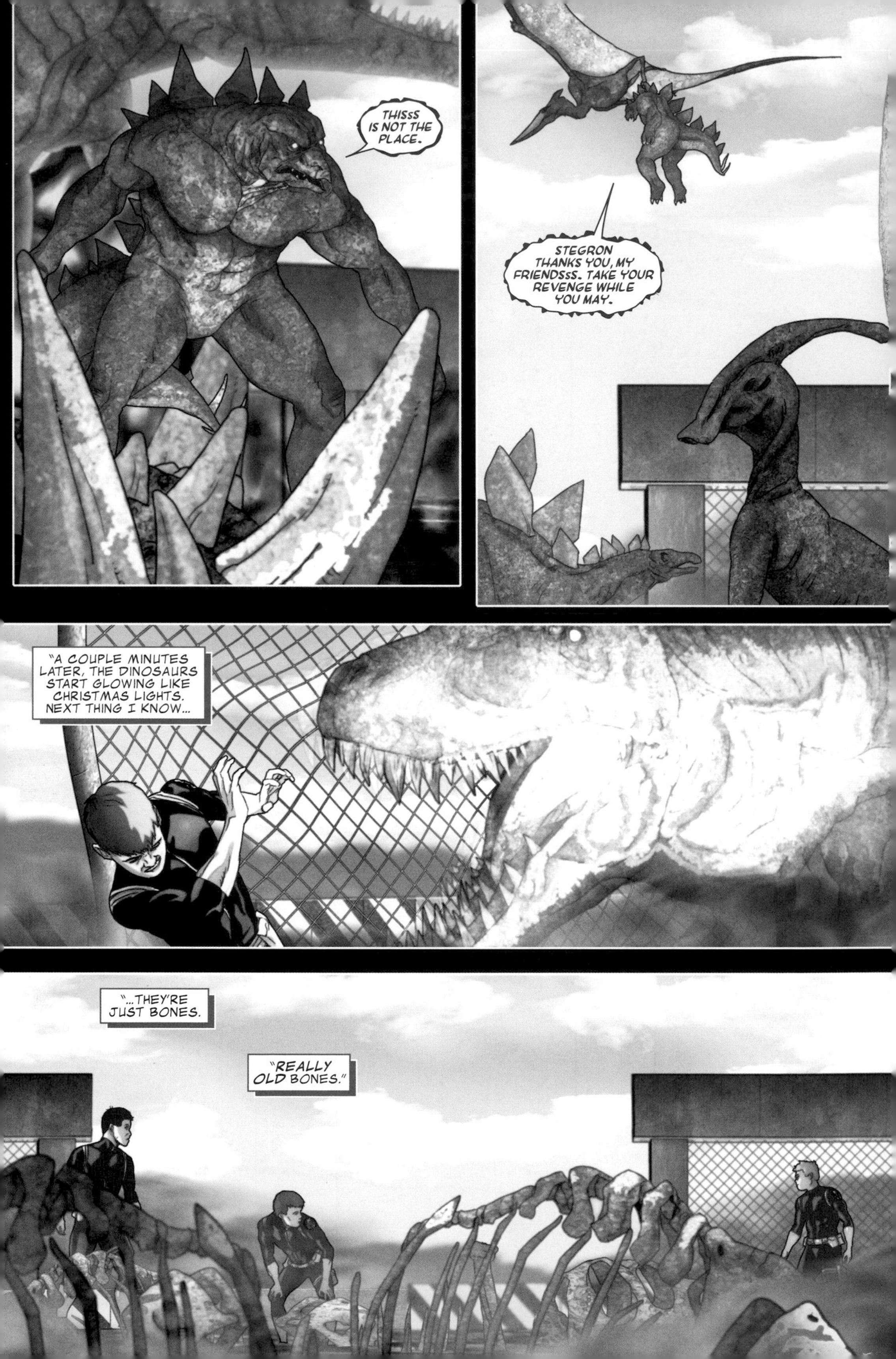
THISSS IS NOT THE PLACE.
STEGRON THANKS YOU, MY FRIENDSSS. TAKE YOUR REVENGE WHILE YOU MAY.
"A COUPLE MINUTES LATER, THE DINOSAURS START GLOWING LIKE CHRISTMAS LIGHTS. NEXT THING I KNOW...
"...THEY'RE JUST BONES.
"REALLY OLD BONES."

Camp Hammond. Briefing Room Alpha.

Tigra: ARKANSAS TEAM LEADER: INSTRUCTOR.

THAT'S CONSISTENT WITH STEGRON'S M.O. HE HAS A METHOD OF REANIMATING DINOSAUR REMAINS.

Dr. Val Cooper: COMMISSION ON SUPERHUMAN ACTIVITIES.

I'D BET THE LOCAL MUSEUM'S MISSING A FEW EXHIBITS.

STEGRON? IT HAS A *NAME*?

DR. VINCENT STEGRON...OR, AS HE'S KNOWN THESE DAYS, THE *DINOSAUR MAN.* HE'S USUALLY OUT TO RECLAIM EARTH FOR THE DINOSAURS, OR DEVOLVE EVERYTHING TO A PREHISTORIC STATE.

IT SOUNDS LAUGHABLE... UNTIL YOU SEE HIS *BODY COUNT.*

OKAY, BUT WHY COME TO ME? ISN'T THIS A JOB FOR THE *RANGERS*?

IT WOULD BE, IF STEGRON CONFINED HIS ACTIVITIES TO TEXAS. BUT HE'S ALSO STRUCK S.H.I.E.L.D. BASES IN COLORADO AND MONTANA.

THERE'S ALSO THE MATTER OF OUR STATE TEAMS BEING IN *TOTAL DISARRAY* AFTER THE SKRULL WAR. HALF OUR PERSONNEL ARE IN THE INFIRMARY, DEAD, OR EMOTIONAL WRECKS.

BUT SOMEONE HAS TO DEAL WITH THIS. I'VE PUT TOGETHER A SQUAD BASED ON RELEVANT SKILL SETS AND READINESS FOR DUTY.

CLOUD 9, GOOD...SHE'S OUR BEST MARKSMAN. SUNSTREAK...OKAY. SHE'S GOT AN ATTITUDE, BUT THERE'S NOTHING LIKE FIRE TO REDIRECT A DINOSAUR HERD.

WAIT A SECOND...

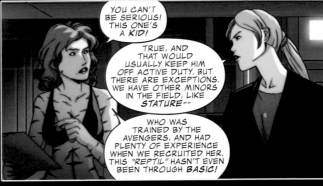

YOU CAN'T BE SERIOUS! THIS ONE'S A *KID*!

TRUE, AND THAT WOULD USUALLY KEEP HIM OFF ACTIVE DUTY. BUT THERE ARE EXCEPTIONS. WE HAVE OTHER MINORS IN THE FIELD, LIKE *STATURE*--

WHO WAS TRAINED BY THE AVENGERS, AND HAD PLENTY OF EXPERIENCE WHEN WE RECRUITED HER. THIS "*REPTIL*" HASN'T EVEN BEEN THROUGH *BASIC*!

LOOK AT HIS POWER SET. HE MAY BE OUR *ONLY CHANCE* OF FINDING STEGRON.

I WASN'T INVITING DEBATE, TIGRA. THERE'S A QUINJET FUELED AND WAITING.

I WANT YOU IN NEVADA BY NOON.

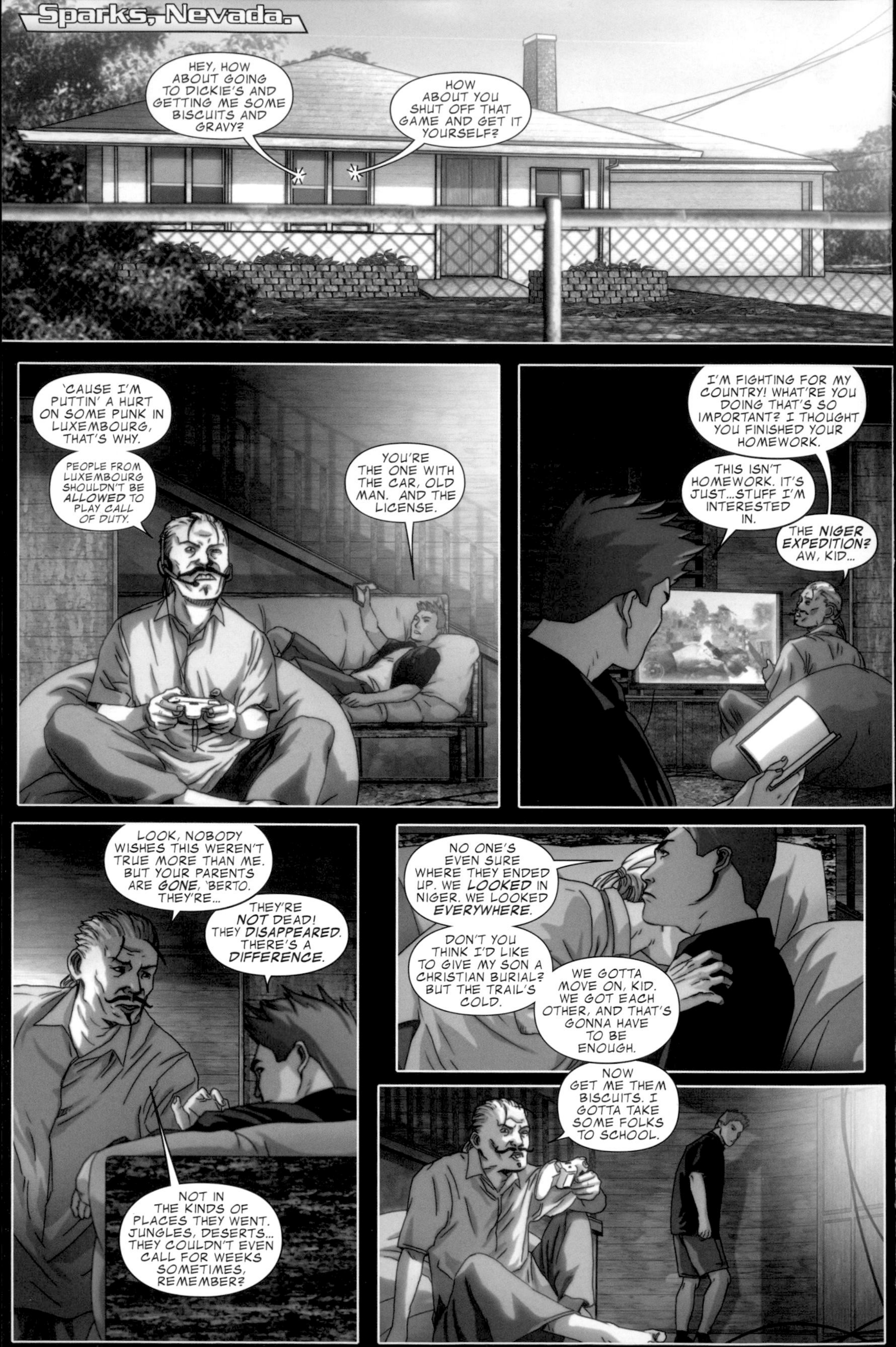
Sparks, Nevada.
HEY, HOW ABOUT GOING TO DICKIE'S AND GETTING ME SOME BISCUITS AND GRAVY?
HOW ABOUT YOU SHUT OFF THAT GAME AND GET IT YOURSELF?
'CAUSE I'M PUTTIN' A HURT ON SOME PUNK IN LUXEMBOURG, THAT'S WHY.
PEOPLE FROM LUXEMBOURG SHOULDN'T BE ALLOWED TO PLAY CALL OF DUTY.
YOU'RE THE ONE WITH THE CAR, OLD MAN. AND THE LICENSE.
I'M FIGHTING FOR MY COUNTRY! WHAT'RE YOU DOING THAT'S SO IMPORTANT? I THOUGHT YOU FINISHED YOUR HOMEWORK.
THIS ISN'T HOMEWORK. IT'S JUST...STUFF I'M INTERESTED IN.
THE NIGER EXPEDITION? AW, KID...
LOOK, NOBODY WISHES THIS WEREN'T TRUE MORE THAN ME. BUT YOUR PARENTS ARE GONE, 'BERTO. THEY'RE...
THEY'RE NOT DEAD! THEY DISAPPEARED. THERE'S A DIFFERENCE.
NOT IN THE KINDS OF PLACES THEY WENT. JUNGLES, DESERTS... THEY COULDN'T EVEN CALL FOR WEEKS SOMETIMES, REMEMBER?
NO ONE'S EVEN SURE WHERE THEY ENDED UP. WE LOOKED IN NIGER. WE LOOKED EVERYWHERE.
DON'T YOU THINK I'D LIKE TO GIVE MY SON A CHRISTIAN BURIAL? BUT THE TRAIL'S COLD.
WE GOTTA MOVE ON, KID. WE GOT EACH OTHER, AND THAT'S GONNA HAVE TO BE ENOUGH.
NOW GET ME THEM BISCUITS. I GOTTA TAKE SOME FOLKS TO SCHOOL.

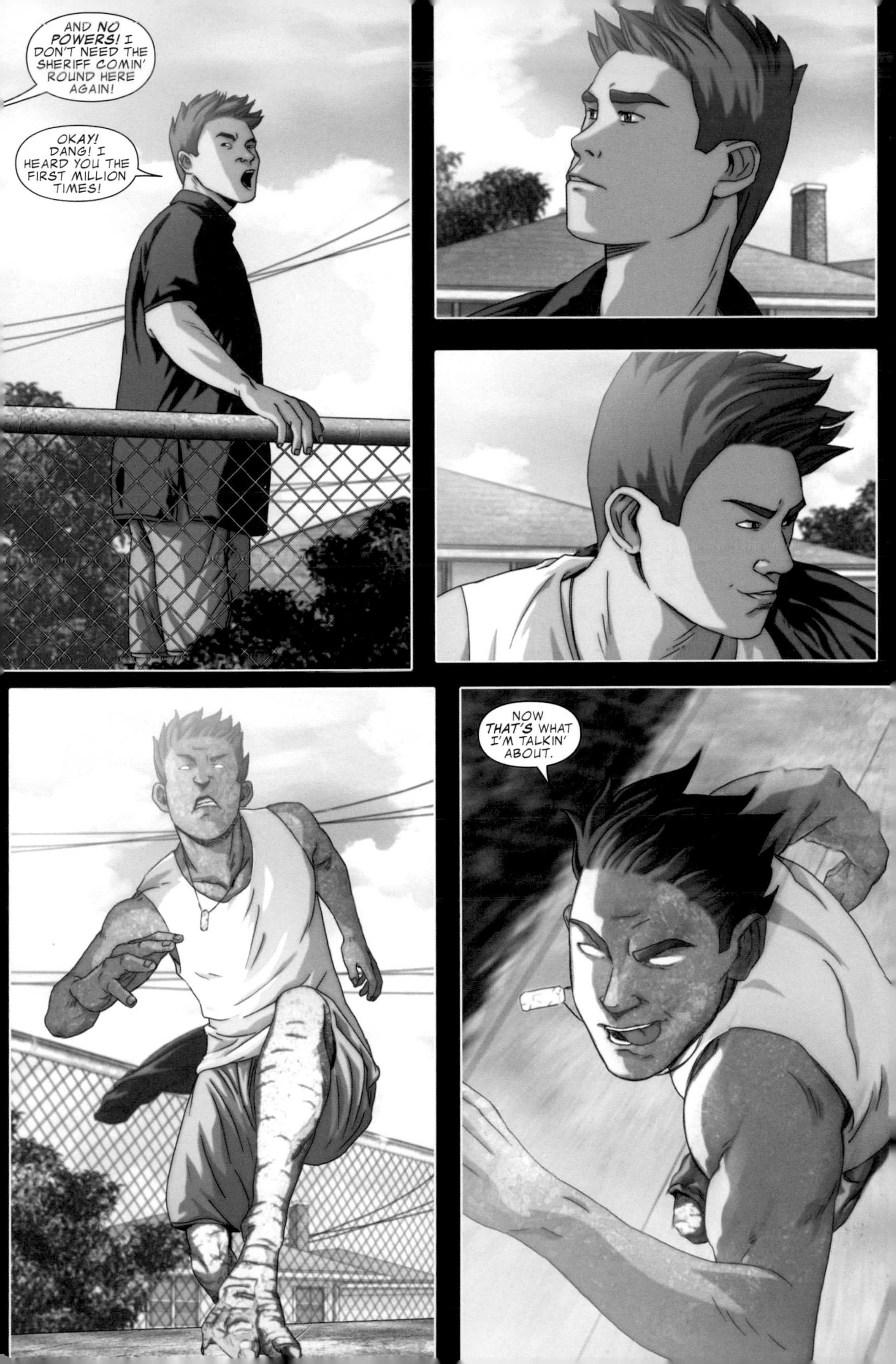
AND NO POWERS! I DON'T NEED THE SHERIFF COMIN' ROUND HERE AGAIN!
OKAY! DANG! I HEARD YOU THE FIRST MILLION TIMES!
NOW THAT'S WHAT I'M TALKIN' ABOUT.

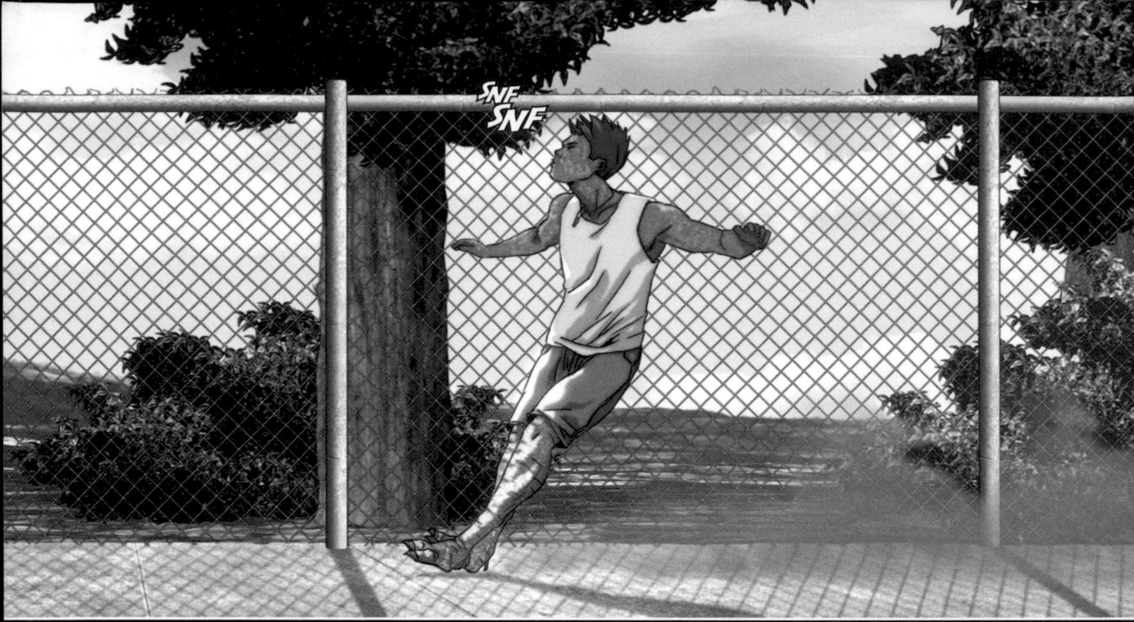
SNF
SNF

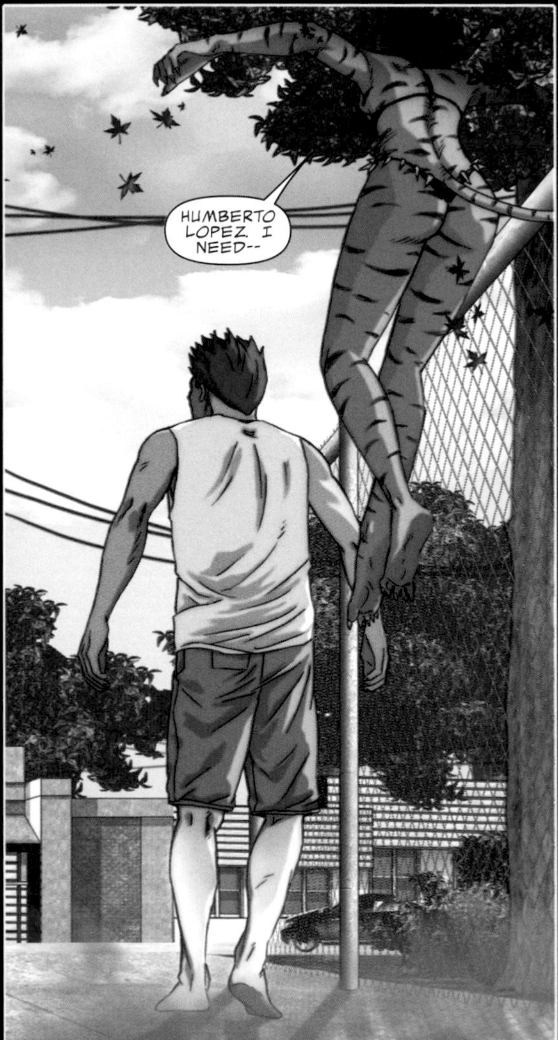
HUMBERTO LOPEZ. I NEED--

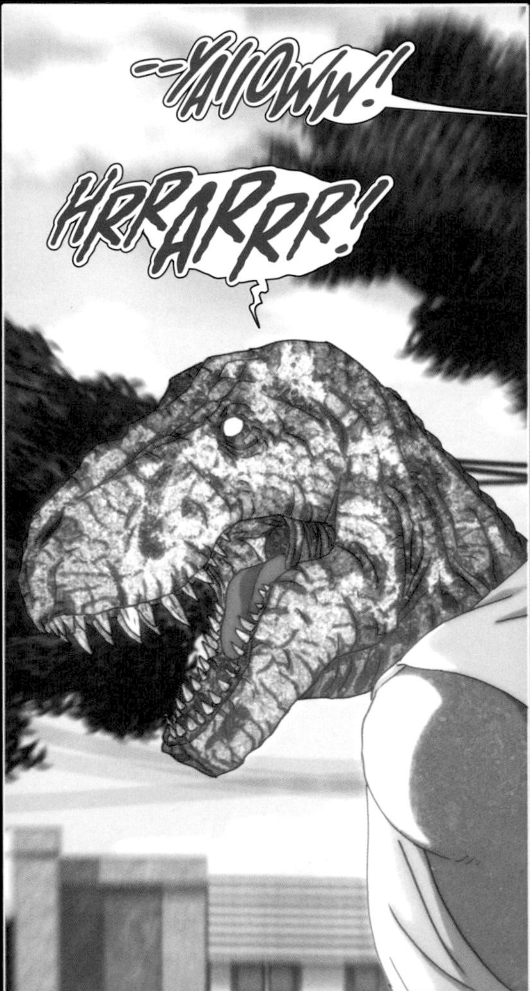
--YAIOWW!
HRRARRR!

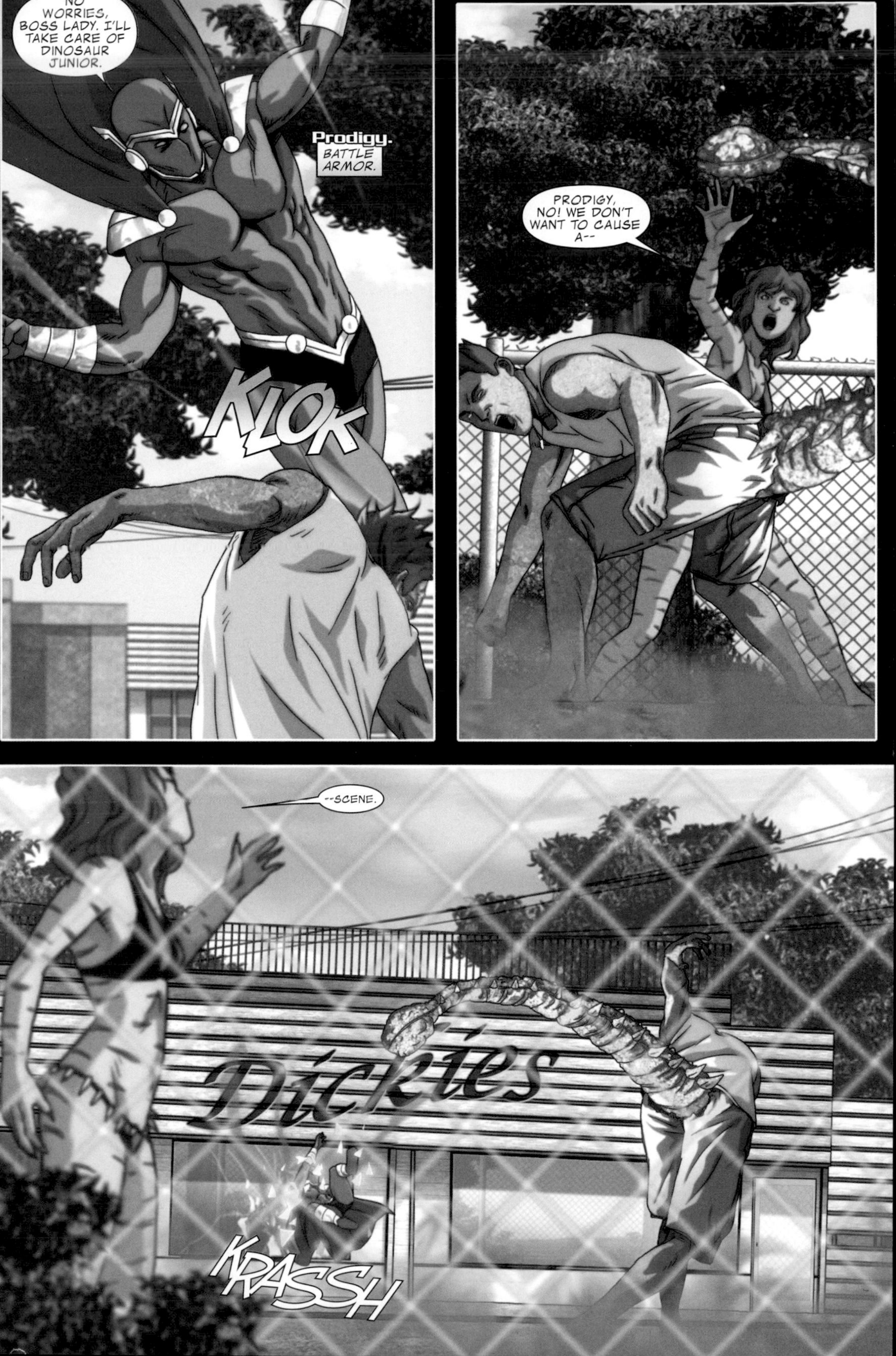
NO WORRIES, BOSS LADY. I'LL TAKE CARE OF DINOSAUR JUNIOR.
Prodigy.
BATTLE ARMOR.
KLOK
PRODIGY, NO! WE DON'T WANT TO CAUSE A--
--SCENE.
Dickies
KRASSH

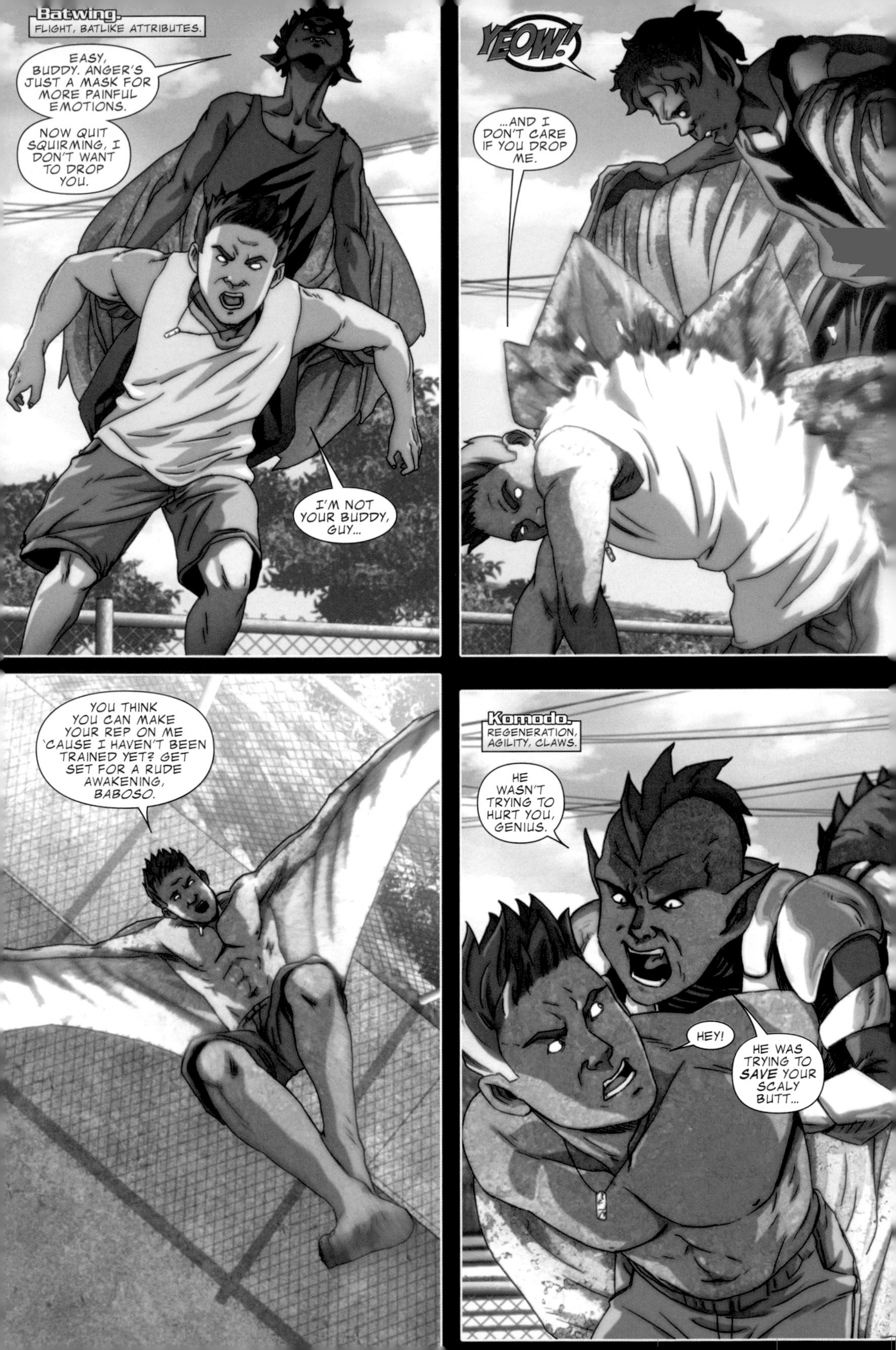
Batwing.
FLIGHT, BATLIKE ATTRIBUTES.
EASY, BUDDY. ANGER'S JUST A MASK FOR MORE PAINFUL EMOTIONS.
NOW QUIT SQUIRMING, I DON'T WANT TO DROP YOU.
I'M NOT YOUR BUDDY, GUY...
YEOW!
...AND I DON'T CARE IF YOU DROP ME.
YOU THINK YOU CAN MAKE YOUR REP ON ME 'CAUSE I HAVEN'T BEEN TRAINED YET? GET SET FOR A RUDE AWAKENING, BABOSO.
Komodo.
REGENERATION, AGILITY, CLAWS.
HE WASN'T TRYING TO HURT YOU, GENIUS.
HEY!
HE WAS TRYING TO SAVE YOUR SCALY BUTT...

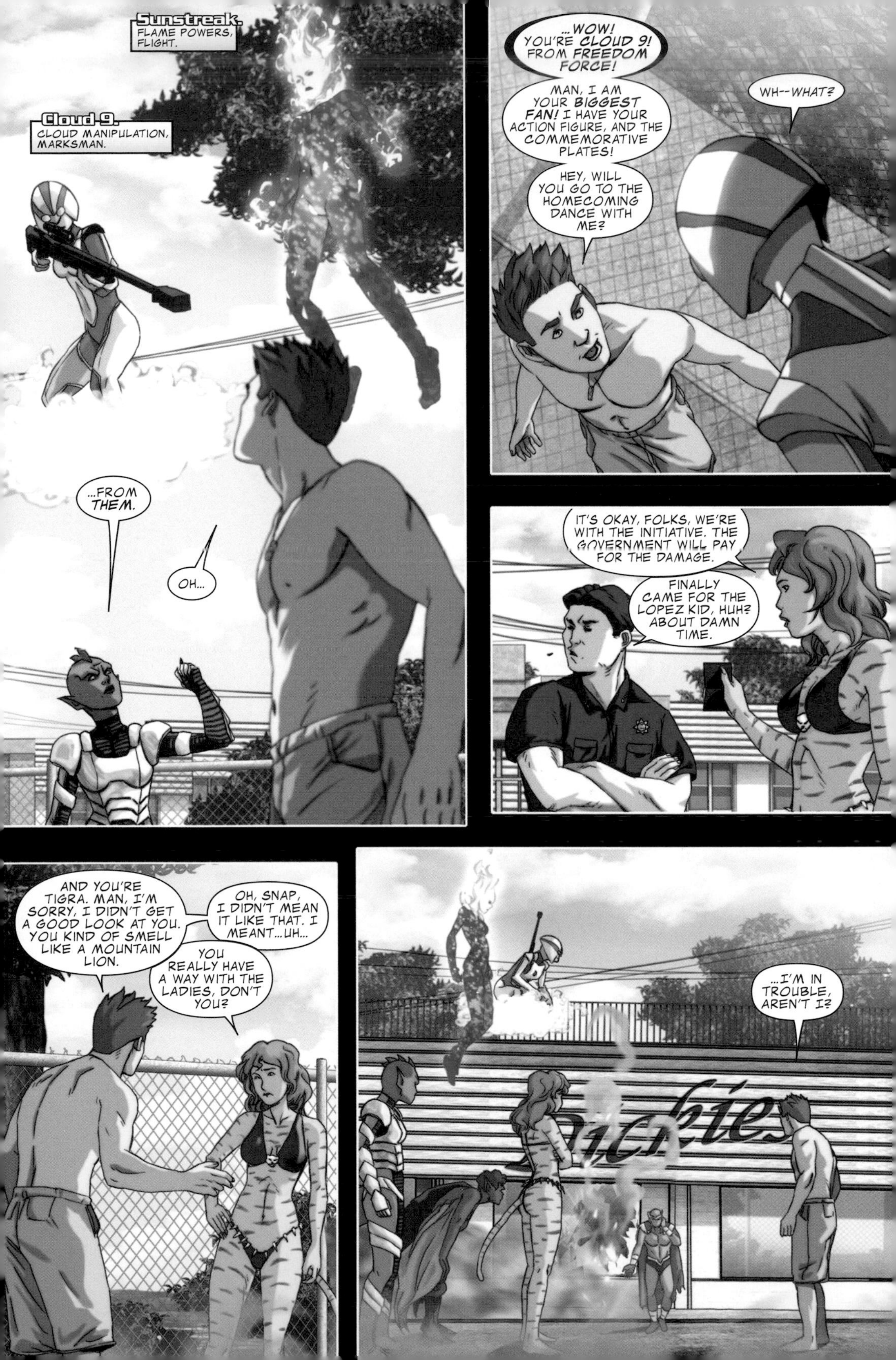
Sunstreak.
FLAME POWERS, FLIGHT.
Cloud 9.
CLOUD MANIPULATION, MARKSMAN.
...FROM THEM.
OH...
...WOW! YOU'RE CLOUD 9! FROM FREEDOM FORCE!
MAN, I AM YOUR BIGGEST FAN! I HAVE YOUR ACTION FIGURE, AND THE COMMEMORATIVE PLATES!
HEY, WILL YOU GO TO THE HOMECOMING DANCE WITH ME?
WH--WHAT?
IT'S OKAY, FOLKS, WE'RE WITH THE INITIATIVE. THE GOVERNMENT WILL PAY FOR THE DAMAGE.
FINALLY CAME FOR THE LOPEZ KID, HUH? ABOUT DAMN TIME.
AND YOU'RE TIGRA. MAN, I'M SORRY, I DIDN'T GET A GOOD LOOK AT YOU. YOU KIND OF SMELL LIKE A MOUNTAIN LION.
OH, SNAP, I DIDN'T MEAN IT LIKE THAT. I MEANT...UH...
YOU REALLY HAVE A WAY WITH THE LADIES, DON'T YOU?
...I'M IN TROUBLE, AREN'T I?

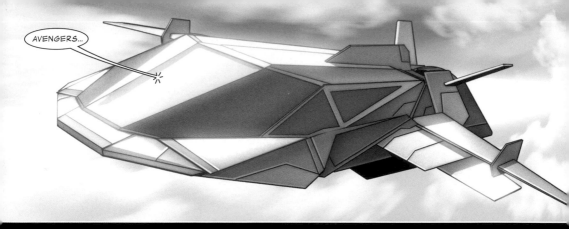

AVENGERS...

...**ASSEMBLE!!**

WILL SOMEONE *PLEASE* SHUT HIM UP?

YOU'RE A LONG WAY FROM BEING AN AVENGER, HUMBERTO.

CALL ME *REPTIL*. MY GRANDFATHER TRADEMARKED IT AND EVERYTHING.

AND I'M *ON THE WAY*, RIGHT? THIS IS THE FIRST STEP TO BEING A FULL-ON SUPER HERO, LIKE YOU AND CLOUD 9.

I HAVE COMMEMORATIVE PLATES?

LET'S SLOW DOWN A LITTLE, REPTIL. TELL ME HOW YOU GOT YOUR POWERS.

WELL, UH, MY PARENTS WERE--*ARE* PALEONTOLOGISTS. I LIKE TO GO OUT TO THE DESERT AND LOOK FOR FOSSILS. YOU CAN FIND TRILOBITES, BRACHIOPODS... ANYWAY, ONE DAY I DUG UP *THIS.*

LOOKS LIKE A PIECE OF CRYSTALLIZED BONE.

THERE WAS A ROCKSLIDE...I RAN TO GET OUT OF THE WAY. IT WAS ONLY WHEN I WAS SAFE THAT I REALIZED HOW FAR I'D GONE AND HOW *FAST.*

I CAN TAKE ON THE ABILITIES OF DIFFERENT DINOSAURS JUST BY THINKING ABOUT IT.

BUT ONLY ONE THING AT A TIME, RIGHT? YOU CAN'T SHIFT COMPLETELY INTO DINOSAUR FORM.

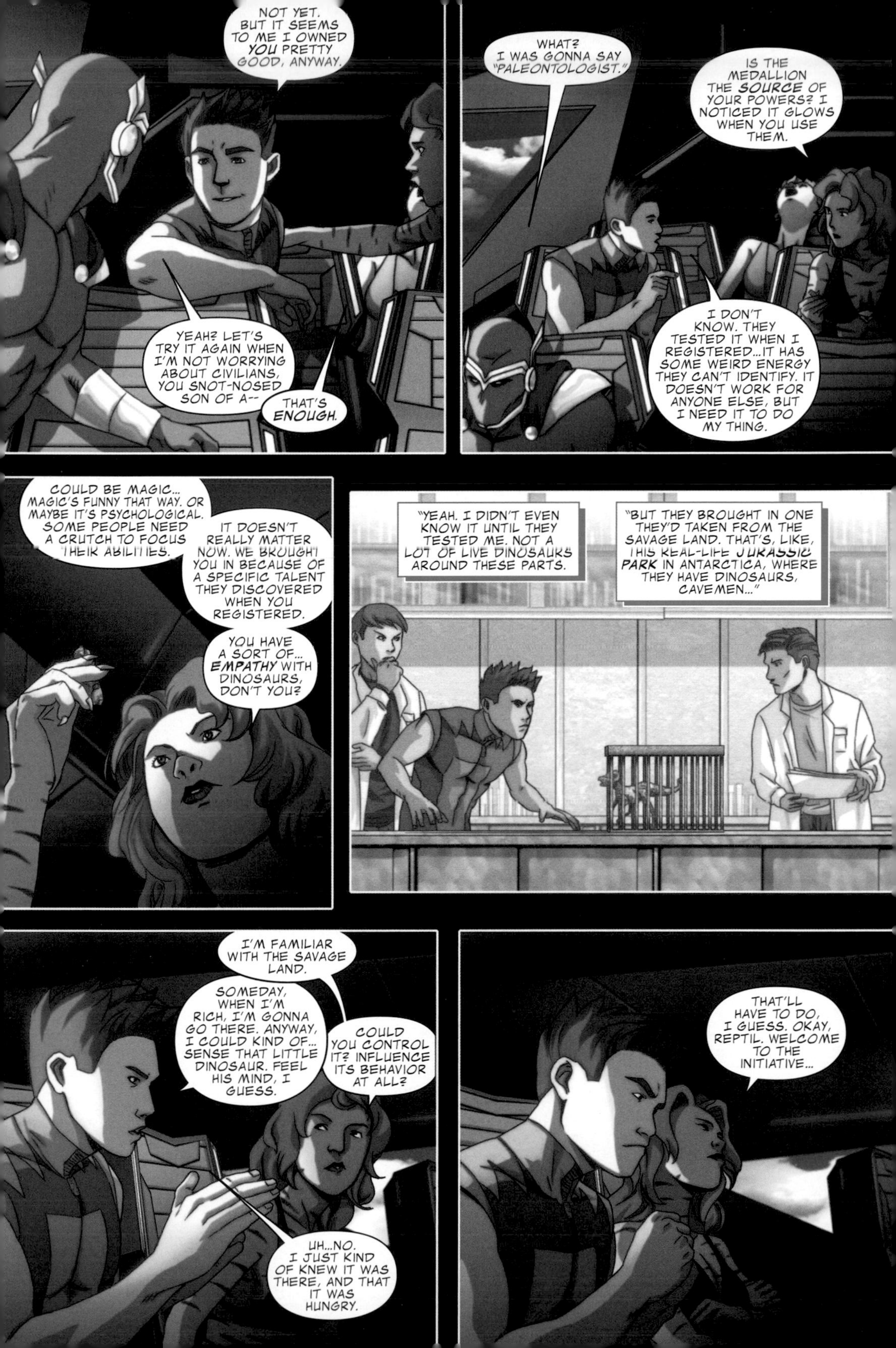
NOT YET. BUT IT SEEMS TO ME I OWNED YOU PRETTY GOOD, ANYWAY.
YEAH? LET'S TRY IT AGAIN WHEN I'M NOT WORRYING ABOUT CIVILIANS, YOU SNOT-NOSED SON OF A--
THAT'S ENOUGH.
WHAT? I WAS GONNA SAY "PALEONTOLOGIST."
IS THE MEDALLION THE SOURCE OF YOUR POWERS? I NOTICED IT GLOWS WHEN YOU USE THEM.
I DON'T KNOW. THEY TESTED IT WHEN I REGISTERED...IT HAS SOME WEIRD ENERGY THEY CAN'T IDENTIFY. IT DOESN'T WORK FOR ANYONE ELSE, BUT I NEED IT TO DO MY THING.
COULD BE MAGIC... MAGIC'S FUNNY THAT WAY. OR MAYBE IT'S PSYCHOLOGICAL. SOME PEOPLE NEED A CRUTCH TO FOCUS THEIR ABILITIES.
IT DOESN'T REALLY MATTER NOW. WE BROUGHT YOU IN BECAUSE OF A SPECIFIC TALENT THEY DISCOVERED WHEN YOU REGISTERED.
YOU HAVE A SORT OF... EMPATHY WITH DINOSAURS, DON'T YOU?
"YEAH. I DIDN'T EVEN KNOW IT UNTIL THEY TESTED ME. NOT A LOT OF LIVE DINOSAURS AROUND THESE PARTS.
"BUT THEY BROUGHT IN ONE THEY'D TAKEN FROM THE SAVAGE LAND. THAT'S, LIKE, THIS REAL-LIFE JURASSIC PARK IN ANTARCTICA, WHERE THEY HAVE DINOSAURS, CAVEMEN..."
I'M FAMILIAR WITH THE SAVAGE LAND.
SOMEDAY, WHEN I'M RICH, I'M GONNA GO THERE. ANYWAY, I COULD KIND OF... SENSE THAT LITTLE DINOSAUR. FEEL HIS MIND, I GUESS.
COULD YOU CONTROL IT? INFLUENCE ITS BEHAVIOR AT ALL?
UH...NO. I JUST KIND OF KNEW IT WAS THERE, AND THAT IT WAS HUNGRY.
THAT'LL HAVE TO DO, I GUESS. OKAY, REPTIL. WELCOME TO THE INITIATIVE...

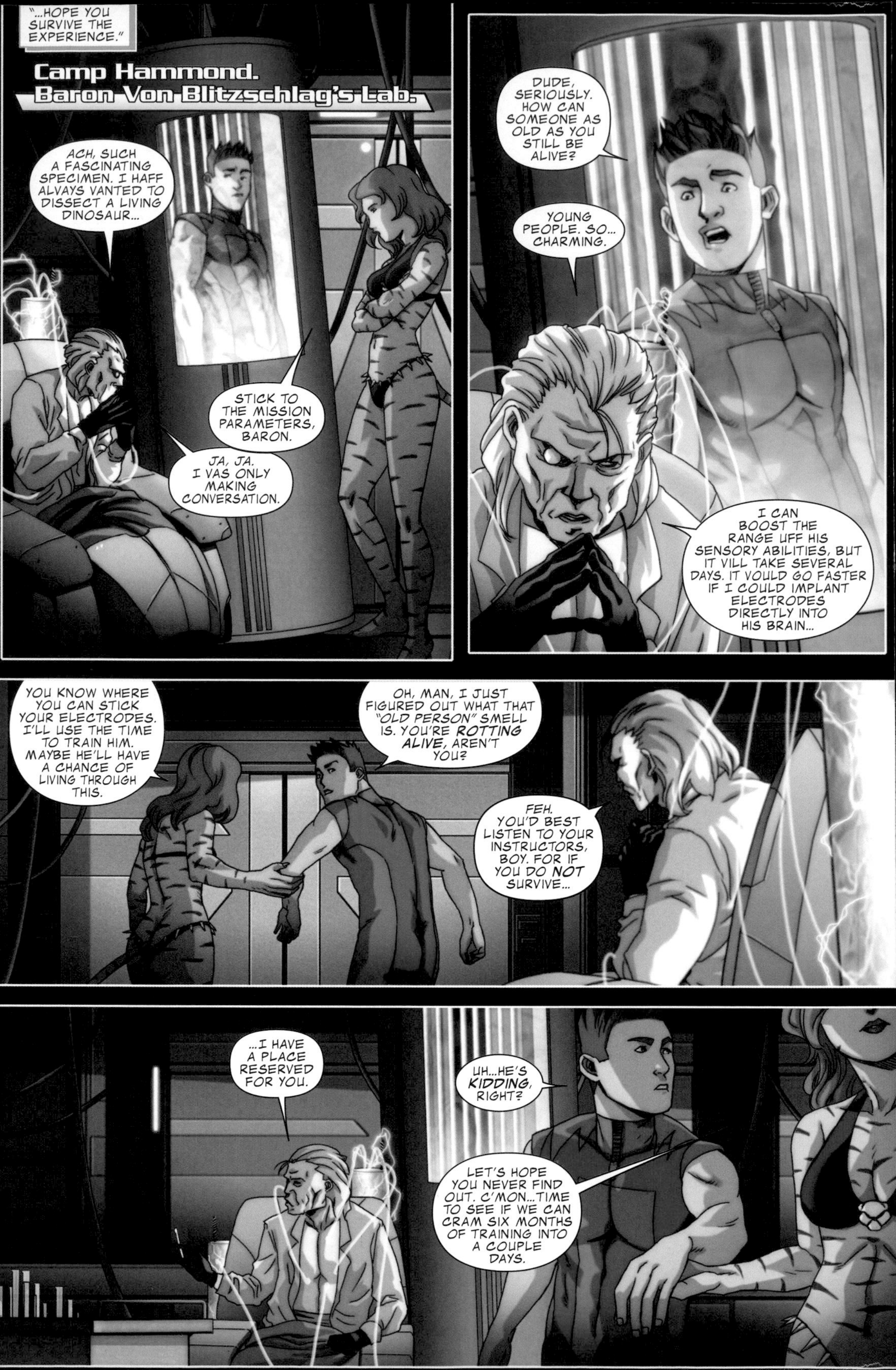
"...HOPE YOU SURVIVE THE EXPERIENCE."
Camp Hammond. Baron Von Blitzschlag's Lab.
ACH, SUCH A FASCINATING SPECIMEN. I HAFF ALVAYS VANTED TO DISSECT A LIVING DINOSAUR...
STICK TO THE MISSION PARAMETERS, BARON.
JA, JA. I VAS ONLY MAKING CONVERSATION.
DUDE, SERIOUSLY. HOW CAN SOMEONE AS OLD AS YOU STILL BE ALIVE?
YOUNG PEOPLE. SO... CHARMING.
I CAN BOOST THE RANGE UFF HIS SENSORY ABILITIES, BUT IT VILL TAKE SEVERAL DAYS. IT VOULD GO FASTER IF I COULD IMPLANT ELECTRODES DIRECTLY INTO HIS BRAIN...
YOU KNOW WHERE YOU CAN STICK YOUR ELECTRODES. I'LL USE THE TIME TO TRAIN HIM. MAYBE HE'LL HAVE A CHANCE OF LIVING THROUGH THIS.
OH, MAN, I JUST FIGURED OUT WHAT THAT "OLD PERSON" SMELL IS. YOU'RE ROTTING ALIVE, AREN'T YOU?
FEH. YOU'D BEST LISTEN TO YOUR INSTRUCTORS, BOY. FOR IF YOU DO NOT SURVIVE...
...I HAVE A PLACE RESERVED FOR YOU.
UH...HE'S KIDDING, RIGHT?
LET'S HOPE YOU NEVER FIND OUT. C'MON...TIME TO SEE IF WE CAN CRAM SIX MONTHS OF TRAINING INTO A COUPLE DAYS.

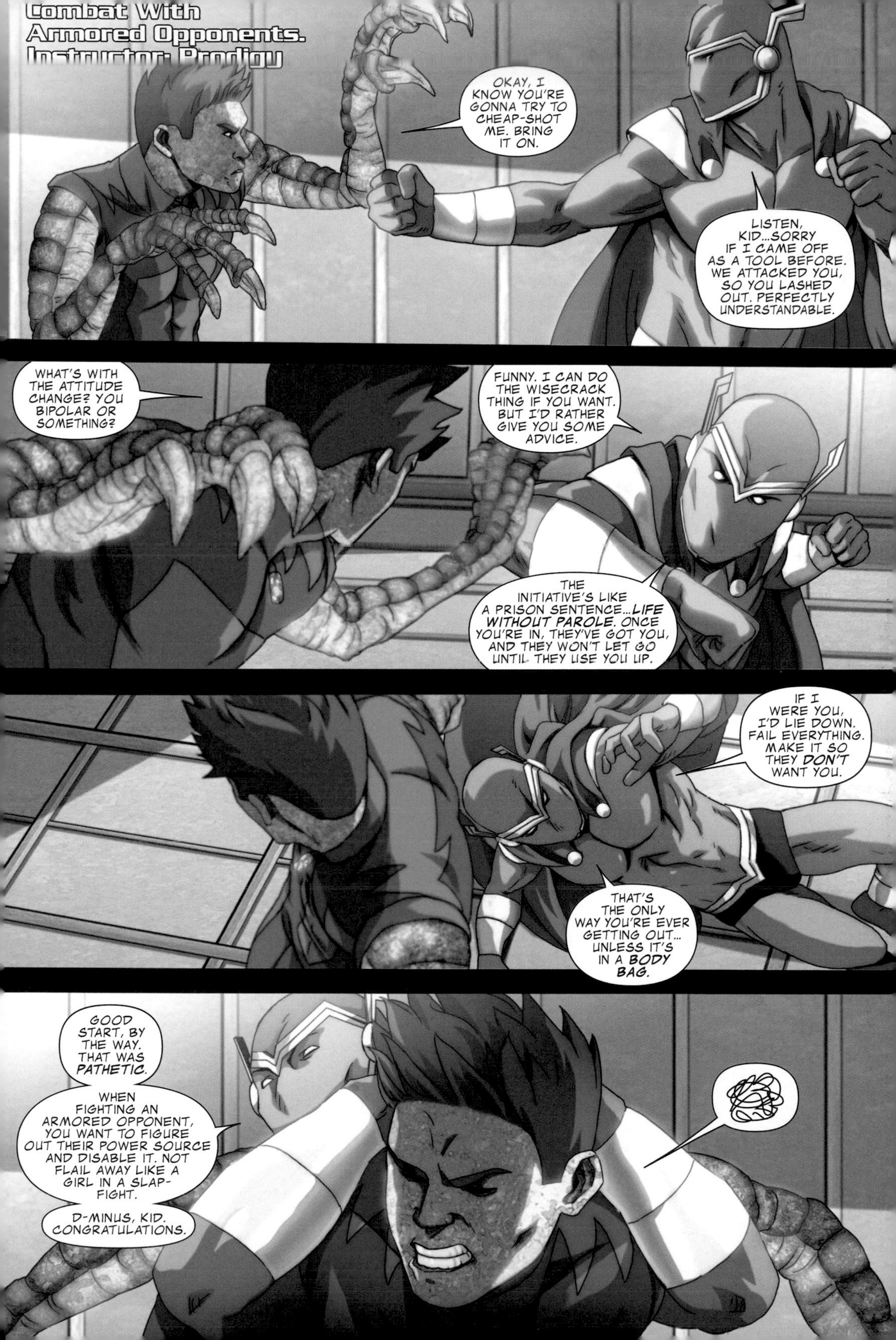
Combat With Armored Opponents. Instructor: Prodigy
OKAY, I KNOW YOU'RE GONNA TRY TO CHEAP-SHOT ME. BRING IT ON.
LISTEN, KID...SORRY IF I CAME OFF AS A TOOL BEFORE. WE ATTACKED YOU, SO YOU LASHED OUT. PERFECTLY UNDERSTANDABLE.
WHAT'S WITH THE ATTITUDE CHANGE? YOU BIPOLAR OR SOMETHING?
FUNNY. I CAN DO THE WISECRACK THING IF YOU WANT. BUT I'D RATHER GIVE YOU SOME ADVICE.
THE INITIATIVE'S LIKE A PRISON SENTENCE...LIFE WITHOUT PAROLE. ONCE YOU'RE IN, THEY'VE GOT YOU, AND THEY WON'T LET GO UNTIL THEY USE YOU UP.
IF I WERE YOU, I'D LIE DOWN. FAIL EVERYTHING. MAKE IT SO THEY DON'T WANT YOU.
THAT'S THE ONLY WAY YOU'RE EVER GETTING OUT... UNLESS IT'S IN A BODY BAG.
GOOD START, BY THE WAY. THAT WAS PATHETIC.
WHEN FIGHTING AN ARMORED OPPONENT, YOU WANT TO FIGURE OUT THEIR POWER SOURCE AND DISABLE IT. NOT FLAIL AWAY LIKE A GIRL IN A SLAP-FIGHT.
D-MINUS, KID. CONGRATULATIONS.

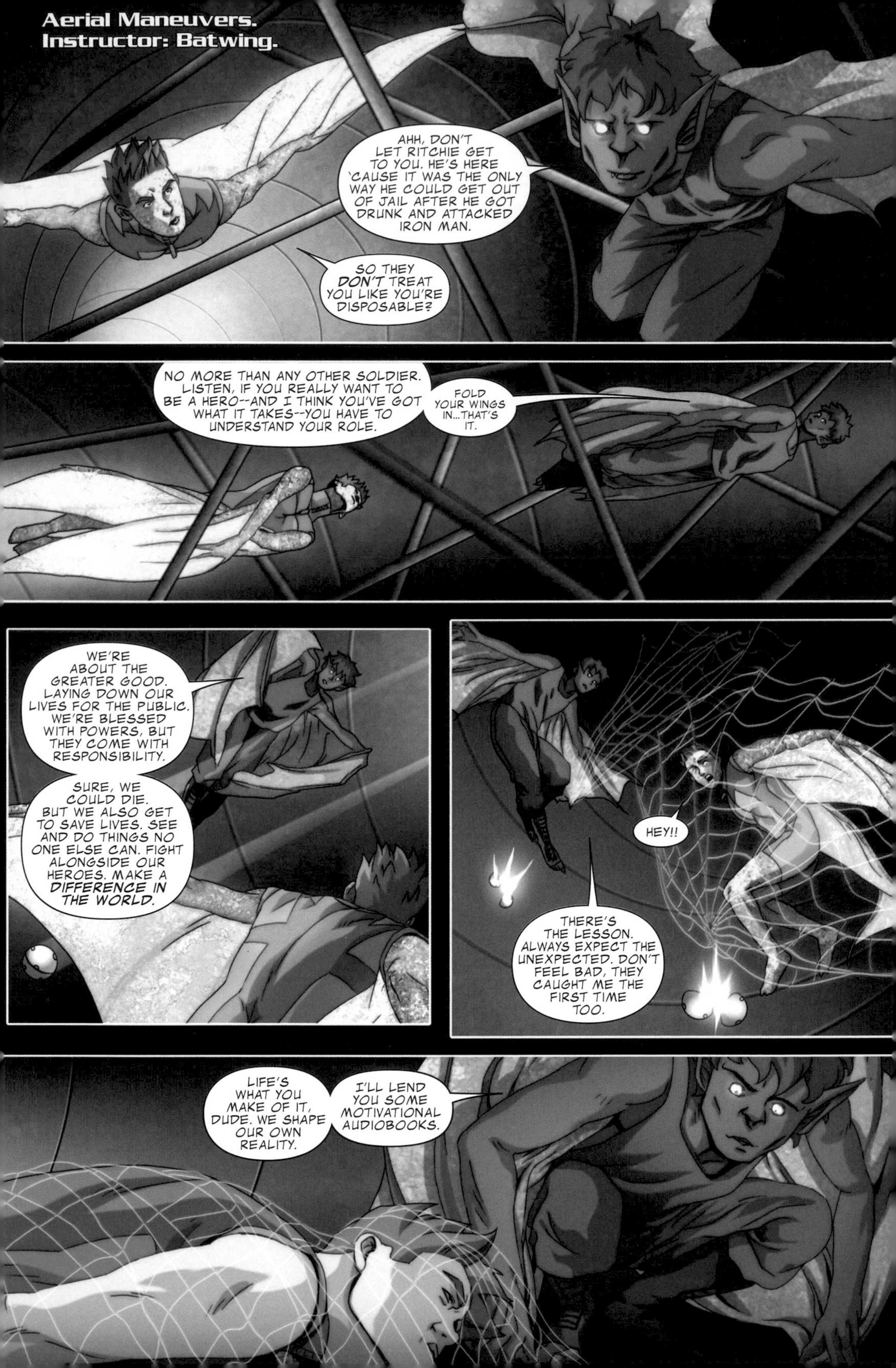
Aerial Maneuvers.
Instructor: Batwing.
AHH, DON'T LET RITCHIE GET TO YOU. HE'S HERE 'CAUSE IT WAS THE ONLY WAY HE COULD GET OUT OF JAIL AFTER HE GOT DRUNK AND ATTACKED IRON MAN.
SO THEY DON'T TREAT YOU LIKE YOU'RE DISPOSABLE?
NO MORE THAN ANY OTHER SOLDIER. LISTEN, IF YOU REALLY WANT TO BE A HERO--AND I THINK YOU'VE GOT WHAT IT TAKES--YOU HAVE TO UNDERSTAND YOUR ROLE.
FOLD YOUR WINGS IN...THAT'S IT.
WE'RE ABOUT THE GREATER GOOD. LAYING DOWN OUR LIVES FOR THE PUBLIC. WE'RE BLESSED WITH POWERS, BUT THEY COME WITH RESPONSIBILITY.
SURE, WE COULD DIE. BUT WE ALSO GET TO SAVE LIVES. SEE AND DO THINGS NO ONE ELSE CAN. FIGHT ALONGSIDE OUR HEROES. MAKE A DIFFERENCE IN THE WORLD.
HEY!!
THERE'S THE LESSON. ALWAYS EXPECT THE UNEXPECTED. DON'T FEEL BAD, THEY CAUGHT ME THE FIRST TIME TOO.
LIFE'S WHAT YOU MAKE OF IT, DUDE. WE SHAPE OUR OWN REALITY.
I'LL LEND YOU SOME MOTIVATIONAL AUDIOBOOKS.

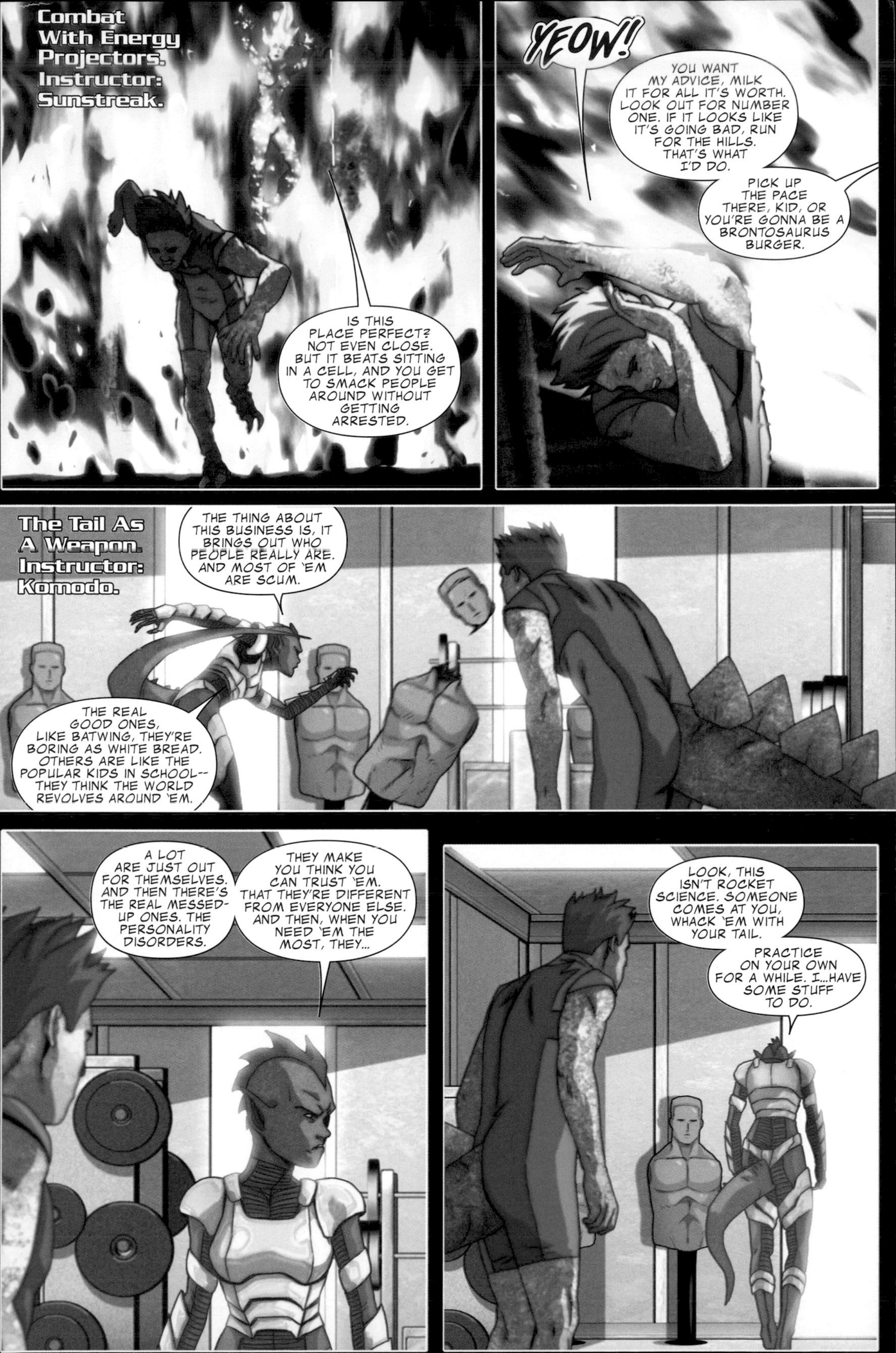
Combat With Energy Projectors. Instructor: Sunstreak.
IS THIS PLACE PERFECT? NOT EVEN CLOSE. BUT IT BEATS SITTING IN A CELL, AND YOU GET TO SMACK PEOPLE AROUND WITHOUT GETTING ARRESTED.
YEOW!!
YOU WANT MY ADVICE, MILK IT FOR ALL IT'S WORTH. LOOK OUT FOR NUMBER ONE. IF IT LOOKS LIKE IT'S GOING BAD, RUN FOR THE HILLS. THAT'S WHAT I'D DO.
PICK UP THE PACE THERE, KID, OR YOU'RE GONNA BE A BRONTOSAURUS BURGER.
The Tail As A Weapon. Instructor: Komodo.
THE THING ABOUT THIS BUSINESS IS, IT BRINGS OUT WHO PEOPLE REALLY ARE. AND MOST OF 'EM ARE SCUM.
THE REAL GOOD ONES, LIKE BATWING, THEY'RE BORING AS WHITE BREAD. OTHERS ARE LIKE THE POPULAR KIDS IN SCHOOL-- THEY THINK THE WORLD REVOLVES AROUND 'EM.
A LOT ARE JUST OUT FOR THEMSELVES. AND THEN THERE'S THE REAL MESSED-UP ONES. THE PERSONALITY DISORDERS.
THEY MAKE YOU THINK YOU CAN TRUST 'EM. THAT THEY'RE DIFFERENT FROM EVERYONE ELSE. AND THEN, WHEN YOU NEED 'EM THE MOST, THEY...
LOOK, THIS ISN'T ROCKET SCIENCE. SOMEONE COMES AT YOU, WHACK 'EM WITH YOUR TAIL.
PRACTICE ON YOUR OWN FOR A WHILE. I...HAVE SOME STUFF TO DO.

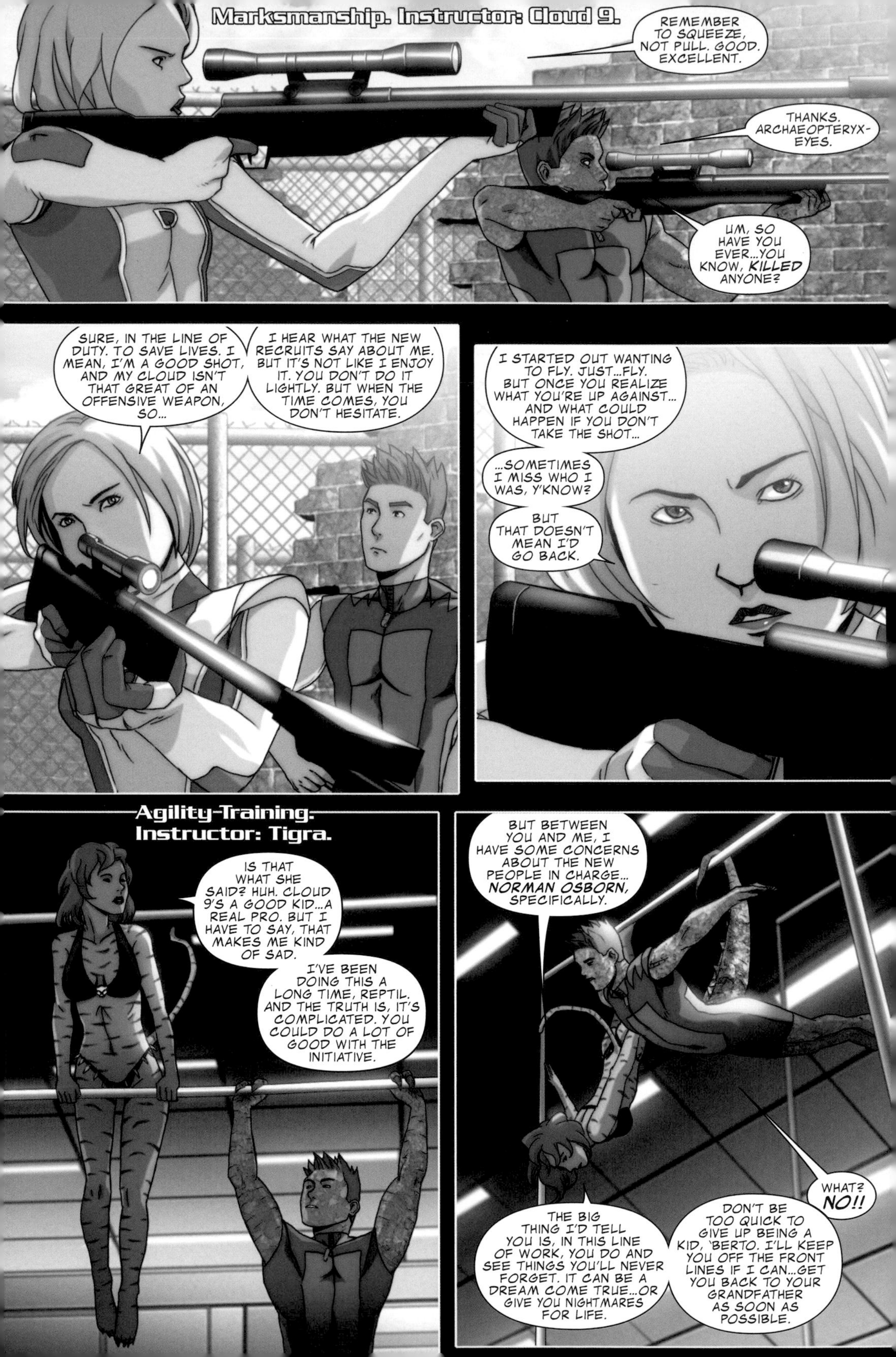
Marksmanship. Instructor: Cloud 9.
REMEMBER TO SQUEEZE, NOT PULL. GOOD. EXCELLENT.
THANKS. ARCHAEOPTERYX-EYES.
UM, SO HAVE YOU EVER...YOU KNOW, KILLED ANYONE?
SURE, IN THE LINE OF DUTY. TO SAVE LIVES. I MEAN, I'M A GOOD SHOT, AND MY CLOUD ISN'T THAT GREAT OF AN OFFENSIVE WEAPON, SO...
I HEAR WHAT THE NEW RECRUITS SAY ABOUT ME. BUT IT'S NOT LIKE I ENJOY IT. YOU DON'T DO IT LIGHTLY. BUT WHEN THE TIME COMES, YOU DON'T HESITATE.
I STARTED OUT WANTING TO FLY. JUST...FLY. BUT ONCE YOU REALIZE WHAT YOU'RE UP AGAINST... AND WHAT COULD HAPPEN IF YOU DON'T TAKE THE SHOT...
...SOMETIMES I MISS WHO I WAS, Y'KNOW?
BUT THAT DOESN'T MEAN I'D GO BACK.
Agility-Training. Instructor: Tigra.
IS THAT WHAT SHE SAID? HUH. CLOUD 9'S A GOOD KID...A REAL PRO. BUT I HAVE TO SAY, THAT MAKES ME KIND OF SAD.
I'VE BEEN DOING THIS A LONG TIME, REPTIL. AND THE TRUTH IS, IT'S COMPLICATED. YOU COULD DO A LOT OF GOOD WITH THE INITIATIVE.
BUT BETWEEN YOU AND ME, I HAVE SOME CONCERNS ABOUT THE NEW PEOPLE IN CHARGE... NORMAN OSBORN, SPECIFICALLY.
WHAT? NO!!
THE BIG THING I'D TELL YOU IS, IN THIS LINE OF WORK, YOU DO AND SEE THINGS YOU'LL NEVER FORGET. IT CAN BE A DREAM COME TRUE...OR GIVE YOU NIGHTMARES FOR LIFE.
DON'T BE TOO QUICK TO GIVE UP BEING A KID, 'BERTO. I'LL KEEP YOU OFF THE FRONT LINES IF I CAN...GET YOU BACK TO YOUR GRANDFATHER AS SOON AS POSSIBLE.

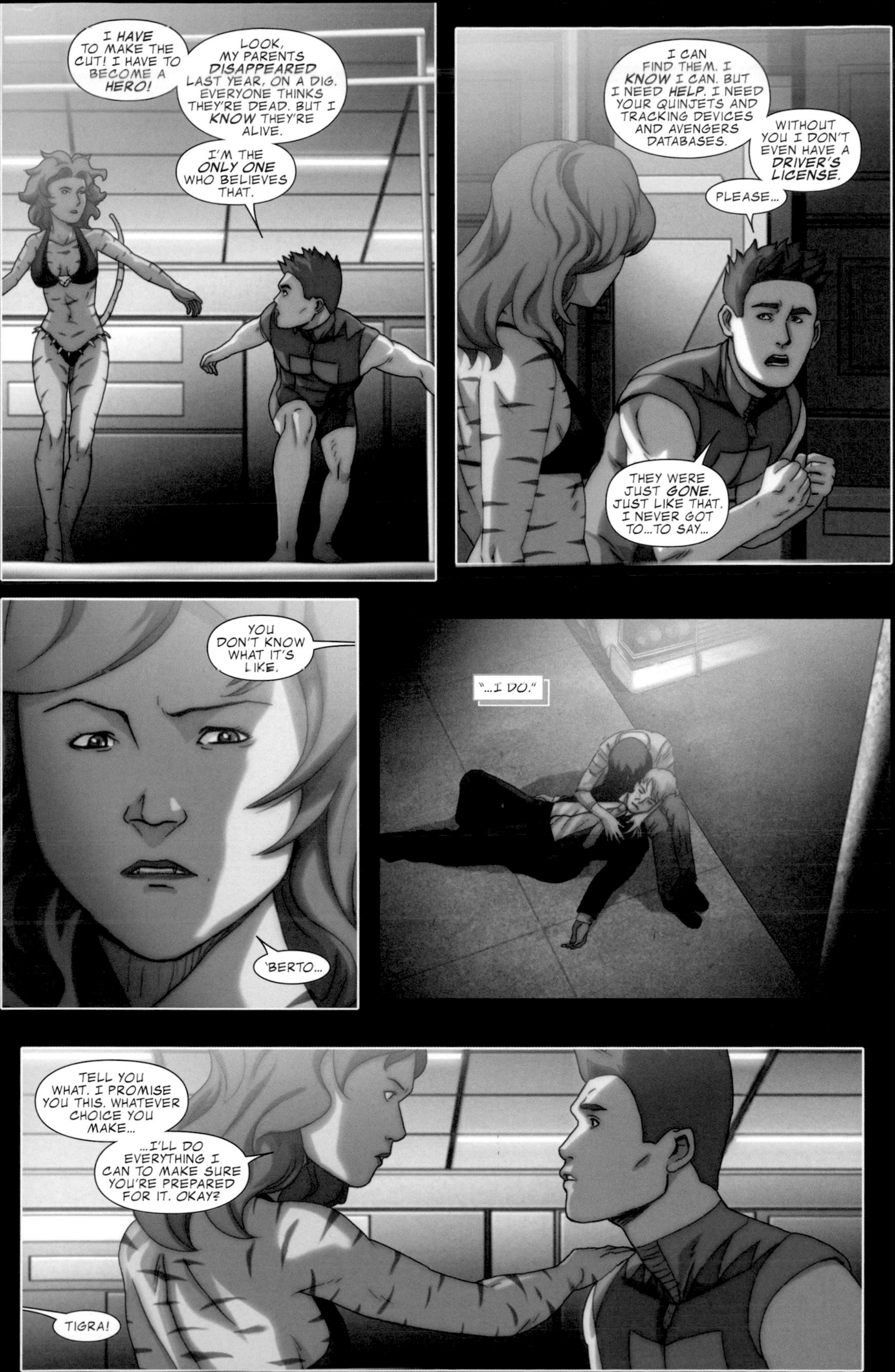
I HAVE TO MAKE THE CUT! I HAVE TO BECOME A HERO!
LOOK, MY PARENTS DISAPPEARED LAST YEAR, ON A DIG. EVERYONE THINKS THEY'RE DEAD. BUT I KNOW THEY'RE ALIVE.
I'M THE ONLY ONE WHO BELIEVES THAT.
I CAN FIND THEM. I KNOW I CAN. BUT I NEED HELP. I NEED YOUR QUINJETS AND TRACKING DEVICES AND AVENGERS DATABASES.
WITHOUT YOU I DON'T EVEN HAVE A DRIVER'S LICENSE.
PLEASE...
THEY WERE JUST GONE. JUST LIKE THAT. I NEVER GOT TO...TO SAY...
YOU DON'T KNOW WHAT IT'S LIKE.
'BERTO...
"...I DO."
TELL YOU WHAT. I PROMISE YOU THIS. WHATEVER CHOICE YOU MAKE...
...I'LL DO EVERYTHING I CAN TO MAKE SURE YOU'RE PREPARED FOR IT. OKAY?
TIGRA!

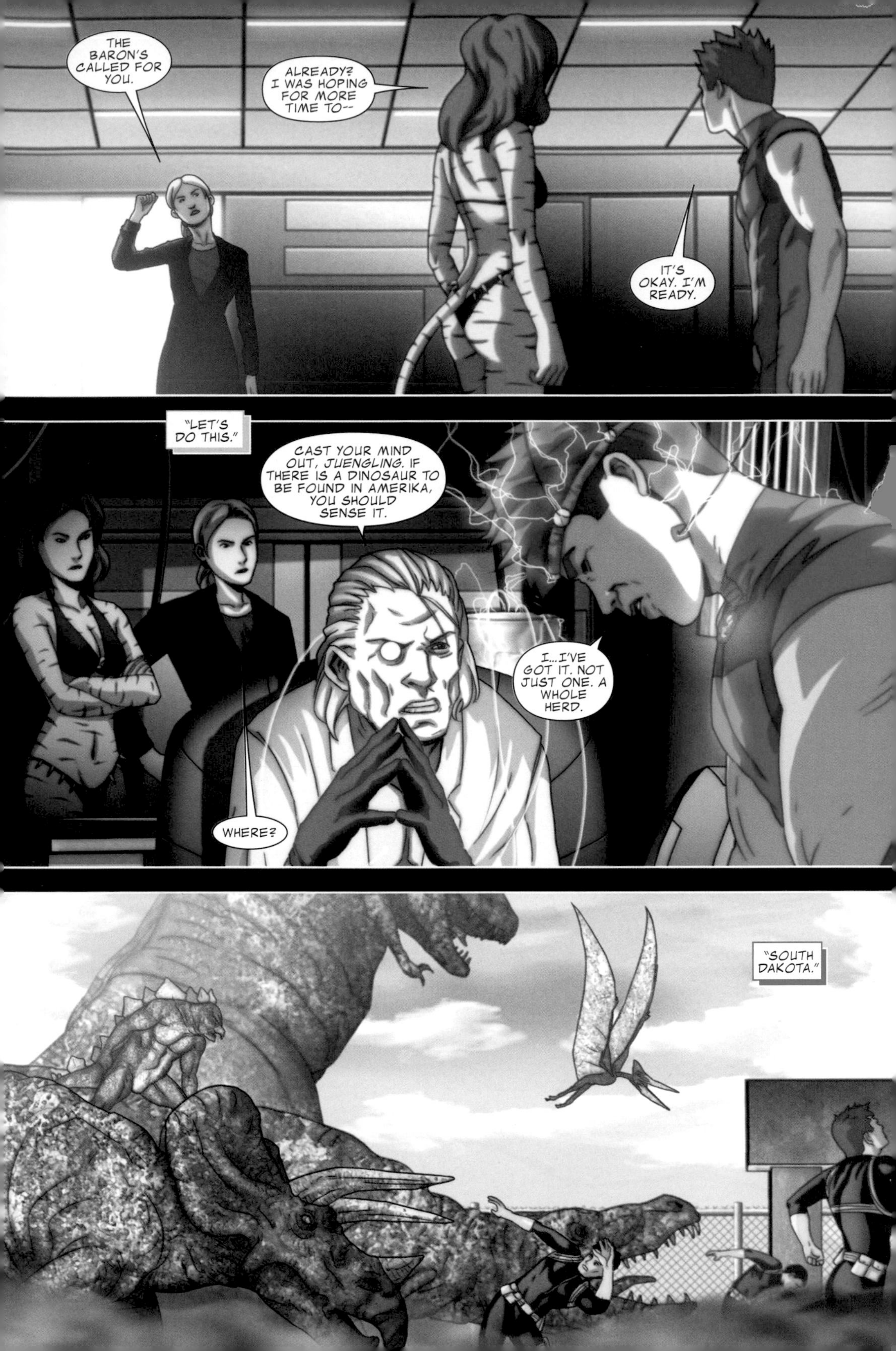
THE BARON'S CALLED FOR YOU.
ALREADY? I WAS HOPING FOR MORE TIME TO--
IT'S OKAY. I'M READY.
"LET'S DO THIS."
CAST YOUR MIND OUT, JUENGLING. IF THERE IS A DINOSAUR TO BE FOUND IN AMERIKA, YOU SHOULD SENSE IT.
I...I'VE GOT IT. NOT JUST ONE. A WHOLE HERD.
WHERE?
"SOUTH DAKOTA."

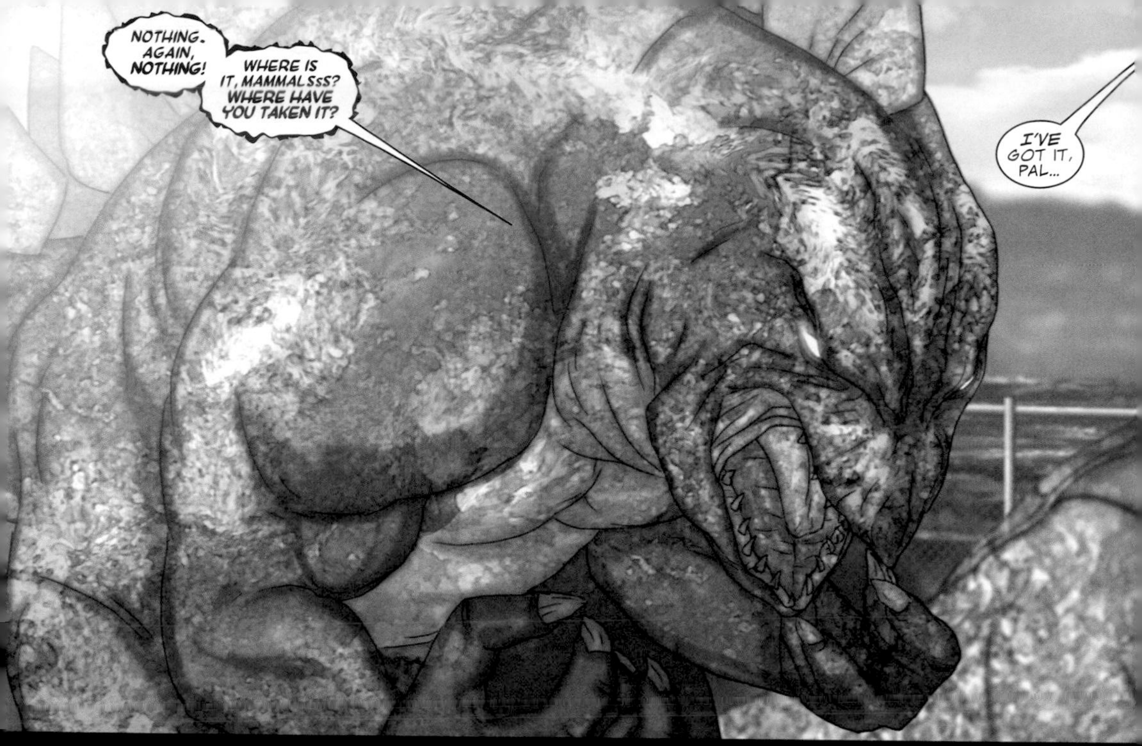
NOTHING. AGAIN, NOTHING!
WHERE IS IT, MAMMALSsS? WHERE HAVE YOU TAKEN IT?
I'VE GOT IT, PAL...

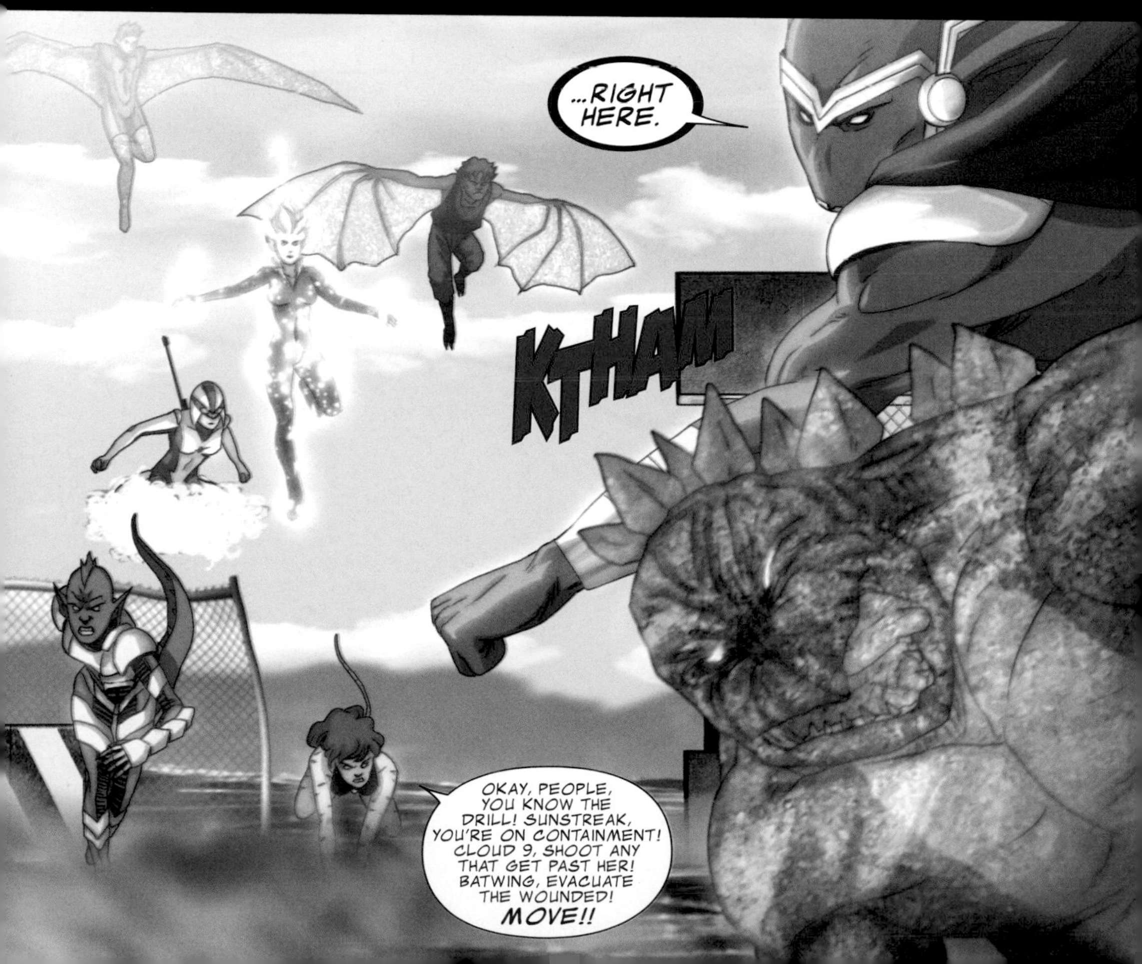
...RIGHT HERE.
KTHAM
OKAY, PEOPLE, YOU KNOW THE DRILL! SUNSTREAK, YOU'RE ON CONTAINMENT! CLOUD 9, SHOOT ANY THAT GET PAST HER! BATWING, EVACUATE THE WOUNDED! MOVE!!

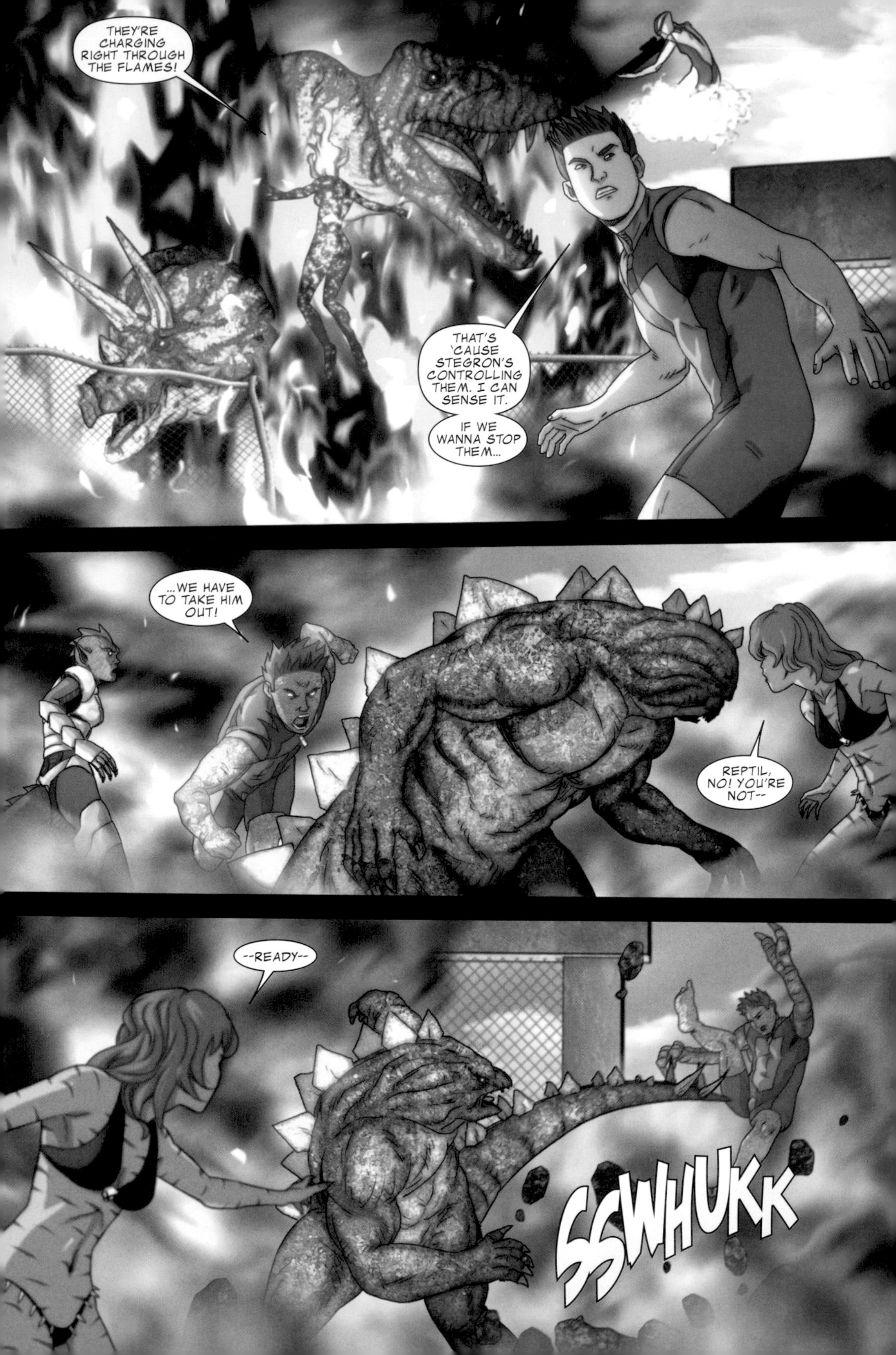
THEY'RE CHARGING RIGHT THROUGH THE FLAMES!
THAT'S 'CAUSE STEGRON'S CONTROLLING THEM. I CAN SENSE IT.
IF WE WANNA STOP THEM...
...WE HAVE TO TAKE HIM OUT!
REPTIL, NO! YOU'RE NOT--
--READY--
SSWHUKK

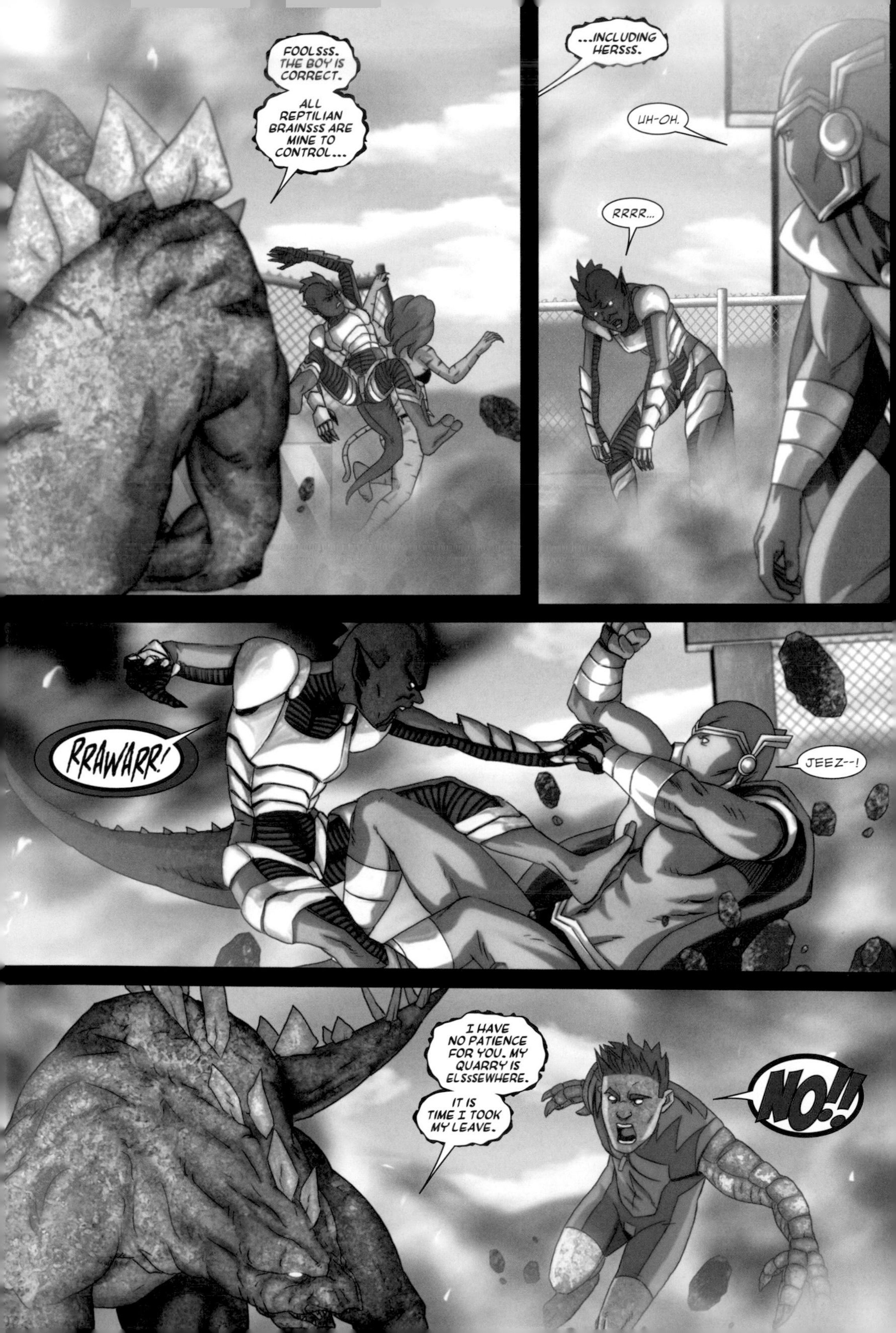
FOOLSsS. THE BOY IS CORRECT.
ALL REPTILIAN BRAINSsS ARE MINE TO CONTROL...
...INCLUDING HERSsS.
UH-OH.
RRRR...
RRAWARR!
JEEZ--!
I HAVE NO PATIENCE FOR YOU. MY QUARRY IS ELSsSEWHERE.
IT IS TIME I TOOK MY LEAVE.
NO!!

SSSTUPID WHELP.

THRAK

YOU PLAY AT BEING ONE OF US.

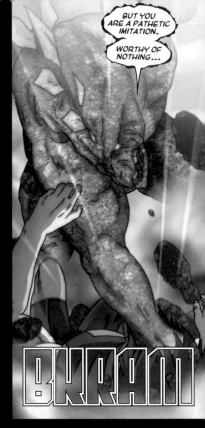

BUT YOU ARE A PATHETIC IMITATION.

WORTHY OF NOTHING...

BKRAM

...BUT EXTINCTION.

OKAY.

SO WE'LL WORK ON IMPULSE CONTROL.

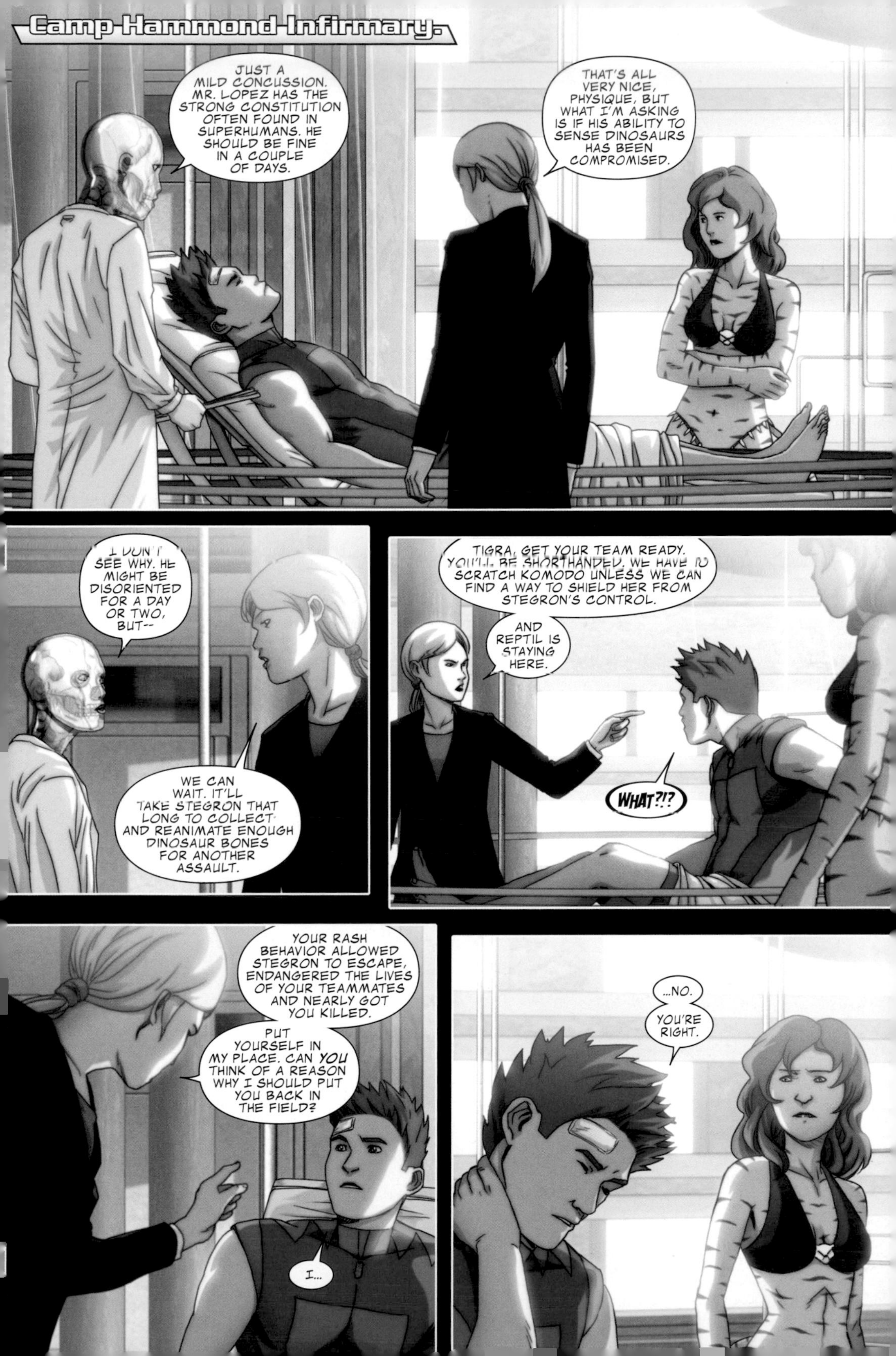
Camp Hammond Infirmary.
JUST A MILD CONCUSSION. MR. LOPEZ HAS THE STRONG CONSTITUTION OFTEN FOUND IN SUPERHUMANS. HE SHOULD BE FINE IN A COUPLE OF DAYS.
THAT'S ALL VERY NICE, PHYSIQUE, BUT WHAT I'M ASKING IS IF HIS ABILITY TO SENSE DINOSAURS HAS BEEN COMPROMISED.
I DON'T SEE WHY. HE MIGHT BE DISORIENTED FOR A DAY OR TWO, BUT--
WE CAN WAIT. IT'LL TAKE STEGRON THAT LONG TO COLLECT AND REANIMATE ENOUGH DINOSAUR BONES FOR ANOTHER ASSAULT.
TIGRA, GET YOUR TEAM READY. YOU'LL BE SHORTHANDED. WE HAVE TO SCRATCH KOMODO UNLESS WE CAN FIND A WAY TO SHIELD HER FROM STEGRON'S CONTROL.
AND REPTIL IS STAYING HERE.
WHAT?!?
YOUR RASH BEHAVIOR ALLOWED STEGRON TO ESCAPE, ENDANGERED THE LIVES OF YOUR TEAMMATES AND NEARLY GOT YOU KILLED.
PUT YOURSELF IN MY PLACE. CAN YOU THINK OF A REASON WHY I SHOULD PUT YOU BACK IN THE FIELD?
I...
...NO.
YOU'RE RIGHT.

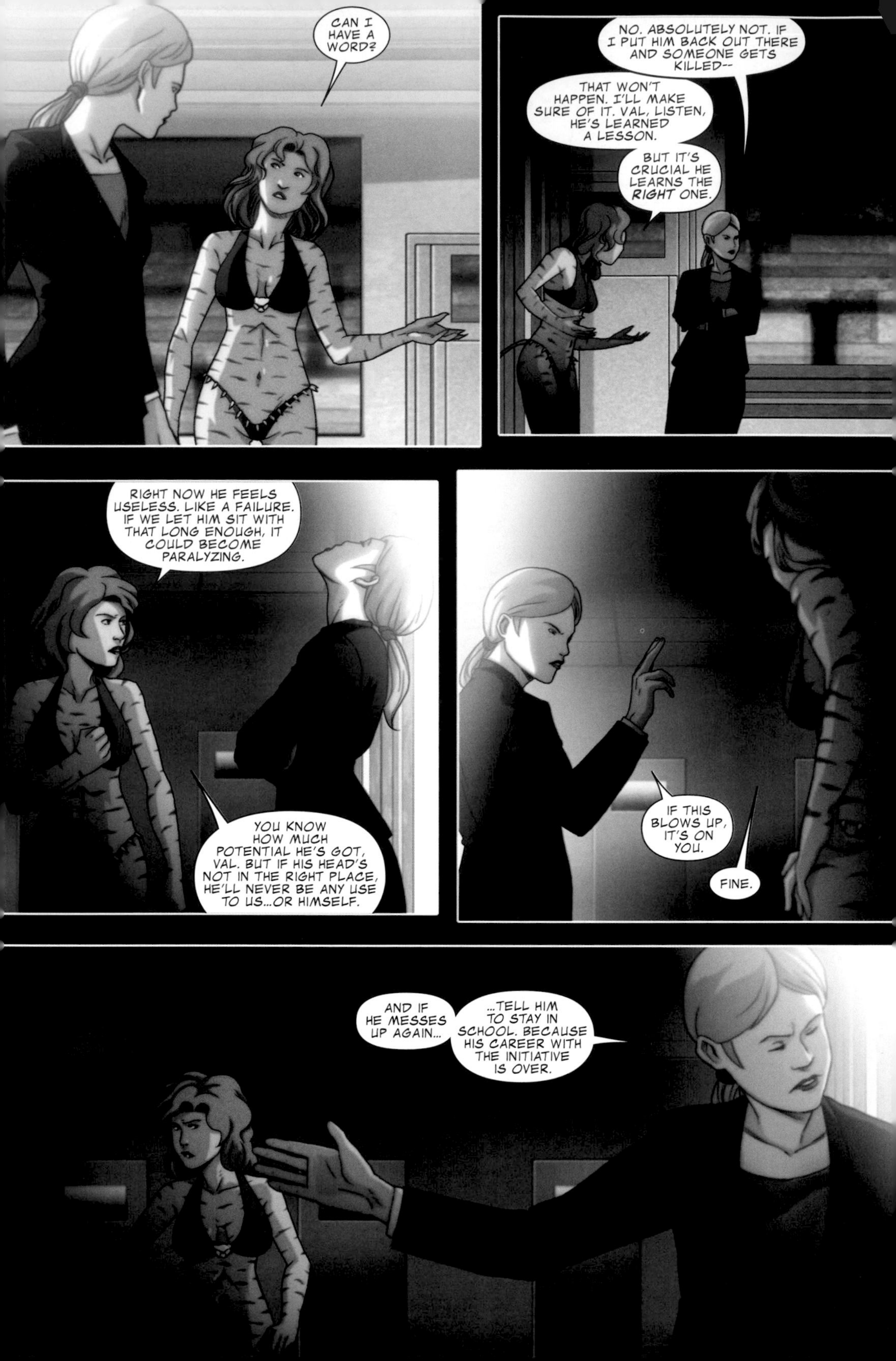

CAN I HAVE A WORD?
NO. ABSOLUTELY NOT. IF I PUT HIM BACK OUT THERE AND SOMEONE GETS KILLED--
THAT WON'T HAPPEN. I'LL MAKE SURE OF IT. VAL, LISTEN, HE'S LEARNED A LESSON.
BUT IT'S CRUCIAL HE LEARNS THE RIGHT ONE.
RIGHT NOW HE FEELS USELESS. LIKE A FAILURE. IF WE LET HIM SIT WITH THAT LONG ENOUGH, IT COULD BECOME PARALYZING.
YOU KNOW HOW MUCH POTENTIAL HE'S GOT, VAL. BUT IF HIS HEAD'S NOT IN THE RIGHT PLACE, HE'LL NEVER BE ANY USE TO US...OR HIMSELF.
IF THIS BLOWS UP, IT'S ON YOU.
FINE.
AND IF HE MESSES UP AGAIN...
...TELL HIM TO STAY IN SCHOOL. BECAUSE HIS CAREER WITH THE INITIATIVE IS OVER.

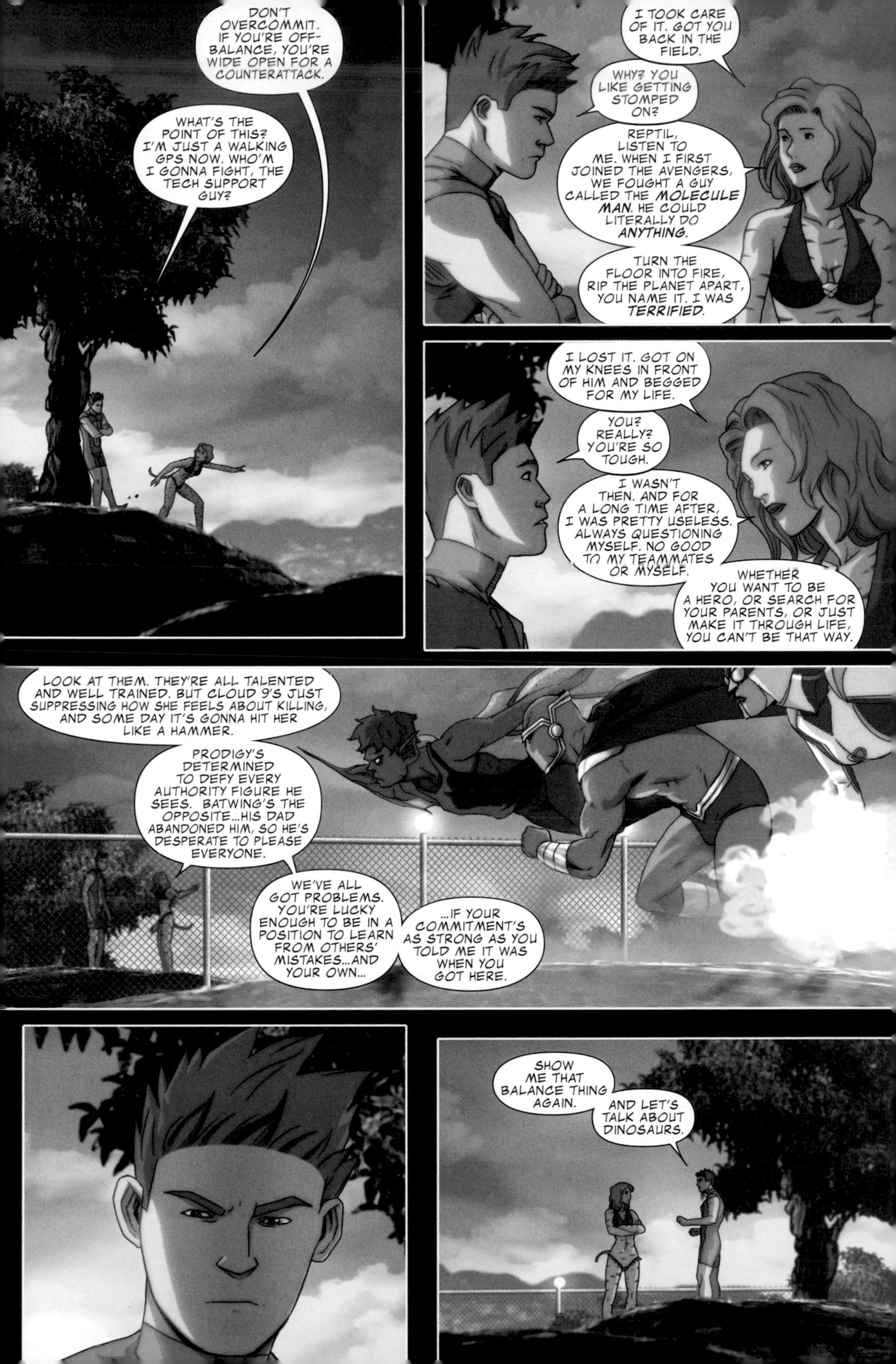
DON'T OVERCOMMIT. IF YOU'RE OFF-BALANCE, YOU'RE WIDE OPEN FOR A COUNTERATTACK.
WHAT'S THE POINT OF THIS? I'M JUST A WALKING GPS NOW. WHO'M I GONNA FIGHT, THE TECH SUPPORT GUY?
I TOOK CARE OF IT. GOT YOU BACK IN THE FIELD.
WHY? YOU LIKE GETTING STOMPED ON?
REPTIL, LISTEN TO ME. WHEN I FIRST JOINED THE AVENGERS, WE FOUGHT A GUY CALLED THE MOLECULE MAN. HE COULD LITERALLY DO ANYTHING.
TURN THE FLOOR INTO FIRE, RIP THE PLANET APART, YOU NAME IT. I WAS TERRIFIED.
I LOST IT. GOT ON MY KNEES IN FRONT OF HIM AND BEGGED FOR MY LIFE.
YOU? REALLY? YOU'RE SO TOUGH.
I WASN'T THEN. AND FOR A LONG TIME AFTER, I WAS PRETTY USELESS. ALWAYS QUESTIONING MYSELF. NO GOOD TO MY TEAMMATES OR MYSELF.
WHETHER YOU WANT TO BE A HERO, OR SEARCH FOR YOUR PARENTS, OR JUST MAKE IT THROUGH LIFE, YOU CAN'T BE THAT WAY.
LOOK AT THEM. THEY'RE ALL TALENTED AND WELL TRAINED. BUT CLOUD 9'S JUST SUPPRESSING HOW SHE FEELS ABOUT KILLING, AND SOME DAY IT'S GONNA HIT HER LIKE A HAMMER.
PRODIGY'S DETERMINED TO DEFY EVERY AUTHORITY FIGURE HE SEES. BATWING'S THE OPPOSITE...HIS DAD ABANDONED HIM, SO HE'S DESPERATE TO PLEASE EVERYONE.
WE'VE ALL GOT PROBLEMS. YOU'RE LUCKY ENOUGH TO BE IN A POSITION TO LEARN FROM OTHERS' MISTAKES...AND YOUR OWN...
...IF YOUR COMMITMENT'S AS STRONG AS YOU TOLD ME IT WAS WHEN YOU GOT HERE.
SHOW ME THAT BALANCE THING AGAIN.
AND LET'S TALK ABOUT DINOSAURS.

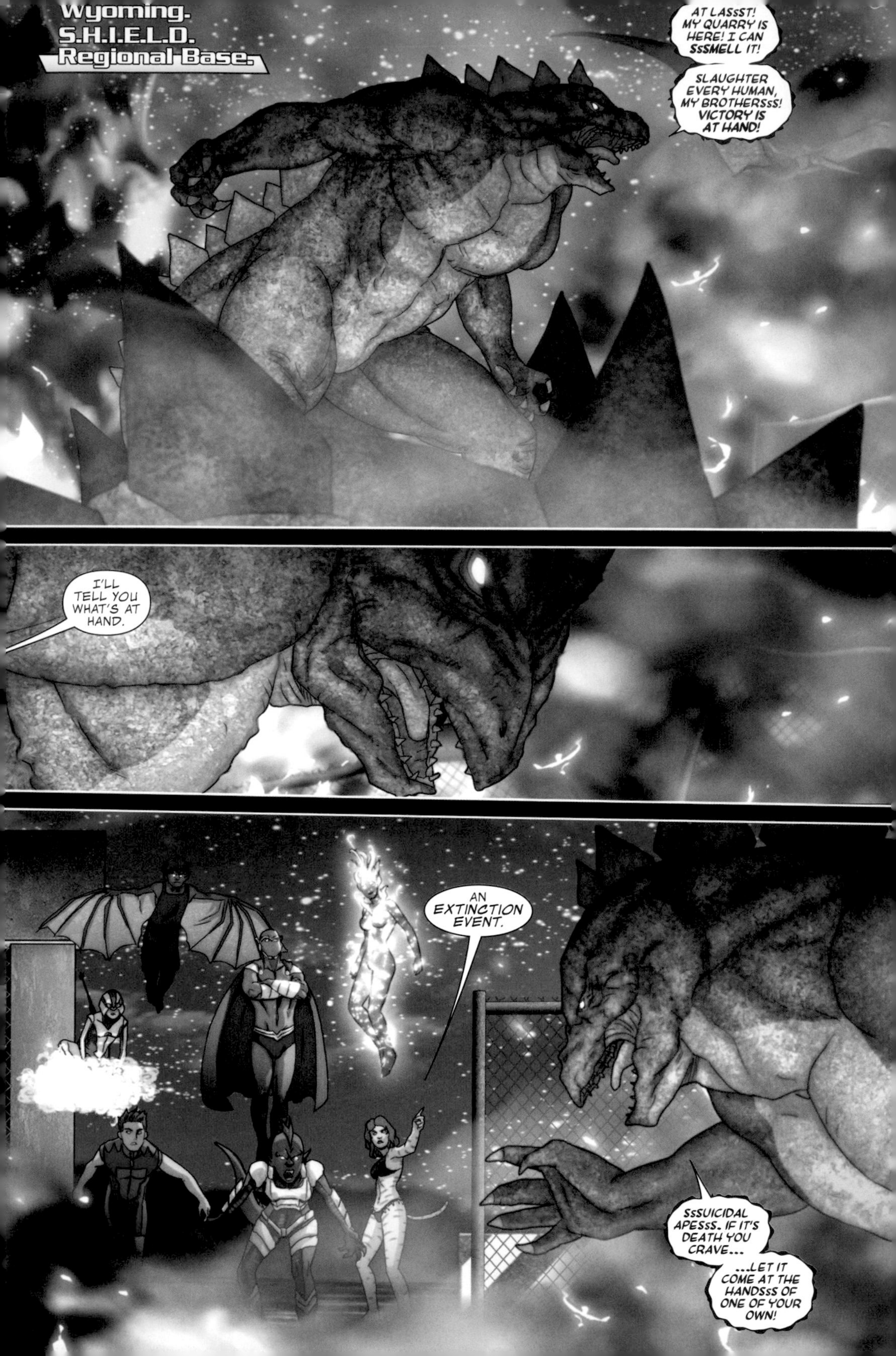
Wyoming. S.H.I.E.L.D. Regional Base.
AT LASSST! MY QUARRY IS HERE! I CAN SsSMELL IT!
SLAUGHTER EVERY HUMAN, MY BROTHERSsS! VICTORY IS AT HAND!
I'LL TELL YOU WHAT'S AT HAND.
AN EXTINCTION EVENT.
SsSUICIDAL APESsS. IF IT'S DEATH YOU CRAVE...
...LET IT COME AT THE HANDSsS OF ONE OF YOUR OWN!

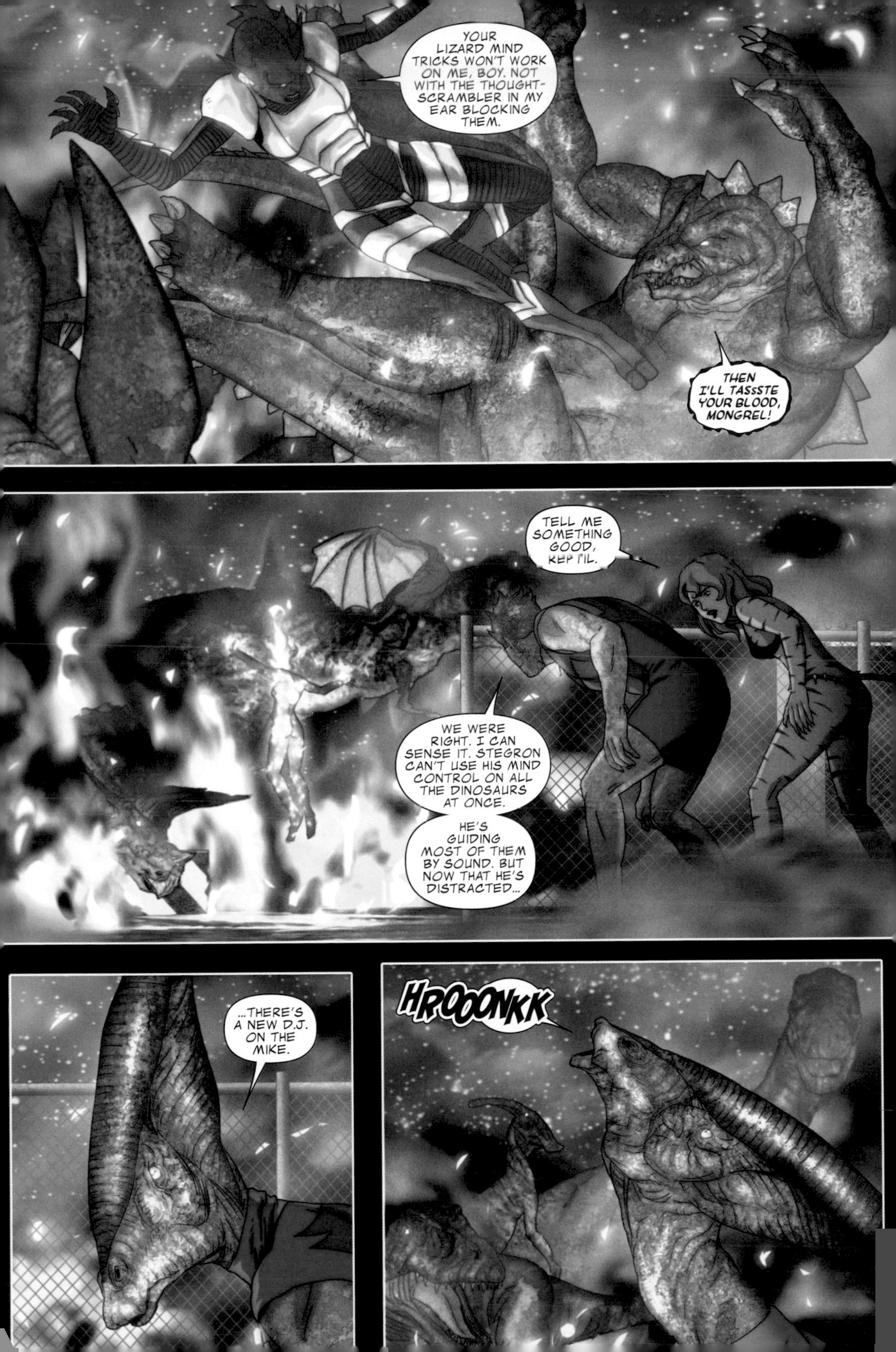
YOUR LIZARD MIND TRICKS WON'T WORK ON ME, BOY. NOT WITH THE THOUGHT-SCRAMBLER IN MY EAR BLOCKING THEM.
THEN I'LL TASsSTE YOUR BLOOD, MONGREL!
TELL ME SOMETHING GOOD, REPTIL.
WE WERE RIGHT. I CAN SENSE IT. STEGRON CAN'T USE HIS MIND CONTROL ON ALL THE DINOSAURS AT ONCE.
HE'S GUIDING MOST OF THEM BY SOUND. BUT NOW THAT HE'S DISTRACTED...
...THERE'S A NEW D.J. ON THE MIKE.
HROOOONKK

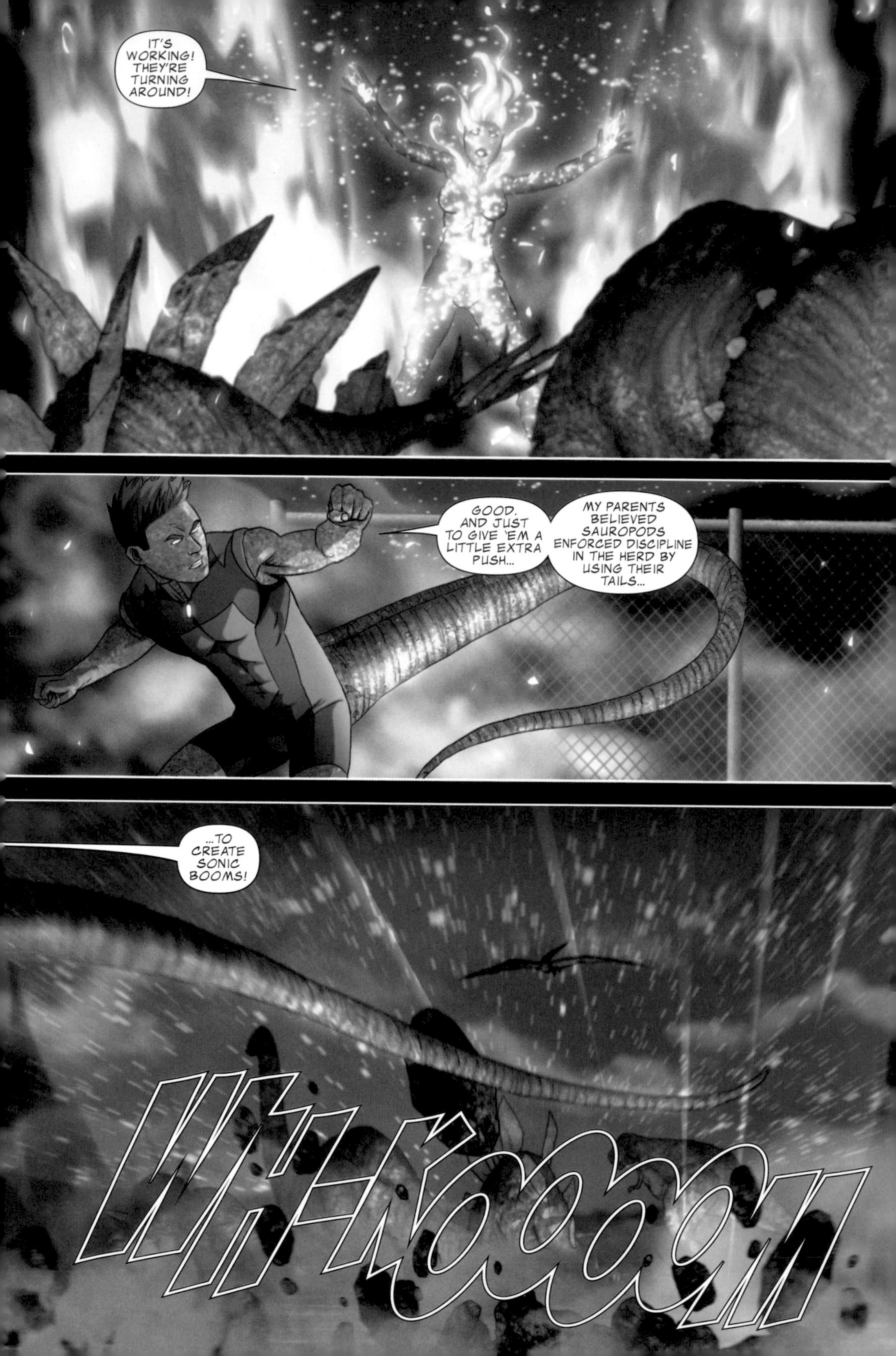
IT'S WORKING! THEY'RE TURNING AROUND!
GOOD. AND JUST TO GIVE 'EM A LITTLE EXTRA PUSH...
MY PARENTS BELIEVED SAUROPODS ENFORCED DISCIPLINE IN THE HERD BY USING THEIR TAILS...
...TO CREATE SONIC BOOMS!
WHOOOOM

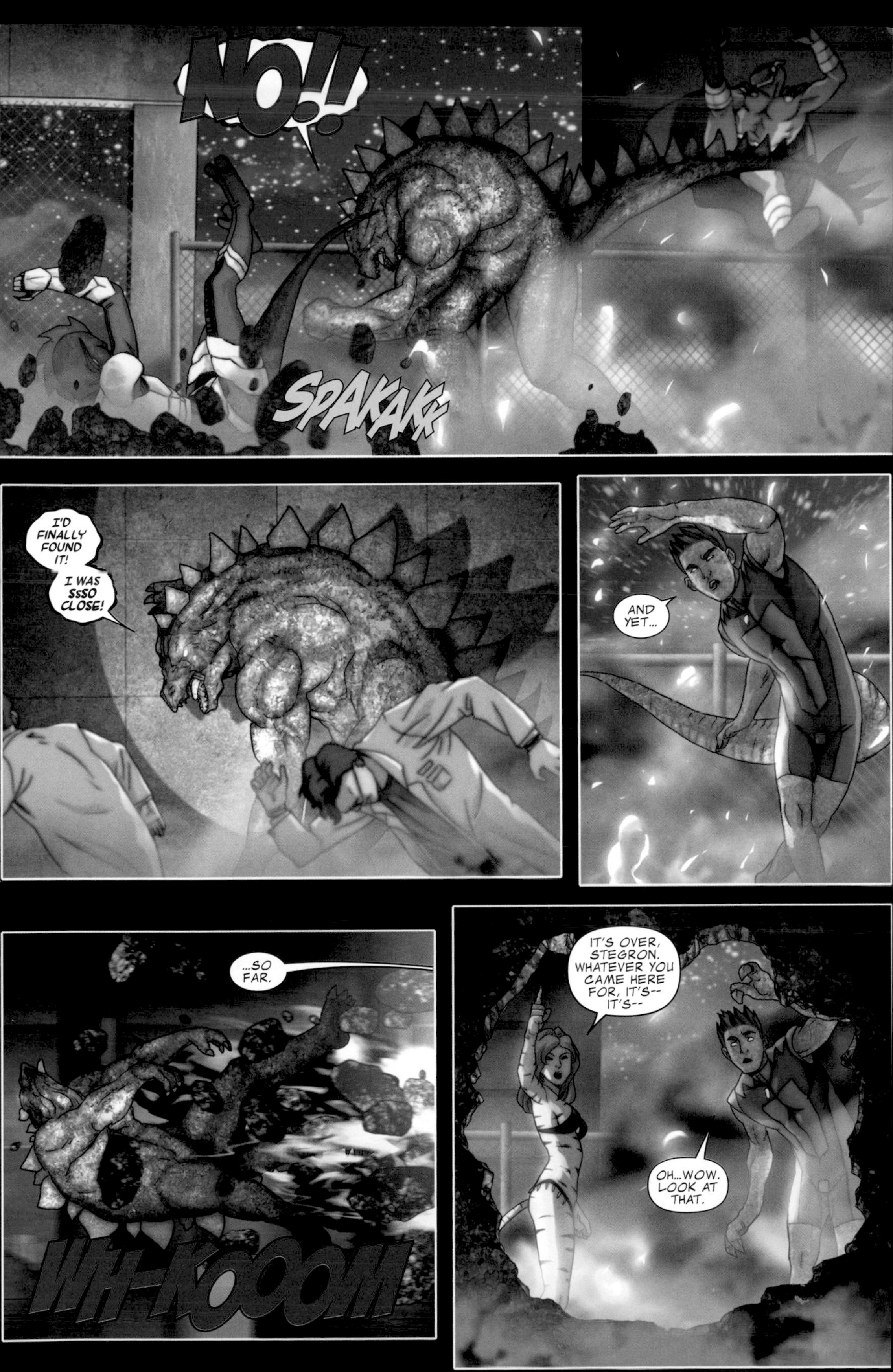
NO!!
SPAKAKK
I'D FINALLY FOUND IT!
I WAS SsSO CLOSE!
AND YET...
...SO FAR.
WH-KOOOM
IT'S OVER, STEGRON. WHATEVER YOU CAME HERE FOR, IT'S-- IT'S--
OH...WOW. LOOK AT THAT.

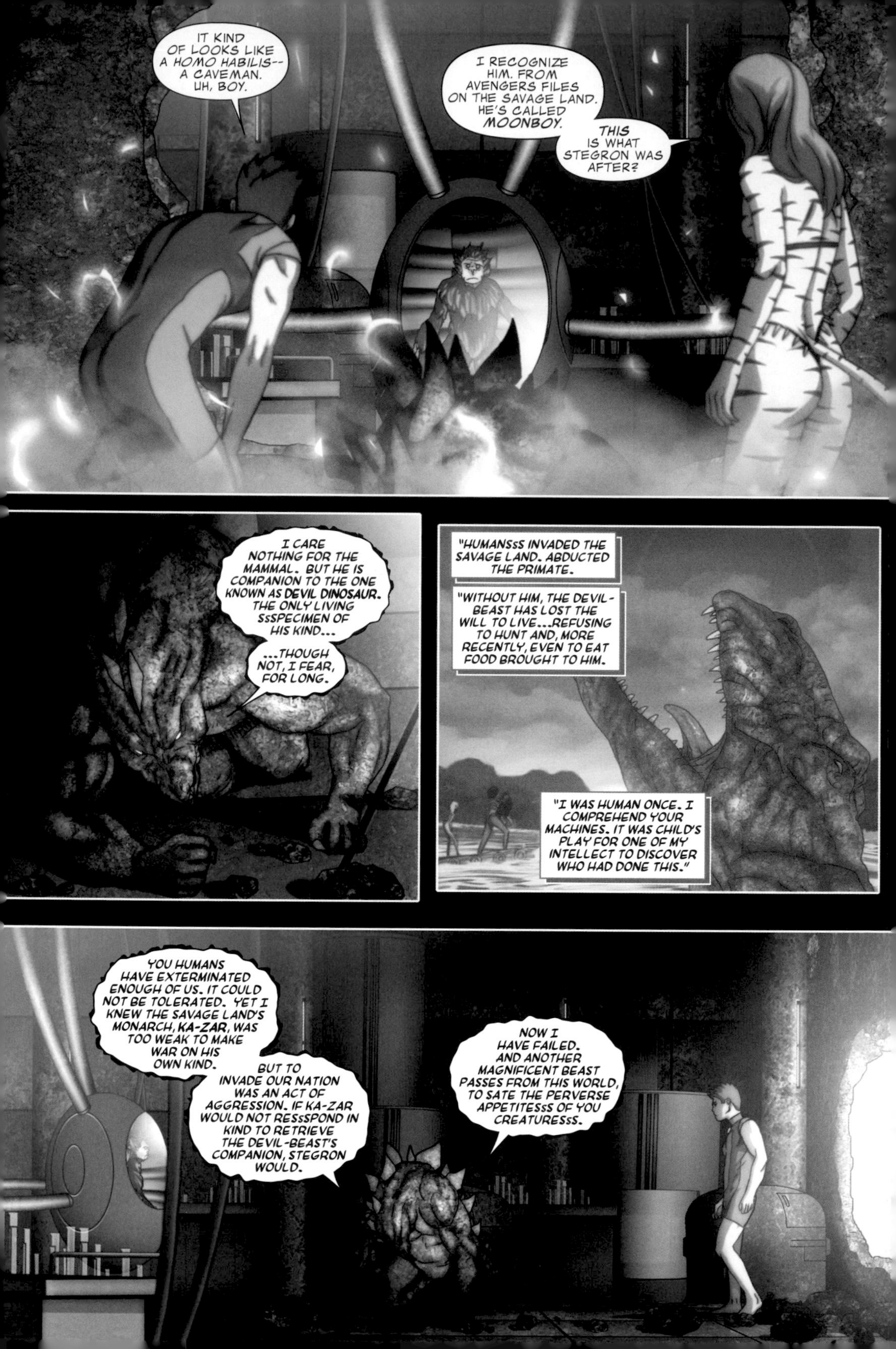
IT KIND OF LOOKS LIKE A HOMO HABILIS-- A CAVEMAN. UH, BOY.
I RECOGNIZE HIM. FROM AVENGERS FILES ON THE SAVAGE LAND. HE'S CALLED MOONBOY.
THIS IS WHAT STEGRON WAS AFTER?
I CARE NOTHING FOR THE MAMMAL. BUT HE IS COMPANION TO THE ONE KNOWN AS DEVIL DINOSAUR. THE ONLY LIVING SsSPECIMEN OF HIS KIND...
...THOUGH NOT, I FEAR, FOR LONG.
"HUMANSsS INVADED THE SAVAGE LAND. ABDUCTED THE PRIMATE.
"WITHOUT HIM, THE DEVIL-BEAST HAS LOST THE WILL TO LIVE...REFUSING TO HUNT AND, MORE RECENTLY, EVEN TO EAT FOOD BROUGHT TO HIM.
"I WAS HUMAN ONCE. I COMPREHEND YOUR MACHINES. IT WAS CHILD'S PLAY FOR ONE OF MY INTELLECT TO DISCOVER WHO HAD DONE THIS."
YOU HUMANS HAVE EXTERMINATED ENOUGH OF US. IT COULD NOT BE TOLERATED. YET I KNEW THE SAVAGE LAND'S MONARCH, KA-ZAR, WAS TOO WEAK TO MAKE WAR ON HIS OWN KIND.
BUT TO INVADE OUR NATION WAS AN ACT OF AGGRESSION. IF KA-ZAR WOULD NOT RESsSPOND IN KIND TO RETRIEVE THE DEVIL-BEAST'S COMPANION, STEGRON WOULD.
NOW I HAVE FAILED. AND ANOTHER MAGNIFICENT BEAST PASSES FROM THIS WORLD, TO SATE THE PERVERSE APPETITESsS OF YOU CREATURESsS.

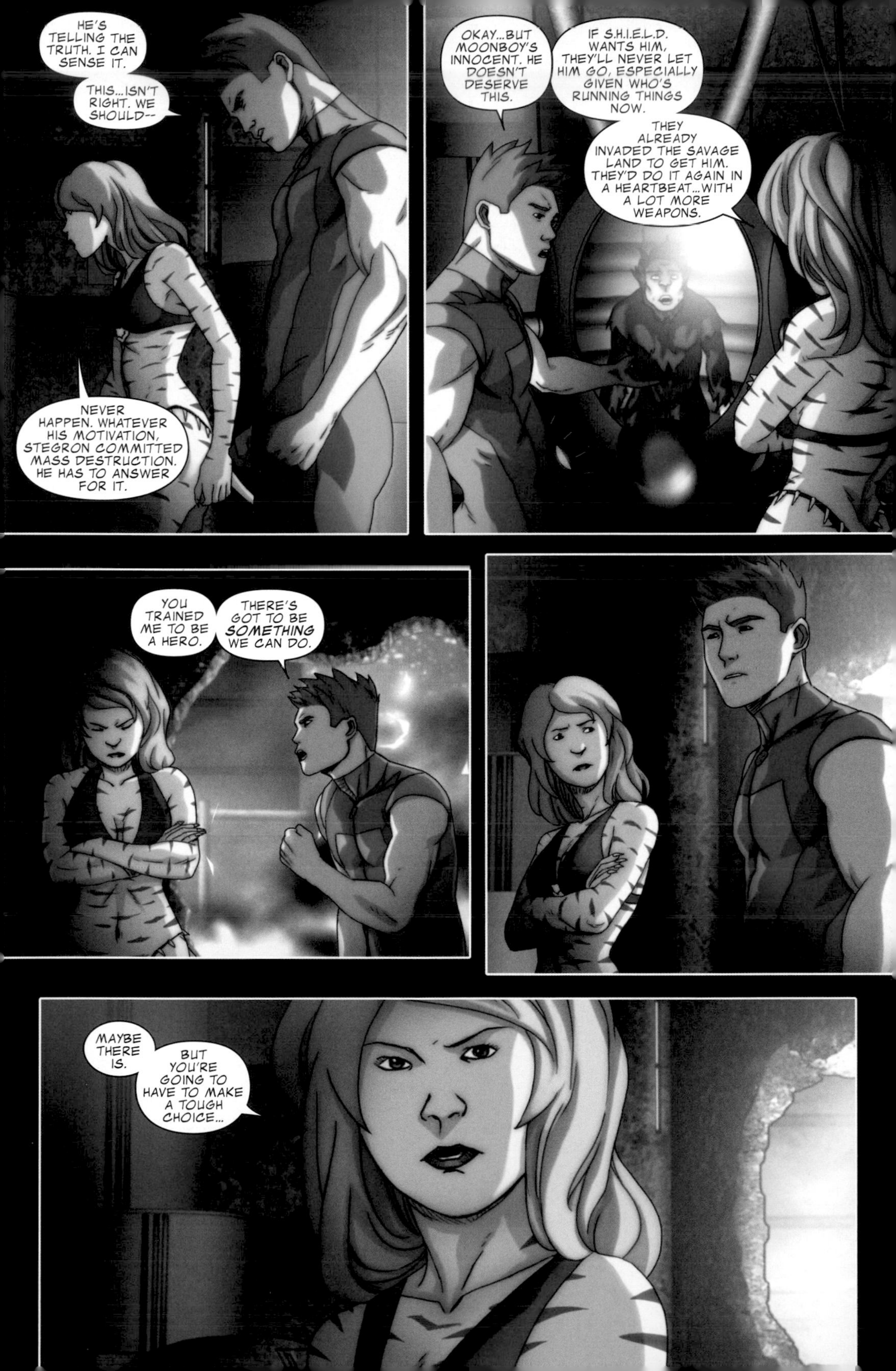
HE'S TELLING THE TRUTH. I CAN SENSE IT.
THIS...ISN'T RIGHT. WE SHOULD--
NEVER HAPPEN. WHATEVER HIS MOTIVATION, STEGRON COMMITTED MASS DESTRUCTION. HE HAS TO ANSWER FOR IT.
OKAY...BUT MOONBOY'S INNOCENT. HE DOESN'T DESERVE THIS.
IF S.H.I.E.L.D. WANTS HIM, THEY'LL NEVER LET HIM GO, ESPECIALLY GIVEN WHO'S RUNNING THINGS NOW.
THEY ALREADY INVADED THE SAVAGE LAND TO GET HIM. THEY'D DO IT AGAIN IN A HEARTBEAT...WITH A LOT MORE WEAPONS.
YOU TRAINED ME TO BE A HERO.
THERE'S GOT TO BE SOMETHING WE CAN DO.
MAYBE THERE IS.
BUT YOU'RE GOING TO HAVE TO MAKE A TOUGH CHOICE...

WELL DONE, TIGRA. IS HE STILL DANGEROUS?

I DON'T THINK SO. HE KNOWS WHEN HE'S BEATEN.

STEGRON SHALL SSSUBMIT TO IMPRISONMENT, MAMMAL. THOUGH HE MAKESSS NO PROMISE TO REMAIN.

THINK YOU CAN BUST OUT OF PRISON 42, HUH, LIZARD LIPS? I'LL ENJOY WATCHING YOU TRY.

WHERE IS HE? WHAT HAVE YOU DONE WITH HIM?

WHERE'S THE HOMO HABILIS?

WHAT, THE MONKEY? ONE OF THE DINOSAURS ATE HIM.

YOU'RE LYING! YOU'VE STOLEN HIM!

ARE YOU SERIOUS? LOOK AT MY OUTFIT, DOC. WHERE EXACTLY DO YOU THINK I'M HIDING HIM?

SEE THAT BLOODSTAIN? TEST IT. I GUARANTEE IT'S A MATCH FOR HIS DNA.

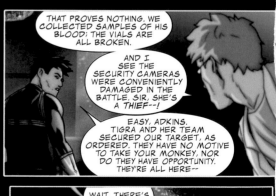

THAT PROVES NOTHING. WE COLLECTED SAMPLES OF HIS BLOOD; THE VIALS ARE ALL BROKEN.

AND I SEE THE SECURITY CAMERAS WERE CONVENIENTLY DAMAGED IN THE BATTLE. SIR, SHE'S A THIEF--!

EASY, ADKINS. TIGRA AND HER TEAM SECURED OUR TARGET, AS ORDERED. THEY HAVE NO MOTIVE TO TAKE YOUR MONKEY, NOR DO THEY HAVE OPPORTUNITY. THEY'RE ALL HERE--

WAIT. THERE'S ONE MISSING. CODE-NAME REPTIL.

THE KID? I SENT HIM HOME.

DR. COOPER WAS RIGHT. ALL HE DID WAS GET IN THE WAY.

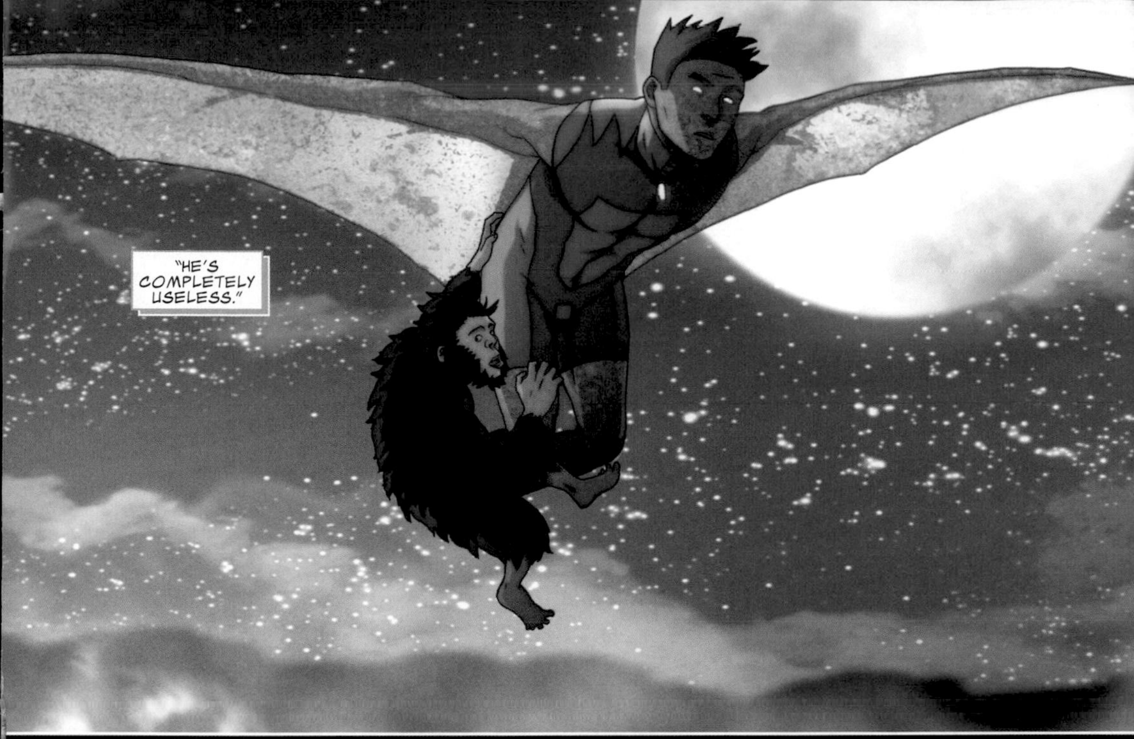
"HE'S COMPLETELY USELESS."

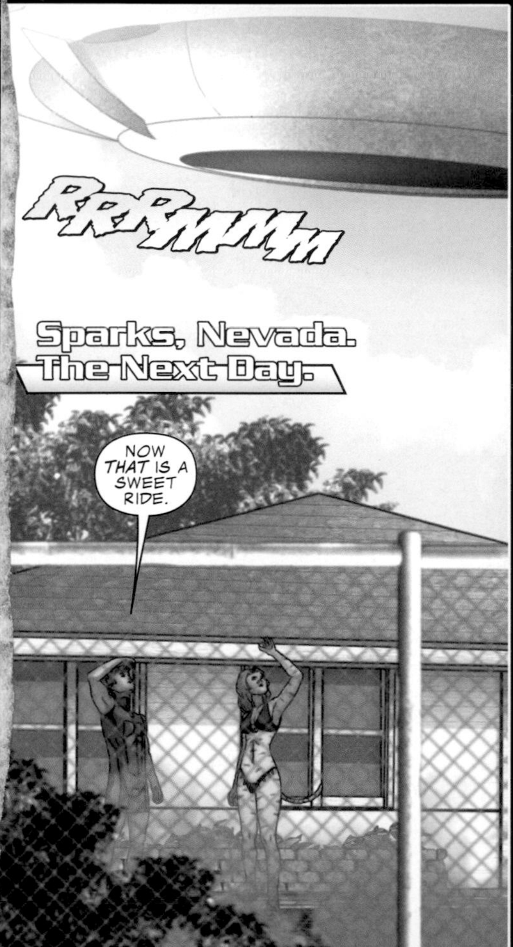
RRRMMMM
Sparks, Nevada.
The Next Day.
NOW THAT IS A SWEET RIDE.

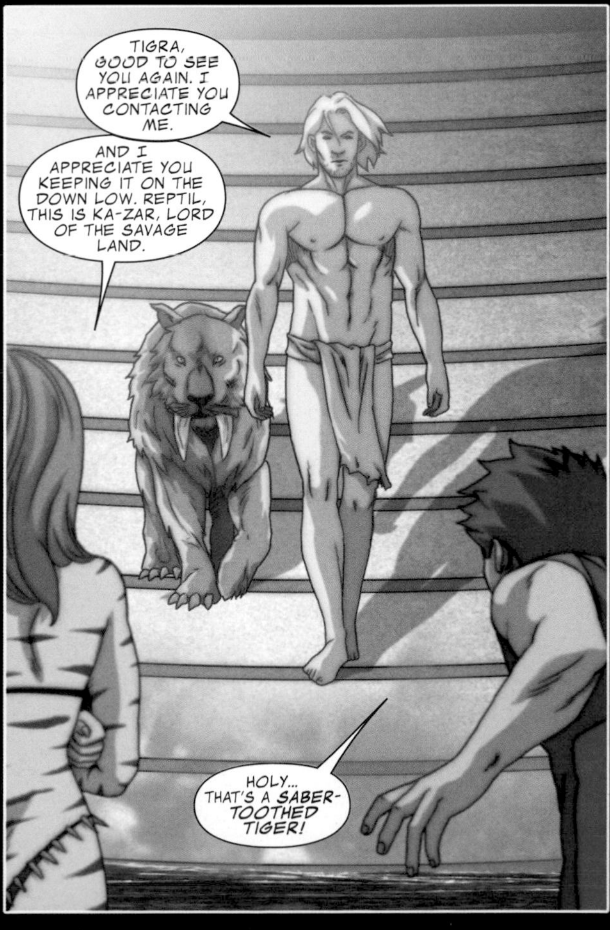
TIGRA, GOOD TO SEE YOU AGAIN. I APPRECIATE YOU CONTACTING ME.
AND I APPRECIATE YOU KEEPING IT ON THE DOWN LOW. REPTIL, THIS IS KA-ZAR, LORD OF THE SAVAGE LAND.
HOLY... THAT'S A SABER-TOOTHED TIGER!

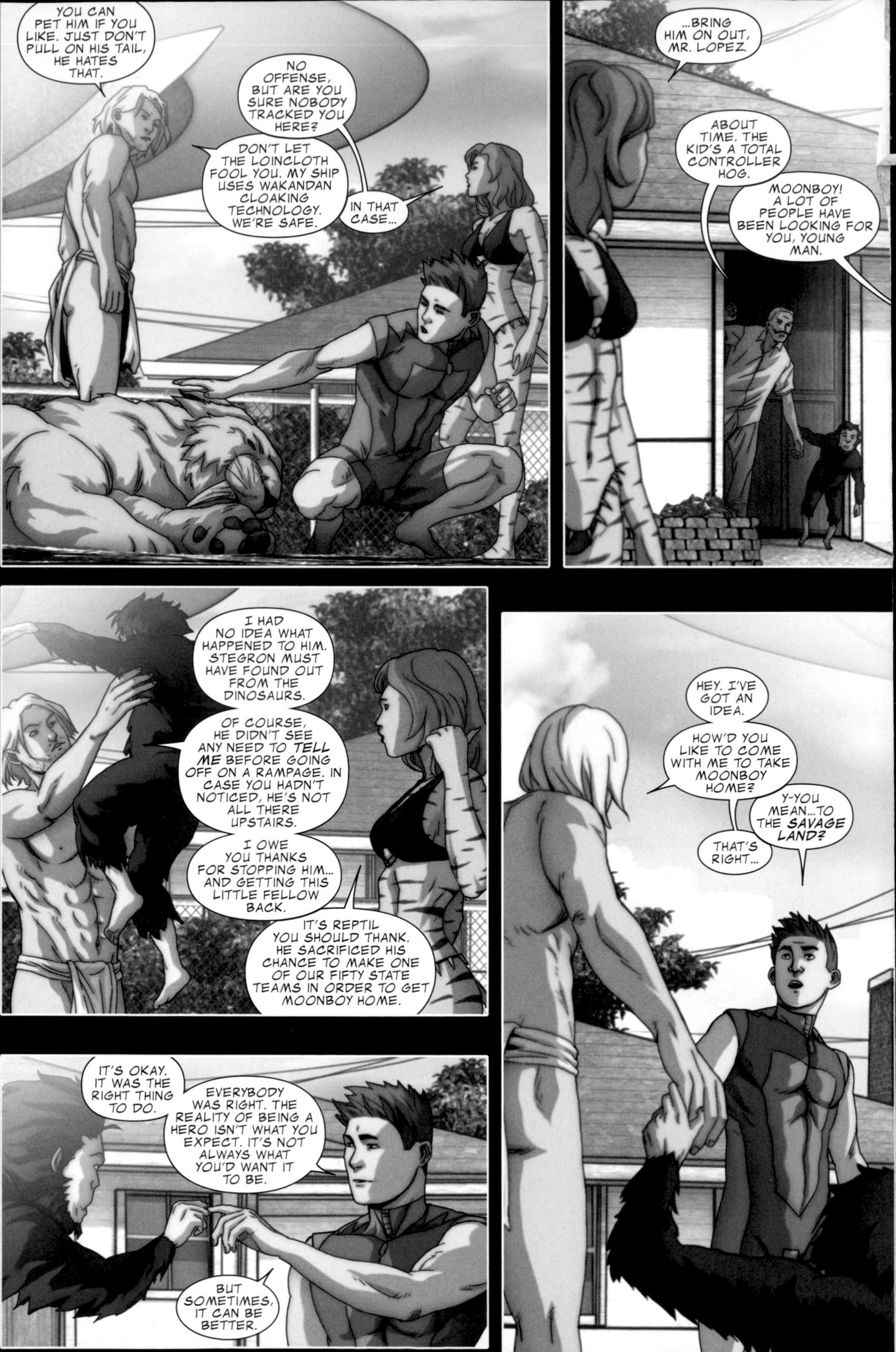

YOU CAN PET HIM IF YOU LIKE. JUST DON'T PULL ON HIS TAIL, HE HATES THAT.
NO OFFENSE, BUT ARE YOU SURE NOBODY TRACKED YOU HERE?
DON'T LET THE LOINCLOTH FOOL YOU. MY SHIP USES WAKANDAN CLOAKING TECHNOLOGY. WE'RE SAFE.
IN THAT CASE...
...BRING HIM ON OUT, MR. LOPEZ.
ABOUT TIME. THE KID'S A TOTAL CONTROLLER HOG.
MOONBOY! A LOT OF PEOPLE HAVE BEEN LOOKING FOR YOU, YOUNG MAN.
I HAD NO IDEA WHAT HAPPENED TO HIM. STEGRON MUST HAVE FOUND OUT FROM THE DINOSAURS.
OF COURSE, HE DIDN'T SEE ANY NEED TO TELL ME BEFORE GOING OFF ON A RAMPAGE. IN CASE YOU HADN'T NOTICED, HE'S NOT ALL THERE UPSTAIRS.
I OWE YOU THANKS FOR STOPPING HIM... AND GETTING THIS LITTLE FELLOW BACK.
IT'S REPTIL YOU SHOULD THANK. HE SACRIFICED HIS CHANCE TO MAKE ONE OF OUR FIFTY STATE TEAMS IN ORDER TO GET MOONBOY HOME.
IT'S OKAY. IT WAS THE RIGHT THING TO DO.
EVERYBODY WAS RIGHT. THE REALITY OF BEING A HERO ISN'T WHAT YOU EXPECT. IT'S NOT ALWAYS WHAT YOU'D WANT IT TO BE.
BUT SOMETIMES, IT CAN BE BETTER.
HEY. I'VE GOT AN IDEA.
HOW'D YOU LIKE TO COME WITH ME TO TAKE MOONBOY HOME?
Y-YOU MEAN...TO THE SAVAGE LAND?
THAT'S RIGHT...

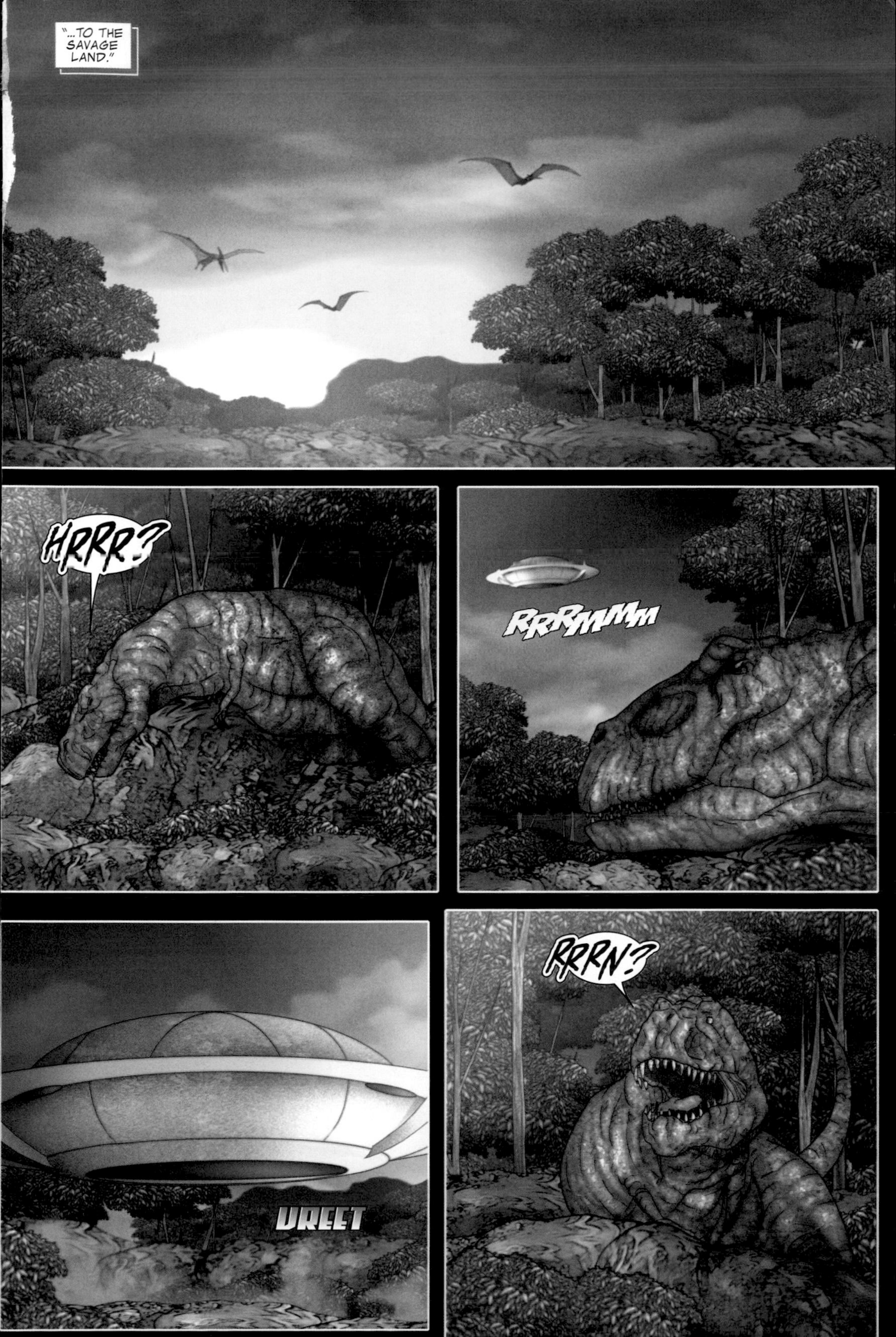
"...TO THE SAVAGE LAND."
HRRR?
RRRMMMm
VREET
RRRN?

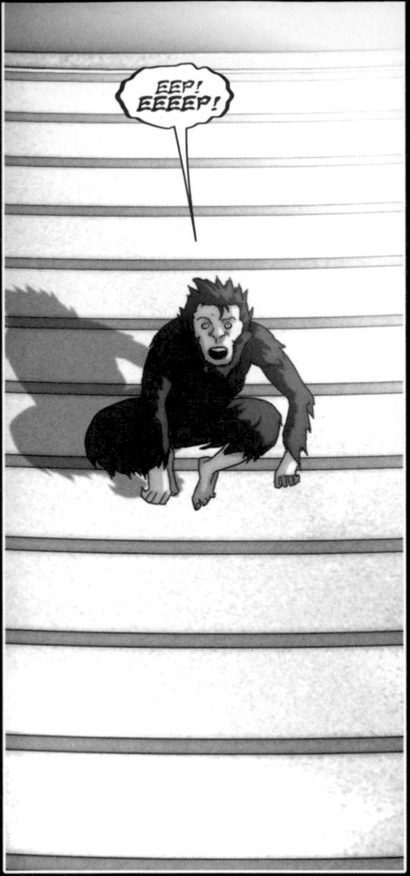
EEP! EEEEP!

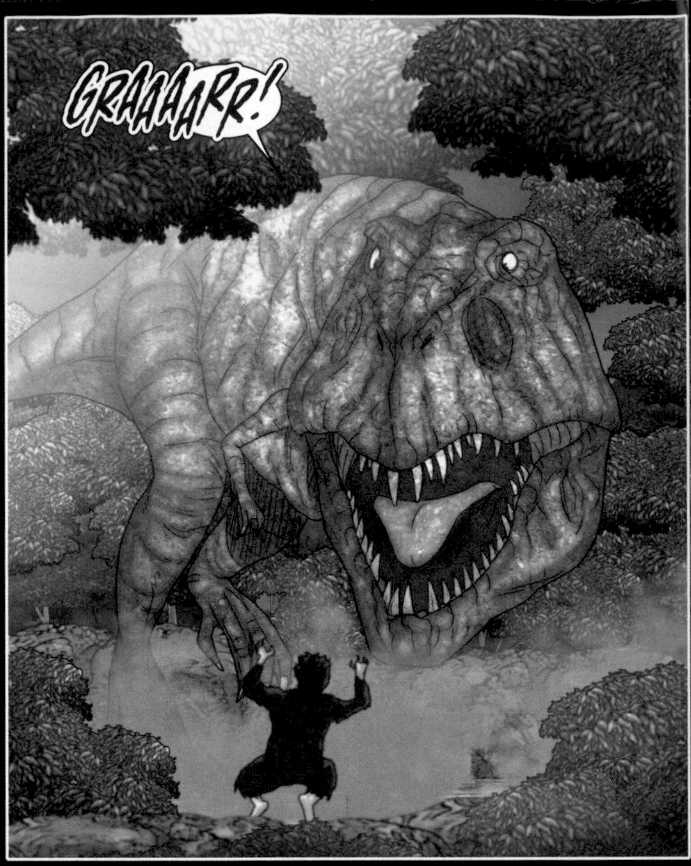
GRAAAARR!

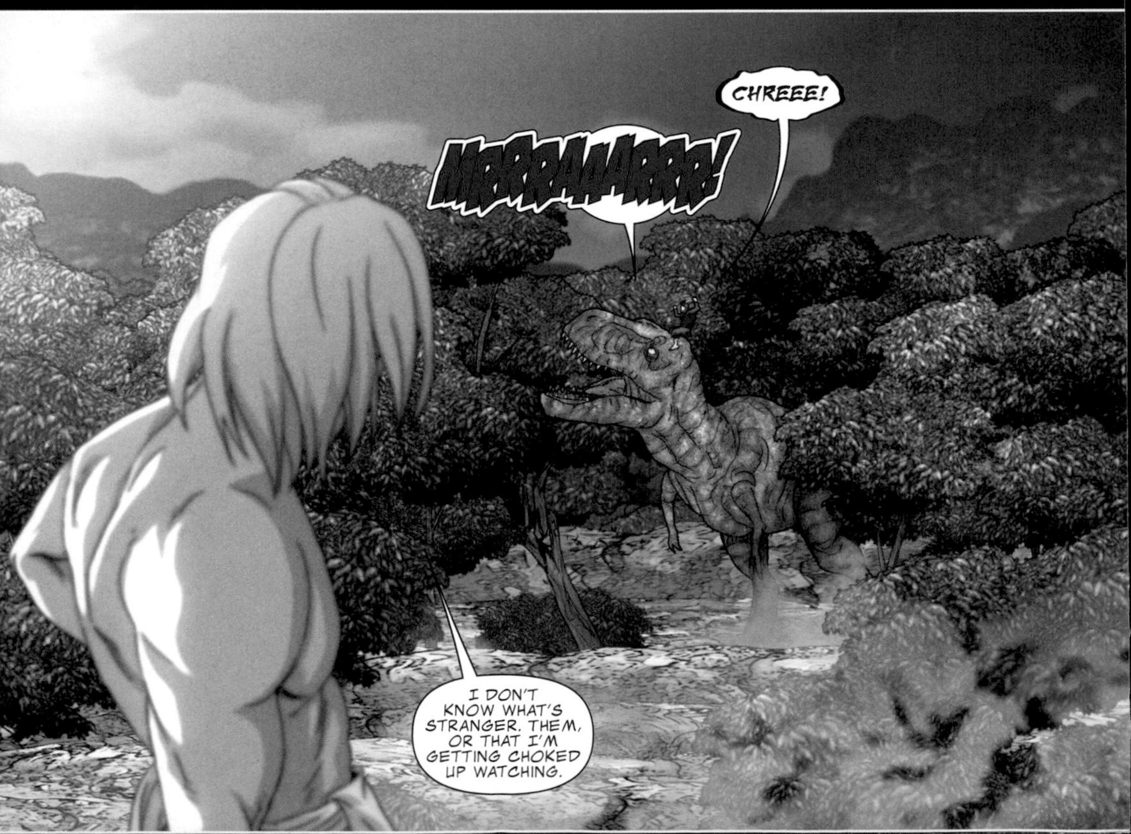
CHREEE!
MRRRAAARRR!
I DON'T KNOW WHAT'S STRANGER. THEM, OR THAT I'M GETTING CHOKED UP WATCHING.

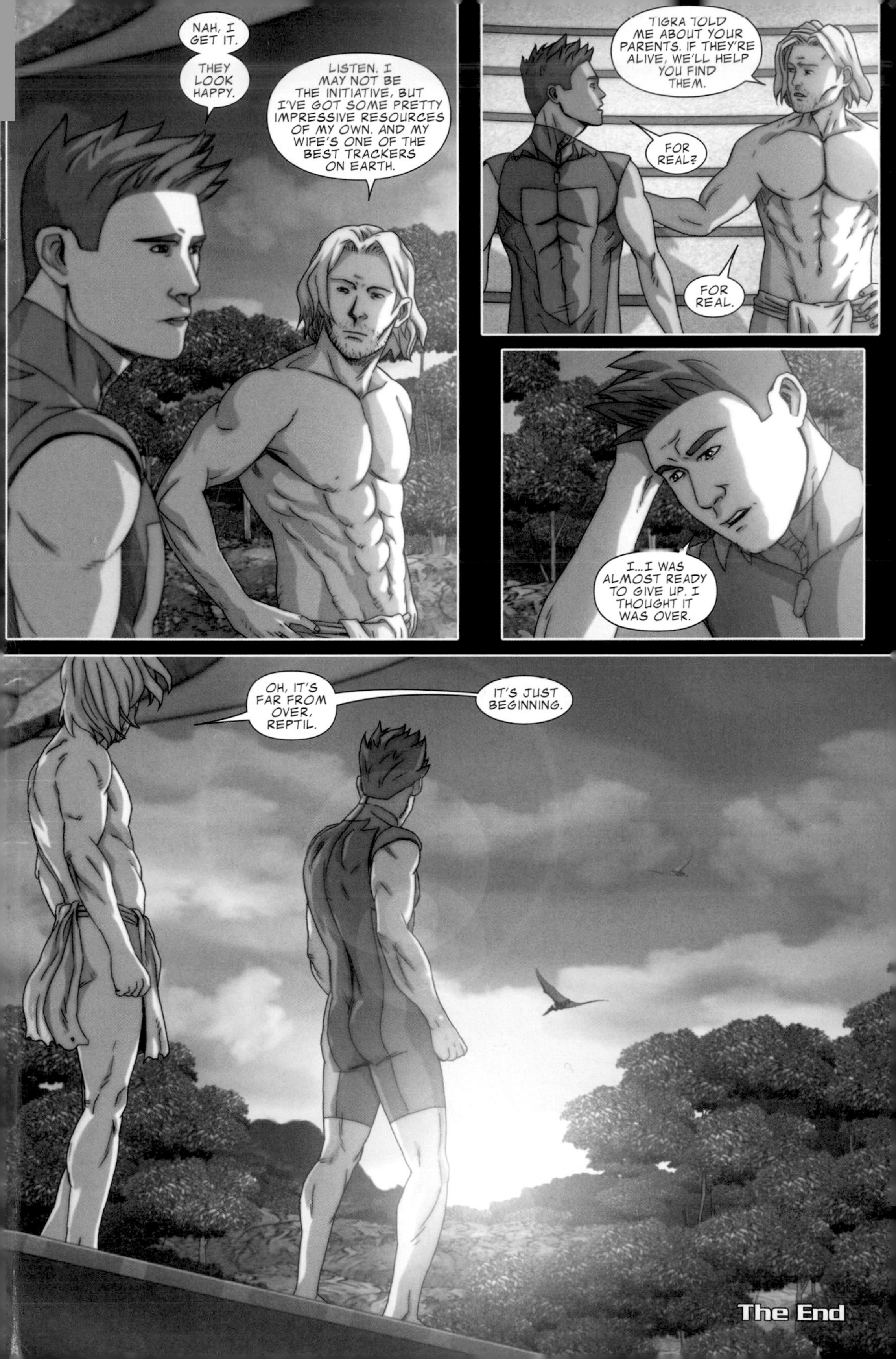
NAH, I GET IT.
THEY LOOK HAPPY.
LISTEN. I MAY NOT BE THE INITIATIVE, BUT I'VE GOT SOME PRETTY IMPRESSIVE RESOURCES OF MY OWN. AND MY WIFE'S ONE OF THE BEST TRACKERS ON EARTH.
TIGRA TOLD ME ABOUT YOUR PARENTS. IF THEY'RE ALIVE, WE'LL HELP YOU FIND THEM.
FOR REAL?
FOR REAL.
I...I WAS ALMOST READY TO GIVE UP. I THOUGHT IT WAS OVER.
OH, IT'S FAR FROM OVER, REPTIL.
IT'S JUST BEGINNING.
The End

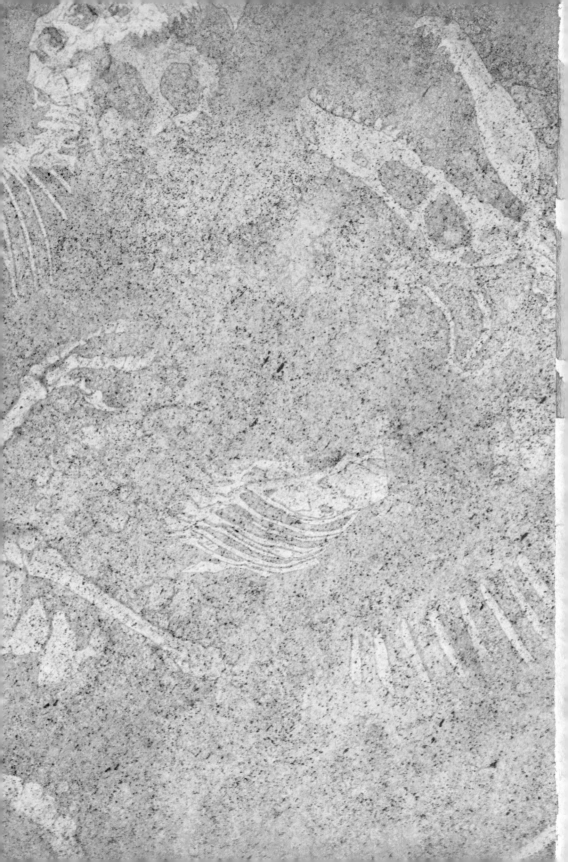